PRAISE FOR
My Soul to Keep

"It's the best ghost story I have read in a long time. Judith Hawkes's sense of atmosphere is beautifully judged and her descriptions lovely."
—Barbara Erskine, author of *House of Echoes*

"Haunting . . . delves suspensefully into the supernatural." —*Library Journal*

"Rich, imaginative and diverting . . . a satisfying paranormal plot." —*San Antonio Express-News*

"Enthralling . . . steeped in atmosphere that chills the reader."
—Marlys Millhiser,
author of *Murder in a Hot Flash*

"A ghost story filled with powers of supernatural perception and moody spirits." —*Kirkus Reviews*

"Clearly delineated characters, moody scene-setting and a perfectly controlled story line. . . . This is the subtle eeriness of Shirley Jackson transplanted to rural Tennessee. Judith Hawkes writes *believable* ghost stories." —*Memphis Commercial Appeal*

PRAISE FOR
Julian's House

"Who wouldn't like to talk to the dead? Who hasn't felt the chill of fear in a dark cellar? . . . Suspense that can make even the heart of a confirmed skeptic beat a little faster." —*New York Times Book Review*

"Convincing intrigue . . . scares up spooky shivers." —*San Diego Tribune*

"A great ghost story and more . . . will continue to haunt you for a long time. . . . I admire *Julian's House* as literature. . . . I urge you to read it." —Annie Dillard

"Elegant writing and an intricate plot . . . a first-class literary work." —*Atlanta Journal and Constitution*

"The reader gets delightfully sucked into a credible, compelling story." —*Library Journal*

"A witch's brew in the tradition of Shirley Jackson. . . . Ms. Hawkes is a true mistress of the macabre." —*Dallas Morning News*

"Chilling, compelling, powerful . . . a vivid tale of relationships between the living and those no longer living but still felt." —*Salisbury Post*

"A chiller. . . . Absorbing, eerie, and profound. . . . This book will scare you." —*Milwaukee Journal*

"Engrossing . . . takes possession of the reader and won't let go." —*Mystery News*

MORE PRAISE FOR
Julian's House

"A ghost story . . . a detective story . . . a dazzling evocation of haunting. . . . Judith Hawkes is most skilled at intersecting the real and surreal."
—*New York Newsday*

"A thinking person's ghost story!"   —*Boston Herald*

"Fascinating, memorable and unsettling . . . an excellent novel in the Shirley Jackson tradition: character-rich, stylish, quietly chilling."
—*Kirkus Reviews*

"A ghost story . . . fashioned of perfect language . . . gives us sexuality . . . apparitions . . . beautiful daytime light and nighttime menace . . . eeriness to creep up your back and break you out in sweats and goose bumps . . . the screws turn even more tightly."
—*Baltimore Sun*

"A 'grabber' of a ghost story . . . shivery!"
—*Columbia State*

"Gripping, readable, and scary as all get out . . . a thriller along the lines of James and Poe . . . a mystery cunningly conceived, wickedly frightening . . . a killer novel that flat out gave me the willies!"
—*Memphis Commercial Appeal*

"Beautiful and horrifying."
—*Roanoke Times & World News*

"Scary . . . sensitive . . . well-written and well-plotted, with three-dimensional characters and a strong voice."
—*Knoxville News-Sentinel*

My Soul
to Keep

Judith Hawkes

Ⓞ
A SIGNET BOOK

SIGNET
Published by the Penguin Group
Penguin Books USA Inc., 375 Hudson Street, New York, New York 10014, U.S.A.
Penguin Books Ltd, 27 Wrights Lane, London W8 5TZ, England
Penguin Books Australia Ltd, Ringwood, Victoria, Australia
Penguin Books Canada Ltd, 10 Alcorn Avenue, Toronto, Ontario, Canada M4V 3B2
Penguin Books (N.Z.) Ltd, 182–190 Wairau Road, Auckland 10, New Zealand

Penguin Books Ltd, Registered Offices:
Harmondsworth, Middlesex, England

Published by Signet, an imprint of Dutton Signet,
a division of Penguin Books USA Inc.
Previously published in a Dutton edition.

First Signet Printing, June, 1997
10 9 8 7 6 5 4 3 2 1

 REGISTERED TRADEMARK—MARCA REGISTRADA

Printed in the United States of America

PUBLISHER'S NOTE
This is a work of fiction. Names, characters, places, and incidents either are the
product of the author's imagination or are used fictitiously, and any resemblance to
actual persons, living or dead, events, or locales is entirely coincidental.

For Mom and Dad

Now I lay me down to sleep,
I pray the Lord my soul to keep.
If I should die before I wake,
I pray the Lord my soul to take.

                    —Child's prayer

December 1968

A white winter silence.

Forested mountain slopes lie blanketed in deep snow, in stillness broken only by the rattle of bare branches in the wind. Shaggy pines bend almost to the ground beneath their cold white cargo, creating unexpected shapes and spaces in the landscape and rendering it unfamiliar even to those who, in other weathers, know it well.

The clear, cold pink of sunset lingers above the ridge as the day slips toward dusk, throwing into sharp relief the skeleton shapes of trees against the white mountainside. The stillness is complete now: rustling leaves and running streams long since silenced by the cold's close grip, animals deep in their lairs. But at this moment, just as the sky begins to fade, a sound breaks the brittle air.

A child's terrified cry, thin as a bird's in the vast snowbound wilderness.

"Anna-bel—!"

From a covert a pheasant flies up with a startled clatter of wings. A masked raccoon peers from the hollow of a tree; a fox stirs in its den. In a distant hollow a keen-eared dog begins to bark and is quieted by a shout from the cabin nearby. But already the silence has settled again, a deep white winter silence that absorbs the sound as if it had never been.

Chapter 1

Nan remembered the hill.

Except that *remember* was much too strong a term. As they rounded the last bend in the wooded driveway and came upon the open vista before them, the flicker inside her head was more like the faint echo of some childhood dream. Old white farmhouse, shaded in front by a huge gnarled oak, sun-dappled lawn sloping down to fenced pasture, in the distance a meandering line of trees marking the creek . . .

Beyond the trees rose the hill. Fired into gold by the slanting afternoon light, its rounded crest blazed against the deep green of the mountains beyond. Without meaning to, Nan stepped hard on the brake, jerking the car to a stop. Beside her, Stephen was saying something.

"Wow! Is that the tree where you had your tree house?"

She nodded, trying to find a reply, but he was already out of the car and running across the grass, making a beeline for the oak in the yard. Nan looked away from him, letting her eyes take in the whole scene again—house, tree, pasture and mountains, ending up back at the hill. Not a dream, not some shadowy memory of a perfect childhood summer complete with tree house, loving grand-mother, best friend. This was real. She was really here.

She took a breath and let it out slowly, forcing herself to see it objectively this time. It would make a pretty photograph. Not her thing, of course; she didn't do land-scapes. But she could certainly live with the view.

Stephen, when she looked again, was poised beneath the oak with arms upstretched. As she watched, he jumped for the bottommost branch and came up short, his fingers just brushing the hanging leaves. Fleetingly overlaid on his small figure she seemed to see another one—jumping to catch the branch above his head, grasping it and pulling himself up in one smooth motion.

(Hey Tuck wait for me)

The vision was gone almost before she was aware of it. Stephen made one last halfhearted attempt, then gave up, and Nan found herself smiling. Just eight this past March, he wasn't quite big enough, although by the end of the summer he might be.

If they stayed that long.

She shrugged off this first tentative touch of doubt. He had left the car door open; she reached over and closed it, then put the Volvo into gear and followed the rutted drive the rest of the way to the house, hearing gravel crunch beneath the wheels. There was a battered red pickup parked next to the house. She pulled up beside it, turned off the ignition and just sat for a minute, listening to the tick of cooling metal, over-whelmed not just by the marathon thirteen-hour drive from New York but by the last few frantic months that now, this moment, seemed to have come to a recogniz-able pause, a quiet space before going on. Journey's end was her grandmother's old white farmhouse, two stories and a gabled roof, weathered wooden steps mounting to a front porch overgrown by honeysuckle vines.

Annabel's house. In spite of the reality of peeling paint and cockeyed shutters, she still had the sense it might waver and melt away at any moment, revealing the too-familiar vista of polluted skies and grimy Manhattan rooftops outside the windows of their SoHo loft. Yet she could smell the honeysuckle from where she sat, and hear birds singing. And even more convincing was the weariness in her bones from the long, exhausting miles they had covered between there and here.

Stephen was yelling something. Nan shook off her fatigue and got out of the car.

"What?"

"I said there's a kid up there."

He pointed up into the tree. She crossed the grass to stand beside him, craning her neck to peer into the rustling green recesses above. A kid? Some neighbor's child, no doubt, playing up in the old tree house, surprised into shyness by their unexpected arrival.

"I can't see him." She raised her voice a notch. "Hello up there! We're your new neighbors."

No reply. As they stood waiting, even the leaves ceased their movement, and Nan was suddenly aware of the profound stillness of the countryside around them. The creak of crickets and distant twittering of birds seemed only to underscore the silence. When she spoke, her voice sounded unexpectedly loud.

"Are you sure you saw somebody, honey?"

"He stuck his tongue out at me." Sunlight flashed briefly on the circular lenses of Stephen's glasses as he looked up at her. He studied her for a moment, then frowned down at the gnarled root under his feet. "You think I'm making it up."

Nan opened her mouth to protest, then shut it. In the increased amount of time she had spent with her young son these past few months, she had noticed that he was often uncannily aware of exactly what was going through her head. Just as she had noticed his tendency to mix fantasy and reality together in a way that Gabe assured her was nothing out of the ordinary for an eight-year-old.

"Look!" Stephen pointed suddenly, and she turned to see three horses standing at the pasture fence, their ears pricked forward. He started toward them at a jog.

"Look out, honey. They might bite."

"Aw, Mom—"

"Well, they might."

She followed him across the lawn. How could you tell if they were planning to bite? They flattened their ears or something. Stephen came to a stop at a safe distance from the fence, a breeze belling the oversized New York Giants T-shirt that hung to his knees, and the horses stretched their necks toward him curiously. A fourth, this one white, was walking up from the ramshackle barn in the pasture below.

"Are they ours?"

"I guess they are now," Nan said. She stopped beside him, marveling at the sweetness of the air. The lawn had been recently cut; she could see the mower's neat concentric swaths. The honeysuckle's fragrance topped the fresh grass smell. The oak tree, when she glanced back at it, still showed no signs of occupancy. Just an eight-year-old's imagination at work? She turned toward the fence again. The horses' ears, four pairs now, were blessedly pointing forward.

"You didn't tell me there were horses," Stephen said.

"I didn't know Annabel still kept horses. She had one when I was little—Blue Moon." The name came unsought to her lips, and she wondered at the mind's capacity to store meaningless details. "But Blue Moon must be dead by now."

"What color was she?"

"White. Like that one there."

The white horse lifted its head as she pointed at it. The dark liquid eyes looked friendly. The others stood swishing their tails. The two smaller ones were a coppery red, the last glossy black with a dab of white on its forehead. Pressing against the weathered fence they were overwhelmingly alive; she could smell them, see the big muscles moving under their glossy hides. In spite of her misgivings, she was moved to admiration.

"They're pretty, aren't they?"

As if in response, all the heads began to toss; the horses made chuckling noises in their throats. Nan took an involuntary step back. Any horse capable of acknowledging a compliment was too much for her. She liked her animals dumb, in all senses of the word.

"They're just sayin' 'thank you, ma'am.' "

The voice came from behind them and she turned quickly, startled again; she hadn't heard anyone cross the grass. The man approaching them was tall, his curly hair and short beard the same coppery color as the smaller horses. At his heels a black and white setter waved its feathery tail in greeting. He put out his hand.

"You Annabel Lucas? I'm Sky Barnett. We're cousins."

Nan had forgotten about being called by her full name that summer—yet now she recalled the elder Annabel insisting on it, as if proud to claim her young namesake. Her newfound cousin was holding out his hand and she shook it. His eyes, dazzling blue, were indeed the same color as the Tennessee sky overhead. "Sky?" she said.

He smiled. "You can call me Schuyler, if you want. Most folks don't."

"Well, actually I don't use Annabel either. It's just Nan." Her hand was still in his. She took it out and put it on Stephen's shoulder. "And this is my son, Stephen Phillips."

"Proud to know you, Steve."

Stephen, too shy to say how much he hated being called Steve, had his hand pumped with a vigor that made the hair flop on his forehead. The dog jumped up at him with muddy paws, subsiding at her master's "Down, Kate." Her tail dropped between her legs but its tip continued to wag. The horses were still nickering and jostling one another at the fence. Sky moved closer, reaching into a pocket of his jeans.

"They don't bite?" Nan said.

"They don't bite people, no ma'am. Just these." A handful of carrot pieces, which he fed to the horses. They settled down as munching sounds filled the air. The white horse pushed its nose gently against Sky's chest.

Stephen had been patting the dog; now he edged closer. "Can I give them some?"

"Sure." Sky gave him half a carrot. "Just hold your hand real flat, so they don't get no fingers by mistake. They ain't much for meat."

He winked at Nan. She was watching Stephen. Breath held, he offered the carrot on his flattened palm to the black horse. It stretched its neck toward him, ears forward, velvety nostrils flaring. At the last instant one of the little reddish horses thrust its nose in and snatched the treat for itself. The black one laid back its ears and nipped at the thief, which skipped off to a safe distance to enjoy its prize. Nan and Sky laughed.

Stephen's face turned red. "That was supposed to be for him—the black horse!"

All at once he seemed on the verge of tears. Nan reached out a hand, but he shied away from the comforting gesture—possibly inhibited by Sky's presence, but she didn't think so. Since becoming a single parent she had been forced, once again, to face the humiliating fact that she wasn't cut out to be a mother. And she was particularly lousy at gauging her child's emotional needs. Even at his best he was moody, and just now he was exhausted from their long journey. What could she offer him? Gabe would have known immediately, but she was at a loss.

Sky simply handed him another carrot. "Here, try again. But remember—you got to watch them ponies. They're a whole mess quicker'n the horses are."

This information distracted Stephen, and he squinted up at the tall bearded man beside him. "The little ones are ponies?"

"Mighty right."

"They're not just baby horses?"

"Nope. Pony's a different breed. They ain't never goin' to get big. Little Bit there—she's Merlin's momma. But see, he's big as she is."

The black horse had successfully taken its carrot. Sky passed Stephen the rest of his supply and stepped back to stand by Nan as the boy was surrounded by eager noses. "You're sure they won't bite him?" she said.

"Relax, Momma. He'll be okay." He watched Stephen for another moment, then turned to her. "Thornton told me you were plannin' on gettin' here today. I figured I'd air the place out for you, make sure everything was workin'."

Thornton Reynolds was Annabel's lawyer, a sprawling signature at the bottom of the letter Nan had received just after Christmas, notifying her that she had inherited her grandmother's house and land in eastern Tennessee. Annabel's house. At the time Nan had put the letter aside out of sheer inability to take it in. A two-hundred-year-old farmhouse in a valley in the Smoky Mountains? She had visited Annabel only once, the summer she was nine, and her memories of the place were so dim that it came as something of a shock to be reminded of its existence. In every sense Corey County was a long way from Manhattan, a classic case of You Can't Get There From Here. Yet in the months that followed, when her life had started to come apart alarmingly at the seams, she found her thoughts returning to the property in Tennessee.

Why not spend the summer there—give herself a chance to relax in the country, away from the pressures of New York life, and think things over? If she focused on the scattering of images floating at the back of her mind, she could get a hazy impression of summer days spent playing with a yellow-haired boy named Tucker in the tree house and barn, on the hill and along the creek—but it was distant and unreal, like a movie she had seen a long time ago. A movie with a sad ending: Tucker's death, a drowning accident . . . There the vague images tailed off into emptiness, leaving her with only an abstract knowledge of the event, like something she had read in a history book. Classic repression, no doubt, and that was just as well. What the property meant to her now was simply a nice chunk of real estate, seventy acres and a house, on which she was obligated to nothing and nobody. And so here she was—and this good-looking country boy, bearded and blue-jeaned and talking with a mountain twang, was her cousin.

"It was nice of you to take the trouble," she said.

"No trouble. I live right across the road—those're my orchards you drove past. I looked after this place for Annabel when she was alive. Feels kinda nice to be doin' it again."

Twenty years since she had last seen her grandmother. The realization made her feel a little guilty in front of Sky, who had known Annabel, been close to her.

"I was pretty surprised when I found out she'd left me the place. I only visited her once. And we moved around so much while I was growing up, I just lost touch with her. I don't even know how she died."

The bright blue eyes met hers steadily. "She just died from bein' old, honey. Heart gave out on her. She didn't suffer none, just stayed in bed a few days and then passed on in her sleep. She knew she was goin'."

Nan shook her head, not knowing what to say, turning instead to admire the view across the pasture once again. "It's beautiful here."

Glancing at Sky she caught the shadow of a frown crossing his face. An unpleasant thought occurred: had he fixed a few hopes on inheriting the place himself? Oops. What kind of family politics had she waltzed into the middle of? She had a moment's panic, then decided she couldn't worry about it now. If he wanted the place, maybe she would sell it to him eventually. For the moment, her plans extended no further than a restful summer in the country.

Stephen had run out of carrots and was carefully patting the horses, which were still nosing him. He looked at Sky. "What's the black one's name?"

"That's Scheherazade, son. It's a mouthful, ain't it? I just call her Annabel's Folly and let it go at that."

"Annabel's Folly?" Nan said.

"Three years old and wild as a mustang." He shook his head. "Annabel was soft in the head over that mare. Wouldn't let nobody break her to ride—why, she's barely halter-broke. Now it's too late to train her. She ain't worth a nickel, 'cept maybe for dog food."

Seeing Stephen's eyes widen, Nan said quickly, "She's pretty, though," and caught a look that might have been amusement flitting over Sky's face. Maybe that was the wrong thing to say about a horse? She decided to drop the topic of Scheherazade. "What's the white one called?"

"That's Joe Lee."

"Joe Lee? Is he some relative of Robert E.'s?"

He looked surprised. "No ma'am, that's French for *pretty*. Joe Lee's a lady horse."

She was too tired not to laugh, but she did her best to turn it into a cough and congratulated herself on succeeding fairly well; at least he didn't seem to notice. In the future she would have to keep an eye out for this kind of culture clash if she didn't want to give offense.

Sky helped unpack the car, toting the two heaviest bags with apparent ease. Nan followed with her camera bag and tripod; he twisted around for a curious glance at the latter.

"I do recall Annabel sayin' you take pictures. She used t' brag on you a good bit. Said you're famous and all."

Nan smiled. "Only by a grandmother's standards. I make a living."

"Fashion pictures, huh? You ain't goin' to find much in the way o' fashion down here."

"Good. I'm on vacation."

When the car was empty he showed them around the house, pointing out its quirks and charms—the enclosed staircase in the south end, the cranky old gas stove in the kitchen, and the temperamental fireplace flue in the living room. The Stephens family, her mother's ancestors, had built the house in stages: the original cabin in the 1700s, the rest a century later. The rooms were spacious, with wide pegged floorboards and beamed ceilings, wood paneling and whitewashed plaster perfectly in tune with Annabel's small, bright rugs and unpretentious antiques. The original small windows of colonial days had been left intact at the front of the house, replaced with larger ones on the back wall that looked out on the mountain ridge. To Nan, accustomed to the wide open look of a Tribeca loft, the wealth of light was welcome.

"Now, this here's Mister Mustard." Sky leaned down to scratch the ears of an orange tomcat that had appeared from somewhere, purring loudly as it honed itself on Nan's shins. "I been makin' sure he don't starve since Annabel passed on, but he'll be proud to have some company around here."

Proud seemed to mean *glad*. With his muddy boots and country speech, Sky seemed like a classic redneck, but she was too travel-fatigued to feel particularly snobbish—and when he opened the refrigerator to reveal the fried chicken and potato salad sent over by his sister Cassie, Nan thought that if this was Southern hospitality, she could learn to live with it.

All at once she realized she was starving, and so was Stephen.

Sky left them ogling the contents of the refrigerator with a promise to stop by in the morning. They heard him calling his dog Kate, who had remained outside during the house tour, then the slam of the truck door and the sound of its engine slowly diminishing into evening quiet.

"Mom?" Halfway through his supper, Stephen looked up, forehead rucked with concern. "The black horse—what did he say she's called?"

"Scheherazade," Nan said, recalling the quirk of Sky's lips around the fanciful name.

"Is that guy going to kill her and make her into dog food?"

"No, honey, of course not. He was just kidding. Besides, she belongs to us now. We'll take good care of her."

She watched his face relax and wished she could vanquish all his fears so easily. The past year had been rough on him as well as on her. Early the previous fall a boy in his class at school had disappeared without a trace, in one of those terrible incidents that periodically make the New York nightly news. A "good" neighborhood, a sunny Saturday afternoon: Brian's parents had let him go unaccompanied to the corner deli to buy a candy bar. Later, witnesses remembered seeing him talking to a man in a maroon car pulled up to the curb, but police efforts to locate him turned up nothing. Over the long months that followed, his picture plastered on bulletin boards and lampposts became a heartbreaking, familiar sight. HAVE YOU SEEN THIS CHILD? Under the words the small face smiled out engagingly, baseball cap at a jaunty angle, while time and weather tattered the posters and hope drained away.

Brian hadn't been a special friend, but the incident scared Stephen, as it did all the children in his class. At the school's request a psychiatric social worker came and talked to them in several group sessions. Nan didn't know if it helped Stephen. After Brian's disappearance he developed a weird phobia about a newsstand on a corner near their lower Manhattan loft. Boarded up when it went out of business, it seemed to terrify him; he would cross the street to avoid passing it. There were nightmares, too, about a weirdo he had seen on the subway wearing four wristwatches on one arm. Preoccupied with a frantically successful career, Nan offered what comfort she could, counting on Gabe to be there for him. And then Gabe had pulled the rug out from under them both.

Now she looked at Stephen again. He yawned hugely, showing the gap where he had lost a milk tooth two weeks ago. He was falling asleep, too tired for any more worrying tonight. Any minute now his face was going to land in his plate, and all other issues were conveniently forgettable in the task of getting him upstairs and into bed.

She put him in the upper chamber of the original cabin, where dark beams spanned the low whitewashed ceiling and small windows recalled a time when there was no such thing as central heating. The bed was covered with a faded summer quilt; on the table beside it, the lamp's yellowed shade boasted a scene of two dragonflies hovering over a clump of reeds and cattails. When she turned it on, the brightening colors made her blink

(down by the creek there are real ones, swooping

and darting over the glimmering water on wings like golden shadows, buzzing so close to my face that I jump back and Tuck laughs at me)

and catch her breath. In the lamplight, within the compass of this little room with its white walls, windows opening onto green country twilight, the forgotten moment came back to her so vividly that she was disoriented. Like a door opening briefly in some dark corner of her memory, behind it a flash of sunlight and the sound of laughter and babbling water. She shook her head to clear it. This was no time to be daydreaming; she needed to get Stephen to bed.

He was practically comatose, too sleepy to object when she put him into his pajamas, something he had become independent about in recent weeks. She took off the wire-rimmed glasses and set them carefully beside the lamp, then lifted him onto the bed and drew the quilt over him, smoothing back the silky dark hair so different from her own brown curls. Without the glasses, his face had the blind, helpless look of a kitten before its eyes have opened.

At the edge of her vision the wings of the painted dragonflies seemed to quiver as she turned off the lamp and went out, leaving the door open to the lit landing in case he woke not knowing where he was. Not a bad idea, either, to leave the light on in the bathroom next door. She flicked the switch inside the room and surveyed it briefly. Shower rig attached to an old-timey clawfoot tub, the kind her friend Bernadette in SoHo had made into a loveseat with the help of a blowtorch and some red velvet cushions. Funky old pull-chain toilet, cracked tiles on the floor. One of the taps in the basin needed a new washer. Water was running feebly, a high-pitched hiss, and she took hold of the handles and tightened them. Useless: a rusty stain marked the porcelain under the faucet, the work of years.

She left the bathroom. Across the landing the enclosed staircase beckoned, and the idea of having a drink carried her down the dark, cramped steps—some thought of keeping to her New York regimen as a way of easing the transition to a strange place. The first floor of the original colonial cabin had been made into a small library. The wooden panel above its fireplace matched the one in the bedroom upstairs—both carved in a sunburst design by, Sky had told her, a traveling journeyman in the 1700s. There was a cabinet in one corner, and she saw glasses and what looked like a decanter of brandy. Annabel's cat appeared, meowed and rubbed against her legs.

She patted it, then got the brandy out. The cut-glass facets caught the lamplight as she poured a generous measure and then a little extra, telling herself she needed to unwind after her long day. To become less vividly aware of the spacious old house with its empty rooms, doors she hadn't thought to lock, the miles of pasture and woods they had driven past without spotting more than one or two other dwellings.

She sipped the brandy, savoring the smooth burn that spread through her without quite reaching her thoughts. With Sky's departure she could feel misgivings beginning to creep out from the dark places of her mind. Night was coming, and she and Stephen were alone here. At this moment the big bad city they had left behind seemed, in comparison, a haven of lights and people.

Oh, don't be such a New Yorker. More than three trees together and you think you're Little Red Riding Hood.

She shivered a little, took another swallow of brandy and went to the window to look out at the front yard. The cat leaped lightly onto the sill and settled there, paws folded and tail tucked around its haunches. The screened window stood open to cool country dusk, green-smelling and voiced with a distant murmur from the creek. In the twilight it sounded secret, less than friendly.

She stood looking out across the lawn, absently stroking the cat's fur. All the greens had deepened to blue and purple; shaggy treetops stood etched in black against a clear lilac sky. To her left, beyond the fence, the pasture faded away in folds of shadow; directly across the lawn the ground rose to orchards and she could see the gnarled shapes of apple trees, trunks pale against their darkening leaves.

As the twilight deepened, so did her sense of isolation. The darkness gathering on the surrounding fields and mountains seemed profoundly impersonal, oblivious to the presence of humanity; she felt oppressed and diminished by it as she never had in the city. From the dark spreading mass of the oak tree an owl hooted suddenly, its eerie quavering call like a shudder transposed into sound. She felt it right between her shoulder blades: two clear tremulous hoots and then a third—rising, hovering, sinking away into a breathless silence in which the noise of the creek seemed all at once thunderously loud.

And in the silence she heard a far-off cry.

Almost like an echo of the owl's call, but human—wasn't it? A child's voice, calling far away in the darkening hills? A lost sound. Forlorn.

The cat's fur had stiffened under her fingers. She heard it hiss softly, sound just at the threshold of hearing, and jerked her hand away in reflex. The cat jumped down from the sill and slunk out of the room. Nan watched it go. All at once the quick-gathering dark seemed full of menacing possibilities.

That sound. Just a child playing, far away—sounds carried in the country. But it had seemed so lost. Hopeless. On impulse she left her brandy glass on the sill and went to the front door. Opened it. Stepped out onto the front porch to listen again.

It was darker now and, except for the shrill rhythmic piping of crickets, completely quiet. Not even a breeze to stir the trees. Standing there, she was aware of wanting to go back into the house, turn on all the lights, lock every door. City dweller's syndrome. She refused to give in to it, forcing herself to remain on the porch a moment longer. The country night, its fall complete now, seemed enormous—filled with unfamiliar sounds and smells that had sharpened in the cooling air. Her earlier awareness of the long, empty miles between her and civilization had returned with a vengeance.

When a gleam flickered somewhere off to her left, she jerked her head to look—but already it was gone. Then it reappeared, multiplied—and the darkened yard twinkled, all at once, with countless fireflies.

Nan let out the breath she had been holding. Watched the glimmer of the tiny, friendly lights a moment more before she stepped back inside and shut the door firmly.

And locked it. Only a New Yorker, she was sure, would bother, here in a part of the country where people probably left their cars and houses wide open and slept out under the stars whenever the mood took them. As she slid the bolt, she knew her actions made no sense—that she was responding not to reason but to a host of nameless fears, shadowy dreads and doubts aroused in her by that lost, poignant cry. What was she doing so far from the world she knew and understood, with a child for whose welfare she was frighteningly responsible? What had ever in a million years made her think she could pull this off?

Settle down, she told herself firmly. You're tired; it's dark out; you've had a long day. It'll all look better in the morning.

The common sense calmed her enough to retrieve her drink from the other room, and she downed it in one gulp. But even while the brandy burned its way to her belly, she could still feel the chill from that distant cry lingering in her bones.

Chapter 2

She woke just before dawn and jerked up in bed, heart thudding against her ribs. She didn't know where she was. And the dream still hovered, shadowy and threatening—the old nightmare of running and not getting anywhere, driven by a terrible, formless urgency, seeing her own breath clouding the air in front of her face.

That was all. But it had never failed to scare the bejesus out of her, and this time was no exception. She sat clutching a handful of sheet, blinking frantically against the unknown half dark surrounding her.

Silence. Silence and dim, unfamiliar space, the shapes of windows defined by a gray glimmer too faint to be called light. At last, little by little, the dream began to loosen its hold and she remembered where she was.

I'm at Annabel's. Annabel's house in Tennessee.

She took a deep breath and released it. The world was utterly quiet. No familiar city noises—wailing sirens, quarreling voices out in the street, megawatt thump of music from a cruising car. Not so much as the rumble of a passing truck over the cobblestones below the loft's windows. In the silence, sleep seemed to be gone for good.

Slipping out of bed, she went to kneel on the deep window seat in the alcove overlooking the front yard.

She caught her breath at the sight of the orchard—gnarled shapes of apple trees rising from a sea of pale mist like an etched illustration from some sinister fairy tale. Her camera bag was on the floor near the closet, dumped there in last night's rudimentary unpacking. She rummaged through it hastily, found the Hasselblad and went back to the window to frame the orchard in the viewfinder, shooting a dozen exposures in quick succession.

The squeal of the motor drive was raucous in the predawn hush, but she was scarcely aware of it, concentrating on capturing the gnomish magic of the scene before her. Before she knew it, she had used up the roll—and, it seemed, her anxiety as well: all at once she was exhausted, too tired even to rewind the film. Dropping the camera on the cushioned window seat, she stumbled back to bed, sleep rising to engulf her like a wave.

When she woke again, the room was filled with sunlight—splashed across the white walls, pooled in the white coverlet rumpled around her on the big four-poster bed, glowing in the cider-colored depths of the wide floorboards. To her left, outside the long window that took up most of the room's back wall, the mountain stretched sunny tree-covered slopes toward a cloudless sky. To her right, the front alcove showed the gray-green tops of apple trees. She sat up and stretched, took a deep breath and let it out slowly.

Maybe this was going to work out after all, the way she had planned: a change of scene to shake both Stephen and herself loose from the past months' misery. Gabe had thrown a fit when she had decided to spend the whole summer out of New York—mostly,

she thought, because he was afraid of losing ground
with Stephen. But she wouldn't put it past him to retain
possessive feelings about her as well, even after he had
offloaded her for that bitch Jennifer as casually as a
worn-out sweater. Of course, he still claimed their
breakup had been her fault as much as his, and on some
level she knew she had to take a share of the blame.
But she shrugged the thought away.

The sight of her camera on the window seat brought
a recollection of her dawn photo session, and close
upon it the memory of her old recurring nightmare. She
hadn't had the dubious pleasure of its company in a
while—yet considering her dismal mood when she had
gone to bed, it was small wonder her dreams had been
dark. She drew up her knees and hugged them,
recalling the wailing, distant cry that she had heard. In
the morning sunlight, a reasonable amount of sleep
behind her, it was easier to dismiss the incident.
Entirely possible it had been not human at all but an
animal—predator or even prey. In her colossal ignorance of the wilderness, she would have recognized
neither.

She shrugged and let her thoughts return to the way
the orchard had looked, floating in mist. A tricky
lighting situation; she hoped the shots turned out. It
had been a long time since she had taken a picture
without being paid for it, for the sheer delight of capturing an image on film, and the feeling came as a
pleasant shock. Anger and depression over Gabe's
betrayal had left her stifled and revolted by her profes-
sion—the models' perfect faces, the fussing of the styl-
ists and makeup people, all the elaborate technical
paraphernalia required by the world of high-fashion
photography.

She swung her legs down from the high bed and went to the back window. The spread of open pasture was visible below, the four horses grazing in a group, tails swishing at flies. No, not four horses. Two horses and two ponies. Thank you, Cousin Sky.

Attractive guy, for a redneck. Gabe considered himself a country music fan, blasting Kenny and Dolly and Hank Junior from the big speakers in the Tribeca loft, but the glorification of booze and trains, he-men in pickup trucks and tough, good-hearted broads had never done much for her. Gabe: she had called him last night, lonely and nervous after hearing that cry in the dusk, and he had been a complete shit, monosyllabic and distant. She had the feeling she had interrupted him in bed with Jennifer. Why didn't he just put the answering machine on?

The sound of an engine chewing the air drew her to the alcove window opposite. Speaking of men in pickup trucks, here came Cousin Sky now, his rusty Ford bouncing over the rutted gravel of the drive. Had she slept indecently late? A glance at the cracked ivory face of the clock on Annabel's dresser told her it was ten minutes to eight. She would have to discourage this sort of thing, but for now—she threw on the jeans and shirt she had worn yesterday and ran downstairs to open the door.

"Mornin'." He stood on the sun-washed porch, smiling down at her. "How'd y'all sleep last night?"

"Great." Birds were singing loudly in the trees; the smell of warm grass engulfed her. She found herself sniffing the air. It was hard not to feel a little like Kate the dog, black nose twitching as she danced at Sky's heels. "Stephen's still zonked. The drive yesterday wore him out."

"I can purely believe it. Sittin' still's hard work for a young'un."

His eyes rested on her face and she returned the scrutiny. He was wearing jeans and scuffed boots, an old white shirt with a frayed collar, the sleeves rolled up to his bulging biceps. Her practiced eye couldn't help seeing him in a spread for one of the top-line sportswear catalogs: the soft blue and white fabrics perfectly complementing his tanned skin, the ruddy hair and short curling beard. She imagined his horror if she were to tell him so, and found herself smiling at him.

"I'd offer you some coffee, but I don't even know if there's any in the house." That should let him know he'd dropped in a little too early.

He didn't seem fazed. "I brought over some of Cassie's buttermilk biscuits, fresh-baked this mornin', and a thermos o' coffee. She figured y'all might wake up hungry."

The biscuits were delicious, the coffee too (although it was black—apparently, for Cassie and Sky, the only way to drink it), and Nan thought she might reconsider her strictures on early-morning visits. They ate sitting at the kitchen table, looking out at the mountain ridge. Nan marveled at the unbroken forest covering the slopes as far as she could see, fading in the distance to the soft haze that had given the region its name. In the presence of such abundance it was a little difficult to believe in the wailings of conservationists about the nation's disappearing forests. She turned to Sky.

"I'd forgotten there were so many trees in this part of the world."

"Yes'm. Tennessee's still got a few." He tipped the thermos to fill his cup again. She wondered if his remark was meant as a cheap shot at New York City and decided it didn't much matter. The Big Apple could take it.

"And we're in the Smokies, right?"

He took a swallow of coffee and nodded. "That's right." Leaning forward to gesture with his cup at the steep slope directly behind the house: "You remember that mountain?"

Nan let her eye trace the forested crest, sunlit tree-tops against a sky of intense blue, and the name came unbidden to her lips. "Sleepy Gal Mountain." She caught Sky's confirming nod and shook her head. "I never really understood why it had that name. If it's supposed to look like a woman sleeping, I can't see it."

His lips twitched. "Well now, you got to understand that ain't how the name come about. Didn't Annabel never tell you that story? Happened this way, see. One of the early settlers in these parts was huntin' possum one night, claimed he found him a gal lyin' up top the mountain underneath a tree, fast asleep."

He put down his coffee cup and settled back in his chair, which gave a comfortable creak. His eyes, improbably blue, watched her face. "Yella hair and dressed all in white. Well, he tried to wake her but he couldn't. Thought he'd pick her up, carry her on home with him—but when he went to lift her, she just melted away t' smoke."

Nan mustered an appreciative smile for this bit of local lore before she realized it was premature. He was still talking.

"Well, when he went to tellin' folks what'd happened, ever'body thought he was drunk or crazy. But he stuck to his story. Kept goin' back up the mountain night after night, tryin' to find her again. Folks down in the valley'd see his lantern shinin' on the mountain, searchin' all over for that gal. One day he just never come back."

He reached for his coffee again, sipped, set it down. Nan waited for the rest of the story, but apparently that was the end. *One day he just never come back.* She wasn't sure she liked it; the legend had a sinister flavor beneath its quaint charm. She looked away from the mountain, her glance catching on the hill beyond the creek, its tawny crest rounded like a child's drawing.

"You know, being back here is really strange for me. The summer I spent here—it's like a dream. I keep thinking I'm going to wake up back in New York."

"Well, take another sip o' coffee. You done gone and inherited yourself a right decent chunk of property. Why, Annabel's land runs clear up to the top of the ridge yonder. Stephenses got here early on in history and grabbed up pret' near everything in sight."

They both laughed. Nan found herself liking him. He was friendly, comfortable with himself and with her; already he seemed less like a redneck, and she could discern no trace of what she had imagined, the day before, as possible resentment that he had been passed over in Annabel's will. Good-looking, sexy in a rough-cut way, with an offhand macho style that would have infuriated her if he had not seemed like a throwback to a past in which there might have been some excuse for it—her women friends in New York would profess to be wildly jealous if they could see her sitting here. But she had made enough changes in her life for the time being. Her appreciation of Cousin Sky was strictly abstract.

As they were finishing their coffee, Stephen appeared, hair sticking straight up in back and pillowcase wrinkles imprinted in one small cheek. He yawned in their faces, a guileless exhibition of eight-year-old tonsils.

"Hi, bud," she said. "Did we wake you?"

"Nope. The cat stuck its whiskers in my nose." His eyes went to the biscuits. "I'm starving."

"Well, sit down and have a biscuit. Cousin Cassie made them especially for us."

"Mornin', hoss." Sky lifted a casual hand.

Stephen's mouth was already full of biscuit. "Hi."

"Stephen, sit down. We want Cousin Sky to think we're civilized."

"Can I have a glass of milk?" He plunked down in a chair.

"We don't own any milk yet. How about a glass of water?"

Stephen wrinkled his nose. Sky lifted the thermos and shook it. "There's a couple drops o' coffee left."

"He's too young to drink coffee," Nan said.

"That so? I had my first cup when I was nine. How old're you, son?"

"Eight. Caffeine gives you cancer."

"Thanks, honey," Nan said.

"Well, Linda says—"

"If Linda says so, it's probably a fact." Nan sipped her coffee. "Third-grade teachers speak only pure truth."

Sky had gotten up to fill a glass of water from the sink tap. He set it down in front of Stephen and took his seat at the table once more, tipping his chair onto its back legs and rocking slowly. "Tell you the truth, my first cup was mostly milk with a little coffee in it, just enough to wake me up to go huntin' with my daddy."

This remark, as it was transparently intended to do,

got Stephen's attention. His eyes went to Sky's face. "What were you hunting?"

"Buck deer."

"Did you get him?"

"Well, yes and no. That's quite a story, son." The blue eyes returned Stephen's gaze, chair rocking back and forth. "See, me and my daddy was out in them mountains from before sunrise till noontime, lookin' to shoot us a deer."

Nan, watching her son's face, got a panicky flash that this was going to be something gory and violent that would lead to more nightmares. As a New York kid Stephen was familiar enough with the idea of humans murdering one another, but she wasn't sure he was ready for a detailed account of some harmless animal's death. She caught Sky's eye, trying to give him some kind of signal, but he only winked at her and went on with his story.

"Now, we'd been trampin' around since dawn, and come lunchtime we had to take a break to eat. Found us a nice sunny clearing in the woods and commenced to see what my momma'd packed for us. Let's see, there was some nice crisp fried chicken, some slaw, and a big ol' cherry pie all wrapped up in foil."

Rock, rock. The movement and his country drawl were hypnotic; in spite of her worry Nan was lulled by the picture his words created: a green forest clearing, drowsy under bright noon sun. "We ate and ate till we figured we'd bust, and we was right in the middle of that pie when we heard a rustlin' sound in the trees. My daddy says, 'Hush. What's that?' "

He paused and made deliberate eye contact with both his listeners: Nan first, then Stephen. She marveled at his timing; he was either a born storyteller or had learned from one. When he spoke again his voice had dropped to just above a whisper.

"Second later, yearlin' deer sticks his head out of the trees and looks us right in the eye."

Another pause while he gave the scene a chance to form in front of them: man, boy, and deer, the moment of confrontation. She saw Stephen wet his lips, about to tumble, about to say *What happened then?* A split second before he spoke, Sky resumed his tale.

"Well, we'd laid our guns down so's we could eat, and they was too far to reach. But my daddy had a mouthful of pie, and he was a powerful spitter. He spit one of them cherry pits at that deer—hit him right in the forehead. Deer gives a great big jump and runs off. We could hear him crashin' through the brush."

He paused again, gauging his listeners. Nan reached for her coffee, relieved that the deer had apparently escaped but distrusting the story's seeming innocence.

Sky was shaking his head. "Well, we never did get us a deer that day. But know what? The next fall I was goin' up the mountain to visit with some folks that lived up there. I was goin' along by myself, real quiet, and I come around a bend in the path and you won't never guess what I saw. There he was. Big buck deer standin' there on the path, and you know what? He had a little old cherry tree growin' right out of his head where the antlers ought to be."

His face was earnest—too earnest. Stephen regarded him owlishly while Nan hid her cynical smile and told herself that everyone could use a strapping second or third cousin to gull them with heroic tall tales. And her innocent little boy was the perfect audience. He had swallowed the story whole.

Then her innocent little boy spoke.

"You're a liar."

Sky's good-natured laugh and her embarrassed "Stephen!" came at the same moment.

"Mom, he's making it up!"

"It's just a story, honey. Telling a story for entertainment doesn't make someone a liar."

He scowled and bit his lip. Nan felt a rush of exasperated protectiveness. If he was difficult at times, who was to blame? He had been almost six years old before they had discovered how drastically nearsighted he was. It turned out that the worried pucker they had grown accustomed to seeing on his small forehead had come from straining to see anything more than a few feet away, and Nan couldn't help thinking the disability must have put a similar pucker in his psyche. At four, he had invented an imaginary friend named Woody who accompanied him everywhere. Therapist friends told Gabe and her to humor Stephen on this subject, so they cooperated when he insisted they set a place for Woody at meals and put up with the occasional screaming fit when Woody was accidentally left behind crossing a busy Manhattan street. With the advent of the thick lenses that corrected Stephen's vision, Woody seemed to fade gradually until at last he disappeared altogether. But Stephen remained moody and withdrawn, as if overwhelmed by the wealth of visual information that had for most of his life been nothing but a blur.

Mothers were supposed to notice these things. Nan blamed herself for not realizing her child's disability sooner, haunted by the guilty feeling that absorption in her career had prevented her from paying proper attention to him. The fact that photography was a visual medium even gave her a superstitious sense of having entered into some unconscious pact with the devil, letting Stephen spend the first six years of his life virtually blind in exchange for her own success.

And success it was, no matter how many times Gabe told her otherwise, how often he bitched that she had sold out, betrayed her talent by playing the high-fashion game. The implication, of course, was that he had remained true to the art they shared. His own work, an obsessive study of textures, was too esoteric to gain commercial success, and he was still working at the high school where they had met as teacher and student. Nan could shrug off his needling with the knowledge that it was her supposed sellout that paid their bills, but toward Stephen the guilt remained.

When the coffee thermos was empty, Sky took his leave. Right away Stephen started nagging her to explore the property, but Nan thought their top priority should be a trip into the nearest town for supplies. That was Breezy, Sky had told her, fifteen miles north on State Road 622. When Stephen sulked, she tried reason.

"Come on, honey. You want to have something to eat for lunch, don't you?"

"Lunch? We just ate breakfast! Can't we at least go see the creek?"

"Stephen—"

"Please, Mom!"

Nan quelled her impatience. Hadn't she just resolved to put her child's needs first? Here was an opportunity to connect with him, help erase the neglect that had been caused, however inadvertently, by her focus on her career. A prescription of sunshine, fresh air, beautiful scenery and righteous mothering to cure all ills.

She looked at her watch: just past nine. Say an hour or so of exploring to keep the kid happy, then drive into Breezy and look around, maybe have an early lunch there, presuming there was an eatery of some kind . . .

"Well, hurry up and get dressed, then," she said. "We haven't got all day."

He ran off through the living room, and she heard his feet pounding up the stairs at the other end of the house. The second, fainter set of footsteps startled her until she realized it was only an echo—one that must have sounded countless times over the house's long history as generations of children were raised here, her own mother and grandmother among them. Bemused and vaguely touched by the thought, she went to fetch her camera.

Outside, under its cool morning skin, the day promised to be hot. Stephen, wearing shorts and a T-shirt, exploded out the back door ahead of her, leaving her to catch the plaintively squeaking screen just before it whacked her in the face. Again the sweet country air took her by surprise. She inhaled deeply and caught, beneath the fragrance of flowers and cut grass, a sharper odor of weeds and rank growth.

Stephen was already climbing the pasture fence, and she quickened her pace to catch up. Beyond his small figure the land sloped steeply down to the creek before rising on the other side. The horses and ponies, grazing together in the green distance, had lifted their heads to watch him, Scheherazade swishing her long tail. Reaching the fence Nan slung the Hasselblad over one shoulder and hoisted herself over the weathered rails into the pasture.

Behind the glaze of sunlight on Stephen's lenses she could see his eyes were big with excitement. Maybe being a mother wouldn't be so hard after all. She smiled down at him. "Ready?"

"Yeah!"

Nan struck off across the pasture, leading the way downhill toward the dark line of trees bordering the creek, but very soon it became apparent that this was going to be more than an easy stroll. They had to push their way through tall, feathery grass loaded with dew, that reached her waist and Stephen's chest. Before they had covered more than a few yards, their bare legs (she had changed into shorts as well) were soaked. Bugs swarmed around their heads, vying to fly up their noses. Every few seconds they had to wave their hands wildly in front of their faces to disperse the mob.

And it was hot—not even a whisper of a breeze. Still they pushed on, the sun like a warm, heavy hand resting on their heads. Birdcalls arced back and forth above them in the still blue vault of the sky, counterpoint to the swish of the grass, the whining insects and sudden whirring flight of grasshoppers all around. The pasture, she thought at one point, was bigger than it looked. Nearing the line of trees at last, they happened across a path made by the horses and followed it thankfully the rest of the way.

Out in the hot pasture Stephen had fallen farther and farther behind; when she reached the trees along the creek, Nan stopped to wait for him. Beneath the rustling canopy of leaves it was blessedly cool. Her skin prickled with sweat from the heat of the open pasture, and she stood still to catch her breath, overcome by her immersion in this much nature, letting her eyes accustom themselves to the shade after the dazzling sun.

At first she couldn't make out much beyond a flecked pattern of quivering light and shadow overlaid on everything around her. Surrounded by tangled green growth, she couldn't actually see the creek, but she could hear it—a contented babbling on the surface of a profound quiet, murmuring of lazy summer mornings, quick-darting fish under the water mirrored by the dragonflies' dance above. It lulled her into a kind of trance, and she moved forward without being aware that she was doing so, scarcely feeling the thick growth that caught at her legs.

(Annabel! Hurry up!

Wait! I have to take my shoes off!

I swear, you're slower'n cold molasses. Whatcha need with shoes anyhow? It's summer!)

The faint voices seemed to flicker in and out of the babble of the water, shifting between illusion and reality as she moved closer to the creek . . .

(towhead Tuck standing barefoot on the opposite bank of the creek, thumbs hooked in the straps of his overalls and his lip curled scornfully

Annabel! Come on!

Okay! I'm coming!

suck in breath as the cold water sluices my legs up to the knee, splash across feeling the pebbly bottom shift beneath my bare soles, then clamber up the cool shady bank opposite, hurrying to catch Tuck, who's already out in the sunshine at the foot of the hill, his hair the same color as the tall golden grass, his voice floating back

Come on! Race you to the top!)

"Mom!"

Stephen's voice, jolting her back to reality. She could hear him crashing through the underbrush.

"Over here." A deep breath and a blink or two seemed to clear both her vision and her head. Stephen came up panting; she reached down to stroke the hair off his flushed forehead. "You okay, buddy?"

He nodded. "It's hot."

The sight of the water seemed to revive him. He plunged toward it and Nan followed, a little shaken by what she had experienced. A dormant memory preserved somewhere in her brain, completely untarnished by handling so that in its awakening she had been drenched by a burst of sensation as intense and immediate as life. Unsettling, both in itself and in its implications of more where it had come from: as if somewhere in the deeps of her memory it still existed, all of it, everything that had happened to the child of twenty years before, only waiting to be sparked into life by the surroundings. Wasn't that what scientific research said—that every experience was stored in the brain, every single experience complete with its own sights and sounds and smells, capable of being triggered by the proper stimulus?

The idea made her oddly uncomfortable and she shook it off, joining Stephen where he stood transfixed by the sight of the creek, wide and shallow, talking to itself as it meandered around rocks and tufts of grass on its way downstream. The flow of movement was everywhere. Runnels and tiny waterfalls spilled down the faces of the larger rocks; there were miniature rapids and placid stretches where the smooth brown stones on the bottom were waveringly visible. Overhead the trees formed a shadowy green arcade shot with sunlight, where gauzy-winged dragonflies darted back and forth and the calling of invisible birds floated above the sleepy trickle of the water.

"Can we go across?" Stephen was pointing. Nan lifted her eyes from the water's surface and saw the hill bulking against the sky, golden against the blue. Its proximity startled her. It shimmered beyond the trees on the opposite bank, suspended in a brightness that didn't seem quite real. A hushed radiance seemed to emanate from it, the scattering of birdcalls and infinitesimal rustlings of the tall grass scarcely grazing the surface of a stillness so profound it set the senses inexplicably tingling.

(grass the color of sunshine almost as tall as we are and together we plunge through it like swimmers our heads bobbing on the surface

take a deep breath—smell the air

tang of pine needles, and something sweet yes ripe blackberries growing at the top of the hill)

There it was again: like a door opening, admitting a wave of vivid recollection before it shut. So real that for an instant she had tasted the warm dark sweetness of the berries bursting on her tongue. She had a sudden dizzying sense of some essential boundary dissolving, allowing an impossible mingling of past and present. Dimly she felt Stephen tugging her arm. "Come on! We can wade across."

Looking down at the small face, made somehow scholarly by the wire-rimmed glasses he had insisted on because they were like Gabe's, Nan forced a smile. "Let's save it for tomorrow, okay? We're running a little short on time."

She congratulated herself silently on sounding just like a typical wet-blanket adult instead of someone whose psyche was performing the classic shake, rattle and roll. Mercifully Stephen didn't argue, just kept glancing across the creek as they started to explore along the bank downstream. The garrulous water kept pace with them, flowing over and around the rocks studding its shallow bed, occasionally giving way to deeper pockets that were smooth as glass. Nan watched Stephen bend to pick up a stick and use it to overturn a rock. He wandered down the shady bank and she followed, trying to watch her footing. A jay squawked loudly on a branch just over her head, then took flight with a clatter of wings.

Remembering her camera at last, she unclipped the lens cap and began to frame shots through the viewfinder. The rippling paths of skating waterspiders on the water's surface, the gleaming texture of a wet rock, lacy fungus growing on a tree trunk—she hadn't taken pictures like this in a long time. The familiar feel of the camera in her hands chased away her jitters, and the universe seemed to shrink abruptly, as it always did when she worked, to exclude everything but what was in front of her lens. Even the squeal of the motor drive scarcely impinged on her concentration. At the water's edge a patch of long, drooping grass fringed with glistening droplets had attracted a hovering dragonfly and she moved closer, holding her breath. The wings were like spun sunlight. Again and again she focused and shot.

(swooping and darting over the glimmering water on wings like golden shadows, buzzing so close to my face that I jump back and Tuck laughs at me)

"Stay there, baby. Don't go away. Just one more . . . and one more . . ." She could feel her lips forming murmured syllables that sank inaudibly into the drowsy background babble of the water. The tiny monster zigzagged back and forth, intent on its own inscrutable business in a timeless microcosm of sunlight and shadow and humid greenery.

Suddenly it darted away. Nan sat back on her heels

and slowly lowered the camera from her face, once more becoming aware of her surroundings—and of her aching thighs urgently protesting their unaccustomed crouch. She stood, wincing, and glanced around for Stephen.

He was gone.

For an instant she stood clutching the camera, paralyzed by panic, and then common sense kicked in. He couldn't have gone far. He had to be just ahead, a little way down the creek bank, probably right around the next bend.

She raised her voice to carry above the sound of the water. "Stephen . . . ?"

A heartbeat went by. Two. Three.

"Stephen! Answer me!" If the little brat was trying to be cute, staging an impromptu game of hide-and-seek, she would wring his neck. All at once the heat seemed stifling, even here in the shade, the air like a moist, invisible blanket clinging to her skin.

"Mom!"

Relief washed over her like a cool breeze. She took a step forward along the bank, then realized her child's high-pitched voice hadn't seemed to come from that direction—or, for that matter, from any specific direction at all. Maybe soundwaves bounced off tree trunks or something. She raised her voice again. "Where are you?"

"Over here!"

This time she got a fix: off to her left and a little behind her, nowhere near where she had expected him to be. It surprised her that he hadn't stuck to the creek, but she shrugged and headed toward the sound of his voice, pushing her way through the woods. As she moved away from the creek, the lush summer growth of leaves and vines formed a thick barrier all around, preventing her from seeing more than a few feet in any direction. Insects whined in her ears. She felt her sense of orientation beginning to trickle away, an insidious unreality taking its place. At dawn yesterday she had been in New York City, the theoretical acme of civilization. Now, just a little over twenty-four hours later, she had managed to lose sight of Stephen in a tract of damp, buggy Southern woods. It seemed impossible, almost insulting.

"Stephen!"

"Here . . ."

Was the voice fainter this time—farther away? Was she going the wrong way? She stopped to listen, all at once unable to hear anything, any sound at all, even the creek. For a breathless moment the silence pressed close on every side. Then there was a sound somewhere at her back—a twig crackling, or a heavy drop of moisture falling from a branch to the ground below . . .

Her skin puckered into goosebumps beneath its film of sweat. Wasn't this where *panic* got its name—the reasonless fear that besets lone wanderers in the forest when Pan, god of the woodland, draws near? Back home in Manhattan this etymological tidbit might seem charming; now she found herself wishing she hadn't remembered it. She touched the camera like a talisman, evidence of modern technology. She needed to find Stephen, and fast. She sucked in a deep breath and called him again.

"Stephen!"

Once the sound of her voice faded, silence returned. A single leaf floated down and touched her shoulder and she jumped. Then a distant cry, scarcely audible, set her heart pounding wildly. Was that Stephen? It sounded so far away . . .

"Where *are* you?" she shouted.

No answer. She wavered, indecisive, reminded of the cry she had heard at dusk the night before, the one she had decided in retrospect was probably some hunting bird. Was that what she had heard just now? Surely it couldn't have been Stephen. How could he have gotten so far away?

". . . Mom . . . ?"

That was Stephen, off to her right this time.

"Coming!" She started toward the sound, shoving branches aside. Damp leaves brushed her face and arms, and the undergrowth caught at her ankles. The camera bounced painfully against her ribs. Without warning she blundered into an enormous spiderweb.

"Aagh—" Trying to wipe the sticky strands from her neck and chin, which had taken the brunt, she could feel a fluttering sensation in her belly, a scream trying to fight its way out. Panic, her mind said helpfully. The fear that besets lone wanderers in the forest when—

"Mom? Where are you?"

Her heart jumped; the voice was startlingly near. She still couldn't see him—but he sounded so close, just yards away. She peered through the thick-growing leaves.

"I'm here, honey. Wait right there. I'm coming." There was the noise of the creek again, doubly welcome after that unsettling stillness. It was maddening that she couldn't see Stephen, but in a moment she would be able to. In a moment this insanity would all be over and she would be able to put her hands on him. Then she heard him squawk in surprise.

"Hey—!"

The yelp ended abruptly in an explosive splash.

"Stephen! What—" Frantically Nan fought her way forward, every instant expecting to emerge onto the creek bank and every instant frustrated. The woods wouldn't end. And Stephen? The only sound was the serene babble of the water . . . but now it seemed to emanate from all sides at once, and she no longer had any idea which way to turn. It was as if the wilderness were trying to keep her from finding her son. The fluttering sensation rose from her belly into her throat. *"Stephen!"* she shrieked.

There was no answer.

Trapped in a maze of sunlit green, she floundered wildly in one direction and then another. In about one second she was going to start screaming uncontrollably. Her breath came in gasps and sweat dripped down her face, stinging her eyes. She wished fervently for napalm, any substance that would obliterate this infuriating jungle of lush growth around her and let her see her way. She needed to find Stephen. That truncated cry—

And then, plunging headlong through what seemed like a solid wall of vegetation, she blundered out onto the creek bank.

Finally. A sobbing breath of relief escaped her. Here it was, just the way she had left it—a winding stretch of water wandering out of sight among the trees. She noticed she had emerged at almost the exact spot where she had first entered the trees: there was the patch of grass where she had photographed the dragonfly. But where was Stephen? From the sound of it, he must have slipped and fallen into the water. Suppose he had hit his head? Knocked himself out? As the horrifying possibilities surfaced in her mind, she was already hurrying along the bank, scanning the water, dread gathering inside her.

When she found him at last, there was a lapse of several seconds before the information made its way from eyes to brain. She became aware of staring down at something beneath the moving surface of the water—something she belatedly recognized as the blurred white face of her son.

"Oh God." The whisper seemed to come from outside her as she stumbled into the numbing water and pulled him to the surface. He lay completely limp in her arms, head lolling. Water streamed from his nose and mouth below the dark hair plastered to his forehead. His glasses dangled from one ear.

Fear had drained all strength from her arms, but somehow she managed to haul him up on the bank, where she laid him on his back and frantically tried to recall what, if anything, she knew about artificial respiration. You tipped the head back, pinched the nostrils shut, breathed into the open mouth . . .

As she bent over Stephen, out of the corner of her eye she caught a glimpse of someone standing in the shadows across the bank. Someone—a small towhaired boy, arms akimbo? Shock jolted through her. And then the leaves rustled and the light changed, and she saw it was nothing. Only air and shadow after all, and bright reflections glancing off the water.

Stephen stirred and made a retching sound. Her heart leaped.

"Stephen? Honey?"

"Mom . . . ?" He blinked and squinted at her, then struggled to sit up. She helped him as best she could; relief weakened her nearly as much as the fear. He retched again and water dribbled down his chin, followed by what seemed like a good gallon of the creek. When he had finished he collapsed, shivering, against her. Nan became aware of something strangling her—her camera strap—and took off the Hasselblad to set it on the ground beside her.

"Are you okay, honey? How do you feel?"

"I'm cold. I can't see."

She located his glasses and he fumbled them into place. Nan hugged him. "We'll get you warmed up. Thank God you're okay. What happened? You slipped and fell?"

He coughed and shook his head. "Somebody pushed me."

"Pushed you?" She held him away from her, peering into his face. Obviously his imagination was on overload. "Stephen—there's nobody around here but you and me."

"I can't help it! I *felt* somebody." His lips began to quiver and he let out a wail. "My knee hurts, Mom."

Glancing down, she noticed his knee for the first time, purple and horrifyingly swollen. He must have hit it on the rocky creek bottom. *Just thank God it wasn't his head.* The thought of what might have happened overwhelmed her all at once, starting her heart racing again, returning her muscles to jelly. She wasn't altogether sure she could even stand, much less help Stephen all the way back to the house. As the two of them huddled there together on the bank, she sensed once more the deep stillness of the woods beneath the sound of murmuring water. Overhead not a single leaf stirred, and even the birds had fallen silent. Across the creek the golden hill loomed against the sky.

The sight of Stephen's knee, growing bigger and

more impressively purple by the second, was what finally gave her the impetus to move.

"Come on, honey. Let's get you back to the house and take care of that bump." Her voiced sounded as shaky as her legs and she steadied it with an effort. "Think you can walk?"

A mute headshake. Nan closed her eyes briefly and opened them on the sight of her wet, miserable child. His nose was running and there was a sodden leaf stuck in his hair. She removed it gently and mustered a fake smile. "No problem. We'll flag a taxi."

With a certain amount of flailing and stumbling she managed to carry him. To her surprise, she found her way through the trees without difficulty this time. The woods seemed less impenetrable; she was even able to glimpse the sunlit pasture shimmering through the trees ahead. It was mortifying to realize that she might have created her own difficulties out of sheer hysteria, and she tried to put the memory behind her.

Out in the open pasture the going was slightly easier. But the slope was steep under a broiling sun, and as she toiled up it her camera seemed to weigh a good five pounds more than it had on the way down. She could hear herself huffing and puffing, the sound punctuated by the rhythmic squishing of her wet sneakers, Stephen's whimpers, the whine of insects around her head. Her only thought was to reach the house, a man-made environment over which she had some control.

The journey seemed to take forever. Her arms began to ache with Stephen's weight, dully at first, then excruciatingly. At last they went numb. Her whole body, even those few parts that had escaped a soaking in the creek, dripped with sweat. The fence wavered in the distance before her eyes, never seeming to get any closer until, unexpectedly, it appeared right in front of her. Somehow she got herself and Stephen over it, then stumbled up the back steps of the house and elbowed the screen door open.

"I'm thirsty, Mom."

"Okay, sweetheart. Okay."

Once she had deposited him on the couch in front of the television set, sensation began to creep back into her fingers. She brought him a glass of water and put him into dry clothes, then went to ransack the bathroom off the kitchen for something to use as an icepack for his knee. By now her breathing had returned to normal, but her arms were still trembling and weak, and closing the door of the medicine cabinet she got a shock: the face in the mirror was wild-eyed, streaked with sweat and grime—not something she wanted to claim as hers.

Deep in the throes of one of his video games, Stephen scarcely seemed to notice when she propped his knee on pillows and packed it with ice. Had he really recovered so quickly from his traumatic experience? She couldn't say the same for herself. She desperately needed a drink, but the fact that it was barely ten-thirty in the morning made her settle instead for a glass of cold water from the sink. Sitting at the kitchen table, she tried to review the incident in its proper perspective.

What had actually happened? They had gotten separated in the woods—her fault, for getting absorbed in her own thing and not keeping an eye on him, the same old shameful story. Her panicky reaction to the situation had prevented her from finding him quickly. And then he had slipped and fallen in the creek, and nearly drowned.

Not a nice picture, however you viewed it. What unnerved her most was the swiftness with which their pleasant outing had turned to disaster—one minute a pastoral idyll, the next a narrowly averted tragedy. She shuddered at the memory of Stephen's white face beneath the water's surface. If she hadn't found him when she did . . .

His odd words returned to her. *Somebody pushed me.*

A shudder went through her and she turned it into a shrug. Absurd. He needed an invisible assailant to blame for the clumsiness that had made him trip and fall. Both Stephen's imagination and her own had been running rampant this morning; he had not been pushed, any more than she had been deliberately led astray in the woods. All said and done, the whole business had been no more than a classic case of city slickers out of their depth in the country. They had blithely embarked on their expedition as if it were a stroll in a city park, complete with asphalt paths, dogs on leashes, trash baskets every thirty feet—and Mother Nature had taught them otherwise. A rough lesson. Draining her water glass, she silently thanked heaven it had been no worse.

Chapter 3

Breezy, Tennessee, fifteen miles away on winding country roads that made it seem at least twice that far, was a smattering of houses and stores (Ikenberry & Garth's General, Breezy Feed & Seed, Bev's Valley Luncheonette), a couple of churches, a gas station and a cider-processing plant. The wide, sunny street in front of the Circuit Courthouse, where a tiny cannon and squat obelisk commemorated dead heroes from the War Between the States, was named Front Street, the one behind it Back Street. Nan had no conscious recollection of the place, although she was sure Annabel must have taken her into town at least once or twice. She accosted two local women for directions to a doctor.

The doctor's office was right on Front Street. Vernon Hales, M.D., who looked like a country medic from central casting with his shaggy salt-and-pepper hair and bushy mustache, listened to her tale of the morning's ordeal with what seemed like minimal interest.

"I don't know how long he was actually under the water, but . . ." she heard her voice trail off. Central casting had supplied Dr. Hales with Ben Franklin half-glasses, but his eyes didn't exactly twinkle over them. They were more on the bleary side, and Nan wondered if the doctor might have a little drinking problem. Just now he seemed to be having trouble staying awake. He grunted, blinked at her, then applied his stethoscope to Stephen's chest.

"Cough for me, son."

Stephen obliged. The doctor moved around to his back and listened some more. At last he straightened.

"No harm done on the inside. Let's take a look at that knee."

To Nan's relief the knee injury proved minor, but Hales advised her to keep Stephen off it for a few days.

"Kids heal quick. He'll be back to normal before you know it."

"And you really think he's okay from . . . from being in the water?"

The doctor's eyes opened fully for the first time. "Relax, missus. He ain't the first youngster ever to rinse out his insides with one of the local waterways. The boy's fine."

His tone was authoritative; Nan felt her doubts subside a little. Hales seemed experienced, at least, and competent enough. And anyway, he was apparently Breezy's only doctor, so there wasn't much choice.

His words lingered in her head as she escorted her limping child from the office. *Ain't the first youngster ever to rinse out his insides with one of the local waterways.* Apparently near-drownings weren't particularly unusual around here—or drownings either, probably. She grimaced, making a sudden connection. *Tucker drowned.* And while the details of that incident were still buried, inaccessible somewhere in her subconscious, she thought it might explain why she had imagined seeing her childhood friend there in the shadows moments after she had pulled Stephen from the creek.

*   *   *

They still needed to buy supplies. Nan discovered
a certain comfort in this practical task, a sense of
regaining control of herself and her surroundings as
she pushed a cart up and down the aisles of Ikenberry & Garth's. She had left Stephen by the double
screen doors in the front, where she could see him
hanging over a glass-topped freezer that contained
every variety of trashy ice-cream bar in the known
universe. She supposed he would want to try them
all, and in her current mood of gratitude that he was
alive, she would be a complete pushover—but it was a
problem she could happily cope with.

Existence seemed to have resumed a manageable
aspect once more. Ceiling fans moved lazily in the
shadows overhead and a calico cat drowsed on a top
shelf. She tried to make a mental shopping list but
managed to fill her cart without being able to shed the
feeling that she was forgetting a dozen essentials. Oh
well, she could always come back tomorrow. The
store's wide, dim aisles seemed to boast, in addition to
food, everything from sewing supplies to hunting gear.

"Y'all hurry back." The plump woman behind the
counter offered the classic Southern injunction, standard in every place of business south of Maryland. On
their drive down, Nan had noted and silently rejected it
as meaningless, a kneejerk response to transacted business. But she smiled and nodded anyway, thinking that
in this case it would probably be necessary.

On the way home in the car, Stephen regaled her
with a description of a three-legged dog he had seen
outside the store.

"He acted like he didn't even know it was missing.
He just went hopping along. But it looked really

funny." He was quiet a minute. Then: "Mom, can I get a dog?"

"Don't forget we have a cat now, Stephen. And Mister Mustard probably doesn't like dogs." She silently thanked God for Mister Mustard. The last thing in the world she wanted was to acquire a dog they would have to find a home for when they went back to New York.

"Linda has a cat *and* a dog. She told us. They love each other. They even sleep together."

Blast that damn third-grade teacher, who—when she wasn't brainwashing the kids on every subject from coffee to dolphins—was always encouraging them to imitate her lifestyle. They were approaching Annabel's driveway and Nan slowed the car, not wanting to miss the entrance, obscured by low-hanging branches. There it was. She touched the brake and turned onto the gravel surface to start down the long, wooded drive.

"Mom?"

"That's nice, honey. But not all cats and dogs get along. And it's not really fair to Mustard, is it? I mean, he was here first."

"But he shouldn't—"

She never found out what it was that Mister Mustard shouldn't do, because at that moment another car appeared around the curve of the shady driveway, coming straight at them and going fast. Some portion of Nan's brain saw dappled sunlight flash on the windshield of the approaching vehicle, noted its damaged front grille as she slammed on the brake and swerved to the right. There was a whoosh of branches sweeping the windshield, then a rapid popping sound as the other car tore by them at breakneck speed. It made Nan think of gunfire; instinctively she reached out and pushed Stephen's head down.

But it was already over. The roar of the other car's engine was audible for a few moments, receding into the distance, and then there was silence except for the whisper of stray leaves drifting down on the hood of the car. For what seemed like the hundredth time that morning, Nan could feel her heart pounding as if it would burst. What had happened to her fantasy of relaxing in the country?

"Stephen? You okay?"

Slowly he uncurled from his crouch. "Was somebody shooting at us?"

Nan glanced out the car window and saw half a dozen small broken branches hanging at drunken angles from the trees on the opposite side of the drive. "No. Those branches caught on his car and broke, that's all." Relief gave way to anger. "Who was that jerk, anyway? He almost hit us!"

"Maybe he was lost," Stephen said.

She started to say something nasty about trespassing rednecks who couldn't drive, then forced herself to swallow it. Children were supposed to learn kindness and tolerance from their parents. Maybe the guy had stopped by for some perfectly legitimate reason, then panicked when he had come upon them so suddenly around the curve. She supposed she should give him the benefit of the doubt. Stephen was peering with interest into the seat behind them.

"Did you buy orange juice?"

"Yes." She tried to twist around but was hampered by her shoulder harness. "Why?"

"Because there's a big puddle of it on the back seat."

* * *

Over the next few days things calmed down considerably, to Nan's relief. Thanks to Stephen's injury, further exploration of the property was put on hold for the time being, and she more or less forgot about the near collision in the driveway as they were invaded by hordes of enthusiastic relatives from a dozen branches of her mother's family. Smiling strangers' faces with equally unfamiliar names, related to her in ways she would have been hard pressed to define without the help of a visible family tree—they arrived in bulk to welcome her and exclaim over Stephen's knee, which had begun to subside to normal size as its color went from purple to green to dirty yellow. The sound of electronic music played a steady accompaniment to these visits, emanating from the living room, where Stephen put his video games through their paces for a gawking crowd of country cousins. Nan served the adults coffee or lemonade outside on the front porch.

They were friendly, these people, all eager to make her feel welcome in their midst, but what she felt was overwhelmed. By their effusive kindness, their gifts of newly caught brook trout and fresh garden vegetables, homebaked pies and cookies, and by their sheer numbers. She couldn't keep them straight. There were Talbots and Vails, Barnetts and Lelands and Thatchers and Garths, and others she couldn't begin to recall. She envied Stephen. The video games gave him a kind of social edge; without them she thought he would have been trampled underfoot by this batch of kids ranging from toddlers to teenagers who spoke with an accent he could barely understand and shared a common mythology of which he was ignorant. He was small for his age, and some of the younger boys towered over him.

For her part, she did her best to take it in stride, although there was no denying that she was daunted by this onslaught of family. She scarcely remembered her mother, killed in a car accident when she was six. For most of her childhood it had been just she and her father. They had led a nomadic existence in which she formed few ties, attending half a dozen schools in various parts of the country. These frequent relocations were connected to her father's work as an atomic engineer; and from somewhere or other she had gotten the vague idea that as a very young man he had played a minor part in developing the Hiroshima bomb. When she told Gabe about this, it became a joke between them. *My daddy made the bomb to blow up all the other daddies. He wanted to be the only daddy.* And: "It's the Only Daddy," Gabe would say, holding his hand over the receiver so her father wouldn't hear. "The Only Daddy wants to talk to you."

The Only Daddy was a spare, undemonstrative man, immersed in the calculations he was constantly jotting on a pad with a mechanical pencil. If he was feeling expansive he would take the silver cap off the end of the pencil and show his young daughter the tiny gray eraser, never used. When she married Gabe, the seventeen-year difference in their ages caused wise head-noddings among friends who said she was still in search of whatever Daddy hadn't given her. Whether or not there was any truth in this, her father had never liked Gabe—never liked the fact that they had gotten married when she was seven months pregnant with Stephen, big-bellied in a bright purple muumuu borrowed from her friend Bernadette. The ceremony was held in the Tribeca loft where she and Gabe had already lived together for nearly a year. Her father left almost as soon as the vows were finished, complaining of stomach pains. Only Daddy, only child: he wasn't much, but he was all she could muster in the way of family.

Until now, when they were everywhere she looked—spilling off the porch onto the lawn, driving up in carloads every afternoon. They all called her Annabel, as her grandmother had done, and she was making slow headway in training them out of using the name. It wasn't that she objected, really—there was something liquidly beautiful in the sound, clipped to a single syllable by her years in the brusque, hurried North. But it wasn't her. The name belonged to someone else—the sassy little girl they all insisted she had been, full of fun and always up to something. She accepted their assurances without protest, unable to confirm or deny them. It was as if they were talking about someone else—a complete stranger to the lack-luster, rootless adolescent she remembered with dismal clarity, or the woman she had since become.

In the meantime she was cultivating a noncommittal smile intended to hide her inability to remember their names and on occasion even their faces. She had absolutely no recollection, for instance, of having met the tall, red-haired woman she encountered emerging from the downstairs bathroom. And a few minutes later, collecting used cups from the now-empty library where a bunch of old ladies (those, she was pretty sure, were Garths) had been holding a tête-à-tête, she heard, from the depths of the enclosed staircase, a voice whisper her name.

"Annabel!"

Nan turned but saw no one. It had sounded like a child—conspiratorial, smothering a giggle. But when she peeked around the corner there was no sign of him. She stifled a sigh. Family or not, the brat needed to stay downstairs with the rest of the guests instead of roaming around the house, probably pocketing anything that caught his eye.

This last New Yorkerish suspicion caused her a twinge of shame. People didn't do that kind of thing here. Still . . . she started up the stairs. No trace of him. Where had he gone? The upstairs landing was empty, and she stood a moment listening to the silence. Her whisperer seemed to have vanished without a trace. Was he hiding, wanting her to look for him? Her heart sank. She wasn't good with kids and had no particular desire to become so. But some of them, she had noticed, were like certain dogs—the less you liked them, the more they sought you out.

The door to her room was ajar and she looked in. Unoccupied except for Mister Mustard, asleep on her bed. She picked up the orange cat; he woke and yawned cavernously in her face, then started to purr. Cradling him in her arms—a dose of animal comfort in the midst of all this weary socializing—she went back out onto the landing.

Still no sign of her young guest. Was he in Stephen's room? She leaned across the threshold to look, and all at once Mustard began to struggle wildly in her arms.

"Jesus!"

She dropped him to keep from being clawed. The cat landed stiff-legged just inside the door, fur bristling and ears flattened against his head, fangs bared as he hissed softly at the empty room. Nan could feel the sound running along her nerves like static. She stood staring down at the animal, disturbed by his sudden transformation.

"Hey. What's the matter with you?" She put out a tentative hand to smooth his fur but he turned wild, dilated eyes toward her, then snarled and dodged away to dart past her down the stairs. She watched his tail disappear around the corner of the staircase. Forced a shrug as she turned back to face the room. Crazy critter, to be spooked by an empty room.

An empty room.

Wasn't it?

Nan swallowed. Sunlight from the west-facing window lay gently on the various surfaces, the narrow child's bed with its nubbly old quilt, the table and lamp, the small rocking chair in one corner. Through the front window, half open, she could hear the voices of her relatives chatting on the porch below. Yes, the room was undeniably empty, and in the golden afternoon light it could not have looked more peaceful. Yet as she stood there she could feel the hair on the back of her neck rising on end, as if in mimicry of the cat's fur. A prickling sensation like the faintest of electrical currents.

"What the hell?" she whispered. She took a step back, and her foot struck something on the floor by the door frame—some small object that gave a metallic *clink* as it slid across the floorboards. She bent and searched for a moment, then spotted it and picked it up.

A crude ring, fashioned from a bent horseshoe nail. A shadow flickered across the back of her mind— impression of a dim sun-shot space, dusty smell of hay. In the barn, up in the hayloft with Tuck. Whispers sounding beneath the rafters, syllables as faint as the sifting light.

(Look—I made you a ring like mine. Remember you said you liked it?

It's for me? To keep?

Yeah. Now we've both got one. That means we're friends for always.)

On impulse she tried the ring on her finger now. Too small. Could it possibly be the same one Tucker had made for her, put aside and forgotten to become part of the flotsam and jetsam of this old house, now jarred loose from some cranny back into the light of day?

"Nan? Honey, where'd you get to? We need to say good-bye."

One of her Thatcher cousins, calling from downstairs, and she put the ring in her pocket and forgot about it.

"Coming."

When the family visits finally began to taper off, she couldn't say she minded, yet with a few of her new-found relatives she felt she had made genuine contact. She would have liked these particular people any-where, and the fact that they were connected to her by blood meant, to her surprise, a great deal.

There was Sky, more than good for his promise to help her with the necessary repairs in Annabel's house. He stopped by every afternoon to work for a few hours, and she was already coming to count on his visits for social as well as practical value. His sister Cassie Barnett Thatcher, whose perfect fried chicken had kept her and Stephen from starving on their first night in Ten-nessee, continued to shower them with food, sending over cookies or muffins or a cake almost every day

with Sky. Mother of five, Cassie had a narrow face set
off by auburn hair that hung halfway down her back in
a rippling ponytail. She treated Nan with sardonic
camaraderie, as if they had known each other for years.

Other than Sky, their most frequent visitor was Lucy
Talbot, whose mother had been Annabel's sister. Lucy
was in her seventies, gaunt and long-limbed, with a
high, cackling laugh and a knot of white hair pinned up
carelessly behind her head. She came several times
during the initial flurry of visits and continued to look
in on Nan and Stephen on a regular basis, usually with
a gift of food. The latest offering was spoonbread in a
bowl. She and Nan sampled it in the kitchen, sitting at
the wide wooden table drinking coffee and talking
while Whit, Lucy's husband, escorted a hobbling
Stephen out to the fence with a handful of carrots for
the horses.

"Honey, it is just so good to see you, I declare. And
you do take after your grandma, especially in the way
you smile." Lucy set her coffee cup down and leaned
her bony freckled forearms on the table. "She was so
proud of you, Nan. She used to buy up them fashion
magazines in the drugstore and show everybody the
pictures you took. 'My granddaughter made that picture,' she'd say. 'She's named after me.' And she'd be
about ready to bust with pride."

"I feel terrible that I lost touch with her," Nan said.
Out the kitchen window she could see Stephen offering
a carrot to Scheherazade, who took it from his palm
with a dainty motion of her glossy black head. "I don't
know how it happened. We moved around so much—"

Lucy wasn't listening; she was glancing around the
kitchen, shaking her head. "Would you just look at
that? That cabinet door hanging clean off its hinges and

this drawer missing a pull. You know, Sky tried to keep this place up for Annabel, but towards the end she was just too ornery to let him. 'Leave it be,' she'd say. 'The place is old, just like me. Leave it be.' "

"Oh, it needs work, all right. And I'm still purging." Nan had been sorting Annabel's things, endless cartons of papers and photographs, boxes of what could only be described as junk—chipped vases, a pink glass darning egg, a pair of black iron bookends in the shape of owls, with staring green glass eyes. At least Lucy and Irene, her married daughter, had taken Annabel's clothes off her hands. She smiled at the old lady now. "Sky's been helping me fix things up."

"Ask me, you'd be better off selling it and buying a smaller place. Around here, of course, honey; now you're here, we aim to keep you. But what do you need with all this land, and a house so old it's falling down? You could find something real nice, something with a modern kitchen, for the money you could get for all these acres. Why, I'll bet you could even afford to build if you wanted to—just start right from scratch."

"But Annabel left me the property," Nan said, surprised that Lucy would suggest such a thing, when the house and land had been in her family since the raising of the original log cabin two centuries before. There was no shortage of local relatives to whom her grandmother could have willed the property, and some—perhaps even Sky—who might have been expecting it. Yet apparently the direct line had meant something to Annabel. "She wanted me to have it," she said.

Lucy's face had gone grim. "You know, honey—sometimes a place can go bad, just like a barrelful of apples. And then it's time to let it go."

The words made little sense to Nan, but she had no

real chance to respond before the kitchen door opened and Stephen limped in.

"Mom! Scheherazade came when I called her!"

"That's wonderful, honey."

"She wouldn't go near Mister, I mean Cousin, Whit, but she came right over to me."

"She must know how much you like her," Nan said.

Whit winked at her. He was well over six feet tall, with a stoop that seemed less the result of old age than a lifetime of too-low dooorways. Thick gray hair, well greased and retaining the marks of the comb like plow furrows, was plastered straight back from his broad freckled forehead. "Young Stephen's got an eye for a fine-lookin' horse," he said.

The Talbots left soon after, Lucy turning back for a moment on the porch. Her old hands, twisted with arthritis, reached for Nan's and held them. "Remember what I said, now."

"I will," Nan said, thinking: She's old. Humor her.

"And come see us. You hear?"

"Okay."

The hands released her; Lucy went down the steps and climbed into the elderly station wagon where Whit sat waiting behind the wheel. It pulled away; Nan saw Lucy look back. She waved, but the old woman did not respond. She wasn't looking at Nan at all, but down toward the creek.

Chapter 4

On their next visit to Breezy they discovered the bookstore. Its hand-painted sign—BOOKS, ETC.—overhung the sidewalk a few doors down from Ikenberry's. The wooden oval was done in a passable replica of what she supposed was Early American style, folk art, or whatever you wanted to call it: no doubt Jennifer, who was reputed to be an antiques buff, would know the proper term. Nan was aware of being an antiques moron herself, but the sign, swinging there over the broad, small-town sidewalk in the midmorning sunlight, had an undeniable appeal. She looked down at Stephen. They had come to town for groceries, but a small detour seemed in order.

"Want to stop in there and pick out a couple of books to read?"

"Books?" Since hurting his knee he had stayed glued to his video games, engrossed in racking up points and dodging forms of computerized destruction so exotic that a mere fall in the creek seemed tame in comparison. It reminded Nan of the first month after Gabe had left, when she had been too depressed to do more than go through the motions of parenting, and all her resolutions of mother-child togetherness had given way to nights of Chinese takeout on the futon sofa in front of the TV. She smiled brightly in an attempt to banish the memory.

"Come on. You can pick one for yourself. Whatever you like."

He shrugged. "Okay."

The store window, equal parts dust and reflection, revealed nothing of the interior. Nan pushed the door open and a bell tinkled overhead, another touch of small-town ambience. Ushering Stephen inside, she had a vague impression of a long narrow room, almost a book-lined corridor, with a high counter across the back. Conical lampshades of green glass were suspended at intervals down the length of the ceiling, providing enough light to illuminate the spines of the books and catch the glint of the elaborate curlique pattern on the antique cash register.

There were rustling sounds behind the counter, and Nan, fully expecting an elderly shopkeeper with a green visor to match the lampshades, was slightly disappointed at the emergence of a stocky, pleasant-faced man about her own age, his thinning fair hair drawn back in a short ponytail. He smiled at them.

"Hi. How're y'all today?"

"Fine, thanks. We're looking for something to read."

"Anything in particular?" He came out from behind the counter carrying a fruit basket, which he set down in a row with several others on the floor in front of the counter. Nan moved closer. The baskets overflowed with a variety of small plastic toys. She saw a purple monkey, an orange kangaroo, a bright pink mouse. Stephen hobbled forward.

"Hey, neat!"

Before she could stop him, he had grabbed one of the toys and was doing something to it. She heard a rasping sound and then he set the toy (it was a kangaroo) on the counter, where it promptly turned a flip and landed on its feet. It was wearing blue boxing gloves. Just as Nan reached for it, it turned another flip. She snatched her hand away. "Jesus!"

Stephen laughed; the shopkeeper smiled. He placed a pink mouse and a deep purple chimpanzee on either side of the kangaroo. The three toys buzzed and flipped busily, occasionally achieving perfect synchronization for their audience. At last the kangaroo ran down. The other two kept going.

"Wish I had that kind of energy," the shopkeeper said. He was holding out a hand, and Nan shook it distractedly. "I'm Cooper Chalmers," he said.

"Nan Lucas." She was sneaking a look over Stephen's shoulder as he delved shamelessly into another basket. "These things are terrific, Mr. Chalmers."

"Oh, call me Cooper. Everybody does. Yup, folks just love 'em." He reached down and retrieved another toy, a hamburger no bigger than a poker chip, with frilly green plastic lettuce and a seeded bun. When he wound it up and set it on the counter, it ran in circles, lifting the top of its bun and extruding a slice of tomato like a rude tongue. There was something faintly obscene about it. Nan laughed.

"Watch, Mom." Stephen had found a set of miniature false teeth, which chattered frantically as they jumped up and down on a pair of pink bare feet. He turned to the store owner. "Have you got the eyeball?"

"Ran out last week. Should be getting more in any day, though."

The exchange mystified Nan. "What eyeball?"

"It jumps around, like the teeth," Stephen said. "It's neat."

"Honey," she said, "where have you seen this stuff before?"

"Dad takes me to a place at home. I've got the kangaroo, the eyeball, and a little car that flips over."

"I've never seen you playing with them."

"They're at Dad's."

"Oh," she said. She looked up to find Cooper Chalmers watching her. Cooper Chalmers—what a name. But it had certainly stuck in her head, which was more than she could say for the names of the relatives she had met recently. "Anyhow," she said, "I'd like to find something for this guy to read. Maybe *The Hobbit*, something like that?"

He nodded. "Over here."

She followed him toward the front of the store, leaving Stephen digging through one of the baskets. Cooper, who wore an appallingly ugly madras shirt, jeans, and high-top sneakers, was a little shorter than she was, his movements economical and somehow graceful in spite of his stockiness. He stopped in front of a section of bookshelf and bent down to run his finger along a row of titles.

"*The Hobbit, The Hobbit*, don't tell me I'm out of it." His finger moved back the other way; he straightened and turned to her with a sigh. "I'm out of it. I could order it for you. Going to be in town long?"

She supposed she shouldn't be surprised that he had instantly pegged her as a non-native. In a town this size they must all know each other, and probably everything about each other as well. Of course her plans were none of his business, but she didn't want to seem unfriendly.

"Well, all summer at least. I inherited some property

near here—my grandmother died last fall and left me her house and land."

"Your grandmother—would that be Miz Annabel Stephens?" His light green eyes fastened on her face, full of lively interest.

"You knew her?"

"Sure did. She was one of my favorite customers. I was real sorry when she passed on. A mighty special lady."

Yet another person who could lay claim to a more recent acquaintance with her own grandmother than she could. Nan tried not to feel defensive. "Yes, she was." One of his favorite customers. The noise of hopping, buzzing, flipping toys from the back of the store offered a whimsical thought. "Don't tell me she was a freak for windup toys."

"Nope. She was interested in the occult. Specifically in survival."

The occult—the term made her think of shabby signs on New York side streets: Madam Dora (Nora, Tara, Lara), Reader and Advisor. Half-curtained windows, plump women in beaded shawls lurking behind. *Read your palm, miss? Only fi' dollah.* It was difficult to connect this image with Annabel. "What—"

"Survival of bodily death," Cooper said. "It's a big issue in the occult—the idea of the spirit living on, after the body dies."

He moved across to a different section of the bookshelf and waved one hand across a row of titles; Nan moved closer to scan them. *The Egyptian Book of the Dead. Out-of-Body Experiences: A Handbook. The Knowable Future.* She turned to Cooper.

"Annabel was interested in spirits? Why?" She couldn't keep the astonishment out of her voice.

"She never really said, not in so many words. We

just talked, in a general way, about survival. It's an interest of mine. She told me she knew it was possible. She had a real open mind."

An interest of his—and, apparently, of her grandmother's as well. Nan shrugged mentally. She knew practically nothing about such matters, vaguely associating them with the kind of people who ate alfalfa sprouts and burned incense. Gabe despised the whole New Age movement, but Cooper apparently didn't share Gabe's prejudices. "You sound as if you liked her," she said.

He smiled. "I did. I liked her a lot."

"Mom?" Stephen was calling her from the back of the store. "Can we get some of these?" A dozen toys leaped and gyrated in multicolored bonhomie on the counter behind him.

"What about a book?" Nan turned back to Cooper with a wry face. He was still smiling at her. Stephen wandered over, and Cooper pointed him toward the shelf of children's books, then faced her again.

"I should be getting more copies of *The Hobbit* in any day now. If you want to leave your number, I can call you . . ."

"Maybe I'll look at home first. It occurs to me my grandmother might have a copy."

"Well, if not . . ."

He seemed eager for more than just the chance of a sale. Nan found herself looking away from his direct gaze and then chided herself for being so coy. After all, these days she was a married woman in name only. But Stephen was holding up a book for her inspection, and she glanced at the cover.

"*Stuart Little*. Oh, that's a good one. It's about a mouse."

"I know." He flipped the book open to one of the illustrations. "He lives in New York."

As they walked back toward the elegant cash register, Nan wondered if maybe his choice was a sign of homesickness. She paid for the book and three windup toys (the chimp, the hamburger, and a teapot that ran in circles, opening and closing its lid) and received her change. If only she could replace the rest of Gabe's offerings as easily as these.

"Y'all hurry back, now." The same stock phrase that she was already well on her way to despising. But as he followed them to the door of the shop and a few steps onto the sidewalk, where his shirt revealed its garish worst in the light of day, Cooper Chalmers seemed to mean it from the heart.

It was late afternoon by the time they got home, the oak tree spreading its giant shadow on the lawn and the hill across the creek ablaze with westering light. Stephen disappeared inside to play with his new treasures, leaving Nan to unload the huge cargo of groceries. This time she had remembered to make a list and, for the first time in her life, to buy in bulk. It was thirty miles, roundtrip, to Ikenberry's—a big change from New York, where you could always run out for a quart of milk from the twenty-four-hour deli on the corner. Ducking out of the car with a precarious grip on one brimming bag and another balanced on her hip, she caught movement out of the corner of her eye and glanced toward it.

The pasture gate was swinging open. As she watched, it made a lazy arc out over the steep slope of the pasture beyond. Somehow it must have come unfastened.

Down in the pasture the horses were standing together in a clump, heads high and ears pointing forward, quivering with attention as they watched the gate's movement. Nan started forward, afraid they might try to get out. She hadn't taken more than two steps when all at once Scheherazade wheeled and burst out of the group, galloping off in the direction of the creek, her tail flying. The next moment the others had followed the black mare, their hooves drumming the ground like the soundtrack of a Western.

Nan watched them go. The heavy grocery bag was sliding off her hip and she hiked it higher. The gate reached the end of its arc, rebounded and began to swing back, the hinges creaking. And out of nowhere she felt a chill rise up her spine.

Out of nowhere. Because it was broad daylight, the pasture grass shimmering in the sun. The horses had disappeared among the trees by the creek, and the wide expanse of green stretched empty as far as she could see.

Empty. And silent. She could hear the silence beneath the rusty creak of the hinges. A fathomless silence that raised goosebumps on her arms and stirred the hairs on the back of her neck.

Ridiculous. She was losing her grip on the groceries—and on reality too, it seemed. The gate's movement might have spooked the horses, but she was a reasoning being. She set the heavy bags on the ground and marched over to the fence on legs that were shamefully shaky, catching hold of the gate as it reached her.

Just weather-roughened boards, nothing more.

At the reassuring feel of solid wood under her hands, her moment of irrational panic began to fade.

Now that she looked, it was easy to see how the gate had come to be open—the catch had fallen apart. A hook on the middle rail was supposed to attach to an eye on the fencepost, but the latter piece had worked its way out and was lying on the ground. It was just a sort of big, rusty staple; she could see the holes in the post where it had been. She picked it up and tried to push it back in, but it still felt loose. What she needed was a hammer.

A hammer. Her grandmother have must owned one, but she had no idea where it was; Sky always brought his own tools with him. Maybe in the barn there would be something she could use. She wedged the gate shut behind her and, on legs still residually unsteady, went down the steep slope toward the ramshackle structure at the bottom.

The barn's exterior was unimpressive: unpainted gray boards and a sagging roof topped by the stub of a broken weather vane. Nan hesitated on the threshold and surveyed the shadowy interior. It was so quiet she imagined she could hear the spinning of the dust motes visible in the bars of sunlight glowing between gaps in the roof and walls. A soft sifting like the hiss of sand through an hourglass . . . like time flowing backward. There at the far end was the crude ladder leading up to the hayloft, where Tucker had given her the horseshoe ring that matched his own.

It's for me? To keep?

Yeah. Now we've both got one. That means we're friends for always.

The memory hovered briefly and then slipped away, leaving her mind a blank. What had she come here for? Oh, yeah. A hammer.

She walked slowly down the barn's central aisle,

glancing into the stalls on either side, looking for a hammer or at least some reasonable facsimile. The first stall on the right contained a mini-tractor, the kind used for mowing a big lawn—or, she supposed, a pasture if you happened to have one. The machine looked well maintained, and she guessed Sky was the man to thank for that. The other stalls were empty except for piles of the same moldy straw that lay in clumps under her feet.

No hammer.

She eyed the ladder to the hayloft. Nothing but a series of two-by-fours nailed to the wall; she couldn't imagine she had ever climbed it with ease, even as a child . . . but it was possible the loft might hold something she could use to fix the gate. She set a tentative foot on the bottom rung, craning her neck to see into the square of darkness overhead. She could make out nothing. Gingerly she hoisted herself up a rung and then another, peering up at the dark opening above. What if there was something creepy up there—bats, for instance? Preoccupied by this unpleasant fantasy as she moved her foot to the next rung, she felt too late that it was loose—felt it give beneath her weight, pulling free from the wall with a rusty squeal. She heard herself make an ugly croaking sound as if in answer. There was one horrible moment in which she hung there knowing she was going to fall, fingers clinging desperately to the shallow rung above her head as her feet scrabbled for blind purchase below.

And fall she did, landing hard on both feet on the dirt floor, stumbling back a few steps and toppling on her ass in a pile of straw. The impact stunned her. As she sat there trying to get her breath

(Tucker's face appearing above her, worried scowl half obscured by the sunbleached hair hanging in his

eyes, while the pain stabbed her ankle and she forced a smile, determined not to be a sissy)

in the silence of the barn a young voice said clearly, "Annabel—you okay?"

The words sounded right in her ear. Her sense of actually having heard them was so strong that her head turned involuntarily toward the sound.

What the—?

She was alone. Alone in the barn, the surrounding silence intensified now by the spinning of the dust motes and by a faint prickling over the entire surface of her skin.

(Hook my toes over the bottom rail, hold tight to the top one while the gate swings out over the sloping ground inside the fence, dizzying depth opening beneath me to whiz past at what seems like breakneck speed. Terror and exhilaration blossom inside my chest and as the gate reaches its halfway point Tuck yells

Now!

and I jump, feeling the gate bounce under my feet as I launch myself into the air and hang there one instant, free as a hawk riding the air high above the mountains)

Nan blinked against the surrounding dazzle of patterned light, trying to orient herself in the present. There had been no voice, except inside her head. Regardless of how audible, how *real* they had seemed, the words had been nothing more than an echo from the past, jarred free—literally this time—from its hidden niche in her head. She ought to be getting accustomed to the startling immediacy of these memories, which had gained an overwhelming potency during their long concealment. Like some exotic vintage ripening over the years, they packed a wallop.

And each time one surfaced, it seemed to fill in another piece of that long-forgotten summer. She had twisted her ankle the first time she jumped off the gate, and Annabel had scolded them both, Tucker and her. But when Annabel wasn't watching they had sneaked the chance to do it again—and again and again, because the thrill of that long, terrifying drop through the air, once experienced, was irresistible . . .

Maybe then, but no longer. She shook off the lingering memory and began to take cautious inventory of her body.

Am I hurt? Don't think so.

Her shinbones were ringing but by some miracle she hadn't twisted an ankle, and the straw-strewn floor had saved her from losing more than dignity in her final landing. She picked herself up and dusted the straw from her legs and the seat of her pants.

No major harm done. She retrieved the traitorous rung from the barn floor and winced at the sight of the rusty nails protruding from it. A dangerous object. Still, she could probably use it as a makeshift hammer. And then, glancing back at the ladder, she noticed something she had missed before—a muddy handprint between the second and third rungs of the ladder, as if someone had braced a hand there for a moment before beginning to climb.

Someone. Sky? Slowly she walked over and placed her own hand on top of the print, seeing with a nasty little jolt that it belonged to someone whose hand, though a good bit wider, was not much longer than her own. A man's, but too small to be Sky's. The mud was dry, flaking off to her touch, but nonetheless she backed away and eyed the loft warily, unconsciously hefting the nail-spiked rung in one hand, remembering the beat-up car with which she had almost collided head-on in the driveway nearly a week ago.

Who was the driver, and why had he been in such a hurry? And if the handprint indeed belonged to him, what had he been doing in her hayloft?

Nan shook her head. If the answer was in the loft, it would have to remain a secret for the time being. She wasn't about to risk that ladder again.

She carried the broken rung up the slope and used it to bang the metal staple back into the fencepost, then hooked the gate firmly shut. And if she recalled her earlier inexplicable attack of nerves at the sight of it swinging open, the memory was obscured by the nagging thought of the stranger who had been trespassing on Annabel's property, and his unknown business in her barn.

Chapter 5

She decided to ask Sky about the stranger. Nearly every day brought a visit from her handsome cousin; he was taking time off from working in his orchards to help her with repairs around the house—mending the various cracked windowpanes and leaky faucets, the faulty electrical outlets and broken hinges, the clogged sink in the downstairs bathroom and all the other minor but irritating problems typical of an old house. Whatever his reasons, whether he was looking out for a possible future investment or simply being nice, Sky manfully tackled these projects one by one. Nan had come to depend on the sight of his truck jouncing down the drive, and not just because of his talents as a handyman. While he worked, they talked, and these brief doses of adult companionship had so far helped squelch her worries about transplanting herself and Stephen to this isolated place. When she told him about nearly colliding with the rundown car in the driveway, he shook his head.

"You know, I'll bet that was Jerry Ray Watkins. He's just an ol' local boy from back in the holler. Used to do a little work for Annabel now and then. Mighta left some tools and such over here and come by to collect 'em. You musta took him by surprise."

"Well, it was mutual. He could have stopped and apologized."

Sky shook his head, blue eyes alight with something that might have been amusement. "Jerry Ray's right shy."

It seemed to explain away her fears, and Nan decided she had been worrying needlessly. She had better things to think about—specifically a project had been lurking at the back of her thoughts since she had photographed the orchard at dawn. And Sky's skill with tools seemed to make it feasible. She wanted to build a darkroom in the basement. When she outlined her scheme he was enthusiastic, even volunteering to drive out in his truck to the lumberyard on the other side of Breezy to pick up the materials.

"But you have to let me pay you for the work."

"You kiddin'? I'm havin' fun."

"But it's taking up your time. And really, it'll make me feel better."

Sky grinned. "Well now, Cousin Nan. I surely wouldn't want t' make you feel bad."

Two days later, he arrived early in the afternoon with a truckload of materials and an assortment of power and hand tools. Nan helped him carry everything down to the basement, where they set up sawhorses and got to work. A few minutes after Sky started to rip Sheetrock with his circular saw, she looked up to see Stephen at the top of the basement steps, peering down.

This was unusual—Stephen had gotten into the habit of avoiding Sky during his frequent visits. He had taken Sky's tall tale about the deer entirely the wrong way, seeming to think Sky had pegged him for a sucker, and no amount of explaining on her part had been able to shake his conviction.

Now the allure of the saw's howl had apparently outweighed his other feelings. The bright, spinning blade bit cleanly through the final few inches of Sheetrock; Nan lifted her half away and set it against the wall, then glanced up to where Stephen was standing.

"Hi, honey. What's up?"

He balanced on one leg on the threshold. "What're you doing?"

"Building the new darkroom. Be careful up there, sweetie. You don't want to fall."

Stephen lowered his other foot to the step. "Mom, can we go down to the creek?"

The saw screeched as Sky touched it to the Sheetrock again. A fine plume of dust flew from the blade's track as, eyes narrowed, he guided it expertly along the line she had penciled. Again she caught the cut piece and put it aside.

"Okay, that was what—four by seven? Now we need a piece three feet by sixteen inches; it can come out of that other sheet."

"Can we, Mom?"

Nan squinted up at him through the dusty air. "Now? I'm right in the middle of this, Stephen."

She couldn't help being annoyed at his timing. In the aftermath of his accident, she had ruled the creek off-limits unless she accompanied him. Yet he had the run of the yard and pasture, from which he had garnered various treasures including several nondescript gray feathers, a large dead beetle with its legs frozen in the classic dead-bug pose, and a dry puffball that broke open and emitted a noxious-smelling yellow powder onto the kitchen table. Why—when she was obviously busy—had he set his sights on the creek?

"We'll go in an hour," she said.

"Never mind." He kicked the doorjamb, not very hard, and she turned away deliberately, making a show of steadying the Sheetrock while Sky started the saw again. Even without looking she was aware of Stephen making a sullen descent, wandering off to the other end of the basement where the saddles and bridles were kept. Then she put him out of her mind. Sky finished cutting the Sheetrock to the dimensions she had calculated, then made short work of the two-by-fours. Together they laid the latter out on the floor to be fastened together.

He stood back and eyeballed the framework. "Where'd you learn about wall construction, anyhow? Most women don't know jack shit about this stuff, pardon my French."

Nan laughed and brushed sawdust out of her hair. "In New York, the housing in my neighborhood doesn't offer frills like interior walls. If you want them, you have to build them yourself."

"Is that so? Don't sound too private."

"Who needs privacy?"

He gave her a half-smiling look that made her suddenly very much aware of their respective sexes. A primitive sense of male and female and what they were designed to do together passed over her like a wave of vertigo. It couldn't have lasted more than a moment. But in that brief interval they had managed to drift far away from the hot, dusty cellar. A voice at Nan's elbow made her jump.

"Mom?"

"Jesus, honey!"

She had forgotten all about him, and her surprise, coupled with her sense of something significant interrupted, made it come out sounding harsh. His face puckered and her conscience stabbed her. "You scared me," she said more gently.

"Can I keep this?"

As he held it up for her inspection, she recognized the horseshoe-nail ring she had found last week on the floor outside his room.

"Stephen, where did you get that? I wish you wouldn't go through my stuff."

"I didn't. It was on the windowsill in my room."

She distinctly remembered taking the ring out of the pocket of her jeans and putting it on her dresser. But right now, with Sky present, wasn't the time to get into a wrangle about truth-telling. She glanced over at her cousin and he winked. She sighed.

"All right. Fine. It's yours."

"Neat. Thanks."

He slipped the ring on his finger, admired it briefly, then turned and ran up the cellar stairs without another word. Nan shook her head, watching him. When he had disappeared she turned to Sky.

"I should walk down to the creek with him. Although why he has to wait until I'm right in the middle of something—"

He scratched his chin. "Why don't you let him go on ahead? I'm willin' to bet he's learned his lesson. He'll be careful."

She sighed. "He's a city kid, Sky. He's just not equipped to traipse around out in the country by himself. If I hadn't been there to pull him out of the creek that first day . . ." She broke off. "I don't even want to think about it."

He was watching her, eyebrows quirked. "Yeah, but he knows to watch his step now. And you know 'bout boys and their mommas' apron strings, Cousin Nan. It just ain't natural. You let him go on ahead. He'll be okay."

Nan's skepticism must have shown in her face. He saw it and smiled. "He ain't goin' to drown, hon. Nor get snakebit, neither—up on the mountain you might find you a rattler or two, but down yonder ain't nothin' but little ol' brown water snakes. He won't come to no harm. Just tell him to keep clear of them pine woods on the far side of the hill. He might get himself lost in there."

He clearly thought she was a typical overprotective mother, and the sharp contrast with Gabe's view of her parenting skills both amused and saddened her. "Are water snakes poisonous?"

" 'Bout as poisonous as a potato chip."

It made her laugh in spite of herself—laugh hard enough to suspect that her response wasn't to his words but to the lingering effects of the unexpected sexual spark between them. If Stephen hadn't been there, what would have happened? Even the recollection was enough to make her a little giddy. She sat down on the cellar steps and laughed until tears came to her eyes, blurring Sky's tall figure against the afternoon sunlight slanting through the high-set cellar window. He started to laugh too, in deeper counterpoint, and the joined sound moved through her like a touch.

When he left an hour or so later, Stephen hadn't reappeared. She heard electronic music in the living room and found him there playing Super Mario. The idiotic blooping and bleeping got on her nerves. She envied Mustard; the fluffy orange cat lay sprawled on Stephen's lap, oblivious to everything but comfort.

"Hey. I thought you wanted to go down to the creek."

He shrugged a little. On the screen Mario's sprightly figure jumped on the heads of a couple of enemy mushrooms and then bounded up a steep flight of stairs to a castle.

Nan had a flash of insight involving the merits of a walk that removed your mother from the company of someone you didn't like, as opposed to one that disrupted an activity you enjoyed. She eyed Stephen's small profile, his lenses reflecting the flickering colors on the screen. He didn't look her way. Was he jealous of Sky and the time she spent with him? The thought gave her a pang. What he really needed was someone his own age to play with, some local kid who knew his way around. Somebody—

Somebody like Tuck.

In the intervening twenty years, the memory of the boy who had been her constant companion for a single summer had paled to a mere outline, like one of those old tintypes whose blacks have faded to silver over time. She had remembered his name, his white-blond hair, the bald fact that the two of them had been involved in an accident in which he had died. That was all, other than a few fuzzy fragments like the tree house, the creek and the hill—which she had employed shamelessly on the drive down in order to whet Stephen's appetite for the place.

But the disconcerting memories awakened by her return to Annabel's were beginning to fill in her sketchy recollections, suffusing them with color and life—and with elusive flashes of emotion as well. For the few dazzling instants in which some random trick of light or sound seemed to conjure Tucker up without warning, she was immersed not only in the sounds and sights of that summer, but in the fierce joys and aches of childhood as well. Scornful, sunny-haired Tucker, her best friend—and her hero, no matter how stoutly she would have denied it. Their friendship had been a heady, nonstop round of teasing, competition and feats of daring; and looking back at it from an adult's perspective, she was touched by the realization that the godlike being she had secretly worshipped had been a small boy, not much older than her own son.

The next day, with Stephen in mind, she asked Sky about children in the neighborhood. But he shrugged and shook his head. "Ain't none to speak of. You got old man Todd over north o' you, he never married. Crenshaws on the south; they got a pair o' baby girls. I'm the only other near neighbor you got. Couple folks livin' way up yonder on the ridge." He seemed to guess she was looking for someone for Stephen to play with. "Hey, my brother Burke's got him a boy 'bout Stephen's size, little bigger maybe. I'll get him over here."

He brought his nephew, whose name was Billy, with him the following day. Billy was a round-faced redhead a year older than Stephen and quite a lot bigger. The two of them didn't seem to have much to say to each other, but nonetheless Nan declared the television off-limits and sent them outside, where they wandered off in the direction of the pasture while she and Sky started to work. The darkroom was beginning to take shape; the walls were complete and the wiring nearly finished. Nan had called Gabe and asked him to strip their unused darkroom in the loft of equipment and supplies.

He had grumblingly agreed. She calculated another week for counter construction, paint and installation.

"Thank God this sink was already here," she said. "I don't think I could have faced plumbing."

Sky had sawdust in his beard. "What do you need with a sink anyway?"

"Well, everything needs washing after it's processed. Film and prints."

He shook his head. "Don't that beat all. I never thought of a picture gettin' washed. Thought you just pushed a button and it came out all done."

"That's only for sissies," Nan said. "Real processing's a whole different ballgame. When everything's set up I'll show you how it works. As much as I can, anyway. Part of it has to happen in total darkness."

Wiring a connection, he looked over his shoulder at her. "Believe I'll hold you to that one."

The thought of standing in the dark with him was suddenly vivid. She looked down at the toolbox on her knees, forgetting what she was searching for. When she raised her eyes he was still looking at her. From the top of the cellar stairs they heard Stephen's voice.

"Mom? We're hungry."

Upstairs in the kitchen she set out milk and some of Cassie Thatcher's sugar cookies for the boys, glancing at Sky. "Do you want coffee? A beer?"

"Milk's fine with me."

She poured three glasses, hesitated, then poured a fourth for herself. Wholesome country living.

"You guys have fun?"

"Yes'm," Billy said. Stephen, his mouth full, avoided her eyes.

Sky took another cookie. "I declare it's a mystery to me how Cassie ever learned t' cook so good. She used to make the most godawful messes in the kitchen when we were kids."

Billy giggled. He obviously thought Sky was terrific, and Nan thought how much simpler things would be if only Stephen felt the same. But—head ducked between his shoulders and eyes lowered—he clearly didn't. Sky finished his milk and gave Billy a poke in the ribs. "Come on, hoss. I told your momma I'd have you home by five."

"Yessir." Billy jumped up and started for the door.

"Whoa! Where's your manners?"

Billy stopped, turned, recited, "I had a good time, thank you." His gaze was somewhere in the vicinity of Nan's feet.

"I'm glad, Billy. Maybe you can come again."

Billy grinned politely. "Sure."

Nan nudged Stephen, who shot her a dirty look and said, "Bye."

When they were gone, the sound of the pickup's engine grinding gradually into silence, Nan sat down across the table from her son.

"I gather you didn't like Billy."

"He's a creep, Mom."

"A creep how?"

Stephen was drawing in a splash of spilled milk on the table top. "He's got a dirty mind. He asked me if I'd ever seen horses do it."

This was too classic. Nan covered her face with her hands.

"Mom?"

"I'm sorry, Stephen. I didn't know he'd be like that."

"He said a horse's cock is as big as a man's arm."

"Okay. We won't ask him again."

"I told you he was a creep."

"I agree," Nan said. "He's a creep."

She took the empty glasses to the sink and gave Stephen a wet cloth to wipe the table. It was a shame about Billy, who might even be a perfectly good companion to those who were not at his mercy. But a city cousin who wore glasses, talked funny and knew nothing about animals had been too great a temptation. Why couldn't Stephen find somebody nice to play with? Somebody who would show him things without laughing at him, without being cruel or trying to scare him? He brought her the crumb-filled cloth and she rinsed it under the tap.

"Is it, Mom?"

"Is what, sweetheart?"

"A horse's cock as big as a man's arm."

Nan turned and looked down at him. The straight dark brows, like hers, were drawn together in an anxious line over eyes like Gabe's.

"Honestly," she said, "I don't know."

She let Sky understand, without going into detail, that Billy's visit had not been a success. In Stephen's book, she knew, Billy was another black mark entered against Sky; and she knew also that there was no point in telling him that this was unfair. She didn't want to appear to be defending Sky to him, but there were times when he made it difficult for her.

"Why's he come over here every afternoon?"

"He's helping me build the darkroom, Stephen. You know that."

"It's taking an awful long time."

"We're almost done," Nan said.

"You know, Mom," Stephen said, "I think he wants to be your boyfriend."

So now at least it had been said. The sexual tension between Sky and her had reached a level obvious even to an eight-year-old. The previous day had been swelteringly hot and he had taken off his shirt and worked bare-chested. She had found herself watching the sinews slide under the tanned skin of his back as if she were a teenage girl ogling a boy at the beach, noticing his hard muscular chest, his flat stomach. She was attracted to him, no point in trying to pretend otherwise. When he passed her the hammer and their fingers touched on the handle, she got the classic million volts. She knew it was mutual, but so far he had made no move, beyond the way he looked at her. And she had to give him credit for that: as if he had somehow divined the conflict in her feelings about him. She knew he was available. He had let her know, in one of their meandering conversations while he worked on the house, that he was separated from his wife, who was at law school in Knoxville.

"Reckon when she gets to be a lawyer she'll go on and divorce me. She's too cheap to pay somebody else to do it."

He sounded more amused than bitter, and she surmised that the decision to call the marriage quits had been more mutual than in her case. Yet in spite of the potent physical attraction she felt toward him, she was still vividly aware of the distance between them in every other sense. She liked him but wasn't sure she could tolerate him in a more intimate relationship. He was so countrified—the way he talked, his manners, his whole mentality.

Stephen was waiting for a response. She sighed. "Look, honey. I'm not in the market for a boyfriend, believe me."

That much was certainly true. She didn't want a man right now; even the idea exhausted her. She needed to relax, recover from the shock of Gabe's betrayal—the last thing she wanted was another relationship. Just Stephen and herself, the two of them: that was enough for now.

So ran the party platform, anyway. Meanwhile she found herself thinking about Sky, structuring her day around his visits, running fantasies about him in some back corner of her mind where she could refuse to acknowledge them. Once in a while they came to the fore and she tried her best to squash them.

Look, he says *ain't*. And if you mentioned Beethoven to him, he'd probably think you were talking about a brand of imported beer.

Oh yeah? Gabe has perfect grammar and a subscription to the New York Philharmonic, and where did that get you?

She gave a mental shrug. If her country cousin seemed to be occupying the center of her thoughts for now—if in spite of herself she was sleeping like a log and waking up every morning with new energy and a sense of buoyancy that wasn't entirely due to the fresh air—well, that would change soon, when the darkroom was finished and Sky wasn't around so much. She told herself that the darkroom was the last major project—that as soon as it was completed she would focus on Stephen, give him the attention he deserved.

But Stephen had apparently grown tired of waiting. On the day she and Sky finished construction on the darkroom and started to paint, he announced at suppertime that he had spent the afternoon playing with Woody.

About to set his plate down in front of him, Nan

barely prevented herself from dropping it in his lap. She put it on the table carefully and then looked at him.

"You did? That's nice, honey." Trying to make it casual. "I didn't know Woody was still around."

"Me neither." He was already digging into his food, his voice matter-of-fact. "He just kind of showed up."

"Great," Nan said, and echoed it mentally: *just fucking great.* Woody had always made her uneasy, even though Gabe insisted that an imaginary companion was the healthy product of a bright, introverted kid's imagination. Children Stephen's age inhabited a world of fluid boundaries between imagination and reality, moving between the two with an ease that would be psychotic in an adult but was perfectly normal for a five-year-old.

Nan had accepted these reassurances. But Woody's gradual phaseout, once Stephen's vision had been corrected, had been a relief—and this unexpected resurfacing hit her with a load of guilt and misgiving. Wasn't Stephen a little too big by now for imaginary friends? Regression spelled insecurity. While she had been spending her time mooning after her handsome cousin, her poor abandoned little boy had been forced to fall back on fantasy.

The telephone, ringing on the wall beside the kitchen table, interrupted her orgy of self-disgust. It was Lucy Talbot, accent twanging like a banjo string at the other end of the line, full of some scheme for giving a party.

"Now honey, you have got to tell me if next weekend is too soon. I want to throw a big old family get-together, to welcome you and Stephen and celebrate my tenth grandchild—well, the little spark ain't due till January, but Danny called me last night and told me Sarah's expectin'. It's their first, and Danny's my youngest, so that makes it just a little bit special, you know? I was thinkin' Saturday night, a good old-fashioned supper in the barn with square dancin' and all. We haven't had one in a good long while, and I realize some of you young folks have never even heard Ellis Whipple play country fiddle. Now that's something you have just got to hear."

Nan, overwhelmed by the rush of words, heard herself accepting Lucy's invitation. Another encounter with the extended family, most of whom she still couldn't recognize on sight: somewhere she would have to find the reserves of social courage to face the onslaught of Southern warmth and goodwill. It wasn't that she was ungrateful. But she was off balance here, out of her element and unsure what was required of her. She was afraid of seeming cold, standoffish, a typical Yankee, hopeless at matching the effusions of relatives who had known her grandparents and remembered her mother and herself as a child. Still, hanging up the phone, she thought the barn supper would be another chance for Stephen to connect with one of his cousins, to make a real friend instead of some pitiful little figment of his imagination.

* * *

Stephen had seen the kid that very first day. Practically the moment they arrived.

Of course, he hadn't known it was Woody then. The impish face with its rude tongue, shadowed by the oak tree's rustling leaves, had vanished so quickly that he had to wonder, along with his mom, if he had just made it up.

But he hadn't.

He hadn't made up the push that had landed him in the creek either. He had felt it, just as he had been aware of the muffled snort of laughter from the bushes along the bank, as if the push were just a great big joke.

And maybe it was. Because afterward things were different. It was as if he could still feel someone there, hanging around at the edge of his thoughts, just beyond reach. But the roughness was gone, and the rudeness—as if whoever it was, was sorry.

The ring he had discovered on his windowsill seemed like a peace offering. Once he had put it on, the sense of someone nearby seemed to sharpen and close in.

A familiar feeling, the same one he used to get from Woody: of a shadowy, friendly presence close at hand. Woody had been like a big brother, someone strong who kept bad things from happening to Stephen. Stephen knew Woody wasn't *real* the way Mom and Dad were real, or his teacher, or the other kids at school. Woody was different. But that difference didn't mean he wasn't there.

And now, as Stephen climbed the fence to head down to the creek, the sense of a soundless, invisible presence beside him made him hesitate for a moment on the top rail.

"Woody?"

There was no answer. But as he started down through the pasture, he seemed to feel Woody walking just behind him—the two of them shouldering the high grass aside under the cloudless expanse of sky, squinting in the sunlight and turning their heads to watch the buzzing grasshoppers sail past them through the air. The pasture stretched around them, a vast expanse of green. Above the trees by the creek, the hilltop seemed to shimmer in the haze, the ridge a mere blue shadow beyond it. Stephen took a deep breath. He could smell pine trees.

"Race you!"

He broke into a run. Suddenly, behind him, he could hear laughter, breathless and nearly soundless, and the rhythmic swishing of the grass. Exhilaration flooded him, practically lifting him free of the earth, and he ran faster. He didn't need to look back.

He knew Woody was there.

Chapter 6

Nan spent the next morning finishing the paint job on the darkroom, wanting to give it plenty of time to dry before Sky came over. He had promised to spend the afternoon helping her bring down the newly arrived cartons that contained the enlarger, safelights, developing trays, powdered chemicals and so on; with hard work she could expect to have a functioning darkroom by evening.

She was surprised by how much the prospect excited her. Back in New York the darkroom in the loft had grown dusty from disuse; Gabe hadn't produced any work of his own in a long time, and hers was handled by a professional color lab. But the shots of the orchard in the mist had been sitting on her dresser for nearly two weeks, and she was curious to see them. And the pictures she had taken at the creek were the kind she had not made in a decade, the kind that had made her Gabe's star student back in high school—black-and-white "found" shots at the opposite end of the spectrum from the carefully created fashion environment.

While the walls and counters dried, she carried the smaller cartons down the cellar stairs. By then it was past noon; Sky was later than usual. No sign of Stephen either—not since breakfast, when he had headed down to the creek. Off to play with Woody, no doubt.

She grimaced and shook her head. This wasn't good. But what could she do? She couldn't limit her activities to the spectrum likely to interest an eight-year-old boy. Maybe he would hit it off with some other kids at the upcoming square dance . . . she could only hope.

Meanwhile, where was he? She went outside and scanned the distant line of trees along the creek bank, shading her eyes against the noontime glare. An unexpected tremor ran along her nerves. It was so *quiet*. Was Stephen out there somewhere playing, or had something happened to him?

The sunlit green pasture drowsed in the heat below the darker rampart of the ridge, breathlessly still, the horses nowhere in sight. A crow cawed hoarsely somewhere off to her left, and the sound was absorbed as quickly as a drop of water in desert sand. Beneath the constant piping of crickets, which sounded to her like miniature sleigh bells, the silence was complete—enclosing the motionless vista of pasture, mountains, sky, not a flicker of movement anywhere. So quiet she could hear the beat of blood in her temples.

Suddenly it was too much. She climbed over the fence and started down through the pasture, not quite running. She just wanted to make sure he was okay. That was all. Just . . . make sure he was okay. As she descended the slope a drowsy murmur reached out to greet her: the voice of the creek.

And then there was a movement among the trees ahead. A small figure emerged and waved.

"Mom!"

Nan slowed her pace, letting out a breath she hadn't

known she was holding. "Hi, sweetheart. I was wondering where you were."

He approached her, breasting the high grass at a trot.
The oppressive silence retreated; a breeze ruffled the
treetops and stroked the pasture grass as a flock of
birds wheeled in the distance. Stephen reached her,
puffing in the heat, and shaded his eyes to look up at
her. "Is it okay if I go across the creek? We want to
climb the hill."

"We?"

"Me and Woody. He showed me a place where it's
easy to cross. There's rocks you can step on and not
even get your feet wet."

Nan blinked down at him. "Maybe you'd better
show me."

He led the way unerringly through the woods to a
spot where a series of stepping stones spanned the
water. "See? You can walk right across."

Nan stood gazing at the smooth brown stones that
gleamed in the sunlight filtering down through the
leaves above. The sound of the lazy, trickling water
seemed to echo in her head.

*(Standing here in the flickering shade of this very
spot, watching Tuck fashion a little boat out of bark.
The final touch is the brave yellow leaf he attaches for
a sail, sunlight catching his pale lashes as he glances
up at me.*

Okay. You ready?

Yes! Hurry up!

*He sets the boat in the water. At once the current
takes it, swirling it away over the creek's miniature
rapids, through the rocks and down. The tiny craft
nearly capsizes, then rights itself, drawing a cheer
from us both.*

There she goes!
Yee-hah!)

"Mom? Is it okay if I go across?"

"I guess so. Just be careful."

The memory still clung to her: tiny boat on its bold voyage, its proportions transforming the creek into a wide river, Tucker and herself into friendly giants running along the shore, yelling encouragement . . .

She glanced down at Stephen by her side. "Do you want me to come with you, honey?"

He shrugged. "That's okay. I'll have Woody."

Ousted by a fantasy. Still, she supposed it might be a healthy thing, some indication of an improving self-image, if he felt confident enough to explore the hill with only Woody for company.

But first he needed to eat lunch. Over his protests, she dragged him back to the house. She noticed he didn't ask to feed Woody—but then Woody had never been much of an eater, even in the tiresome days when Stephen had insisted on having a place set for him at every meal. Now Stephen bolted his peanut butter and jelly sandwich and downed a glass of juice in one gulp.

"Bye, Mom. Be back later." He dashed off across the pasture just as Sky's pickup came down the drive.

Perfect timing. Yet even though her child seemed to be in excellent spirits, her conscience wouldn't quit smarting.

I'll make time for him soon. I swear I will.

But two hours later, when she and Sky had finished carrying down the final cartons and were relaxing over a couple of beers on the porch, she found herself guiltily grateful for the absence of Stephen's eagle-eyed disapproval. The conversation might have been lazy and meandering, but the male-female vibrations were loud and clear.

"So I'm assuming you'll be at this barn-supper thing of Lucy's on Saturday," she said.

"You bet. Gonna dance with me, ain't you?"

Nan shrugged, studying the label of her beer bottle. "I'm not much of a dancer. And I have to tell you, I hate parties. In New York I usually skip them."

"Well, you can't skip this 'un. Lucy's got her heart set on it. She's pleased as punch to have y'all around. And she ain't the only one."

"No? Who else?"

He didn't answer, just put the bottle to his lips and took a long pull, keeping his eyes on hers. She held the look, aware of a distinct sensation of tiny warm bubbles clustering and bursting all along her nerve endings. Exactly the effect he had intended, no doubt. She dropped her eyes at last.

"Well, if you're going to be there, at least I'll know somebody besides Lucy and Whit."

He smiled, accompanying it with a blue-eyed look that caused the bubbles to return in force. "That you will."

*   *   *

Stephen was having fun.

At first he hadn't liked it here in Tennessee, so far away from New York and his dad. The place and the people were strange, and the feelings he could sense coming from his mom were so mixed up that he felt a little nauseous all the time, like the time Dad and his new girlfriend had taken him sailing. He hadn't puked, but he had felt the whole time like he wanted to.

That was how it had been the first couple of weeks in Tennessee. His mom was worried all the time—cheerful and worried one minute, sad and worried the next. He didn't know how to make her feel better. If he let on that he could feel her feelings, it seemed to make it worse. But he couldn't help it. Sometimes it was like he could see inside people, everything they were feeling—as if all of a sudden their skin turned to clear plastic, like the Visible Man model they had at school with his red muscles and blue veins and yellow organs.

Stephen couldn't see other people's guts—he was very glad of this—but at certain moments, which seemed to hit him out of the blue, other people's feelings washed over him in a wave. It happened even when he didn't like them. Like Ricky Brand, a kid in his class at school who had gone after another kid with a pair of scissors. Everybody thought he was really mean, but Stephen could feel how scared he was, his heart beating fast like the class hamster when you held it in your hand.

And then there was Cousin Sky. Even though he acted so friendly and sweet with Stephen's mom, Stephen could tell it was partly an act. Cousin Sky was hiding something.

But today he had forgotten about all that. Woody was here, and they were having fun. They sat on the creek bank for a while, watching the light sparkle like tiny diamonds on the water, occasionally plunging their arms in up to the elbow to retrieve smooth brown stones from the cold creek bottom and throw them back in with a satisfying *plop* that punctuated the water's soft continuous babble.

In the dappled shade of the bank, Stephen was pleasantly surprised to find he could see Woody. A couple of years earlier, before he got his glasses, he hadn't been able to see Woody at all—but he hadn't seen much of anything clearly then. Now, though, especially if he didn't try too hard, if he let his vision soften in the light that was scattered on the creek bank like round gold coins from a pirate's treasure chest, he was able to get quite a clear picture of Woody.

Woody was a little bigger than himself. His hair was very light, like the coins of sunshine, and he was barefoot. He wore overalls, frayed around the cuffs, and a T-shirt. And he had a horseshoe-nail ring just like Stephen's.

"Come on," he said now. "Let's climb up the hill."

Stephen eyed the stepping-stones. "Think I ought to take my shoes off?"

There was no answer. Looking up, he saw with surprise that Woody was already on the opposite bank.

"Hey! How'd you get there so fast?"

"I swear, you're slow as cold molasses. How come you need shoes in the summertime, anyhow?"

Stephen considered the matter, then shrugged. "I don't know. In case I step on something creepy, I guess."

Woody snorted. "Just look out where you step."

He laughed and Stephen found himself laughing too. He untied his sneakers and took them off, then peeled off his socks. The stepping-stones were cold and faintly slippery beneath his bare soles. Once his foot slipped into the creek and he gasped.

"Wow! It's cold!"

Woody didn't answer. Reaching the other bank at last and scrambling quickly up it, Stephen caught a momentary clear glimpse of his face. He was grinning, and there was a little chip off the inside corner of one front tooth. He turned and ran out from under the trees into the bright sunshine and Stephen followed, blinking against the dazzle.

Then something strange happened. He couldn't see Woody anymore. For a moment there was silence, a hush in which even the murmur of the creek seemed to sink away to nothing, and in that moment he felt terribly alone. The golden hill and the bright blue sky behind it seemed to press down on him with a tremendous weight of solitude. Then Woody's voice reached him, drifting back like an echo.

"Race you to the top! Last one there's an old maid!"

* * *

By the time Sky left that night, Nan was forced to admit to herself that she was desperate to go to bed with him. It might be crazy, but the chemistry was just too powerful. Then again, why was it so crazy? She liked him. He was a nice down-to-earth guy, not sophisticated, but she had had her fill of sophistication for the time being. Of course he was her cousin, but what did that matter? She wasn't planning to marry him or have his children. It was just that her body, more honest than her mind, seemed to have made its decision.

He had stayed to supper and she had made a quick pasta primavera, wondering if the dish would seem hopelessly prissy to him. He seemed like the meat-and-potatoes type. Oh well, let him eat again when he got home, if he was still hungry.

Stephen, forgetting to sulk in Sky's presence, chattered about his excursion to the top of the hill with Woody. Sky listened without comment and she was grateful to him for not asking questions; she didn't feel up to explaining about Woody just now. Back in New York, where a good number of Stephen's third-grade classmates were in therapy, Woody was run-of-the-mill. But for Corey County he was pretty exotic, and she didn't want Sky thinking Stephen was some kind of nut. She tried to focus the conversation on the landscape.

"Aren't there blackberry bushes at the top? I seem to remember—"

"Yeah, but the blackberries aren't ripe yet. Woody says they'll be ready by the middle of July. If the birds don't eat 'em first."

Nan accepted Woody's know-how on this subject with a large grain of salt. "And what's on the other side?"

Stephen giggled. "Christmas trees."

"Stephen—"

Sky glanced up from piling a second helping of pasta onto his plate. "He's right, y'know. Annabel planted ten acres of pines for a Christmas tree crop, but she never had the heart to let anyone cut 'em. Just let 'em go. Turned into a right healthy pine forest by now." Pointing his fork at Stephen: "You be careful, young fella. Don't you go playin' in there, hear? Might get yourself lost."

Nan, seeing defiance in Stephen's scowl, spoke up. "Okay, bud. The Christmas trees are off-limits. Got it?"

"*Okay.*" He heaved a disgusted sigh and Nan, glancing at Sky for sympathy, received instead a lazy grin that reduced her bones to the consistency of the al dente pasta.

*   *   *

A Cheshire Cat grin, it began to seem, as the rest of the week went by and she saw nothing more of Cousin Sky. He left that night just at Stephen's bedtime, almost as if he didn't want to be alone with her. Did he have his own reservations about the two of them becoming involved? Hers had been effectively drowned out by the racket her body was making.

Wednesday she was mildly surprised when the whole afternoon went by without his appearance, although the darkroom was now completed and they had made no other plans. By the middle of Thursday she was annoyed. The pleasure she took in her new darkroom was diminished by having no one to help her admire the enlarger in its metallic splendor, the processing trays set neatly side by side on the counter, boxes of paper and bottled chemicals shelved along one wall. But Stephen was off entertaining himself with Woody, and Sky was—absent.

She had been looking forward, she realized, to keeping her promise of showing him how to print a photograph from a negative, not least because the process took place in the dark—prime territory for an accidental touch that could lead to more contact, less accidental. This realization added to her discomfort. She felt desperately uncool, like a high school girl with a crush, plotting and scheming for whatever she could get. Did he know he had her dangling, and had he stepped back to enjoy the sight?

The thought swamped her with humiliation. She leaned back against the counter, feeling the hot blood rise in her face and grateful no one else was there to see it. She didn't need this. Didn't need some redneck Romeo dumping on her, not after what Gabe had put her through. To hell with them both. With the whole rotten sex. All the thoughts of Gabe, more or less successfully kept at bay since the move, ambushed her now as she stood feeling the darkroom's black walls close around her like a palpable depression.

*   *   *

They had lived together nine years, been married for the last eight. From the beginning, their relationship seemed to possess its own momentum, a comfortable current that carried Nan along. After studying photography with him in high school, she had gone on to something like a career in the field, working for a fashion photographer who paid her slave wages. She and Gabe had reencountered each other, after a four-year hiatus, at a school reunion, and after the party she had ended up going home with him. When she moved into his loft downtown several months later, it was without really having made any conscious decision—so many of her belongings had migrated there that finally it seemed silly not to follow them.

Exposure to the lifestyle of a man seventeen years her senior had come as a revelation. Although the salary from his part-time teaching job was far from handsome and only rarely did he sell one of his photographs, he managed to stretch his finances to cover what he called "the essential luxuries"—Colombian coffee beans, good French cheeses, the best sound system money could buy. His loft, ceiling soaring far above the unfinished plank floors (it was her earnings, later on, that replaced the splintery pine with oak), seemed like a prairie compared to the tiny dark Chelsea studio where she had spent her evenings eating frozen pizza and watching bad TV movies on the nights she didn't have a date with some poor slob of a School of Visual Arts student as young and unlicked as she was.

She liked living with Gabe. Liked the cafés and shops of nearby Little Italy and Chinatown, the cobblestone streets outside the loft; liked spending most of every Sunday reading the *Times*, with coffee and fresh brioche from the bakery on the corner. Unofficially he seemed to retain the role of teacher in their relationship—from him she learned that the best bagels came not from Zabar's but from Yonah Schimmel's on the Lower East Side; that it was fine to pay a restaurant check with a credit card but considerate to tip in cash. He introduced her to foreign cuisines—Japanese, Thai, Indian, Ethiopian—and taught her how to drive a stick shift, open a lobster, wire a lamp and make a decent salad.

He had read everything, heard and seen everything, was at home discussing everyone from Black Elk to Wittgenstein. His friends were sculptors and musicians, a famous linguistics scholar, a Central American poet. She listened and learned and accepted his values, his judgments, his analyses and summations. He defined her for herself: bright, the most talented student he had encountered in twenty years of teaching, but damaged by her mother's early death, her father's coldness. The withdrawn, tentative self she showed the world was completely at odds with the creative, irreverent boldness of her photographs.

"It's like you have this other person, this wild woman, hidden away inside. And when you pick up the camera, she takes over."

He was very excited when she became pregnant. He didn't actually propose to her, just started talking about their marriage as a given; and she found herself borne along on the tide of his enthusiasm and the approval of his friends. It was only after they had legalized their union and Stephen was born that she discovered her own paralyzing doubts about her ability to be a mother.

The baby made her nervous. She was filled with fears that she would make some mistake in his care, inadvertently cause him some terrible injury. Much as she wanted to feel warm and maternal, the best she could muster was a timid yearning for his approval. He always cried when she picked him up.

"You're too tense," Gabe would say. "That's why he's crying. He can feel it." She could tell he was beginning to share her misgivings. "Just relax," he would say, frowning, and take the baby. Against his broad chest Stephen always quieted and fell asleep at once.

When Stephen was two, her career in fashion photography unexpectedly took off. All along there had been a continuing trickle of jobs from her early connections—a couple of department store catalogs here, the occasional trade magazine there—provoking acid comments from Gabe about prostituting her talent but adding welcome funds to their family budget. Then one afternoon she got a call from one of the top sportswear magazines; someone had seen a spread she'd done for Bloomingdale's, liked it and wanted her to shoot for their fall issue on location in Montana. Without consulting Gabe, she accepted at once.

That was the beginning. The catalog was a big success and suddenly she was hot, with more offers than she could comfortably handle. Gabe, already contemptuous of the fashion scene, bitched about her frantic schedule, gave her grief when she had to travel, and sulked when she was too tired to make love. As usual he was ready with an analysis of the situation—something about avoidance and denial—but Nan shrugged it off and spent increasing amounts of time on her work. She enjoyed it. With the camera in her hands, her insecurities melted away and she felt competent and assured. To the standard fashion formula she brought a quirky, offbeat style that made people notice her photographs. The response was so enthusiastic that it took her aback at first, but gradually she learned to accept it, to gain a measure of confidence and enjoy the company of colleagues and models, the hobnobbing with clients who were delighted by what she was doing for their product. When they tried to get her into bed, she used Gabe as an excuse, vaguely aware of the irony of the situation.

After a while she noticed things improving at home. Gabe gradually retrenched, dropping his angry demands on her and concentrating instead on Stephen, taking up any parenting slack left by her busy schedule. He became more a companion than a lover, and Nan could only be relieved. She loved him, of course, but the sex had lost what magic it possessed after the first six months. It was his emotional commitment—to her as a friend, to Stephen as a father—that mattered; and of that essential fidelity there seemed to be no doubt. Until this past year, when he had started seeing Jennifer.

Jennifer was a high-powered child psychologist who subscribed to the opera and alternated her weekends between flying to Paris and antique-hunting upstate. Gabe met her at a bookbinding course he was taking at the Y uptown. She was exactly Nan's age—twenty-nine—and recently divorced from an actor who had decided he was gay. Over glue pots and utility knives and sheets of marbled endpaper she and Gabe began a flirtation, which he reported to Nan with a wry, self-mocking air, characterizing himself as an aging Casanova.

It seemed primitive to feel jealous, and Nan didn't. She trusted Gabe, felt herself and Stephen secure in their position as his emotional center, and didn't much care where he parked his cock. When the flirtation expanded into a sexual liaison she even claimed part of the credit for encouraging Gabe; she knew she was less than satisfactory in that area and had a confused wish to prove she wasn't selfish. They were adults, after all, and New Yorkers. They could handle themselves in what might have been, for a less sophisticated couple, a sticky situation. The memory of all that self-congratulation made her cringe now. One icy evening last March, after Stephen was in bed, Gabe had sat her down on the futon sofa in their loft and told her he wanted a divorce. He was in love with Jennifer. They wanted to be married. Surely she had guessed.

The shock was as if he had suddenly attacked her with some primitive weapon, a knife or club. Stunned, then furious, she struggled to say that she depended on him, counted on him to be there for her—that it was fine to flirt with Jennifer, to have sex with Jennifer, but not to fall in love with her.

"Come on, Nan." Shaking his head. "You want to put in your emotional spare change and have it earn top interest. It doesn't work that way. Nobody gets something for nothing."

"You bastard!" she had shouted, indignant as any criminal caught in the act. He looked sorry for her, and she couldn't stand that. She looked around for something to throw at him, but there was only a pile of the fancy architectural magazines he liked on the coffee table. When she flung one, the startled flutter of its pages sounded like a flock of birds taking flight.

Most of her fury at him, she could see by now, was at herself—for being a smug fool, a classic chump, tripped up by the corniest cliché of them all. *Never miss the water till the well runs dry.* Her friends were sympathetic, but she could tell they weren't surprised.

They thought she was naïve not to have seen it coming. And so she had been: infatuated with the idea of her own sophistication, taking it for granted that Gabe's devotion would never waver.

The panic of losing him had turned her offhand sense of motherhood into fierce possessiveness, and when he offered to take Stephen off her hands she refused vehemently. They reached an arrangement in which the boy spent weekends with Gabe and Jennifer, the rest of his time with her. Stephen, innocent victim, didn't like Jennifer, but Nan couldn't take much consolation from that. Depression and lack of sleep made the career that had taken so much of her time for the past six years seem hollow, an exercise in futility conducted against the filthy, dangerous urban backdrop. The idea of retreating to Annabel's property in Tennessee, to heal and reevaluate, had come as an inspiration. Except that now she was here, she found herself once again at risk of being jerked around by some man. Well, she wouldn't have it. Enough was enough.

The resolution went a long way toward pulling her out of her depression—enough, anyway, to develop the films of the orchard and creek. Once they were dry, she made a quick contact sheet of each and began to pull work prints, pleasantly surprised by their quality. A wet creek rock with a gleaming sycamore leaf plastered to its surface; a water spider skating into a shaft of sun. The series of the dragonfly was magical, uncannily reminiscent of the painted scene on the lampshade in Stephen's room. And the shots of the orchard more than fulfilled their promise—the goblinlike trees cloaked in luminous mist, a scene of spectral enchantment.

This was what had first drawn her to photography: the delight of seizing a spontaneous moment and capturing it forever. Seeing the images in print, their halftones arrestingly different from the numbing color of her fashion spreads, she was excited by them. And as she fine-tuned the focus on the enlarger and reset the timer for another print of the orchard, she told herself firmly that this brand of excitement was a lot more dependable than the kind she had been heading for with Sky.

Chapter 7

In the waning light of sunset the Talbot barnyard looked like a used-car lot, full of shabby station wagons and pickup trucks with their noses aimed haphazardly in the direction of the fence. Nan parked outside the gate in what she thought would be a good getaway spot; then she and Stephen picked their way past rusty bumpers and dented fenders toward the big white barn, passing a chicken coop topped by a wooden whirligig of a scarecrow with a large crow stationed on its head. The painted figures were motionless at the moment, but she guessed that a gust of wind would start the outsize bird pecking its sad-faced companion. Just beyond the coop they noticed a dark shape lurking behind a stretch of fence.

Stephen stopped to investigate, waggling his fingers through the fence rails. "Hi, goat."

The black billygoat ignored his overtures. Above unblinking yellow eyes, its horns rose in a sinister curve that made Nan think of Satanic cults. She caught a whiff of it and wrinkled her nose, glancing toward the wide-open barn door from which a buzz of talk and laughter spilled into the quiet country evening. The sound made her cringe inwardly. Much as she appreciated Lucy's gesture, she couldn't help regarding the coming barn supper as more of an ordeal than a recreation. And Stephen, lingering face to face with the smelly and unresponsive goat, clearly felt the same.

"Come on," she said at last. "Let's just do it."

The barn's spacious interior was illuminated by kerosene lanterns hung at intervals along the walls, scattering ruddy light across the faces of the crowd inside. Overhead the vaulted roof soared into shadow above a hayloft bristling with bales. The hardpacked dirt floor had been neatly swept, benches and folding chairs set up along the walls; toward the far end were trestle tables covered with picnic cloths and loaded with food. There were easily a hundred people already present, standing in noisy groups or seated on the benches with full plates on their laps, children running among them wild with excitement. Nan saw Whit Talbot, Cassie Thatcher, Sky's brother Burke and his son Billy, a few others she recognized.

The faces of the old people especially drew her gaze. Antithesis of the smooth, perfect faces of the models she was used to photographing, these were lined and weathered, mapped with long seasons of living but free of the confusion and defeat she was accustomed to seeing in the faces of old people in the city. Suddenly she wanted to photograph them— capture the quality, some mixture of innocence and wisdom, that kept their eyes alive. Then Lucy appeared out of the crowd and came over to kiss her, pressing a hard, wrinkled cheek to hers.

"Well, come on in, you two, don't dawdle there in the doorway! You're my guests of honor, after all." Her big-knuckled hand patted Stephen's shoulder. "Y'all just march on over and get you some food 'fore the dancing starts. Don't you miss my peach pie, now."

She steered them through the crowd. Faces turned

and smiled, calling greetings; hands reached out to touch them. Nan moved forward in a daze, smiling and nodding in response, feeling the tight clutch of Stephen's fingers on hers. As they closed in on the food she realized she was famished. There were platters of fried chicken and barbecued beans, steaming corn on the cob and candied yams, a ham the size of a small suitcase; buttermilk biscuits and cornbread, string beans in some kind of marinade, black-eyed peas and sliced tomatoes. A third table was devoted to cakes, pies, cookies and cobblers galore. Stephen dropped her hand and headed straight for it. She grabbed the back of his shirt and hauled him back.

"Eat some real food first, big guy."

Lucy had turned away to talk to a blond woman in a pink dress. Nan took plates for Stephen and herself from a stack at the end of the first table and made sure he took some chicken and a piece of corn. Once he had made a beeline for the dessert table she helped herself to a sampling from every dish in sight, her plate precariously near to overflowing. She would have to come back for dessert, unless she exploded first. She joined Stephen on an empty bench, noting the additions on his plate: a piece of chocolate cake, six cookies, a generous wedge of pie.

"Finish the chicken first, Stephen. And the corn." She supposed he would have a roaring case of the sugar blues shortly, but there was nothing she could do to prevent it. She was planning to engineer one for herself.

They ate under a bombardment of Southern friendliness—greetings and introductions to which Nan responded automatically, forgetting the names as soon as she heard them. The unfamiliar faces blended into one another, ruddy and smiling, drawled phrases echoing the same theme.

"Honey, I'm so proud to meet you. You know, your momma and I went to grammar school together. She was just the sweetest person. It was a cryin' shame she passed on so young."

"About time y'all came back to see us! Ain't right for folks to live so far away from fam'ly."

"I guess you don't remember me, hon. Last time I saw you, you was—what? Nine years old? Lord, but time does fly."

Whenever there was a momentary lull, she took in the scene in front of her. All the women seemed to be wearing dresses and she was glad she'd put on a skirt. The men wore jeans, white or checkered shirts, many with string ties. Most of them wore boots, some wide-brimmed hats. Giggling little girls in frilly white dresses dodged in and out among the groups of adults, pursued by redfaced little boys dressed as replicas of their fathers. Stephen was the only boy wearing shorts and a T-shirt, but she didn't think he'd noticed. He had made short work of his chicken and corn. Now he was stuffing his face with Lucy's peach pie, his eyes following the movement of the crowd.

"Nan! When'd y'all get here? Hey there, Stephen." Cassie, wearing a dark red blouse and black skirt, joined them on the bench, giving Nan's clothes a quick glance. "Hon, you look great. Better watch out for Jackson Talbot—he's already drunk as a skunk and he grows extra hands when he's like that. I swear, one year at the church picnic he got hold of the preacher's wife, and if she hadn't hollered loud enough to split wood I don't know what-all would've happened."

Jackson, Lucy's eldest son, heavy and fiftyish with a

plum-colored sweating face, was across the room in a loud group producing regular bursts of laughter. He had his arm around the waist of the woman on his left. As Nan watched, his free hand strayed to the buttocks of the woman on his right. She slapped it away without bothering to look back. Nan met Cassie's grin.

"Nice."

"Ain't it? We got us some real classy boys around here." Sky's sister shook her smooth head, then half rose to greet an old man making his way toward their bench.

"Well, hey there, Uncle Jim! You come out to shake a leg tonight? Bet you're going to dance all us girls into the ground, that right?"

Uncle Jim wore immaculate faded overalls and a flannel shirt of the most hideous green plaid Nan had ever seen. He looked about ninety. His hairless head trembled on a scrawny neck, the lenses of his glasses catching the lantern light as he beamed at Cassie, patting the hand she put on his arm. He resembled a superannuated baby bird, and Nan could not imagine him shaking a leg, much less dancing anyone into the ground. She didn't recall him among the hordes of relatives who had come to the house to welcome her. He might be a relative of Cassie's husband, Tom, although Tom, of course, was related to Cassie—and therefore to Nan as well—in some distant, genetically acceptable way by blood as well as by marriage, so Nan supposed that on some level she was also related to Uncle Jim. In any case Cassie was introducing them, a wicked gleam in her eye as if she not only guessed Nan's confusion but was enjoying it, and Nan felt the old man's dry, clawlike hand grasp hers gently.

At the back of the barn a flurry of movement caught

her eye. She saw the big wooden doors begin to slide open, felt Stephen pull at her arm.

"Mom—what's going on?"

"They're bringing in a truck for Ellis and Nancy," Cassie said. She leaned over to Uncle Jim and shouted into his ear. "Ellis Whipple's going to play, Uncle Jim."

The old man cracked a grin, revealing a set of terrifyingly perfect plastic teeth. Nan, unsure of the purpose of the truck, saw that one was indeed backing into the barn, its flat bed empty except for a few wisps of hay. It came to a stop and a monkeylike man in a straw hat climbed onto the bed amid cheering and applause. He reached down, offering his hand to a woman standing beside the truck—a woman much bigger than he was, Nan saw; taller and several times as wide, her pony-tailed hair an improbable orange. He struggled to haul her up, and the two of them teetered on the edge of the truck bed for a moment while the cheering rose a notch; then willing hands from the crowd supplied the needed push. The pair beamed and waved in triumph. A fiddle and guitar were handed up, two folding chairs, and the bandstand was complete.

The honey-colored curves of the two instruments reflected the lantern light as the musician pair took their seats and tuned up with half a dozen squawks and twangs. Nan sat watching, detached but curious, enjoying the spectacle. A space had been cleared in the center of the barn and people were shuffling into position. She saw Sky with the blond woman in the pink dress who had been talking to Lucy earlier. Another lucky recipient of those lazy looks from those so-blue eyes? His white shirt was open at the neck, sleeves rolled high on his muscled arms, and he was laughing, leaning forward to catch something she had said.

His legs in their clean faded jeans looked about nine miles long.

As he straightened again, his eyes met Nan's across the room and she felt the blue, even if she couldn't actually see it at that distance. He held her gaze for a long moment. *Corny,* her mind said, even while the muscles in her legs started to dissolve. Then the fiddle's bow scraped across the strings, and Sky's partner touched his arm and he looked away and started to dance. Above the music Nan heard the caller's voice announcing the figures: "Swing your partner! Allemand left! Grand right and left—meet your partner and promenade!"

Stephen seemed mercifully unaware of her exchange with Sky. "Mom, can I get another piece of peach pie?"

"Maybe you should ask Lucy, Stephen. She might want to save some for other people."

"Okay."

He jumped up and she watched him edge past a group of old men who had occupied the far end of the bench and were puffing on pipes. The lighthearted music was infectious and she stopped trying to resist its charm. It was plain the dancers were enjoying themselves. She looked for the caller and picked him out: a youngish, balding man standing next to the truck, his head bobbing in time to the music, a sheen of sweat already on his freckled forehead.

"Ring, ring, pretty little ring, break that ring with a corner swing!" The dancers circled, holding hands; then the men turned to the women on their left and swung them around. Nan glanced around for Stephen. Lucy Talbot had just put another enormous platter of fried chicken on the table and was bending down to listen to his request, her arm encircling his shoulders. He whispered in her ear and she straightened, laughing and nodding her white head, hands on her hips as she answered him. A lantern on the wall behind her outlined her profile with tender light. Some combination of her spirited pose and lit profile made Nan see her suddenly as she must have looked as a young woman, all her life before her, and the vision made her catch her breath.

The piece he brought back this time was obscenely large.

"Oh, Stephen."

"Lucy said to have as much as I want."

"Let me have some of that."

"Mom—she said God made boys to eat pie. You're a girl."

"Girls eat pie too." She reached for his plate.

"Promenade that pretty little girl, promenade all around the world! Promenade all around the floor, promenade home, there ain't no more!"

The dance came to an end with a flourish on the fiddle. Ellis tipped back his hat and wiped his face with a red bandanna. Nancy leaned over the side of the truck and let loose a hefty gob of spit onto the barn floor. Averting her eyes, Nan caught sight of Sky's blond partner in the milling, laughing crowd, but not Sky himself. Beside her Stephen started to put half the pie into his mouth at once.

"Stephen! That's too much."

Laughing, he tried to cram it in anyway. Part of it went in his lap. Nan handed him her napkin. "You slob."

A touch on her shoulder then: she looked up and Sky was standing over her. "Will you dance, Cousin Annabel?"

"I don't know how to square dance, Cousin Schuyler."

"It's easy. Come on."

He caught her hand and pulled her to her feet. She had a glimpse of Stephen's scowling face and then she was on the dance floor, people all around her, the fiddle sounding a long note. She heard the caller's twang. "Bow to your partner, bow to your corner."

She managed a curtsy, but after that she was lost. The next five minutes were a blur. Music, the stamp of feet on the dirt floor, lantern light on breathless faces, the caller's voice high and clear over the strident singing of the fiddle.

"Wave to the ocean, wave to the sea, wave that pretty girl back to me!"

It was gibberish to Nan, but it didn't seem to matter. Friendly hands pushed and turned her, sent her here and there until she was laughing and out of breath, finding herself in Sky's arms for a moment and then in some other man's, surrounded by faces flushed and smiling.

Will you dance, Cousin Annabel? Sky's bearded face among the others, blue eyes holding hers. This was his place, his world, and he fitted it seamlessly. All the gestures and phrases that seemed hokey and countrified in terms of urban sophistication were perfectly appropriate here, now. He danced well and she danced well with him, the slightest movement of their bodies attuned. His hands on her waist, turning her this way and that, then taking hers to swing her around.

"Hand over hand around the square, then promenade your lady fair!" Even the dance calls charmed her— although she supposed, objectively speaking, they were sexist and degrading to women, the whole *schtick*. But somehow in the rosy lantern light with her skirt swirling around her as she danced, she was enjoying a guilt-free sense of *being* a pretty girl, a lady fair—as if the old-fashioned language in its innocence had returned them all, men and women alike, to an earlier, more romantic era. Now Sky put his arm around her waist, pulling her close to his side; pressed against him Nan could feel his heart beating, hers matching its rate, and not just from the fast-paced dancing. "You swing Sal and I'll swing Kate! Hurry up boys, don't be late!"

Then it was over; people were laughing and talking, wiping hot foreheads and moving off the floor for refreshments. Nan looked around and saw Stephen still on the bench, his face glum. His plate was empty. Cassie and Uncle Jim had disappeared, and she wondered disbelievingly if they had joined in the dancing. She went over to Stephen.

"You okay? Stomach hurt?"

He shook his head without speaking. He really can't stand Sky, she thought.

"Listen, the square dancing is fun. Some of the other kids are doing it. Want to try?"

Another headshake. Nan sat down beside him. "Let's sit awhile, then. I'm pooped." As she said it she couldn't help scanning the crowd, trying to see if Sky had asked the blond woman to dance again. But no—he had chosen Lucy Talbot this time and was leading her out onto the floor, her hand in his, while she laughed and held out a fold of her skirt flirtatiously with her free hand. Nan smiled involuntarily, then caught an abrupt movement out of the corner of her eye as Stephen, who had been watching her, turned away.

It was too bad, really a shame, that he felt that way. What he needed down here was someone just like Sky, a man to take an interest in him, do all the things with him that Gabe had done. She could tell he missed Gabe, who had made a point of staying part of both their lives even after the split. If only Stephen liked Sky, Sky could . . . she caught herself. Sky could what? Take Gabe's place? Was that what she wanted for herself as well as for Stephen? He was attractive, sure. But she seemed to recall that she had decided against the idea of getting involved with him.

He asked her for the next dance; but she said, with an eye on Stephen, that she was tired. Sky seemed to understand, got himself another partner and went back into the fray. Her refusal visibly perked Stephen up. Once the dancing started he even left the bench and stood on the fringes, tapping one sneakered foot and bobbing up and down in time to the music.

Nan tried without success to keep her eyes off Sky. It wasn't just that he was a skillful dancer. It was his complete ease in the situation, his air of being at home with everyone and everything—calling joking comments to the other people in his square, laughing when a little girl ran up behind him and pulled his shirttail out, clapping time with the others in some maneuver that called for each couple to take a turn crossing the square. He knew exactly what was expected of him, that was it, and was confident of being able to deliver. That lazy male assurance attracted her powerfully—especially here in an environment unfamiliar to her, where more sophisticated standards seemed jaded, almost decadent.

"All join hands and circle eight, eight hands around the ring!" She recalled the sensation of his hands touching her waist and let her imagination go a little, then pulled herself up abruptly. Another minute and all her good intentions would melt into nothing. She made herself look away from him.

Stephen had become involved in some game with Billy Barnett and another boy, dodging around the edge of the dance floor, and that was a relief. She drank some punch, danced with towering Whit Talbot (Sky was a different square), then sat and chatted with her hostesses, Lucy and Irene. Cassie joined them, puffing, her face a deeper red than her blouse; Uncle Jim, her partner, didn't seem to have so much as broken a sweat. The pace was slowing down as the evening went on. Stephen appeared, panting, and she smoothed the damp hair off his forehead. At last Ellis Whipple stood up and tapped the back of his chair with his bow.

"Ladies and gentlemen, Nance and me're going to take a little break now, but 'fore we do we'll take a request for one last tune."

Half a dozen voices called out song titles. To Nan's surprise, Stephen's was one of them—clear childish treble rising audibly above the others. "Play the White Rose Waltz!"

The fiddler peered in their direction, then tipped back his hat and nodded. "Little feller wants the White Rose Waltz, folks. That's a good tune, but we haven't played 'er in a good while. Let's see if we can remember how she goes . . ." He bent toward Nancy for a moment's murmured consultation, then straighted. "Folks, the White Rose Waltz."

Stephen was standing beside her and she touched his arm. "How do you know that tune, honey?" The name was unfamiliar and she wondered if he had heard it from Gabe, who had a thing for country music. Stephen smiled at her. Flecks of gold, lanterns reflected in miniature, swam on the lenses of his glasses. "Woody whistled it for me."

Too slow for square dancing, it was a real waltz tune, gentle and lilting. People sat listening, tapping their feet or nodding in time. Stephen leaned against Nan. She drew him onto her lap and put her arms around him, resting her cheek against his hair and rocking him slowly to the music. Lucy's son Danny led his wife out onto the floor, taking her in his arms carefully as if cradling her unborn child between them; and the sight of the young couple, accompanied by the sweetly raucous sound of the fiddle, made an actual physical sensation in Nan's chest—as if she really possessed heartstrings and the tune was tugging at them.

Through sudden tears the room blurred; the lanterns on the wall were transformed into spangles of golden light. She blinked the tears away, looking at the faces around her. There was a resemblance among them that came less from physical likeness than from a lifetime of shared knowledge and custom that had left its stamp on each. The old fiddle tune had put a wistful look on every face, from the smallest child's to the oldest adult's—on Stephen's and, she realized, even on her own. A sense of belonging touched her. She savored it, letting her eyes go around the room again—and felt her gaze snag sharply on one face.

It was Lucy Talbot's. The old woman was not looking, as everyone else was, at Ellis and Nancy Whipple. Instead she was staring straight at Stephen, and she did not look wistful.

She looked frightened.

Chapter 8

Nan opened the door of the corner cabinet and took out the decanter. "Brandy?"

"Believe I will, thank you, ma'am."

She poured two glasses and handed one to Sky on the library sofa, taking her seat at the other end. She couldn't help being acutely aware of Stephen sleeping in the room above.

"It's never done that before," she said. "I hope it's not something major."

Her car had refused to start after the square dance. Something—the battery?—was completely dead. Nothing at all happened when she turned the key. She and Stephen had sat there cursing in the cricket-noisy dark until Sky had showed up and offered them a ride home in his truck. After that, it was only civil on her part to invite him in for a drink.

"I'll take a look at it for you tomorrow," he said.

"That was fun tonight," she said. "I think people in New York have forgotten how to have fun at parties."

Sky smiled without answering. Nan sipped her brandy, set the glass down and leaned over to take off her sandals. He intercepted her on the way back up. His lips, soft in the crisp hair of his beard, were warm and tasted of brandy. He put his tongue in her mouth.

It was, she supposed, the inevitable point toward

which the evening had been headed. *Will you dance, Cousin Annabel?* That had been the beginning of the end. Now all her rationalizing about not getting involved with him was only the fuzziest memory. Her body had simply taken charge and was doing exactly as it wanted. As their embraces grew more intense, she was aware of being taken over by a kind of dreamy fatalism. The last time she had necked with this kind of fervor had been in high school, and it had ended in her losing her virginity on a picnic table during a summer thunderstorm. Matters seemed to possess a similar momentum now.

"I got a real good idea," he said at last, against her mouth. "But it kind of needs a bed."

"There's a bed upstairs," Nan said.

"I know."

His tongue was in her mouth again and she realized that of course he knew. He knew the house intimately, much better than she did. And the bed was Annabel's, the one she had died in. Nan was too far gone at this point for the fact to make any difference. She let him pull her to her feet.

On the cramped staircase, wanting to take some measure of control, she went first. Halfway up he stopped her, hands on her waist, and she turned. She was a step above him, enough to give her a height advantage. She rested her forearms on his shoulders and they kissed. Sky slid his hands up her legs and under her skirt.

They almost didn't require the bed. He took her on the edge of it with his jeans still on, fly hastily unbuttoned. Her pleasure when he entered her was so acute that it took away her breath, suspending her for a long moment in exquisite limbo before orgasm released her.

She arched against him with a gasping cry. He caught his breath, said, "Sweet Lord Jesus," and came.

When they could move again they undressed and got into bed. He kept looking at her, touching her. "You're some lady, Cousin Nan."

She tried to stifle her laugh and failed. "A lady wouldn't have had sex with you just for giving her a ride home."

He looked down for a moment and she thought she might have shocked him. Then, without a hint of a smile: "Guess you musta been real grateful."

She laughed again; she couldn't help it. She felt weightless and a little drunk. Watching her he smiled at last. She realized helplessly that he was going to make love to her again, and that she wanted him to. He leaned over her and their mouths met.

That was when Stephen screamed.

He was sitting straight up in bed, eyes wide, but she saw immediately that he was still asleep. She pulled her hastily belted robe more closely around her; then, without turning on the light, sat on the edge of the bed and put her arms around him. He was shaking.

"Stephen." She drew his small body against her, stroking his hair. He gave a start and then a wail.

"Mom—"

"You were having a bad dream. It's okay."

She rocked him. He was still half asleep, mumbling against her shoulder, trying to tell her about it. She could make out almost none of what he was saying, just a word that might have been "cold."

"What, honey? I can't understand you." She remembered Gabe saying it was better to let him verbalize the nightmares, get them out of his system. She levered him away from her shoulder so she could see his face. The eyes were glazed.

"I was trying to run," he mumbled. "Trying . . . but I couldn't. And it was cold. I could see my breath . . . all frosty—"

Nan felt her reassuring smile waver and collapse. He was describing *her* nightmare—wasn't he?—the one that had plagued her as far back as she could remember. That suffocating sense of trying to run and getting nowhere, seeing her own breath clouding the air in front of her face. Part of the terror came from never knowing if she was trying to run toward something, or away . . .

She couldn't imagine she had ever told Stephen about it, yet how else could his dream resemble hers so closely? Unless it was classic somehow, one of those archetypes that everyone experienced in common . . . and what else *could* it be?

"You're okay, sweetie." She held him close, beginning to rock him again, talking as much to her own fear as to his. "It was just a dream. That's all. Just a bad dream. You're safe in bed. Now try to go back to sleep."

She felt him relax a little, lulled by the rocking and her murmured words. Then he tensed again.

"Mom!"

He was fully alert now, staring over her shoulder. Her heart jumped; she turned quickly and recognized Sky's silhouette in the doorway, black against the light from her bedroom across the hall.

"It's just Sky, honey. He stayed for a drink."

Stephen kept staring and she wondered if he had noticed she was in her bathrobe, naked under it.

Sky lifted a hand. "Hey, there, hoss."

Stephen didn't answer. After a moment he hid his

face against Nan and stayed motionless. Her gaze met Sky's. He gave a little nod and disappeared from the doorway.

When she came downstairs nearly an hour later, having finally gotten Stephen to sleep again, he was fully dressed and sitting on the sofa drinking brandy. He picked up her glass and offered it to her. "Little fella okay now?"

Nan nodded, accepting the glass, and sat down. "Just a nightmare. He used to have them a lot in New York. This is the first one he's had since we've been here."

"Hope I didn't scare him."

She cupped the brandy glass in her palms. "No. It was probably just too much of Lucy's peach pie, although I guess it's possible he heard us in his sleep. The rooms are right next door to each other. I should have thought of that."

Sky drained his glass and set it down. "You sorry it happened?"

She considered a moment, then smiled. "No. I'm just sorry it didn't happen again."

"The night is young."

She looked down, then up at his face. The bright blue eyes were unreadable. She wondered if he thought he had said something suave. She didn't know him at all: that was borne in on her with force at this moment. She shook her head, remembering to smile. "I don't want to risk waking him again."

"I'll say good night, then." He stood and held out his hand. As she got up to take it, he pulled her to him gently and kissed her. During the kiss she was aware that if he didn't let her go at the end, she wouldn't try to break free. But he did let her go, releasing her hands last of all, walking slowly backward into the living room and all the way to the front door with his eyes on her, so familiar with the house that he could carry off such a maneuver, cornball Hollywood-romantic, without a hitch. At the threshold he lingered a moment, holding her gaze, and then was gone without a word. When the door closed after him she sat down on the sofa, ignoring the trembling in her thighs, and reached for the brandy bottle.

The next morning she had just made herself a cup of coffee and settled at the kitchen table when Lucy Talbot appeared, tapping and yoohooing at the kitchen door.

"Hi, Lucy. Come on in. Coffee?"

"Why, thanks, honey, I believe I will." The sight of Nan still in her nightgown brought the old lady up short. "I'm sorry I came by so early . . ."

Nan glanced at the clock; it was past nine. She had a blurry memory of hearing Stephen banging around in the kitchen a while ago, and there was the evidence: a half-eaten bowl of cereal on the counter, generous splash of milk beside it. She should have joined him for breakfast, but instead she had let herself drift back to sleep, deliciously relaxed after last night's encounter with Sky. The hovering memory was still so vivid she was afraid Lucy would be able to read the details in her face. She turned away to pour the old lady a cup of coffee.

"I guess I slept late. All that square dancing must have worn me out."

"Did you have a good time, honey?"

"I had a great time." Nan brought the coffee cups to

the table and they sat down. "It was really nice of you to include us, Lucy."

"Include you! Why, Nan, y'all are family! I'm just glad you're back among us again." Lucy hesitated, seemed about to speak and then bit her lip. Finally she said, "Did you like the music?"

"Loved it."

"And Stephen—I heard him ask for the White Rose Waltz. Wherever did he learn that tune?"

Woody whistled it for me. Yet obviously there was some other explanation, and Nan seized on the likeliest. "His father's a fan."

"Oh, I see." Lucy seemed oddly relieved. Ordinarily Nan might have wondered about the exchange, but just now she was finding it hard to keep her mind on the conversation: memories of last night kept intruding, punctuating the tame social exchange with explicit images that sent residual quiverings along her nerves. It was a good thing Lucy couldn't read her thoughts. The idea brought hot blood to her cheeks and she ducked her head.

"Hon, let me ask you something else," the old woman was saying. "That ring Stephen's wearing. Where did he get it?"

Nan forced her attention back to the here and now. "Ring? Oh, I found it and he wanted it, so I gave it to him. I think it's something I had as a kid. I seem to remember . . . you know that boy I was friends with that summer—Tucker? He made it for me."

"Oh. Oh, yes. And you just found it in the house?"

Bewildered by Lucy's belaboring of such an insignificant topic, Nan started to laugh. "On the floor in the hall, actually. I must have lost it the summer I was here, and it got kicked into a corner or something.

I guess Annabel wasn't the world's best house-keeper . . . What about the ring, Lucy?"

Now it was the old lady's turn to blush. "Nothing, honey. Nothing. Well, just . . . I mean . . . as long as you're happy, and everything seems . . . you know. Normal."

"Normal?" Nan said blankly.

"Never mind." Lucy seemed embarrassed by her own choice of words. "If you say everything's all right—"

"Oh, everything's all right," Nan said. She had had enough of this odd, pointless conversation. A warm shiver went through her at the memory of Sky's hand sliding up her thigh, and she spoke with more force than she had intended. "Everything's *fine*."

A little later, when she walked Lucy out to her station wagon, the Volvo had miraculously appeared in the driveway. Once the old lady had said her farewells and driven off, Nan got into the car and turned the key. The engine caught on the first try. On the front seat were half a dozen shallow pink roses, just spilled there—nothing so sissy as a bouquet from Schuyler Barnett. She had a sudden suspicion that he had sabo-taged her car somehow the night before, that the whole thing had been a setup. But she couldn't say she minded if it had.

She spent the day drifting between recollection and anticipation. Stephen was off on his own, and she had nothing to distract her from her thoughts. In retro-spect, all her logical reasons for not getting involved with Sky seemed hollow. He seemed easy, ready to accept whatever role she might offer him in her life for now. And the sex had been incredible. In any case, it had happened almost on its own. She supposed that

on some level, protestations aside, she had been ready
for it.

By the time supper had come and gone that night,
she was more than ready. She hoped Sky would wait
until Stephen was asleep before putting in an appearance; she wasn't prepared to deal with her child's reaction yet. But when Stephen's bedtime finally came, he
wanted to chat.

"We saw this big turtle, Mom. Down by the creek. It
went into its shell, but Woody took a stick and poked
it. And then—pow! It shoots its head out and bites off
the end of the stick!"

"A turtle bit off the end of a stick?"

"It had a beak like a parrot! Woody said it was a
snapping turtle. He said it could bite off my toe if it
wanted to."

His imagination, she thought, was amazing. How
much of the incident had actually happened? She supposed he might have actually seen a snapping turtle,
but there was slim likelihood that her little city boy had
actually possessed the nerve to approach it. She ruffled
his hair.

"You be careful. Don't go making enemies among
the local wildlife."

He fell asleep at last. Nan took a quick shower, put
on a light cotton dress that looked simple and cost an
insane amount in a SoHo boutique, and went downstairs to sit on the porch. It was twilight, and the gathering dark was filled with honeysuckle fragrance. She
stationed herself in the porch swing, pushing off with
one foot and let it rock her, feeling like Scarlett
O'Hara. As she rocked she saw the first lightning bug
wink against the darkness of the orchard. Another. And
another.

She went on rocking. The setting was almost too perfect; doubts began to creep into her sense of expectation. Suppose Sky didn't come? Suppose he decided there was too much competition from Stephen, that he didn't want the hassle? In that case she was a fool to be sitting out here on the porch in the summer darkness waiting for him, her body's earlier lassitude replaced by taut anticipation. For a time the rhythmic creaking of the swing was the only sound in the dusk.

A pale shadow darted across the shadowy lawn— the cat in soundless pursuit of some small doomed creature—and the owl called in the oak tree, eerie quavering cry. She shivered suddenly, hot and cold at once, a nameless dread running like quicksilver over the surface of her desire. It was as if the familiar dreamlike surroundings caught and amplified her emotions, returning them to her at a pitch so intense she scarcely recognized them as her own.

Then he was there, standing at the foot of the porch steps. She could see his white shirt in the dark.

"Hi," he said.

"Hi." She stayed where she was, touching her foot to the boards beneath her to halt the swing. "I didn't hear your truck."

"I walked up through the orchard. It's a beautiful night."

The words sounded in her head, evoking a vivid mental picture of him approaching the old white farmhouse through the shadowy trees, and with that image her sense of the night expanded suddenly outward from the porch to encompass the tranquil country night, sky overhead black and full of stars, mountains bulking over the soft hollow of the valley where only a few lights burned. The darkened porch on which she sat seemed the center and focus of it all. Her life outside this moment dwindled and sank away.

"It is," she said.

Chapter 9

Of course she'd heard of sexual chemistry, but now, with Sky, the phrase seemed to take on a whole new dimension. She had never experienced sex the way it was with him. None of her previous lovers had prepared her for this, and she had thought herself reasonably experienced, had been to bed with a dozen different men, even excluding the high school boy whose awkward destruction of her virginity could not be accounted lovemaking. She had experienced affection, boredom, frustration, release on a par with a good healthy sneeze, but no more than a glimmer of what all the fuss was about. And in her recent years with Gabe, sex—or her indifference to it—had become such an issue that at times she had honestly wished it had never been invented.

Now it was as if the top layer of her skin had been stripped away and all her nerve endings exposed, as if she had taken some wild sensation-enhancing drug. When he touched her, she actually felt her head spin. She lived these days in a kind of sensuous fog, aware of her body in a way she had never been before.

And there were other surprises, too. For the first time in her life she was a vocal lover, producing an array of alley-cat noises that both amused and faintly shocked her. Every time they made love she found herself moaning and yowling, unable to contain herself as he urged her toward climax. When she confessed to Sky that this was a new thing for her, he laughed.

"Why, honey, I purely love to hear you holler. And I'll tell you why."

They were in bed. As he talked, his mouth moved slowly from her shoulder to her hip.

"It's 'cause I like to see you lose control a little bit, Miss Big Shot from New York City, where everybody's seen everything. You come on down here to ol' Tennessee, and you got a little surprise. You found out there's times when things go a certain way and you can't do a blessed thing but lay back and let 'em. So you learned something new. Now didn't you?"

At the time she was too distracted by his mouth and hands to respond to what he was saying, but it came back to her later and she thought about it. She supposed it wasn't surprising that he should think of her as a big shot who needed to learn a lesson, in particular a lesson from him. In spite of their physical involvement, she had taken care to make it clear enough that her life was her own: that she controlled all entry thereto, and that his access was limited. She thought that might be a new and slightly shocking thing for Schuyler Barnett. Meanwhile she was enjoying the affair for what it was worth—the attentions of a handsome, virile man in his prime.

Because of the noise she made they couldn't use her bedroom; it was too near Stephen's. Instead they used the spare bedroom at the other end of the house, above the kitchen. The bed was a single, but it was all they needed. Although they kept the door closed while they made love, she could imagine that something still got through, that Stephen in his sleep heard the racket and connected it with Sky. He made it clear enough, daily, that he liked Sky less and less. And considering his position, she couldn't blame him.

These days, as soon as breakfast was over, he invariably headed across the creek to the hill, where he seemed perfectly content to spend long hours with only Woody for company. Nan was nervous about explaining Woody to Sky, afraid he would think Stephen was nuts, but he didn't even blink.

"Kids're somethin', ain't they? All that imagination. Well—" he leaned forward to kiss her "—least it keeps him out from underfoot."

In all honesty Nan had to admit this was true: Her son's absorption in his fantasy friend dovetailed conveniently into her own infatuation. But the idea of his spending so many hours on his own still made her feel guilty, and she made a genuine effort to put in some time with him.

Their outings usually took the form of driving into Breezy and heading for Cooper Chalmers's store. The windup eyeball had arrived—a bright-blue doll's eye, skittering awkwardly around the countertop on bare plastic feet. She found it surreal, but Stephen greeted it like an old friend.

"Here, boy. Here, boy." He held cupped hands at the counter's edge in case the grisly thing tried to leap off. Nan grimaced and glanced at Cooper, who was watching with a half smile. He was endlessly tolerant of Stephen's hard usage of his merchandise. Out of gratitude she had started buying a windup toy every time they came into the store—but to do Cooper justice, she didn't think his patience stemmed from this trickle of three-dollar sales.

The eyeball avoided Stephen's hands and threw itself off the countertop. Cooper caught it and put it back. "It tropes to the right, Stephen. The mechanism adds a little extra weight on that side."

Nan couldn't help noting this small lesson in How Things Work, the kind of male thing that Stephen would never have accepted from Sky in a million years. She watched him wind the toy again and set it down, eyeing it narrowly as it hopped in an arc to the right. As it neared the edge of the counter, he adjusted the position of his hands to catch it, his face lighting with satisfaction as the eyeball landed safely in his cupped palms.

Nan glanced over at Cooper and met his smile. Unlike Sky, he was someone she could share with Stephen. Also unlike Sky, there was no overwhelming physical attraction to create a paradoxical emotional distance between them. Although she sensed a certain amount of male interest from Cooper, he didn't push it. He was, she realized, the closest she could come to a potential friend within the radius of a thousand miles. During visits to the store, while Stephen put the toys through their paces and customers wandered in and out, they had exchanged scraps of background. She told him about Gabe and her muddled reasons for this summer's retreat to Tennessee, learned that he had studied philosophy at Duke University and that his wife had died four years ago.

He usually ended up accompanying Nan and Stephen for ice cream at Bev's Valley Luncheonette, half a block down Front Street, a no-frills place with a counter and a single row of wooden booths against a long plate-glass window. While a teenage waitress hustled the orders, Bev herself, lanky and in her forties, leaned on the counter leafing through a magazine and exchanging quips with her customers. Cooper seemed to be a regular, and Nan thought she detected something slightly proprietary in Bev's attitude toward him.

Today, as they took their regular booth, Stephen slid in beside Cooper. Nan was surprised; up until now he had always sat with her. But no doubt he missed Gabe, and Cooper helped fill the void. Once the waitress had taken their order she sat back and observed the two of them, Cooper listening closely as Stephen chattered about a windup golf ball he had seen in New York. It struck her that Stephen looked like a different boy from the pale, tentative waif she had brought with her a little more than a month ago. He had filled out some; there was color in his cheeks and he looked into Cooper's face as he talked. Of course there were trade-offs—nothing as bad as his fall in the creek that first day, but a constantly renewed collection of cuts and bumps she did her best to doctor. Currently he had an enormous scrape on one elbow (tripped and fell running up the hill) and pink islands of calamine lotion decorating the backs of both hands (poison ivy along the creek bank), but Sky had laughed at her when she expressed concern, assuring her that these were badges of normalcy for a boy growing up in the country.

"Hell, I can't hardly recollect a time when wasn't one of us with a cast on his arm from fallin' off a horse or out of a tree. Didn't hardly slow us down a minute."

Their ice cream arrived and Stephen dug into his with gusto, apparently finding it as tasty as the fancier brands he was used to back home. Nan picked at hers, glancing idly out the greasy window at a car pulling up outside. Something about the snaggle-toothed look of the broken front grill jogged her memory and she looked more closely. Wasn't that the junkmobile that had almost hit them head-on in Annabel's driveway?

On close examination it looked even worse than she remembered, the front bumper tied up with twine and the rusty exterior splotched here and there by patches of pale primer reminiscent of the calamine lotion on Stephen's hands.

She watched as the driver's door opened and a man emerged. She caught a glimpse of his hat, but that was about all. A moment later he came into Bev's and she got another look at him.

He was short and thick, his belly straining the side buttons of a pair of worn overalls. A filthy yellow baseball cap was pulled low on his forehead, hiding his eyes; the lower part of his face sported a patchy ginger-colored beard and mustache. He ordered something at the counter, then lounged on a stool. As he glanced up, eyes darting the length of the restaurant, Nan was finally able to see his face: fleshy whiskered jowls, a mean little mouth, eyes cold and flat under brows so pale they almost didn't exist. All at once she realized he had noticed her scrutiny and was returning a truculent stare. She quickly dropped her gaze.

"Your ice cream okay?" Cooper was giving her a rueful smile as if he knew Flavo-Brand, or whatever this was, wasn't what she preferred. She glanced at her fast-melting bowlful and shrugged.

"It's fine. Coop, not right now, but in a minute, can you sneak a peek and tell me who that guy at the counter is—the one with the yellow cap?" She was pretty sure she recognized the car, but she wanted to make certain. What had Sky said the man's name was? Something very redneck-sounding.

Stephen, of course, had twisted around immediately, but fortunately the man's order—it looked like coffee to go—had arrived and he was delving into the pocket of his overalls for change. Cooper glanced over his shoulder, then turned back to her.

"You mean Jerry Ray Watkins?"

"That's the one."

"Good Lord, Nan. What have y'all got to do with him?"

"Nothing, really. Except that he almost ran us down in our own driveway. By accident," she added, seeing Cooper's worried expression. "Apparently he used to do some work for Annabel." His face didn't relax and she said, "Coop. What's the matter?"

"Well, nothing, I guess. It's just that he's fresh out of prison."

"Prison!" The word hit her with a jolt. Sky hadn't mentioned anything about Watkins being in prison. "What for?"

"Making moonshine whiskey, from what I hear. He had a still set up back in the mountains, where he lives. Shot off his mouth about it and got caught."

"Oh." She felt herself calming down. A moonshiner was quite a different animal from a rapist or a murderer. Compared to what she was used to in New York, making illegal whiskey struck her as a quaint, almost picturesque form of crime. Still, she wished Stephen hadn't heard the exchange. He was gaping at Watkins, but the man was on his way out by now. Nan touched her son's shoulder to get his attention.

"You understand why he went to jail, right, honey?" She didn't want Watkins showing up in one of his nightmares. "He's been making booze and selling it without paying the government tax. That's a crime, but it's sort of a little crime, like—"

"Oh, I know." Stephen dropped his spoon into his empty bowl with a rattle. "Like keeping the quarter when the pay phone gives it back to you by mistake. Linda says you could go to jail for that. But it doesn't mean you're a bad person."

"Right," Nan said weakly. She caught a glimpse of Cooper's amused face. By the time they had paid their check and left the restaurant, Watkins's car was gone.

But it stayed on her mind while she went grocery shopping—not so much the car and its scruffy owner as Sky's failure to tell her that Watkins was an ex-con. What could be his reasons for withholding such information? Was it just that he didn't want to worry her? She would have to let him know she didn't appreciate being protected in that way. She preferred to know the facts, whatever they were.

She consulted her list: milk, eggs—Stephen could get those, but he had already wandered off on his own, probably to the cookie aisle. On her way to the dairy section she ran into Cassie Thatcher with her two youngest in tow.

"Hey there, Nan! What you been up to? You have a good time at the dance?" Cassie took a package of cookies from her brimming cart, tore it open and handed down a cookie to toddler Susannah, who clung whining to her leg. Lucas, a year or so older, dashed up for a cookie of his own and then ran away making artillery noises. As always, Cassie seemed the calm eye of a storm. She had, Nan remembered, five children in all. In another set of circumstances she might have become a close friend, but their busy separate lives had so far kept them from making a real connection.

You have a good time at the dance? At moments Nan had wondered if knowledge of her liaison with her cousin had somehow filtered out to their dozens of shared relatives. She had absolutely no clue what, for instance, Lucy's attitude would be—if the old lady would approve or disapprove, or consider rightly that it was none of her business. But of all people Cassie, her brother's confidante, would be most likely to know about their affair. Was she probing for confirmation? Nan found herself suddenly determined not to give it: a reflection, probably, of the mixed feelings she harbored about the relationship.

"It was fun. How about you? Did Uncle Jim dance you off your feet?"

Cassie hooted. "That old coot! I swear, what a lech. I hope I've got that kind of juice in me when I'm ninety. Lord a mercy!"

A familiar clicking distracted Nan and she glanced down in time to see the windup eyeball emerging from behind a shelf of canned goods. Next Stephen and Lucas came into view, following the toy's jerky progress across the wooden floor. Its feet caught in a space between two boards and it fell over in convulsions. The two boys collapsed laughing.

"What in hell is that?" Cassie wrinkled her nose. Nan retrieved the eyeball, holding it up for inspection, and Sky's sister pushed her hand away in disgust. "That is the ugliest thing I have *ever* seen. Where in heaven's name did it come from?"

"You know Books, Etc., on Front Street?" Nan handed the eyeball back to Stephen, and he busied himself rewinding it while Cassie watched in fascinated revulsion.

"Oh, you mean Cooper Chalmers's store? I thought that was supposed to be a bookstore, for cryin' out loud. I declare, since Laura died Cooper's always into something weird. I have *got* to wonder about him sometimes."

Nan felt curiosity stir. *Since Laura died—*

The eyeball skittered away with Stephen and Lucas in giggling pursuit. Susannah took a few steps after them before Cassie pulled her back. "Honey, you stay here with Momma. Let them nasty old boys chase after that ugly thing by themselves."

"Her name was Laura? Cooper hasn't really told me much about her. Just that she died four years ago." Nan hesitated, then gave way to impulse. "What happened to her?"

Cassie gave Susannah another cookie. "Hung herself, hon. She was—you know, one of them depressives. It was in her chemistry, Doc said. Cooper and her'd been sweet since grammar school. Lord, he loved her—depression and all, I guess. Anyhow, she quit takin' her pills for some reason we'll never know. Cooper'd gone off huntin' with his buddies for the weekend, and when he came home he found her." She grimaced. "That's surely enough to make anyone weird."

Shocked by the story, Nan was moved to defend Cooper. "I don't think he's weird. I like him."

"Lord, Nan. We all like him. But he's weird. He got drunk with Buddy Dale one night and said Laura came back to see him the night after she died. Ever since then he's been into spirits and séances and whatnot, all that spooky stuff. He drove all the way to Brownsville to talk to a psychic lady and see could she put him in touch with Laura again. I know he misses her, but still, Nan—it *is* weird."

So that was the explanation for Cooper's interest in the supernatural—an interest Annabel had apparently shared, since she had purchased books on the subject. Nan agreed it was weird, although away from Gabe's influence she was discovering her prejudices to be mere cheap imitations of his, all surface and no substance. And because she liked and respected Cooper, she was inclined to forgive his oddities. After all, what he had suffered with his wife's death was enough, as Cassie said, to make anyone weird.

*   *   *

Woody wasn't there.

Stephen felt a pang of loneliness as he searched the shadows on the other side of the creek in vain for his friend, whose companionship he had come to depend on. He liked the windup store and the ice-cream outings, and he really liked Cooper a lot. But he liked playing with Woody best.

Woody was more fun now than he had been before, when Stephen was younger. He wasn't afraid of anything—not even the slim brown water snakes they sometimes encountered by the creek. Sometimes he would catch one behind its narrow head and toss it into the water, where it quickly swam away. He showed Stephen how to hurl a rock against a tree trunk with such force that it made a satisfying *thunk* and birds rose squawking in the air. He could whistle like a bird and run like the wind. Stephen was willing to bet Woody was even brave enough to make the tempting but daunting climb to the tree house hidden high in the oak tree in the front yard.

But where was he?

Stephen hesitated a minute longer, then took off his shoes and socks and left them on the bank while he splashed across the cold creek. If Woody didn't wear shoes, why should he? The first few times he had tried going barefoot, it had really hurt—every little blade of grass had stuck into his foot like a pin. Now he scarcely felt them at all. Once he had even stepped in horse poop. He had thought he was going to be sick until Woody told him it was only chewed-up grass.

He trudged up the hill by himself. It seemed steeper than usual. Maybe, when he finally reached the top, he would find Woody waiting for him.

But this hope went unanswered. The hilltop was deserted, and he stood there chest deep in the waving golden grass, the blue sky overhead seeming so far away that it made his chest ache. Except for the breeze stirring in the sunlit grass and the distant, repetitive calling of a bird from the pine woods, he was completely alone.

"Wood—ee!"

The wind snatched his cry and spiraled it away in a high thread of sound. Stephen sank down on his haunches in the high grass. A lump was growing in his throat and he tried unsuccessfully to swallow it. Oppressed by the vast emptiness of the blue sky, he hid his face on his knees, hearing the grass whisper around him.

Little by little, he began to realize that the sound in the distance, the one he had taken to be a mournful, broken birdcall, was the sound of someone crying.

He lifted his head and listened. Now it sounded like a bird again, but if he lowered his head to his knees the crying was unmistakable. Was that Woody? He sounded desolate, unconsolable, and Stephen felt his own eyes smarting in sympathy.

"Woody, what's the matter?" The words came out in a whisper. But Woody must have heard him, because a whisper came in answer.

"I'm all by myself."

The loneliness hit Stephen in a wave, twisting his heart in his chest. "No, you're not. I'm here. I'm your friend, Woody. I'll always be your friend."

"No, you won't."

"I will too!" Indignation brought Stephen's head up from his knees. He looked around for Woody but couldn't see him. "I will!" he said.

Woody didn't answer. The tall grass swayed whispering in the wind.

*　　*　　*

Trying to explain to her young son about social obligations, Nan found herself getting frustrated. Ever since the square dance Lucy Talbot had been begging her to let the boy spend an afternoon, promising him a taste of farm life, and Nan had finally arranged it. But when she told Stephen, he kicked up a royal fuss about abandoning Woody.

"Honey, Woody won't mind."

"He will. He gets really sad sometimes, Mom. I think he's lonely."

For *he,* read Stephen Phillips—you didn't have to be a big-bucks child shrink, like Jennifer, to figure that one out. Yet he hadn't connected with any of his cousins and there were no children living nearby. What was she supposed to do? This was a wrinkle she hadn't foreseen when she had brought him to Tennessee, and it was a bad one. A child needed friends, someone to play with. Yet now that she was involved with Sky, the idea of pulling up stakes and returning to New York was nearly inconceivable. She looked down at her son's frowning face and sighed.

"Well, I think he'll survive without you. It's only one afternoon. And Lucy's feelings will be hurt if I tell her you don't want to go."

When she called Sky and told him she had a few daylight hours free, he took the afternoon off and the two of them went riding. Mounted on Jolie and Sky's gelding Joker, they ambled along dirt roads and through fields of daisies and black-eyed Susans, the two horses moving side by side under a cloudless blue sky.

They didn't talk much. Occasionally Sky pointed out a local landmark or mentioned the name of the family whose property they were currently crossing, but for the most part they rode in silence. On the subject of Jerry Ray's prison term, Nan had decided to simply ask him straight out why he hadn't told her—but out here in the country air, the sun on her shoulders, she was unwilling to interrupt the serenity of the moment. And the presence of this faint shadow between them, she was forced to notice, did nothing to diminish his attraction for her. Whatever the movement of the horses brought their legs into momentary contact, she felt her erotic temperature rise.

The way home took them through Sky's orchards, long rows of gnarled silver-green trees following the contours of the gentle hills. There was a distant chug of machinery. Catching sight of a man operating some kind of spraying machine at the far end of one leafy aisle, Nan reined in Jolie and stopped to watch.

"Who's that?"

"Bob Comer. He works for me."

"What's that he's spraying—some kind of insecticide?"

Her distaste must have been evident in her voice. Sky grinned. "Yes, ma'am, that's bug killer. You rather eat worms?" He clucked to Joker. "Come on, let's get goin'. I got a surprise for you."

"Like what?" she said as they rode on.

"Wait and see."

They emerged from the orchards into the graveled yard where the apples were packed. Over to one side was a low-roofed open shed and Nan saw piles of apple crates stacked against one wall. Sky rode toward the shed.

"If you're going to offer me an apple, you've got your roles mixed up," she said. "Eve's supposed to offer the apple."

He turned in his saddle to look at her. "I ain't goin' to offer you no apple. You New York gals're already too smart for your own good."

There wasn't time to consider the implications of this statement; Joker's glossy rump had disappeared around the back of the shed and Nan followed on Jolie, rounding the corner and catching the gleam of chrome in the shadow of the overhanging roof. A glimmer of white and flamingo pink. Sky had dismounted and was grinning at her. She stared in disbelief.

"Jesus. Is that Estelle?" She had all but forgotten about Annabel's old car until this moment, when the name came instantly to her lips.

"Mighty right. I been tunin' her up, restorin' the paint job. Looks pretty, don't she? Runs good too. I guess she's yours now."

"Oh Christ, no—you should keep her."

She dismounted and looped Jolie's reins around one of the shed supports, moving slowly toward the car. FORD FAIRLANE, read the chrome letters in stubby fifties' script above the radiator grille, and she ran her fingers over them, then opened the passenger-side door and got in. Sky slid in behind the wheel, jingling a set of keys.

"Want to hear her purr?"

Nan nodded only to be polite, caring nothing for the workings of the engine but entranced by seeing Estelle once again. She passed an admiring hand over the flamboyant curves of the yellowed plastic dashboard, its gauges and controls set in lovingly polished chrome, and touched the oddly emaciated steering wheel and plump bench seats upholstered in pink leather. Once Sky had started the engine (a low throb that sounded like nothing special to her untutored ears), he clicked on the radio and she recognized the whiny, staticky signal of WKMT in Gaylesville, the nearest sizable town. She turned to him, smiling.

"What a great surprise."

"You're mighty far away." He reached for her across the roomy bench seat; they kissed and then kissed again. "Mmm." He slid one hand up her back, under her shirt. "Reminds me of high school, out parkin' on a country road. Some of them gals was mighty sweet to me. Mighty sweet."

"I'll bet they were." Nan felt herself sinking into the depths of the seat. He was half on top of her, nuzzling her neck, his hands roaming around inside her clothing. She let his weight bear her down on the car seat, half closing her eyes against the dazzle of sunlight glowing between the boards of the shed wall beside the car. A sweet, lingering smell of apples permeated the air. The radio signal, struggling across the mountains, disappeared briefly in a crackle of static and returned with Crystal Gayle singing "Talking in Your Sleep."

Nan looked at Sky through her lashes, very much aware that the handsome face so near hers was that of a stranger, one she had a certain amount of reason to distrust. The thought acted as a perverse goad to her desire. She gave an involuntary nervous laugh. He opened his eyes and looked at her.

"What's so funny?"

"I don't know." She could hardly confess the truth. "I just never got a chance to do this when I was a teenager. None of the kids I knew had their own cars."

"Well, we'll just have to fix that little lapse in your education."

As he spoke he was wrestling with her clothes and she tried to help him, suddenly wild to feel him inside her. Even their awkwardness was erotic, in this classic setting with its savor of forbidden fruit. Suppose somebody caught them?

"What about that guy spraying the apples? What if he walks in on us?"

"Honey, Bob's all the way t' other end of the orchard. Even you can't holler that loud." He finished unbuttoning her shirt. "Now just relax. I'm a little rusty on this, but it's all comin' back."

Afterward, they levered themselves upright and lolled on the car seat, too spent to move further. Outside the shed, birds called in the orchard and there was the occasional jingle of a bridle as one of the horses shook off flies.

"Did we know each other that summer I was here?" she said. "I don't remember you."

"Well, I remember you. You had pigtails and you was just as wild as a little deer. I wanted to kiss you."

"Come on. I was nine years old."

"Well, I was eight. My mind just naturally ran on that sort of thing."

"It still does," Nan said.

He stretched lazily and rested his arm along the seat

behind her head. "Mighty right. I waited a long time for this."

"Well, I'm glad I made such a big impression. And I apologize for forgetting you. The fact is, I don't remember much about that summer. Some of it's been coming back to me since I've been here, but only in bits and pieces." She paused; then: "Sky . . . do you remember Tucker?"

He shifted his weight on the bulging seat. " 'Course I remember him."

"Who was he, exactly? Was he part of the family? I know it sounds ridiculous to ask. I know we were best friends. But my memory's so damn flaky—"

Sky cleared his throat. "His daddy was Annabel's hired man. He used to bring Tuck with him when he came to work. They lived up on Sleepy Gal Mountain, just the two of 'em—Tuck's momma was dead. I'm not surprised you might think he was family, though. Annabel set high store by Tuck. She must'a been real tickled when y'all two hit it off."

Nan struggled to remember. But the memories, she knew by now, came on their own whim, not hers. She found herself saying, "Do you know exactly how he died? It's pretty weird to have to ask you. I think I was there. But I can't remember it at all."

"Well, tell you the truth, I don't remember the story all that well myself. But I believe the two of you was playin' on the ice in that old flooded quarry up behind Annabel's. The ice broke, and Tucker fell in and drowned."

"Ice?" The word jarred her. "How could there have been ice? It was summer."

He cocked his head. "You sure?"

"Well, I know I was never here in the wintertime."

Sky shrugged. "Maybe I got it wrong, then—maybe y'all were swimmin' and he drowned. Mostly what I remember is how hard Annabel took it. Seems like she was always wipin' away tears after that. Caleb, Tucker's dad—he moved away. Place just held too many memories for him, I guess."

Nan was silent. Then: "I wish I could remember."

"Why? Better you don't. Musta been pretty grim."

"I know, but Tucker and I were so close. It seems like the least I could do—" She broke off, not really knowing what she meant. Sky eyed her sideways with a look that said the conversation was too morbid for his liking.

"I'd concentrate on the good parts if I was you. For instance—he ever kiss you?"

"Now, *that* I really don't remember. But I'm sure he didn't. We were little kids. He wasn't as precocious as you."

He offered her an exaggerated leer. "Don't you believe it, hon. All little boys're precocious that way." Pretending to reconsider: "But you know, the way I recollect ol' Tucker, he was a real mountain boy. Maybe his idea of sexy was his daddy's hog."

She shoved him backward toward the door. Laughing, he caught the back of the seat to save himself. His opposite elbow hit the horn and it let out a plaintive blast, shattering the peace of the orchard and making them both jump.

"You're disgusting," Nan said. In spite of herself she was laughing, but the crude joke had shocked her. Sky saw it and his face changed; he reached for her, encircling her wrist with his thumb and forefinger but making no effort to draw her closer to him.

"Y'all were good friends, huh?"

Soft words conjuring a memory: the hayloft in Annabel's barn, sunlight filtering through the roof, glint of metal and a ticklish sensation like a waiting sneeze behind her eyes . . .

Friends.

For always.

Chapter 10

The bumpy dirt road that switchbacked up the wooded mountainside was barely wide enough for Sky's truck and he drove much too fast, one hand on the wheel and the other resting loosely on the gearshift. Nan braced herself on the turns, a protective hand gripping the camera in her lap. She pitied Kate the dog, crouched low in the truck bed. The radio blasted Hank Williams and sunlight flashed through the trees on either side as they barrelled along. It had rained the night before, and the leaves glowed like chips of stained glass; every now and then there was a break in the thick foliage and she saw the valley below for a moment, tender patchwork of living greens and golds, a few houses tucked into the folds of the land. Until this summer she had forgotten there were so many shades of green in the world. She craned her neck, trying to see Annabel's house, and instead caught the distant glint of water through the trees.

"What's that water down there?"

Sky, whistling through his teeth along with Hank's yodeling, glanced past her. "That's the quarry. Where your buddy Tuck . . ."

"Oh." She looked again but the glint was gone. "What's a quarry doing with enough water in it to drown somebody?"

His eyes flicked toward her briefly. "Workers hit an underground river, sometime near the beginning of the century. Ground caved in and the quarry filled up."

They went over a bump and Nan bounced, feeling the top of her head graze the ceiling of the truck cab and clutching the camera in protective reflex. She saw Sky grinning at her near concussion. He had offered to bring her along on this visit to two old women, friends of his, he said, "from way on back," because he knew she wanted to photograph the mountain people.

Since the square dance, when the lived-in faces of her relatives had struck her with such force, she had done portraits of Whit and Lucy Talbot, and she was deeply pleased with them. But she was tempted by the idea of photographing the people who lived on the ridge and in the "holler" beyond. She had caught glimpses of them in Breezy, loading their trucks with supplies and—aside from Jerry Ray Watkins—she had been impressed by what she had seen. They had an untamed, independent air that seemed to separate them from the "bottomland folks" by more than simply topography. When Sky had mentioned driving up Sleepy Gal to check on Pen and Flutie Larkin, she had jumped at the chance to go along.

Hank launched into "Your Cheatin' Heart" as the truck bore left, off the dirt road and onto a steep, grassy track among the trees. Sky drove more slowly now, but there was no noticeable improvement—the ride was worse, if anything. Ruts beneath the wheels had the truck pitching and rolling like a ship in a storm and she could hear the overgrown center strip clawing at the undercarriage. Low-hanging branches whipped the windshield as sunlight flashed code, too fast to decipher, through jewel-bright leaves overhead. Unseen birds sang around them, joining the radio's mournful fiddle.

They went over a rise in the track, then a dip—and there it was . . . a little cabin actually built of logs, standing in a clearing. Its sloping shingle roof extended over a sagging porch. Beside the cinder-block step, a worn truck tire had been turned into a planter, sprouting pink and yellow snapdragons from its center. Sky brought the truck to a jolting halt beside the cabin; Kate jumped out of the back and began to run in circles.

Nan got out and stood looking around the sunlit clearing. Birdsong poured from the trees all around, sparkling on the surface of the profound forest silence like water spilling down the face of a rock. Behind the cabin the mountain reared a protective bulwark, green and still under the noon sun. Speckled orange butter-flies fluttered among rows of plants in a neat vegetable garden, where a tinfoil pan hung on a long string from a pole.

"Sky?" She pointed. "What's that for?"

"Poor folks' scarecrow."

As if to demonstrate his words, a breeze tossed the pan, making it rattle and glitter in the sunlight. A rusty black dog came around a corner of the cabin and gave a single hoarse bark before approaching Kate with its tail wagging.

"How do they get around?" Nan said. "Do they have a car?"

Sky grimaced. "Don't neither one of 'em know how to drive. They used to have this ol' mule—called him Frank. Pen'd ride him down to the E-Z-Way on Route 9. But he up and died this past April. A few of us been takin' turns lookin' after 'em since, but I purely hate to think what they'd do if there was trouble. I been tryin' to talk 'em into a CB radio, but they won't have it. It's right worrisome."

The sound of the cabin door opening caught Nan's attention. A dumpy old woman in a faded print dress came out onto the porch and squinted toward them in the sunlight.

"Hey there, Pen." Sky reached into the back of the truck and lifted out a cardboard carton filled with groceries. "Brought y'all some of them tangelo things Flutie likes so much. And a pound of Ike's peppered bacon."

Her squint deepened to a scowl. "Hey yourself, Sky Barnett. What you pesterin' us poor old women for? Ain't you got enough to keep you busy?"

"Never too busy to pester y'all." Grinning, he came around the truck, touching Nan's arm, bringing her forward. "Pen, this here's Annabel Stephens's granddaughter, Nan. Come all the way from New York City to live down yonder at Annabel's with her little boy."

"New York City. Well, I declare." Pen Larkin's bony hand grasped hers and Nan looked into eyes so pale that their blue was only a hint. Time had knotted and gnarled Pen like an apple tree. Her nose and chin were trying to meet in front of her sunken mouth, and her arms stuck out at a scarecrow angle from the shapeless dress. Her scowl was ferocious but her warm grip seemed to belie it; she shook Nan's hand in quick syncopated jerks, like a maraca. A younger woman appeared in the shadowed doorway behind Pen and stood watching in silence. Sky reached into the carton and took out a tangelo.

"Look here, Flutie. Brought you a present."

She reached out and he put the bright fruit in her hand. As the motion brought her into the light, Nan saw that in reality she was not much younger than Pen. It was just that she had aged more gently, kept the time-blurred presence of a slim young girl. Silvery brown hair streamed over her shoulders, and a thousand tiny lines clustered around her mouth and radiated from the corners of her pale eyes. She wore a conglomeration of clothing—a cotton dress similar to Pen's, topped by a long patchwork skirt and a motheaten red cardigan.

"Flutie, this here's Annabel's granddaughter," Sky said. Nan remembered what he had told her: the two sisters, last of the once-thriving Larkins, lived together in the old family cabin, Pen caring for her retarded sister. Among the mountain people Flutie had a certain reputation for having second sight or some such thing. Nan smiled at her.

"Hello, Flutie," she said. Without answering, the other woman clasped the tangelo close to her chest and ducked back into the cabin.

"She don't talk much," Pen said, grudgingly making an excuse for her sister. "She don't mean nothin' by it. That's just the way she is."

Inside, the cabin was small and dark but somehow festive, its walls papered with overlapping pages cut from magazines—ads mostly, glossy sophisticated scenes wildly at odds with the woodstove, worn wicker rocking chair and sagging sofa. Through a doorway Nan saw a double bed covered with a faded quilt that would have brought a fortune in a New York antique shop. She was ushered to the rocker. An ancient refrigerator hummed in one corner, its enamel worn away in a ragged circle next to the handle, showing dull metal underneath. Pen saw her looking at it.

"Jack Carson give us that fridge near sixteen years ago. We used t' keep our clothes in it till the power line come through and give us some electric to run it on. Flutie likes them orange Popsicles they have down at Ike's, and it keeps 'em from turnin' to mush. It sure do make a racket though, don't it, Flu?"

Flutie nodded. Perched on the edge of the sofa, her long faded hair straggling around her, she looked like one of those old Julia Margaret Cameron photographs from the nineteenth century—sylphs and muses and drowned-looking ladies draped in white. Nan was tempted to try to imitate them, with maybe an orange Popsicle for a grace note. She smiled at Flutie, trying to estimate the available light in the cabin, not wanting to use flash if she could possibly avoid it. Three small windows, one on either side of the front door and another behind the sofa, offered only limited illumination.

Sky was clumping around the cabin, his boots echoing hollowly on the floorboards, peering at something behind the stove as he talked to Pen.

"That pipe holdin' okay now? Y'all haven't had no more trouble with it, have you?"

"No. It don't hardly get smoky a-tall in here since you fixed that ol' pipe." Pen's bad temper was gradually revealing itself to be a facade. She turned to Nan. "Afore he fixed it, used t' get so bad, the smoke got all in our clothes and ever'thing. Flutie says to me one time, 'You smell like a side o' bacon.'" She laughed, a short, high-pitched wheeze that reminded Nan of a baby's squeeze toy.

Sky gave the pipe a final pat and straightened. "Pen, Nan's a photographer back in New York. Gets her stuff in magazines and all. She wants to take yours and Flutie's picture."

"You're foolin' with me, Sky Barnett." Pen folded her arms, scowl back in place. "Why in the good Lord's name would you want to put a picture of two old women in a magazine?"

"This wouldn't be for a magazine," Nan said. "Maybe a book of pictures of people from around here, something like that . . ."

She heard herself with a shock. A book of her own photographs, portraits and landscapes from this place where she felt awakened and renewed? Her fashion colleagues would hoot. Nan Lucas, known for the cool, hard color of her magazine spreads, the bitchy get-lost look on the models' faces, the quirky, parodied eroticism of the poses. Yet the images of this place, of the past few weeks, had begun to work a change in her. Set against the dozen or so work prints she had pulled in the newly completed darkroom, her fashion work seemed garish and cheap—a slick trick calculated to stimulate envy and desire. In contrast she was pleased, deeply so, with the portraits of the Talbots, starkly composed in black and white: just the people themselves, no longer young, offering no apologies and no promises. The early-morning shots of the orchard, too, just coming up out of the mist, gave her real pleasure.

Excitement stirred inside her. Had she hit upon a way to stay here, extend this pleasant interval into a way of life? A series of vignettes flashed before her: herself in boots and a duffel coat, a regular at the Feed & Seed store, her own pickup truck parked out front. *The usual, Nan? Yeah, put it in the back.* Mountains gold and copper in the fall, then blanketed in winter white. Stephen red-cheeked, building a snowman in the front yard, sledding on the hill. Spring, the orchards bursting with a pink froth of apple blossoms.

"A book?" Pen seemed awed but dubious.

Sky was grinning. "It's your big chance, girls. Y'all can get famous. Buy yourselves a Cadillac car."

It struck Nan as the wrong tack and she put a hand on his arm. "Would you mind getting that black portfolio from the truck? Pen and Flutie might like to see some of the things I've done here."

"Yes *ma'am*." He knew, of course, that he was being gotten rid of, and she would pay for it later; that was obvious. She watched him duck under the low door and swing off the porch, the sunlight on his coppery curls, then felt a moth's-wing touch on the back of her hand and turned to find Flutie beside her. The mountain woman's eyes, pale blue like her sister's, didn't blink. With her long gray-streaked hair and motley clothing she looked like an aging flower child.

"You grew up purty, honey." The words were almost a whisper, the smile an echo. Nan mustered a smile in response.

"Do you remember me, Flutie?"

"Sure I do. Them long braids."

"Did I visit you here?" Yet another experience to add to her long list of forgotten events. But Flutie was shaking her head.

"I was down yonder t' Annabel's one afternoon, lookin' to find me some coachie-ann leaves to cook with supper. Run into you and young Tucker Wills playin' by the branch. Y'all made me some tea— branch water and dandelions." Her smile widened. "You still got the recipe?"

"I'm afraid not."

Flutie shook with silent laughter. "That tea was mighty fine, hon. Mighty fine."

Nan felt her smile waver. Flutie's fixed, empty gaze was at odds with her friendly words, making her eyes and mouth seem almost like separate entities. The impression was unsettling, not to say bizarre—but Sky was back with her portfolio, and she turned away from Flutie with a feeling of relief, taking the case on her lap to unzip and open it.

The print of the orchard was on top, gargoyle trunks lifting from the mist, whole scene silvery as an etching. She felt Pen and Flutie looking, standing over her on either side of the rocking chair, and heard one of them take in breath.

"Looks like a dream, don't it?" It was Pen speaking. "But that's just what it do look like. Some mornin's you can walk out yonder to th' road and see the whole valley like that."

Nan had not felt like this, showing her photographs, since her student days with Gabe—vulnerable, tremulous, craving approval so deeply that she felt every word like the rush from some powerful drug. In her fashion work she was detached, businesslike, coolly weighing the factors that would achieve the effect she wanted, manipulating the formula until it delivered. She remembered Gabe throwing her first *Vogue* spread across the room, yelling "Just don't ever tell anyone I was your teacher!" Recalled, too, that she had felt a contemptuous pity for him, his idealism. Because this was *Vogue* magazine; this was success. Now she turned the prints over one by one with cold fingers, desperate to please these two old mountain women and her country lover, hanging on their reactions as if they were a board of the fiercest art critics.

The pictures pleased them. A word now and then, murmurs behind her—she turned and looked up to see

Flutie smiling down at the final print, the portrait of Lucy Talbot with her beloved he-goat, Black Billy.

"Well, what do you think? Would you let me take your picture? The two of you together, maybe here in the cabin, and out on the porch?" She looked at one sister, then the other. "I'd be honored if you would."

"Gal, I can't for the life o' me see why you want two ugly old women like us. But if you're crazy enough—" Pen, spokeswoman, glanced at her sister. "You best take off that ol' sweater, Flu."

"No, please—she looks wonderful just as she is. You both do. Please don't change a thing."

They were perfect subjects, gazing into the lens with no attempt to pose, no trace of self-consciousness. Safely behind the camera, Nan found Flutie's empty eyes intriguing. She started to enjoy herself. The first shots were outside on the porch—she backed off and got the whole setting, then closed in for a series of the sisters together on the old car seat that served as porch furniture. Indoors: Flutie in the rocking chair and Pen standing behind her, a splash of bright sun on the floor at their feet. The exposure was tricky but she thought the result would be worth it.

Click of the shutter, creak of the floorboards beneath her feet as she moved from one angle to another, feeling relaxed and confident as she always did with the camera in her hands—the session was going flawlessly when she unwittingly brought it to an end. A bright jumble of fabric in a basket beside the sofa caught her eye, and she saw it as the perfect prop.

"What's that—a quilt? How about if Flutie holds it on her lap while—"

She had crossed the room, had her hands on the quilt before their shocked faces registered.

"That's Flutie's seein' quilt." Pen sounded horrified.

Nan pulled her hands away, mystified but repentant. *Seeing quilt?* "I'm sorry. I didn't mean—"

"She didn't know, Pen," Flutie said. But Pen seemed deeply affronted, stomping over to the basket and making an elaborate ritual of refolding the quilt, which Nan had hardly touched. "She didn't know," Flutie said again, and Nan made another apologetic murmur. Pen nodded brusquely, her face averted, accepting excuse and apology at last; but the rapport of a moment before had been destroyed. Nan blamed herself for forgetting where she was, behaving like a professional hotshot. Still, she knew she had gotten some nearly perfect pictures.

By the time she had rewound the film and gathered up the contents of her portfolio, the atmosphere had eased and she was cordially bidden to come for another visit any time.

"I'll bring you proofs of the pictures. You can pick the one you like best and I'll make you a copy." She would have offered this courtesy in any case, but she wanted to make up to Pen for whatever obscure crime she had committed by touching the quilt in the basket. She had scarcely dared look at it after that, aware only of a bright intriguing blur at the edge of her vision. A seeing quilt? She had gotten only a brief glimpse of it, just enough to see that it was pieced to resemble a landscape, apparently the local one—she thought she had recognized the silhouette of Sleepy Gal Mountain.

"Lordy, hon," Pen was saying. "We don't even own a lookin' glass. Old and ugly as us, it's a blessin' not t' see yourself."

"According to my camera," Nan said, "you're beautiful."

She meant it, but the old women cackled gaily. Sky called Kate, and they got into the truck; there were waves and good-byes, and they jounced off through the trees.

"What in God's name is a seeing quilt?" Nan said as the cabin disappeared from sight.

"Hell if I know. Something she uses to predict the future, I guess. Folks around here'll swear Flutie's got the sight. They come ask her all kinds o' things. Whether their baby's goin' to be a boy or girl, stuff like that."

"Well, I really screwed up when I touched it. They acted like it was going to explode."

"Future's a dangerous thing," Sky said. He sounded serious, but Nan saw his lips twitch and glanced more closely at him. There were moments, this one of them, when she found herself wondering if she had underestimated this man. When she had finally asked him why he hadn't told her Jerry Ray Watkins was a jailbird, he had said with a kind of stiff dignity that he didn't think the poor bastard ought to be saddled with his past. "Hell, everybody's entitled to a few mistakes. Ain't that so?"

But this kind of rustic simplicity occasionally took on what seemed like a tinge of mockery that made her suspect him of exaggerating it for her benefit. Since they had become lovers, his attitude toward her had gained a teasing, antagonistic edge that had been lacking before, reminding her more than anything else of boy-girl relations in junior high, when a jeer meant "I like you." It was only natural that their relationship should have undergone a change with intimacy; still, she was surprised by what seemed to be an attempt to hide his deeper feelings behind such a childish ritual. Was he in love with her? She didn't know. She knew she wasn't in love with him, but she enjoyed him, found him attractive. And that was plenty for now.

He drove more slowly going downhill. She found herself enjoying the country radio station (Patsy Cline now) and the truck's rough ride—the feeling of being a real down-home gal. It looked as if it might rain again this afternoon; dark clouds were massing over the valley. The truck rounded a bend and the flash of water again caught her eye—the flooded quarry partially visible at a distance through the trees.

"Sky, stop. Pull over a minute."

The engine growled as he downshifted and pulled over to the side of the road. "What for?"

"I want to go look at the quarry."

He gave her an incredulous look. "What the hell for?"

"I don't know. I just do."

He sat staring at her as if she had suddenly sprouted horns. The impulse that had made her speak was already fading, but his resistance aroused a certain stubborn perversity in its place. She put her hand on his thigh. "Come on. It won't take long."

His leg was tense to her touch. "It's hard to get at," he said. "Ain't all that near the road."

"So we'll hike," she said.

"Might be poison ivy."

"We'll hike carefully."

"Snakes."

"*Very* carefully."

He shook his head and she squeezed his thigh. "How come you're acting so weird?"

"Me? You're the weird one, wantin' to go there,

after what happened. Why in tarnation would you ever want to see that place again?"

"I don't know. To see if I can remember, I guess."

"Look, Nan. If you don't remember, just count it a blessin'. Don't go stirrin' up something that's been buried with good reason."

"Look," she said. "I'm an adult, okay? I don't need your advice on this. All I'm asking is for you to show me where it is."

She knew she was being obnoxious, but the urge to oppose his wishes, on any subject at all, was suddenly overpowering—probably rooted in the fact that he was resisting her, refusing to be head over heels in love and eager to show it. She felt at a disadvantage here on his turf. At times she suspected him of having methodically seduced her, just to see if he could.

They stared at each other for a long minute and suddenly he grinned, a tight angry baring of teeth in his coppery beard.

"Okay. You got it."

He killed the engine. Around them the birds' clamor suddenly seemed twice as loud in the dense summer woods. Leaves hung heavy on their branches, and a stickyhot green smell made the air almost palpable. Sky opened the door and got out. "Stay, Kate."

The dog whined once, then lay down in the truck bed and settled her nose on her paws.

Nan climbed out on her side, into thigh-deep undergrowth still wet from last night's rain. Remembering his remarks about snakes and poison ivy, she moved cautiously around the truck to join him. He stood scanning the woods on the down-mountain side of the road for a moment, then moved forward into the trees.

She followed. In spite of their acrid exchange and

the day's growing humidity, the idea of a walk in the woods held a certain appeal. Ever since her freak-out along the creek that first day, she had toyed with the idea of a rematch, a chance to prove to herself, and maybe to Nature, that she could handle herself in this environment.

But now, as the lush, dripping jungle of vegetation surrounded her on all sides, she could discern nothing that resembled a path; it was as if she and Sky had been unexpectedly transported from North America to the Vietnam she had seen in war movies. Or maybe to Tarzan's Africa? Ropy vines hung down from some of the trees, seeming to invite a swing.

"Sky? Are those grape vines?"

He didn't turn; his answer floated back. "Poison ivy."

Nan eyed the vines—easily as thick as her wrist— with new respect. Overhead, successive tiers of leaves blocked the sunlight, creating a humid green twilight. The air was thick with tiny insects. They formed a cloud around her head and she waved them away, but seconds later they were back. She was wearing shorts, and the sensation of the wet undergrowth slapping her bare legs as she passed was highly unpleasant—

Worse than unpleasant. "Shit!" she said suddenly, feeling a slash of pain and glancing down to see quick beads of blood forming across her shin, where a thorny vine had raked her leg just below the knee. The thorns, when she examined them, were at least an inch long. Sky, a dozen feet ahead, glanced back briefly but didn't stop, shouldering past the low-hanging branches for all the world like a testy rush-hour commuter, leaving them to drip their cargo of moisture down her neck as she followed. The scratch on her leg stung like fire. Hot and miserable as she was (and still uneasy about snakes; he seemed to be stirring them up on purpose for her to step on), she refused to give in and ask to turn back. She wouldn't give him the satisfaction.

She didn't notice exactly when the birdcalls stopped. The silence of the woods around them was borne in on her little by little. She became aware first of her own breathing, then the edgy whine of the gang of persistent little bugs that seemed to have voted her their personal project for the day. At least Sky seemed to know exactly where he was going. He was crashing along ahead like a bear; it must be his commotion that had frightened the birds. The silence was nervous-making and she started to wonder where he was leading her—if he had some corny notion of losing her in the woods to teach her a lesson. It wouldn't be hard. Uneasiness stirred at the pit of her stomach: the memory of her earlier unpleasant escapade by the creek was suddenly vivid. Surrounded by impenetrable green growth, she could barely tell up from down, much less determine any more relevant direction. Ahead of her, Sky had stopped and was motioning her forward.

His face was set, unsmiling. She told herself he was acting a part, trying to spook her so he could laugh at her. And it was close to working; she was acutely aware of the fact that she was a million miles from nowhere, alone with a man she didn't know particularly well, except in the physical sense. As she reached his side he grabbed her elbow and she barely suppressed a yelp. Holding her arm he drew her roughly forward.

"Look out. It drops off real sharp."

His voice was hoarse, as if he hadn't spoken for hours. This close she couldn't miss seeing how tense he was— the deep lines around his mouth, quick movements of his eyes. The curly hair at his temples was dark with sweat and she realized that she was sweating profusely too; the humidity was intense. She swiped at the bugs again. Looked ahead. Caught her breath.

They stood almost at the brink of a stony cliff dropping sheer to water far below—water filling a roughly oval pit ringed by unbroken forest.

The quarry.

The sun had disappeared behind clouds and the surrounding wall of trees had a somber, secretive look. On either side of their vantage point the excavated stone walls angled down, tawny and ash-gray behind their summer cover of tangled vines, following the descending slope of the mountain; on the low side opposite, the edge of the pit appeared to be no more than seven or eight feet above the water.

She edged forward to peer over the cliff and moved back hastily. They were at its highest point; the water was a long way down. Pale green algae blotched the motionless surface here and there.

Nothing was familiar. She had been expecting—and dreading, uncertain what perverse impulse had made her seek it out—a sudden vivid flash of memory like the others she had experienced, but she might as well never have been here before in her life. The place had an abandoned, sinister air, but it was abstract, not personal. She shook her head.

"I just don't remember. I mean, I know it happened. But it's like a story I've heard. And this place doesn't ring any bells at all."

Sky pointed across to the low side and she saw a crevice where the rock had eroded, forming a steep channel down to the water.

"Yonder's where kids used to go in to swim."

"Did a lot of kids swim here?"

"Weren't supposed to, but they did."

He paused, obviously seeking a change of subject. "You know, the Stephens family made a pile o' money out of this quarry in the 1800s. It's located right on your property. That hill across the creek—well, if you go through them pine woods on the far side of it, then cross the north fork o' the creek and follow it a ways, you'll come out right over there on the low side. The railroad used to come back in there when the quarry was in business. They'd load the stone onto flatcars." He was still holding her elbow, his eyes darting here and there over the surface of the water. "Okay. You seen enough?"

She freed her arm and moved away from him, aware of a coiled tension inside her. In part it was due to her unanswered expectations about seeing the quarry, and probably to the barometic pressure, the heat and humidity as well. But it was also sexual. Once again, the sense of Sky as a stranger was doing something kinky to her libido.

"It's very private here. Have you noticed?" As she spoke she pulled her shirt over her head and flourished it. At the sight of his startled face she couldn't suppress a smile.

"You're fuckin' crazy," he said. He covered the distance between them in one step and grabbed her shoulders. "Put your goddamn shirt back on. Let's get out of here."

She reached up to ruffle his beard. "What are you so jumpy about? Nobody's going to see me. Except you." She let her hand slide down his chest and come to rest on his belt buckle.

"You crazy bitch."

His eyes were wild and he seemed to be having a hard time breathing. He twisted his head in a frantic look over one shoulder, then the other, as if he thought someone might be watching them. Then he pushed her back against a tree trunk, yanking her pants down.

The rough bark scraped the tender skin of her buttocks and she closed her eyes, clutching his shirt, hearing her own ragged breath and the muttered obscenities punctuating his. He pushed against her, but when she reached down to guide him he was flaccid. She opened her eyes and found his a few inches away, glazed and bloodshot.

"It's this place," he said. "This goddamn place."

She stared at him, feeling desire drain away. She could smell the fear on him now. Its stench, his impotence, the hollow look in his eyes all combined to dispel the perverse mood that had seemed to possess her as soon as she had glimpsed the quarry from the road. With its passing she was overcome by an unexpected dread of their surroundings: the silent woods, the deep, still pool at the foot of the cliff. Whether she remembered it or not, her best friend had drowned there. *Drowned.* The memory of Stephen's white face underwater . . . She pulled up her pants with hands that were suddenly unsteady. Sky set his own clothing in order, then retrieved her shirt from the ground where she had dropped it.

"Get dressed. Let's get the hell out of here."

By this point she was more than ready. But just as she pulled the shirt over her head, the heavy air was cut by a faint, wailing cry. Nan's heart jumped. She yanked the shirt down and looked wildly at Sky.

"What the hell was that?"

His eyes narrowed. "What was what?"

"Didn't you hear it?"

He swallowed. "I didn't hear nothin'."

Nan took a tentative step closer to the cliff edge. "I thought I heard . . ."

The same cry she had heard before. Probably nothing more than the call of a hunting bird—so commonplace that Sky had not even been aware of hearing it, had simply tuned it out, the way she did with car alarms back in New York. Her voice trailed off as she looked down at the algae-mottled surface of the water below. Among the pale patches she could make out the wavering reflection of the trees that ringed the quarry. There was something wrong with the way they looked. She took another cautious step forward, narrowing her eyes.

"Sky?"

"What?"

"Would you come here and look at the reflection in the water? Does it look . . . funny to you?"

"Funny?" Twigs crackled underfoot as he came to stand beside her.

The reflected trees hung upside down, suspended from the water's surface, their branches etched in spidery tracings against a submerged sky. Nan kept staring at them, then at the leaf-laden branches of the actual trees above, comparing the two. They didn't seem to match. But that wasn't possible. Her mind, confronted with the anomaly, continued to chug and churn like some machine that had run up against a wall, wheels turning but getting nowhere.

"See that?" she said. "It's like they don't match." She would have preferred to come up with a smart remark at this juncture, something to ease her own tension at least, but the impulse had utterly vanished. Instead she was aware of a squirming sensation at the base of her spine, as if a nest of miniature snakes had been disturbed. When Sky's fingers grasped her arm she jumped.

"Shit," he whispered. "The ones in the water—they're *dead*."

At the word Nan felt an involuntary shudder go though her. Their eyes met. Of one accord they turned their backs on the quarry and plunged into the woods, heading back toward the truck. Sky took the lead, moving quickly but not quickly enough for Nan; her heart was pounding wildly and she was sweating all over, possessed by a senseless urge to flee headlong through the trees. The only thing preventing her from shoving Sky aside and crashing ahead on her own was a total ignorance of the truck's whereabouts. She didn't want to get lost in the woods again—least of all *these* woods.

Yet as they thrashed their way through the trees, putting distance between themselves and the quarry, she was dimly aware of common sense struggling to make itself known. What were they running from? There was nothing chasing them. Nothing behind them but a tragedy long past and an odd, anomalous reflection in the water that had to be nothing more than some kind of optical illusion.

The logic had a calming effect. Her impulse to flee faded; her pulse rate began to slow and she reduced her frantic pace, still keeping Sky well in sight but no longer trampling his heels. As they left the quarry farther behind, the lush green woods around them seemed less menacing and she began to hear birds calling here and there among the trees. A certain heaviness lingered in the atmosphere, as if the quarry's sinister aura were emanating outward through the trees; but of course the clouds and weighted air meant nothing more than another rainstorm on the way.

When the truck came in sight at last, Kate greeted them with a frenzy of barking and tail wagging. Sky ignored her. Nan peeked at his face. He looked hollow-eyed. They got back into the truck without speaking.

He started the engine and spoke without looking at her. "I told you we oughta stayed away from that place." His voice was flat. "It's haunted."

Chapter 11

Their descent from the mountain was made in silence. Just as Sky turned down the gravel drive to his house, the heavy skies opened: a burst of rain drumming the roof of the truck cab, washing in sheets across the windshield. Nan was grateful for the noise. In the aftermath of his announcement about the quarry being haunted, the lack of conversation in the truck had been uncomfortable.

She thought back to what she had seen. No, the trees in the water hadn't matched their counterparts above—but to describe the leafless reflections as *dead* seemed to her an unnecessarily grim way of putting it. The distorted, spidery images must be caused by something in the water—maybe its alkaline content, something like that. At the time, she had to admit, the anomaly had shaken her. But in retrospect it seemed obvious there had to be a better, more scientific explanation than Sky's wild assertion that the place was haunted.

She had tried to say something along those lines, but he had brushed her words aside, driving the rest of the way home with his jaw set and his eyes on the road. It was clear he was deeply disturbed, and she could think of nothing else to offer in the way of comfort. The sight of the Volvo parked in front of his house was a welcome one.

"I'd better go get Stephen. Call me, okay?" She leaned across the seat and kissed his cheek; he made a movement that might have been flinching. Then she was out of the truck, running through the rain to her car with her camera cradled against her chest, glad to be safely out of his presence.

Stephen's first visit with the Talbots had been such a roaring success that she had arranged another for this afternoon, thinking he would enjoy it more than the trip up the mountain in Sky's company. He would have preferred, of course, to spend the day across the creek, pretending to play with Woody, but she thought it was high time to start phasing Woody out. The Talbots, well into their seventies, might not be the ideal friends for her eight-year-old. But at least they existed outside Stephen's head.

She had dropped him off at the farm before driving over to Sky's and leaving her car at his house for the trip up the mountain in his truck. If the maneuvering seemed unnecessarily complicated, it was a price she was willing to pay to avoid rubbing Stephen's face in the fact of her relationship with Sky. Of course he knew perfectly well whom she would be spending the day with, but neither of them mentioned any names.

And she couldn't say the outing had been entirely enjoyable, not by a long shot. Pulling up at the Talbot farmhouse, she saw light in the kitchen windows beyond the wind-driven sheets of rain sweeping the yard. She parked as close to the house as she could and made a dash for the back porch. As she opened the screen door, the wind tried to yank it out of her hand, then banged it behind her.

Lucy, kneeling on the floor beside the stove, looked

up and smiled. Feeble peeping noises arose from a cardboard box in front of her. Nan moved closer and saw a dozen half-drowned baby chicks inside.

"Stephen and Whit just brought them in," Lucy said. "Didn't that rain come on sudden!"

The wet chicks resembled wads of sodden paper towel; Lucy was using a pink plastic hair dryer to dry them. Seeing Nan's expression, she cackled.

"I know, I'm terrible. Irene would snatch me bald-headed if she saw me usin' her hair dryer on a bunch of chickens. She's in town all day, givin' Marge a hand at the store while Ike's laid up with a bad back. I'll just sneak it back to her room and she'll never know."

Nan sat cross-legged on the floor beside the box, letting herself relax and enjoy Lucy's company, finding the old woman's down-to-earth chatter a perfect antidote to her recent foray in the woods. In Lucy's presence it was hard to believe she had let herself be spooked, however briefly, by something as harmless as a reflection—no matter how sinister it might have seemed at the time. And the tacky, cluttered kitchen was equally comforting: the blue-and-white gingham curtains and matching tablecloth, salt and pepper shakers shaped like baby ducks wearing bonnets, and a dime-store sampler reading "Bless This Mess" hanging on the wall above the stove.

She turned her attention back to the drying process. Under Lucy's persistent ministrations the chicks were slowly beginning to fluff. "Did Stephen behave himself?"

"Lord a mercy, yes. That's a wonderful young'un you've got there. He's out yonder in the barn right this minute, helpin' Whit fix a leak in the roof. I declare, he's been such a help today we ought to pay you cash money for him."

"He loves coming here," Nan said. "You and Whit are really the only people he's hit it off with down here. I wish I could find a way to get him connected with some other kids."

Lucy put the chick she was holding back into the box and glanced Nan's way. "He hasn't taken a fancy to any of his cousins?"

"Not really. Sky brought Billy over one day, but it was pretty much of a disaster."

Lucy chuckled. "That Billy can be a handful. There's times I've thanked the good Lord I've got the jump on him by a couple of generations. Poor little Stephen—bless his heart! What's he been doin' for fun?"

Nan hesitated. All at once the urge to share her worries about Woody with someone like Lucy, who radiated common sense and had raised four children of her own, was overwhelming. She found herself talking without having made a conscious decision to do so.

"Actually, he's . . . resurrected this imaginary friend he used to have a couple of years ago. He seems perfectly content to spend all day playing by himself, pretending he's with Woody. He goes down to the creek, climbs up the hill . . . even makes up stories about the stuff they do together." She shrugged. "At least he's getting exercise and fresh air. And people have assured me it's not abnormal for a kid Stephen's age to have an imaginary friend. But I just wish—"

Lucy had turned the hair dryer off. In the silence that followed her trailing sentence, Nan could hear the patter of rain outside.

"Honey, you have to stop it," Lucy said at last. "You can't let him do that."

Nan felt as if she had been kicked. Of all possible responses to her confession, she had never envisioned such flat condemnation. Now, paradoxically, she was moved to defend the relationship, to convince Lucy that Stephen wasn't some kind of demented little freak.

"It's just a coping thing," she said. "He'd actually outgrown Woody, but I guess he's been so lonely here, he needed to bring him back. Actually I've been told it's supposed to be pretty healthy—"

Lucy was shaking her head vehemently. She put the hair dryer down and faced Nan, her mouth compressed to a thin line. "Hon, I have to tell you something. I've been on the verge of telling you ever since you got here, but it's just so crazy I couldn't bring myself to say it." She swallowed, then said shakily, "Nan—right before Annabel died, she told me something real strange. She said she believed her property was haunted."

Nan felt her jaw drop. The common sense she had been seeking was nowhere in sight; instead Lucy was talking gibberish. For a moment they stared at each other. Then Lucy looked down into her lap and started to pick at a loose thread on her apron.

Nan tried to form her mouth into a reassuring smile, the kind you offer a crazy person. "Lucy . . ."

"She told me she'd seen him around the place—oh, a dozen or more times."

"Seen who?" Nan said, completely lost, and all at once the old woman's eyes focused on her, bleak and bottomless.

"Young Tucker Wills."

It was so obvious the old lady wasn't joking that Nan was shocked at herself for starting to laugh. But she couldn't help it. All her relatives seemed to have picked this afternoon to go stark raving mad. First Sky and his absurd reaction to the reflection in the flooded quarry, now Lucy babbling about ghosts. And not just any ghost—Tucker's, no less. Her childhood friend, cast in the role of lurking phantom. She had to laugh or cry.

She put her hand over her mouth, hearing a faint peeping from the box beside her and noticing that the hair dryer, lying on the floor nearby, resembled a ridiculous pink pistol.

Lucy was shaking her head. "Lord knows, I can't blame you for laughin'. I can hear myself just how crazy it sounds. When Annabel told me, I thought she'd gone round the bend. But I couldn't get it out of my mind. And then at the square dance, when Stephen asked for the White Rose Waltz—honey, that was Tucker's favorite tune. He asked for it every chance he got, every square dance and picnic and church social— so much that nobody's had the heart to ask for it since he died. But then you said Stephen learned it from your husband—"

Woody whistled it for me.

Nan's head started to spin. "He didn't," she heard herself say flatly over a rushing sound in her ears.

"Didn't?" Lucy echoed.

"Didn't learn it from my husband. Or maybe—I don't know. He told me Woody whistled it for him."

"Oh, my Lord," the older woman said. "Dear Lord God."

Nan found herself in the middle of a mental process akin to pitching a tent in a howling windstorm: as soon as she got one corner of her thoughts pinned down tidily, another escaped and started flapping.

Woody's imaginary.

He doesn't exist outside Stephen's head.

Stephen must have learned the tune from Gabe and just given Woody the credit.

The fact that the tune was Tucker's favorite was just coincidence—a whopping coincidence, an incredible one.

But still more credible than a ghost.

She opened her mouth to say all this, but Lucy was clambering stiffly to her feet, motioning her without speaking into the living room. It was dark in there, shadowy furniture bulking in the gloomy light from the windows. Without stopping to turn on a lamp, Lucy went straight to a tall secretary desk in one corner, where she bent and opened the bottom drawer. Nan, hesitating in the doorway, saw it brimming with what looked like piles of papers. Papers and photographs. Lucy was taking them out in handfuls, letting them fall to the floor heedlessly, searching for something.

"Lucy?"

The old lady didn't answer, and Nan's uneasiness mounted. Had Lucy snapped? She wondered if she should go out to the barn and get Whit, but she didn't want to leave Lucy alone. Instead she went and knelt beside her, taking the drift of papers and trying to stack it neatly, not knowing what else to do. Letters and receipts and old church bulletins, maps and recipes and tattered postcards. From the photographs faces looked out at her in the dim light, some strikingly like her own. Formal portraits: a woman and child in frilly old-fashioned clothing, a young man in riding dress. Snapshots: two men on the creek bank, a bunch of people around a truck. Whit, as a young man, holding a hunting dog by the collar.

"Here. I knew I had it here."

Lucy had found a bulky brown envelope and was fumbling it open. Out came a short newspaper clipping, tea-colored and brittle, flaking at the edges as she thrust it at Nan, who received it carefully.

LOCAL BOY GIVES LIFE FOR FRIEND read the headline. Nan glanced up at Lucy, then back at the article in her hand.

Annabel Lucas, nine-year-old granddaughter of Corey County resident Mrs. Amos Stephens, is alive today thanks to the selfless act of Tucker Wills, ten, son of Caleb Wills of Sleepy Gal Mountain. Annabel, who lives in Connecticut, is visiting her grandmother for the holidays. Late yesterday afternoon the two children were playing on the frozen surface of an abandoned quarry on the Stephens property when the ice broke beneath them. Young Wills managed to push the girl to safety before succumbing to the freezing water. His body has not yet been recovered. As the Bible tells us, "Greater love hath no man than this, that he lay down his life for a friend."

Winter.

Sky was right. It had been winter—not summer, as she had assumed all this time, based on the only fact she remembered: that Tucker had drowned.

Winter. Bare branches reflected in the quarry's deep water.

The newsprint seemed to slip in and out of focus before her eyes. She had no memory, none at all, of visiting Annabel that Christmas. But here was the evidence, incontrovertible. A line of text came clear momentarily: *playing on the frozen surface of an abandoned quarry.* In the margin of the clipping were handwritten the words *Gaylesville Record, December 23, 1968.* The ink had faded to a coppery color.

She looked up. Lucy was fumbling in the envelope again, bringing out a shapeless rust-colored object. When she held it out, Nan saw it was a child's hard-used mitten.

"Come spring, they had people divin' down in the quarry, trying to bring up his body," Lucy said. "But this was all they ever found. Annabel had it, and the newspaper clippin', at her bedside when she died. She'd kept 'em all this time. She loved Tucker, you know. I think she'd always wanted a little boy of her own."

Nan swallowed as best she could. Her mouth and throat felt gluey and her thoughts had stalled. She sat holding the square of old newspaper in her fingers, acutely aware of its dusty texture, listening while Lucy talked.

"She said the first time she saw him, it was maybe a month after he died. She was comin' down the driveway in her car, and all at once there was this boy in the road right in front of her. She jammed on the brakes so hard she hit her chin on the steerin' wheel and saw stars, but she said she was too shook to black out. Because she'd recognized him. And it was Tucker Wills.

"She said she thought her heart would fly right out of her mouth. He was standin' right there in the road. Annabel said she just couldn't move. It was like her hands were froze to the wheel. She said she didn't know how long she sat there starin' at him, and him just lookin' back. But she must've blinked or somethin', because all at once he was gone.

"After that, she said, she used to see him around—not often, but ever' once in a while. Sometimes a year or more might go by and she wouldn't see him at all. Then she'd see him twice in a week. Sometimes just a glimpse of him, down by the creek, or climbin' that tree in the front yard. A couple of times she saw him swingin' on the pasture gate the way he used to, and she said even when she didn't see him, she used to find that gate open ever' so often, like he'd been there.

"She said the plain truth of it was, she got used to him. After that first time, he didn't scare her no more. She saw a book about ghosts at the bookstore in town and bought it to read. She said the book said sometimes when someone dies suddenlike, their spirit is confused and doesn't know where to go. So they just stay around someplace that's familiar to 'em. Someplace they know. She said he didn't do any harm."

A memory nudged Nan: Cooper, telling her Annabel had been interested in the spirit's survival of bodily death.

She said she knew it was possible. She had a real open mind.

Or a flaky one. While she sat listening to Lucy, Nan's sluggish thoughts began to move again, and finally logic kicked in. Annabel's grief over the death of the boy she had loved must have weighed heavily on her all those years. Small wonder she had sought comfort in a fantasy that Tucker still existed, safe and happy in some limbo of perpetual childhood, forever climbing trees and swinging on gates.

Swinging on gates.

She thought of the afternoon she had seen the gate swinging open in its slow arc. The rusty creaking of the hinges. A frisson ran over her and she squelched it firmly.

Come on. The catch was broken, that's all. That's *all*.

"Lucy," she said gently. "Don't you think it's possible Annabel just imagined seeing Tucker? Don't you think that's a lot more likely than the idea of a ghost?"

Lucy shook her white head. "Honey, I don't know. When she told me—Lord knows, I felt just the way you do. I didn't want to believe it. And that's why I didn't say anything to you. I thought— well, maybe it was all in Annabel's mind. But when Stephen fell in the creek and almost drowned . . . I'll tell you, I started to wonder. And then he asked for that tune—and he showed up wearin' that ring like the one Tucker used to wear—and now you tell me he's been playin' with some little boy . . ."

Somebody pushed me.

Wasn't that what Stephen had said, that first morning when she had pulled him out of the creek? And hadn't she looked up and seen—*imagined* seeing—Tuck standing on the opposite bank?

Impossible.

"Lucy, for God's sake. The creek business was an accident; Stephen slipped and fell. As for the ring—*I* gave it to him. And the little boy he pretends to play with is a make-believe friend he invented three *years* ago, long before we came here. Don't you see? There are two different kids here. One belongs to Stephen's imagination and the other to Annabel's. But neither one of them is a real ghost."

"No?" Lucy said. "Then answer me this, honey. How did Stephen know that fiddle tune?"

That damn tune. Nan could feel her logic surrounding it, unable to close in. *Woody whistled it for me.* Irritation flooded her. The unlit room, its window panes rattling intermittently, lashed with rain, was the perfect setting for a ghost story, but she was definitely not in the mood. In the murky light Lucy's face was stark, grim, a stranger's countenance. Nan was suddenly aware of how little she really knew this woman.

"I don't know," she said sharply. "But I'm sure there's an explanation. And I'm sure it has nothing to do with ghosts."

Lucy's mouth opened, but her rejoinder remained unuttered. There was a sudden loud *whump,* and the window beside the desk blew in with a splintering crash.

"Lord a mercy!"

The old woman clutched at Nan as the wind burst into the room, scattering the stack of photographs into a whirling white storm and rattling the pictures on the walls. Across the room a tall lamp swayed drunkenly, then toppled and fell with a crash. A book on a table blew open, its pages snapping madly, and the rocking chair was set in vigorous motion.

Nan bit her lips to keep from bursting into laughter that she recognized was probably hysterical. Her heart was pounding wildly. It was only the wind, for God's sake, but the timing had been impeccable, and in Lucy's mind there must be no doubt that the ghost was showing its displeasure.

"Have you got a bedsheet? Something to keep out the rain?" She had to shout over the racket, but at least Lucy wasn't too far gone to listen. She nodded and stumbled to her feet, hurrying into the kitchen to return a moment later with a crumpled sheet in her arms.

Nan took it from her. It was warm, probably fresh out of the dryer. "Good. Now we need some tacks, pushpins, something like that. To tack it to the window." Lucy gazed distractedly at her and Nan gave her a little shove. "Tacks, Lucy. Go find some."

While the old lady was gone, she examined the shattered window as best she could without getting soaked by the rain blowing in. Only the bottom pane had broken, and it looked as if it might have been cracked already. A touch at her elbow: Lucy was there, holding out a plastic container of colored pushpins.

Nan took it from her. "Perfect."

In the end it turned out they didn't really need them. The wind was already beginning to die down before they had finished tacking the sheet into place, and by the time Whit and Stephen had returned from the barn to exclaim over the destruction in the living room, the storm was over and the sun had come out, making bright mirrors of the puddles in the yard.

*   *   *

On the drive home, Nan's thoughts were in a spin. What a day! That ill-conceived pilgrimage to the quarry where Tucker had died, topped by Lucy's grisly fantasy that his restless ghost had somehow managed to hook up with Stephen. All at once the tragic death of her childhood friend seemed to have moved from the distant past to overwhelming proximity. She had been stunned by the revelation that the accident had happened not during the summer, as she had always assumed—but in the winter, during a second visit of which she had absolutely no recollection. None whatever. When she tried to focus on what she knew about the accident, she met nothing but a blank. A smooth and featureless wall with no discernible door . . .

She grimaced as she slowed the car and made the turn off the road onto Annabel's driveway.

"Do you, Mom?"

Belatedly she realized that Stephen had been chattering at her all the way home; she had simply tuned him out. "Sorry, honey. Do I what?"

"I said, do you think all this rain'll make the creek overflow? Woody says last year it overflowed and flooded the whole pasture."

Woody says . . .

They were bumping down the drive, between trees that formed a high green tunnel, leafy branches crisscrossing far overhead. A shaft of sunlight pierced the leaves to spill down on the windshield, a sudden dancing brightness that temporarily blinded her. For an instant she had the sensation of falling. She gripped the wheel, touched the brake, but by then it was gone. "I don't know, Stephen. I don't think so. It's stopped now."

A child's imagination at work, nothing more. This past March, outside their Manhattan loft, the sewers had backed up during a heavy downpour and the whole street had flooded.

A simple explanation, perfectly obvious. But not to Lucy, full of tales of a ghost child. Or Sky, with his vision of death in the water at the quarry where Tucker had drowned. Ghosts and haunted quarries. All at once Nan was appalled at the gulf that had seemed to open this afternoon between her and the people with whom she had formed relationships in this new place. Of course it had been there all along, but until now it had seemed small and easily bridged. Now it yawned like a chasm.

She stopped the car beside the house and Stephen jumped out. Nan leaned into the back seat to retrieve her camera. The strap had gotten wrapped around a seat belt and she had to untangle it, emerging a minute later to see Stephen over by the pasture fence, unfastening the gate. That surprised her; he never used the gate, always climbed the fence. Then she saw him push off with one foot, riding the bottom rail, clutching tight to the top one as the gate swung out over the steep decline of the land.

A couple of times she saw him swingin' on the pasture gate the way he used to, and she said even when she didn't see him, she used to find that gate open ever' so often, like he'd been there.

Something any kid would do—the gate and its placement practically begging for such a stunt. But standing there motionless in the afternoon sunshine, the camera dangling by its strap from one suddenly nerveless hand, Nan was suddenly aware of a sensation like dozens of tiny cold fingers laid tentatively along the length of her spine.

*   *   *

"Ride it all the way out to the end," Woody said. "Then jump off."

Stephen eyed the pasture's sharp drop-off inside the fence. "It looks kind of steep."

"It's fun," Woody said.

He pushed the gate and Stephen felt himself swing out. His stomach did a flip in slow motion. He clutched the top rail with white-knuckled hands as the ground went zooming past beneath him. From here it looked like a really long way down. He remembered how he had fallen off the monkey bars once at school, how the ground had rushed up at him. He had twisted his knee badly. He could still remember the sickening pain.

"Now!" Woody said, but Stephen's fingers refused to loosen their grip. With a rusty squeak the gate reached the end of its arc and began to swing slowly back. "Jump!" Woody said.

But Stephen couldn't. The gate returned to solid ground at last and he dismounted with a sense of heartfelt relief.

"How come you didn't jump?"

"I dunno."

"Chicken," Woody said.

Stephen winced. The insult, offhand and apparently friendly, was still intensely painful. Woody had never said anything like that to him before. But he knew it was true. He was a chicken.

He turned away from the gate, feeling a lump growing in his throat, and his gaze was caught by the oak tree in the yard. Its leafy crown rose higher than the roof of the house, casting an enormous dappled shadow on the green lawn around it.

There was a tree house up there.

Ever since his mom had told him about it, the idea of a house way up in a tree had both fascinated and frightened Stephen. He didn't like the thought of being way high off the ground. He guessed that meant he was chicken. But if you were in a little house, it might be sort of fun . . .

"Lots of fun," Woody said.

And suddenly Stephen could feel, hovering there behind Woody's words, all the enchantment of being up in the tree house. Surrounded by rustling green leaves, hidden from everybody on the ground, stifling your laughter to keep your whereabouts a secret, while far below the rest of the world went its unsuspecting way. A wave of longing passed through him. He tilted his head back, looking up at the tree. A breeze blew, and its branches seemed to whisper and beckon.

"Hey!" Woody had mounted the gate. "Gimme me a push, huh?"

Stephen complied, thankful not to be the passenger this time. "You gonna jump off again, Woody?"

But Woody was no longer riding the gate. Stephen looked around in surprise. Where had he gone? The breeze had died down, and the only movement in the whole still, sunny afternoon was the slow swing of the gate, creaking rustily out to the end of its arc. Then, behind him, the green branches of the oak began to rustle and sway. As if someone were high up in the tree, and climbing higher.

Chapter 12

That night, after Nan had put Stephen to bed, she poured herself a brandy and collapsed on the sofa in the library. She had been looking forward to processing the film she had shot that afternoon at the Larkins' cabin, but she was too edgy to concentrate and too exhausted by the antics of her relatives.

First Sky, then Lucy. What had gotten into them? In a single afternoon they had revealed themselves as superstitious yokels, raving about hauntings and ghosts, the corniest possible stuff. The recollection of her flight through the woods in Sky's wake made her cringe with embarrassment. It was tempting to put the blame on him for her own momentary surrender to panic. Why couldn't he have supplied a level head instead of being so damn suggestible? His line about the reflected trees being dead had undeniably spooked her, and she was ashamed of herself for sinking, no matter how briefly, to the level of a credulous country bumpkin.

Yet—and here was the real bite—with the advent of darkness outside the windows, the whole ridiculous business of the supernatural took on a certain substance, a certain weight it did not possess in daylight. Every little creak and snap in the house was making her jump. She found herself thinking of those faint cries that came drifting out of the distance every so

often, chilling her heart each time . . . The memory made
her shiver, aware of the impulse to go to the window and
look out.

Don't get up. Don't you dare move. There's nothing
out there.

Nothing you can see, anyway.

She shook a mental fist at this rejoinder. Of course
she didn't *believe* the story of Tucker's ghost haunting the property. She was a thinking adult, a New
Yorker, sophisticated, educated, with a successful
career, and a child, and even the ultimate statistic—a
looming divorce. And things like ghosts didn't exist
outside the fevered imaginations of writers and the
makers of horror movies. She didn't believe it at all.
It was just . . . the night was so huge, so dark outside
the house, that it seemed almost anything could be out
there.

Almost anything.

But not a ghost.

*Even when she didn't see him, she used to find that
gate open ever' so often, like he'd been there.*

Oh—phooey.

She drowned her involuntary shudder with another
swallow of brandy, wishing she could summon a good
strong surge of skepticism instead of these feeble
protests.

How can a ghost call out?

How can a spirit unlatch a gate?

But the rational approach didn't bring the comfort
it should have. In the quiet house isolated by dark
countryside, with only the cat for company and Stephen
asleep upstairs in his room, the mere suggestion of a
phantom child was tenacious, and all attempts to laugh
it away stuck in her throat.

*When Stephen asked for the White Rose Waltz—
honey, that was Tucker's favorite tune.*

Woody whistled it for me.

How can a bodiless being whistle a tune?

She put the glass down on the table beside her
harder than she meant to, wincing at the impact.

*There has to be an explanation. A logical explana-
tion. And instead of sitting here scaring yourself, like a
big-eyed kid around a campfire, you need to find it.*

She got up and went into the kitchen, punching in
Gabe's number with a forefinger that undeniably shook
a little. When it started to ring she closed her eyes and
prayed that Jennifer, damn her anyway, wouldn't
answer.

"Hello?"

"Gabe—"

"Hi! How's it going?" He sounded genuinely glad to
hear from her—quite a difference from the last time
they had talked—and for this she was pathetically
grateful.

"Okay." Did she sound as shaky as she felt? She
didn't think so. "How about you?"

"Okay." A pause. "What's new?"

"Well, I've been taking some pictures." It was astonishing how the mere sound of his voice could put things
in perspective, making her worries of a moment ago
seem faint-hearted and ludicrous. "The local people—
their faces are amazing. I've been trying some portraits.
Totally different from anything I've ever done before."

"Yeah? I'd like to see some."

"Well, I've only done a few work prints. We just
finished building the darkroom about a week ago."

"We?" Gabe said.

"One of my relatives gave me a hand." The

thought of Sky's hands and what they had been doing recently made her stumble over the next words. "Uh, we, um, it's down in the cellar along with a conglomeration of junk, old saddles and riding trophies and stuff."

Absurd for her to feel guilty about Sky. After all, she and Gabe were definitely no longer together. He had Jennifer; why shouldn't she have someone?

"How's Stephen doing?" he was saying.

"Fine," she said automatically.

"What's he been up to?"

"Oh, you know, exploring and stuff. We've been riding a few times."

"You've got horses, huh?"

"Two horses and two ponies."

"Far out," Gabe said.

Silence.

"Well, sounds like you're doing okay."

"How about you?" She didn't want him to hang up. He belonged to a part of her life when things had been complicated in a simpler way. Gabe was Manhattan and the loft in Tribeca, where Nature was represented tamely by a single ficus tree in a pot on the polyurethaned oak floor, the memory curiously comforting against the vast summer night outside, crickets singing in the darkness that hid the pasture where the creek flowed, hill and mountains rising invisibly beyond.

"What have you been up to?" she said.

"Nothing much. Spent last weekend at the beach. Other than that, just working."

She could translate his spoken shorthand easily enough: *the beach* meant Jennifer's house in Easthampton, *working* meant working at the school. His three-day-a-week teaching job there was his only relationship with photography these days. He hadn't used a camera seriously in four or five years and seemed to take a masochistic pleasure in referring to himself as dried up, sterile. It had been another problem between them: that his photography was talk, hers action. Even though he hated the work she was doing, at least she was doing it.

Now there was another pause. Then he said, "Is Stephen asleep?"

"Yes."

"Oh. I would have liked to talk to him. Give him my love, okay?"

There was a sudden lump in her throat and she couldn't answer, could only nod idiotically into the phone. Gabe said, "Nan?"

"Yeah, I'm here. Gabe, I have to ask you a question. It sort of has to do with Stephen."

She heard him take a breath and then say, "I'm listening."

"Did you—do you remember introducing him to a bluegrass tune called the White Rose Waltz?"

There was a beat of uncomprehending silence and then he exhaled on a loud, relieved laugh. "Did I *what*? Christ, Nan! You scared me. I thought you were going to ask me for sole custody."

"Well, did you?"

"Did I what?"

"Play him that song. The White Rose Waltz."

"Never heard of it," Gabe said.

"But you like country music, don't you? Maybe it's on some old record you played him—"

"Listen, my dear, you overrate me. I like the glitzy Nashville sound, not the authentico stuff."

"Are you sure?" she said.

"Of course I'm sure. What's this all about?"

Nan told him.

She thought she told it with the right amount of skepticism, but even so it got to her in the retelling, the way a scary movie could do on occasion. The phone receiver was slippery in her hand when she finished. Gabe was silent. Then he said, "Holy shit."

All at once she realized how badly scared she was. Her heart clenched, a convulsive fist. "What—"

He laughed then, and she let out a shaky breath. "Get a grip, Nan," he said. "Your grandma was either out of her tree or else she was pulling Lucy's leg. Spinning her a spooky yarn. Listen, wasn't Edgar Allan Poe a Southern boy?"

"But the tune. The White Rose Waltz. It was Tucker's favorite, Gabe. And if you didn't play it for Stephen—who did?"

Woody whistled it for me.

Gabe grunted. "Well, for starters he could have heard it on the radio. Or from one of those seven billion relatives of yours. Damn, there's a hundred places he could have heard it."

"I guess you're right," she said.

"You bet I am. But it's more fun for Stephen to pretend Woody taught it to him, so he does. End of mystery."

"But what about the gate? Who showed him how to swing on it?"

"Nan. No child, especially no male child, has to be shown how to throw a rock, climb a tree, or hang on a gate. Those actions are encoded in the genes."

"All right," she said, smiling a little. "Okay." His

scoffing was a comfort she sorely needed right now. "Just one more thing, O Great Debunker."

"Shoot."

"About Woody resurfacing. Do you think it's ... normal?" She hesitated, then decided to come clean. "It's not a great situation for Stephen down here. He hasn't hit it off with any of his cousins, and we're really isolated—a long way from neighbors, from town. I try to spend time with him, but there's a limit to how much I have to offer ... Obviously what he really needs is a friend his own age. But Woody?"

Gabe seemed to be thinking it over. Then: "Look, you said he's outside playing all day. And he seems pretty happy?"

"Yeah ..."

"Well, that's got to be your yardstick. I wouldn't worry yet. It's not like he's got a lot of alternatives. If Woody's still hanging around when he turns thirty-five, then I think we have to start worrying. But for now, I'd let it be. Okay?"

"Okay," she said.

"And keep me posted." Putting on a fake Yiddish accent: "Don't be a stranger."

"Okay." The lump was back in her throat. Talking to him was giving her a roaring case of homesickness—not necessarily for the city with all its noise and mess, but for a general mind-set that excluded belief in the supernatural. Was this what happened when you went beyond the city limits—was everyone you met agog over UFOs and messages from beyond? Her relatives, lovable as they were, were members of a superstitious subculture in which legends and tall tales were accepted on some level as truth. Their heads, not the surroundings, were haunted. Gabe, on the other hand,

could be trusted—even after all the unpleasantness
between them—not to turn weird on her, not to start
spouting nonsense about ghosts of dead children or
spooky reflections of trees. The new life she had
embraced so blithely seemed to have gone sour, and
she suddenly wanted, more than anything on earth, to
go home.

But at least now she felt calm enough to sleep. In
fact, all at once she was so tired she could hardly keep
her eyes open. She went back to the library, doused the
lights and ascended the enclosed staircase to the lit
landing above. Stephen's door was shut. But as she
started toward her bedroom door, she heard his voice.

Apparently he wasn't asleep after all. Nan glanced
at her watch. Past ten: he should have been out long
before now. But she could hear him talking away—to
Woody, no doubt. All at once he laughed, a child's
high, delighted laugh, and in spite of Gabe's recent
megadose of common sense she felt the back of her
neck prickle at the sound. She crossed to his door, gave
a quick tap and opened it.

"Stephen? What are you doing still up?"

He was sitting on the floor beside the empty fireplace, his collection of windup toys spread out in front
of him and his face still showing a trace of a smile.
That laugh. Eight-year-old imagination. Only that.

"It's way past your bedtime," she said.

"Aw, Mom. We're having fun."

Nan retrieved his pajamas from the foot of the bed
and tossed them to him, refusing to rise to the bait.
But the prickling sensation that had begun at the back
of her neck was spreading like wildfire to envelop
her whole body, making every hair stand on end.

Stop it, she told herself firmly. You're doing this to yourself. This is the power of suggestion. So just knock it off. Mind over matter. Her nerves ignored her. She remembered the cat crouched hissing on the floor.

"Mom, Woody wants you to say hello to him."

There was a gold film of reflected lamplight on the round discs of Stephen's lenses, hiding his eyes. For a split second she saw him as a stranger, someone she didn't know: a small bespectacled boy clutching a pair of white pajamas patterned with blue rocketships to his chest.

"What do you mean, Stephen?"

"He just wants you to say hi."

Nan swallowed with difficulty. This was about validation, about recognizing her child's needs. That was all. Just do it, she told herself. Just say *Hi Woody*. But the words stuck in her throat. Her heart was pounding. She turned slowly and looked around the softly lit old room. At the ancient beams crossing the low ceiling, the small windows open to the night. Lopsided bookcase in one corner. Rocking chair. Fireplace with its carved sunburst. On the table by the bed, the lamp cast a circle of light that gave way to luminous dusk in the corners.

The wings of the dragonfly on the shade seemed to quiver. Without warning Nan seemed to sense, among the old room's gentle shadows, one that did not belong. A presence she could neither hear nor see, only perceive obliquely through the insistent tingling of her nerves.

When she spoke her voice was harsh with tension. "Listen, Stephen. It's late, and I'm tired. I want you to just go to bed."

* * *

Windowed with moonlight, Stephen's room was quiet except for the rustle of sheets as he sat up and peered into the silvery shadows.

"Woody?"

There was no answer. Stephen lay back and rested his head on the pillow with a sigh. He had seen his friend standing right beside his mom, touching her arm, wanting her to pay attention to him. But she had refused to speak to him, probably because she was mad about them staying up too late, playing. Now he was worried that Woody's feelings were hurt. For the second time today, his friend had left without saying good-bye.

But just as he was drifting off to sleep he thought he heard a whisper somewhere in the room, no louder than an exhaled breath, so faint it almost seemed to issue from the moonlight itself.

"Annabel . . ."

* * *

"I'm sorry to be calling you back so late," Nan said. "But I think I've got a serious problem here."

At the other end of the long series of wires connecting them through endless miles of darkness, Gabe made a sound but she overrode him.

"Just listen a minute, okay? Woody's imaginary. Right? Then how come I can feel him?"

She found she had to take a breath, and Gabe broke in. "What are you talking about?"

Nan tucked the receiver against her shoulder and tried to warm her hands by rubbing them together. She could feel waves of trembling passing through her, like aftershocks of the sensation she had experienced in Stephen's room. She heard herself give a tense, humorless laugh. "I think I'm talking about a ghost."

There was a long pause. Finally Gabe said, "Why don't you tell me exactly what happened?"

"I'm trying to. I went upstairs and Stephen was still up. I told him it was time for bed. He asked me to say hi to Woody."

"Nan." His tone was soothing. "He was pretending, okay? What's wrong with wanting you to pretend along with him?"

She took a breath and tried to let it out slowly. "Gabe. There was something in his room."

"Something—?"

"I could feel it. I got goosebumps all over. For no reason at all. It was like . . . a presence."

"Nan—"

"Look, don't you think I know how crazy it sounds? I didn't *want* to feel it, for God's sake. But I did. Gabe, I swear I did."

"Okay, okay. But just try to calm down a minute and think. Think about the kind of day you've had. Pretty rocky, right?"

"Right," she said shakily.

"Well, maybe this was just the last straw. I mean, you spend the afternoon getting an earful from this hysterical old lady about how your house is haunted. And the ghost, no less, is a kid you actually knew— whose death you apparently witnessed, even if you've pretty much repressed it. So you're already feeling jumpy. And then you find Stephen talking to thin air. I'm not surprised you got the heebie-jeebies. You're on overload, my dear."

"The cat feels it too," she said.

"The cat?"

"I've seen Annabel's cat freak out in that room."

He made a noncommittal sound. "I'm not going to try to analyze the cat's behavior. I'm just telling you, you've had a hard day. Bigtime in the stress department. If I were you, I'd sleep on it before calling Ghostbusters."

The waves of trembling were beginning to subside, but another one came just as she spoke. "Right now I can tell you I don't feel a lot like sleeping."

There was a long pause. Then he said, "Look. It's an old house, and you're alone there with that flaky kid—and a flaky cat—and I don't blame you for being freaked out. Maybe all three of you could use some company. What if I came down?"

The offer astonished her and she didn't answer at once. He read her silence as refusal.

"Hey, a spacey eight-year-old wouldn't be my first choice for sole companionship if I was stuck out in the boondocks. And maybe the kid could use a man in his life. You know? The old father figure?"

A man in his life. She started to snap at him, but the thought of Sky kept her quiet.

"How about I check the flights and call you tomorrow?" Gabe was saying.

Old resentment flared. He thought he could abandon them, then just stroll right back into their lives when he took the notion. She wouldn't demean herself by saying Jennifer's name.

"This is my house," she said. "Don't you think you could wait till you're invited?"

"Nan, please. I'm not trying to barge in. You just sound like maybe you could use some support, that's all."

Fine. She was a little frightened by the relief she felt

at the idea of Gabe showing up—as if all strange notions and happenings would instantly cease, driven off by the simple fact of his presence. A dim vision flitted across her mind, hinting at the complicated logistics of carrying on her affair with Sky while someone who was still her legal husband was staying in the house, but she dismissed it.

"Just remember you'll be a guest here."

"I'll bring my company manners," he said.

Chapter 13

Sky called the next morning. Nan was down in the darkroom, working on the prints of Pen and Flutie, when she heard the phone ringing in the kitchen and dashed upstairs to answer it, thinking it must be Gabe with news about his flight. The male voice, not his, was momentarily unfamiliar.

"Hey there. How 'bout I come by for some coffee?"

"Hello, Sky." Her last sight of him, grim and tight-lipped after their visit to the quarry the day before, rose in her mind's eye and she pushed it away. "Sure," she said. "Come on over."

When he arrived ten minutes later, she had coffee brewing and a couple of muffins warming in the oven. Clomping into the kitchen, letting the screen door bang shut behind him, he seemed to have returned to his old confident self. He grinned at her and she got the familiar trite weakness in her knees. He made no attempt to touch her. They sat on opposite sides of the table and drank their coffee while he finished the muffins in two bites.

"Brought you Annabel's car. She's parked out front. Thought you might need her, 'case yours starts actin' up again."

Remembering her suspicion that he had intention-ally sabotaged the Volvo she gave him a close look, but he raised innocent eyebrows. Maybe she was being ungracious. Maybe this was a peace offering after yesterday's shenanigans.

"Well, that's very nice of you. But don't you think poor old Estelle deserves to retire?"

He grinned. "You kiddin'? That car'll last a thousand years. You ever want to get rid of her, you're gonna have to drive a stake through her heart." He leaned back in his chair and surveyed the kitchen, eyes finally returning to rest on her face. "So what's new? How'd your pictures of the Larkin gals come out?"

"As a matter of fact I was just working on them. Want to see?"

"Sure 'nough."

He followed her down the basement steps and over to the sink against the wall, where the work prints were spinning around in the washer. She picked out one of the sisters posed together on the porch, their faces solemn, and offered it to him, still dripping. He took it and peered at it.

"Ain't they sweet. You got to love them gals."

Nan, expecting fulsome praise for her photographic skill, had no answer but he didn't seem to notice. He glanced up from the picture. "Where's Stephen at?"

She took the photograph from his fingers and put it back in the washer. "Oh, across the creek—with Woody."

"You don't sound too happy about it."

Nan swallowed. "There've been a couple of developments on the Woody front."

"Developments?" He was bending over the washer, poking at the other prints, trying to see them. She leaned against the sink and watched his face.

"Yeah. Lucy Talbot thinks he's a ghost."

That got his attention. He looked at her and started to laugh. "Say what?"

"You heard me. And here's the punch line. Not just any ghost. The ghost of Tucker Wills."

Sky's eyebrows shot up. His smile disappeared. *"What?"*

Nan took a deep breath. Her take on yesterday's events was still uncertain. Her instinctive resistance to Lucy's tale had been badly undermined by that weird business in Stephen's room last night—and contrary to Gabe's reassurances, a night's sleep had not helped her regain much in the way of rational perspective. She wasn't ready to say she believed in ghosts. But, ghost or not, the sensation she had experienced was something completely outside her ken. She told herself maybe there was some scientific explanation for it, something electrical or magnetic. But nonetheless the recollection still gave her the willies.

"Did Annabel ever—" She found herself already out of breath and had to start again. "Did she ever say anything to you about seeing Tucker's ghost?"

He was still gaping at her. "Hell, no."

"Well, just before she died, she told Lucy she'd been seeing him on and off for years. Hanging around here. Haunting the place."

He gave a low whistle, then stood with his hands jammed in his pockets, staring at nothing. After a moment she touched his arm and he muttered, "Damn if she ever said a word to me."

"Maybe she thought you'd laugh. Or think she was crazy."

He shook his head. "Annabel had her head on straighter'n just about anybody I've ever known. If she said she saw him, I believe she did. But what's all that got to do with Woody? I thought he was just—you know. Pretend."

Nan took a deep breath. "Do you remember when Stephen asked for a tune at the square dance—the White Rose Waltz? Apparently it was Tucker's favorite. Stephen told me he learned it from Woody."

Sky tugged at his beard. "Is that all?"

"Well, basically. Except—" Against her better judgment, she tried haltingly to describe her experience of the night before.

"Last night I went up to tell Stephen to go to bed. He was gabbing away to Woody, and all of a sudden I got this really weird sensation. Not just a creepy feeling. An actual physical sensation, like a low-grade electrical shock. My hair actually stood on end. I've seen it happen to the cat, too—seen him hiss at thin air in that room. And that's how I felt last night. Like there was something there. I couldn't see it. But I swear I could feel it."

"Something? You mean—a ghost?"

"I don't *know*." She sighed. "You know, back in New York nobody believes in ghosts. I mean, that kind of thing is just a joke. When Lucy started telling me all this stuff, I laughed. I thought maybe she was pulling my leg. But she wasn't. She's really freaked out."

"Well, hell, I guess she is."

Nan made herself shrug. "Why? Whoever he is—Woody or Tucker—Stephen's crazy about him. And God knows the kid needs somebody to play with. Ghost or imaginary friend, what's the difference?"

She was trying to inject a lighter note into the discussion, but it came out sounding bleak. There was a silence, during which Sky glanced sideways at her. "You sorry Annabel left you the house?"

"Well, that depends." Nan lifted her hands and let them fall helplessly to her sides. "If having a ghost in the family is part of the deal, I don't think I'm up for it."

He didn't smile and she thought it was partly his fault that her feeble attempts at humor kept falling flat. Undispelled by laughter, the words hung in the air and she heard the truth in them. Sky reached out to squeeze her shoulder. Nan grabbed at his hand and he folded her into his arms.

"Y'know, honey, Flutie Larkin might be somebody worth talkin' to about all this. These kind of doings're right up her alley."

Remembering the mountain woman's vacant eyes, Nan wasn't encouraged. She said nothing. In the silence he stroked her back and she pressed closer to him. He felt so warm, so solid—all at once she wanted him, wanted to escape, however temporarily, from this whole crazy business. She put her hands on his buttocks, feeling the firm muscles under the worn fabric of his jeans. He got hard immediately. Nan came partially to her senses.

"We can't do this. What if Stephen comes back?"

"He's got to come up through the pasture," Sky said. "We'll stay right here where we can keep an eye on him."

He turned her so she could see out the dusty basement window set high in the wall above the sink, then pulled her shorts down and moved against her from behind, reaching up inside her shirt and taking her breasts in his hands. Nan clung to the edge of the sink and closed her eyes, trying to lose herself in physical sensation, then winced and opened them again as he pushed roughly into her. Above the ridge enormous white clouds floated against the blue, shadowing the green mountaintops. A breeze stirred the crowns of the trees along the creek, leading her gaze to the bright summit of the hill beyond.

Sky moved inside her, his tempo increasing. He was going deeper now, his breath exploding in hot bursts against her neck. She felt disconnected from his frenzied use of her body, unable to summon a response.

(as we turn in circles faster and faster arms outstretched around us the tall grass a bright dazzle in our eyes and the mountains a singing green blur beyond faster and faster falling down at last to lie flat on our backs and feel the earth rocking rocking beneath us while high overhead in the blue sky a hawk floats on a current of warm air above our spinning golden hill)

Sky gave a little yelp. His hands tightened on her breasts; then he slumped against her back. She felt his spent penis slide out of her. He rested his weight on her a moment, then straightened and pulled her around to face him.

"Hey, lady. You're a million miles away."

"I'm sorry, Sky. I just can't stop thinking—" She was silent, fixing her clothes. He did the same. Their eyes met.

"I knew somethin' was wrong," he said. "You didn't holler for me."

He was trying to get a smile out of her and she forced one, but it wouldn't stay. He tried again. "Look, honey, it's not the end of the world. It's not like anything bad's happened."

She shrugged. "Another thing," she said. "Gabe's been calling. I told him what's going on. He's coming down here."

"When?"

"Soon," she said.

"You tell him 'bout us?"

She shook her head and he put a hand under her chin and lifted it.

"You plannin' to?"

"It's none of his business," she said. "Anyway, he's coming down here for Stephen, not for me."

"Good." He dropped his hand. "I'm a selfish bastard. I purely hate to share."

Chapter 14

The passenger terminal of the Tri-Counties Regional Airport outside Gaylesville was a corrugated tin building that stank of gasoline and body odor. Out along the runway a chain-link fence kept onlookers, and presumably wildlife, from wandering into the path of the planes. Nan watched as the twelve-passenger puddle jumper from Kingsport landed and taxied to a stop, wings wobbling as if they might drop off any second.

Gabe was the first one off the plane, appearing in the open hatch dressed in chinos and a loose black jacket over a faded blue T-shirt, his thickening midsection disguised by the fashionably baggy clothes. Above his forehead the thistly peak of hair had more gray in it than Nan remembered, and she saw with a little shock that the clipped beard along his jawline, shorter than Sky's and entirely different in texture, was now completely white.

She watched him jump down and turn to assist a buxom blond woman in a leather jacket—the pilot—who didn't seem to need his outstretched hand but took it anyway and held onto it, breaking into a laugh when he leaned close and said something in her ear. Pleasant little flirtation during the short flight, sexy older man . . .

Nan grimaced. Take a number, honey.

She stood waiting by the gate with her arms folded. The pilot caught sight of her, gave Gabe's arm a pat and tactfully veered off in the direction of the hangar. Reaching the fence, Gabe let himself through the gate and left it open for the other passengers beginning to straggle across the tarmac.

"Christ, this is really the sticks." He kissed her cheek, scowled at her, then smiled. "You look good."

"Is that the only bag you brought?"

His battered leather satchel, long strap slung over his shoulder. Knowing him, it contained mostly books (he had a habit of reading three or four at a time) wrapped in a couple of changes of clothes. He glanced down at it, nodding, then cocked his head at the rusty terminal. "State-of-the-art facilities, I see. Where's Stephen?"

"At a friend's house. I didn't tell him you were coming."

"Didn't tell him? Why the hell not?"

"In case Jennifer wouldn't let you," Nan said.

He took her chin between his thumb and forefinger and shook it gently. "Fuck you. Okay?"

She had parked beside a black pickup with a shotgun rack and Dixie license plates. Gabe eyed his neighboring vehicle but made no comment. As they turned out of the parking lot onto the county highway and started south toward Breezy, his head turned to take in the shady cemetery across the road. "Hey, that's a nice touch. Must be a real comfort to folks when they go to board their flights."

"See that big stone Bible there in the middle?" Nan found herself enjoying the role of tour guide. "There's an electric eye hidden in the base. When you get close enough, it sees you and a tape starts playing Tennessee Ernie Ford singing 'The Old Rugged Cross.' "

"You're lying," Gabe said. "Did you actually experience this?"

"No. Someone told me about it."

Sky had told her. Gabe rested his arm across the back of the seat, saying nothing. When she glanced his way he was watching her, one eyebrow raised. She turned her attention back to the road.

The drive took nearly two hours, and he used part of the time to fill her in on Jennifer's professional opinions about Stephen. He didn't ask if she wanted to hear it, just launched into his spiel.

"He's had a lot of trauma recently—Brian disappearing last fall, then you and me splitting up, and now this move to a new place—we're talking bigtime stress factors here. Jennifer thinks Woody's return is a positive manifestation rather than otherwise. He's familiar, a reference point in a strange place where Stephen feels lost. He's not vulnerable like Brian; he won't disappear. And he belongs completely to Stephen."

A reference point in a strange place where Stephen feels lost. Nan winced. Wasn't that supposed to be her job? Gabe's discussion of Woody left no room for the supernatural interpretation; he seemed to take it for granted that she had recovered from that particular blip in her sanity. And for the time being she tried to see the situation in his terms. Okay, so Stephen's loneliness—compounded by her infatuation with Sky—had forced him to haul Woody out of storage. And the rest of it: the fiddle tune, the cat's weird behavior, her own attack of mega–goose bumps? Nothing but a hodgepodge of coincidence and misinterpretation, explicable in some perfectly logical way.

The conversation switched to a different mode, light and civilized. He caught her up on New York gossip, managing to keep Jennifer's name out of it, and she contributed an edited account of her own doings, including the square dance and the visit to Pen and Flutie Larkins'. In their brief silences he seemed to be admiring the scenery on either side of the country road—forested ravines and hillsides giving way to open vistas of rolling hayfields, rocky pastures dotted with cows, rusty-roofed farm buildings. Above it all rose the mountains, their green slopes dominating the horizon and fading to a delicate gray-blue in the distance.

Again Nan was amazed at how much comfort she could take from Gabe's presence, even while she still felt emotionally betrayed by him. It was more than the old-shoe syndrome: with him beside her in the car, the boundaries between possible and impossible seemed once more firmly set. She didn't think any ghost could survive that skeptical raised eyebrow.

Reaching the Talbots', where she had left Stephen, they encountered Whit at the end of the driveway collecting the mail. Nan leaned out the car window to introduce Gabe.

"Proud to know you, sir." Whit lumbered around to the passenger side and reached in to shake hands. "Your young'un's up at the house, spoilin' his dinner with a fresh batch of sugar cookies. Y'all hurry on up there and you just might be in time to get you one."

"Can we give you a lift back to the house?" Nan said.

"No, honey. I got to check the culvert down thataways. It keeps gettin' clogged and I need to see what's what. Y'all go on ahead."

He waved them on. As they drove away Gabe twisted around to look back at the tall, stooped figure. "Christ, he's in good shape. How old is he?"

"Mid-seventies," Nan said. "Think you'll last that long?" It was a cheap shot, but relieved as she was to have him here, resentment still lurked just beneath the surface. He gave her a sideways glance and said nothing.

And her punishment, if she had believed in such things, was swift: when she pulled open the screen door to the Talbots' kitchen and stepped aside to let Gabe in, the blaze of joy on Stephen's face hit her like a furnace blast, searing her heart. He burst out of his chair at the kitchen table and hurled himself at Gabe. "Dad!"

Nan herself might as well not have existed. Gabe hugged him wordlessly while she stood watching, feeling the first scorching pain diminish to a dull smolder. Lucy Talbot stood beaming by the stove, hands clasped on the bib of her flour-dusted apron. Nan felt a wave of disgust but she knew it wasn't fair; she had told Lucy nothing about her marital situation and had no right to expect the older woman to grasp the nuances. She tried to concentrate on keeping her emotions from showing in her face.

Stephen was still wild with excitement by the time they finally extricated themselves from the Talbots and headed for Annabel's. As they drove along the winding road past orchards and fields he talked nonstop: his room, the cat, the horses, the pasture and creek—eager to share his new world with Gabe. Nan listened, expecting a reference to Woody at any moment, but heard none.

Once at Annabel's, Gabe demanded a drink. They settled in the library and Nan gave him a scotch.

"Ah. Civilization." He sipped, put the glass down. "Very decent. Is this Granny's scotch?"

"Nope. Mine."

That raised eyebrow again. Years ago she had tried to learn to raise hers in answer but had never been able to get the proper muscles to cooperate. Stephen hung on the arm of Gabe's chair.

"Dad, don't you want to see Scheherazade?"

"Who? Oh, the horse. I didn't come to see horses, Stephen. I came to see you."

Nan watched their faces, the eyes identical behind matching granny glasses. Gabe's hair had been as dark as Stephen's, before the onslaught of gray. There was no mistaking that they were father and son; and in spite of the fact that she had given birth to Stephen, she often felt he was more Gabe's child than hers. Gabe's feelings about him always had seemed so much more definite, in every area from shoes and toys to schooling and nutrition—and Stephen, as if sensing this, had always responded more to Gabe. Feeling outclassed, she had retreated into the career in which she knew herself to be an expert, relieved on some level to let Gabe be Stephen's mother in all senses but the strictly biological.

Now she was paying the price, having her nose rubbed in her child's deep attachment to his father. A literal attachment at the moment: first he hung on Gabe's shoulder, then climbed into his lap for the duration of this drink and the next. By then it was getting close to suppertime, and Stephen dogged Gabe's steps while, true to his promise about company manners, he attempted to help Nan set the table for supper.

After their third near collision Gabe handed the kid a quart of milk he had just taken out of the refrigerator. "Here, make yourself useful. That big glass is yours. Fill it."

Stephen carried the red and white carton to the table. "Dad, are you going to be staying with us now?"

"You mean, for good?" Gabe hesitated, shot a glance at Nan that said she should have explained all this. Then: "I can't, son. You know New York would collapse without me."

Nan, seeing Stephen's stricken face, cursed herself for not having handled the whole business differently—she should have told him Gabe was coming and specified a short visit. But Gabe had betrayed them once, with Jennifer; and he could easily have done so again—changed his mind, called and said he had plans, couldn't make it after all. And Stephen took things so hard. Right now he looked as if he had been punched. It hadn't occurred to her that he would assume Gabe had come to Tennessee to live with them. In New York he had seemed to understand the separation, accept Gabe's assurances that, between the two of them at least, nothing had changed. Now apparently he had taken his father's unexpected appearance to mean they were going to be a family again.

"How come you can't just stay with us?" There was an audible quaver in Stephen's voice as he thumped the milk carton down on the edge of the table and turned to face Gabe, who gave a small sigh.

"Hey, champ. I'm here now. Isn't that something?"

He moved forward, arms open to embrace the boy, but at the last moment Stephen jerked away. One outflung hand hit the milk carton and it teetered and fell, landing on the floor at Gabe's feet with a resounding *splat*.

"Jesus!" He jumped back. Stephen let out a wail and ran out of the room while Nan and Gabe stared in shock, hearing his footsteps pound on the stairs. Milk spread in a rapidly widening white pool across the floor. Mister Mustard appeared from nowhere, gave Nan an inquiring look and began to lap it up appreciatively.

Nan got a wet cloth from the sink to mop up the mess, glancing up from her kneeling position to find Gabe watching her. "Nice going."

He opened his hands. "Was that my fault?"

Chapter 15

Front Street was blazingly hot in the late morning sun, and the tinkle of the shop bell at Books, Etc. made Nan think longingly of ice-cream trucks as she pushed open the door and peered into the recesses of the store. After the glare outside it took a couple of seconds for her eyes to adjust to the gloom. She heard a grinding noise and looked down to see a small red car driving across the floorboards in her direction. As it neared her the horn blew raucously and the headlights flashed. The vehicle came to a stop near her left foot.

She peered into the depths of the store. "Coop?"

"Hi, Nan." He rose from his crouch behind the counter at the back and came forward, looking slightly sheepish and pleased with himself at the same time. "Like it?"

She picked up the car and examined it. Mickey Mouse was the driver, Minnie the passenger. "Cute."

He took the car, smiling at her, his eyes crinkling at the corners. "I was just thinking y'all hadn't been around in a while. What's new?"

"Oh, this and that. I just came in to do some shopping."

An hour spent tagging after Gabe and Stephen had left her feeling utterly superfluous, and she had fled with the excuse that she had to pick up some supplies in town—but what she honestly needed was to spend a little time with someone who knew she was alive. Of course she was being hypersensitive. The novelty of Gabe's presence would wear off if he kept the promise he had made Stephen this morning, of two weeks' stay. But right now it grated on her to see Stephen hanging on everything he said, following him around like a puppy.

Cooper offered her his stool behind the counter while he sat on the floor opening cartons and trying to match their contents to a stack of crumpled purchase orders. "Where's Stephen?"

She made an effort to pull herself together. "At home. His father's here visiting, and they're doing some heavy-duty male bonding."

He glanced up from a carton brimming with pink plastic mice to offer her a rueful smile. "Three's a crowd, huh?"

A little sympathy was enough to just about undo Nan. She gulped and pretended interest in the shipment of mice. "How many of those things are there?"

"Four dozen." He took one out, wound it and set it on the floor. Instead of flipping all the way over, it jumped and fell on its face. Cooper sighed. "They've been doing that lately. Don't tell me I've got another four dozen duds."

Nan started to laugh and he joined her. From where he was sitting on the floor behind the counter, he wasn't visible from the door; and it occurred to her that any customers entering right now would see her sitting there by herself, laughing her head off. It made her think of Stephen talking and laughing with an invisible presence in his room, and she felt the smile fade from her face.

Cooper was looking at her. "It's got to be more than

just a little male bonding that's getting you down, Nan.
Want to talk about it?"

She took a breath and started to examine her nails.
"Coop, can I ask you something?"

"Shoot."

She wouldn't have asked if she hadn't already been
fairly certain of his answer. His talk of "survival,"
Cassie's story about his efforts to communicate with
his dead wife—what more evidence did she need that,
to him, the supernatural was a matter for neither scorn
nor laughter?

But she wanted to hear him say it. Because then she
could allow herself to confess her heart-clutching fear
that maybe it was true—that maybe Stephen had somehow, impossibly, been befriended by the restless spirit of
the boy she had known as a child. Faced with Gabe's flat
dismissal of the supernatural, her fears tended to be
shamed into retreat, but they had an insidious way of
slithering back as soon as she was out of his presence.

Now she took a deep breath and said, "Do you
believe in ghosts?"

Cooper didn't respond. He sat there at her feet
without saying anything, looking down at the plastic
toy in his fingers. She couldn't see his face, only the
top of his head, the pink scalp visible through his thinning blond hair.

"Why?" he said finally.

The flat word seemed to imply that it was none of
her business. In a panicky effort to justify her question,
she found herself blurting out the real reason for
Gabe's sudden visit, spilling the whole business from
Lucy Talbot's ghost story to the frightening sensation
of presence she had experienced three nights ago in
Stephen's room.

While she talked, Cooper took another mouse from the carton and tried it out. It jumped and fell on its face.

Nan shifted on the hard stool. "I don't know what to believe anymore. It seems impossible. But I keep thinking . . . even discounting everything else—what Annabel told Lucy, and the feeling I had in Stephen's room—there's that business with the fiddle tune. *Where* did Stephen learn it?"

Cooper glanced up from the defective toy at last. "One of the first things a real parapsychologist would tell you is that *any* explanation is preferable to a paranormal one. They'd tell you Stephen could easily have learned the tune from a living person, maybe one of his relatives, and the fact that it was also Tucker's favorite is just a coincidence. They'd say maybe there's something about that particular tune that appeals to little boys."

Seeing her face, he stopped with a wry smile. "I'm not much help, am I? I can't tell you what to think, Nan. I do know your grandmother believed in Tucker's presence. She told me she knew a spirit could survive bodily death. We discussed it several times." He held her gaze for a long moment before dropping his own. "I guess you've heard the stories about me."

"Well—"

"I know folks talk. I don't care. Because I saw Laura—saw her and talked to her, the night after she died." He fiddled with the mouse in his hands, doing something to the winding mechanism, then tried it again without success.

"I wasn't drunk," he said. "I hadn't started that stage yet—I was still too numb. I was sitting on my front porch. It was just about dusk and I was sitting there kind of dazed." He looked up and seemed to focus on Nan for a moment. "I didn't really feel much of anything, you know, until a lot later on. When I found her, it was like I'd always known it was going to happen." The pain was so apparent on his face that she had to look away. After a moment she heard his voice go on.

"Anyhow, I was out there on the porch, and I heard her say my name, the way she'd said it a million times. I looked up and she was sitting there on the railing. I was so numb, I wasn't even that surprised. You know? She looked as real as you do. I said, 'Laura?' and she sort of smiled and said, 'Come home soon, Coop.' Then she just kind of faded out, faded into the dark."

He took a shaky breath and Nan kept her eyes averted, afraid he was on the verge of breaking into tears. "Did you ever—see her again?"

When he didn't answer, she sneaked a glance and saw him shaking his head. "No. I tried to contact her, but—no. But I think— well, at first I thought she was just, like, repeating what she said when I went away for the weekend. You know, like an echo. She always said it when I went anywhere without her. Come home soon. I tried not to leave her behind much. Maybe . . . Anyway, I don't think it was that. It was more like she was telling me, *I'm home now. Really home, and everything's okay. And I'll be waiting for you.*"

He swallowed audibly and looked down at the mouse again, obviously without seeing it. Nan discovered an incipient hangnail on her left thumb and began to pick at it ferociously. His recital seemed to have circumvented her ability to believe or disbelieve and gone straight to her heart. Finally she reached out and touched his shoulder. He put his hand over hers and squeezed it convulsively, then tossed the defective mouse back into its carton, where it landed with a tinny rattle.

"So, all I can tell you from my own experience is that, yes, it's possible you have a ghost, and that this ghost is somehow in contact with Stephen. But if you want proof—"

He smiled and lifted his shoulders in a shrug.

As she left the bookstore, her mind was still on matters no sane person could entertain with any degree of comfort. At first she didn't notice Sky's truck parked in front of Breezy Feed & Seed. Then it registered: the familiar rusty red vehicle, Kate's inquisitive nose poking out the back and the unmistakable broad-shouldered silhouette of her country hunk behind the wheel. She hadn't seen Sky for a couple of days; now might be a good time to go over and reassure him that she hadn't forgotten about him. She had been partly irritated, partly touched by his remark about not wanting to share her. Primitive as it was, on some level she appreciated the sentiment.

She had just stepped off the curb, about to head across the street toward the truck, when the door of the feed store opened and a familiar figure emerged. Unpleasantly familiar: Jerry Ray Watkins. He was hefting a bulging burlap bag on one shoulder. As Nan watched in astonishment, he dumped it into the back of Sky's truck, then walked around and climbed in the passenger side door of the cab, dirty overalls bulging across his fat behind.

Feeling like the heroine of a bad movie, Nan backtracked and ducked into the recessed doorway of the drugstore nearby. What was going on? She had accepted Sky's explanation for not having told her about Jerry Ray's stint in prison—but he had mentioned nothing about a close association with the man. Was she being a fool, a chump? It seemed he could tell her as much or as little as he pleased and expect her to swallow it and be satisfied.

The truck pulled out of its parking spot and drove past in the street, heading out of town on the road she herself would take on her way home. She watched it from the shadow of the drugstore awning. There they were, the two of them, Sky driving and Jerry Ray in the passenger seat. Tweedledum and Tweedledee. What was going on here?

" 'Scuse me, please."

A woman with a baby in a stroller was politely waiting for her to stop blocking entry into the drugstore. Nan moved aside with a murmured apology and stepped out into the hot sunshine of the sidewalk, where she stood trying to gather her wits, with no particular success.

Chapter 16

The Talbots had invited her little branch of the family for dinner that night, and on the way over in the car Nan found herself slightly unnerved by how pleasant it felt to be part of a threesome again. She had managed to convince herself that neither she nor Stephen needed Gabe, and she still believed that. But in this place where she was unsure of herself, and where extremely odd things were starting to happen, there was no question that his presence was a solid comfort.

And a social asset as well. Conversation at the dinner table was lively, their hosts taking instantly to Gabe—possibly, Nan thought, because her lack of a visible husband had been bothering them and they were relieved to see someone filling the gap. But there was no question that Gabe was at his most charming, waxing enthusiastic about the beautiful countryside and the wonderful local people—of whom, Nan noted sourly, he had met exactly these two. It occurred to her, while they were on the subject of the locals, that Whit and Lucy might be able to shed some light on Sky's apparent association with Jerry Ray Watkins.

"You know that Watkins guy, sort of a sleazy character who used to work for Annabel?"

Whit, to whom she had addressed the question, gave

her a puzzled look, his wide jaw still working on a mouthful of Lucy's superb fried chicken. "Watkins?"

"Jerry Ray Watkins? Fat guy with a beard?"

Whit swallowed and wiped his mouth with his napkin. "I know who you mean, honey. But he never did no work for Annabel. No, ma'am."

"I thought he used to do odd jobs for her," Nan said.

From the other end of the table Lucy's laugh was abrupt. "Not likely, hon! That boy never did an honest day's work in his life. And Annabel had no use for him— she never would suffer a fool, and she'd a' run him clean off her property if he'd so much as showed his sorry face. Did he try to tell you he worked for her? Why, the idea!"

Nan mumbled something and let the subject drop. Chalk up another lie to Sky's account. Had he told her anything about Watkins that was true? His name, but that was about all. But there was something even more disturbing than this further evidence of Sky's dishonesty. If Watkins had never worked for Annabel, what had he been doing on her property?

She resolved to find some answers, and soon. Meanwhile the dinner party was going on its merry way without her participation. Gabe was in the middle of what seemed to be a monologue extolling the wonders of New York, and she listened while he sketched a colorful picture of glittering skyscrapers and wisecracking cops, philosophical Bowery bums and street musicians, subway graffiti, Chinese laundries, Broadway shows, Italian street fairs, standup comics and unicyclists and fire jugglers in Washington Square. Whit and Lucy seemed fascinated, and Nan found herself listening in a daze. He made it sound magical, and even though she knew this picture was highly selective, still she felt a twinge of nostalgia. She sneaked a glance at Stephen.

Did he miss everything they had left behind? But, smiling a little, lost in his own thoughts, he didn't even seem to be listening.

When the meal was over, Lucy accepted her offer to help clear the table. They carried one load of plates into the kitchen, and Nan was starting back for more when Lucy stopped her with a hand on her arm. "Honey, I know I'm butting into your business, but I've just got to ask you—"

She hesitated and Nan said, "Ask me what?"

Lucy released her arm. "If you're keepin'—well, keepin' a close eye on Stephen."

"Oh, Lucy—"

"I know you don't believe me," Lucy said. "Honey, I must seem like a crazy ol' coot to you, full of tales about ghosts and such. But believe me, I have your happiness at heart."

"I know you do." Nan was touched. She wanted to say or do something that would relieve the older woman's obvious concern, but how could she reassure Lucy when she was uncertain exactly what she herself believed? "I think we've got the situation under control," she said.

The old woman closed her eyes, her face crumpling into a web of wrinkles, and Nan was painfully reminded of the moment at the square dance when she had seemed to see Lucy's younger self glowing inside her like a light inside a dusty shade. Now she looked a hundred instead of her feisty seventy-three.

When she opened her eyes they had a hollow look. She reached out and grasped Nan's wrist. "Honey, I've lived a long time, and the one thing I've learned is that we live in a mystery. I don't guess there's any-body can say why Tucker Wills hasn't passed on to heaven—why his spirit isn't at rest. Maybe it's because they never found his body to give it a proper Christian burial. We'll never know. But I do know one thing. It's not natural for the dead and the living to keep company. Tucker is *dead*, Nan. If you're set on stayin' at Annabel's, you've got to keep him and Stephen apart."

Nan was shaken. Lucy's belief had a primitive force that flattened logic, her gaunt figure in its faded print dress seeming for a moment to cast an enormous shadow on the kitchen wall. Her grip was icy. Nan swallowed, aware of her thoughts swirling around and around the obstinate memory of standing in Stephen's room and sensing, among the shadows, one that did not belong.

"You gals need some help in there?"

Whit's voice from the dining room broke their tableau. Nan took a breath and shook her head to clear it. Lucy released her wrist and gave it an awkward pat. "Please," the old woman said softly.

Nan hugged her, the gesture almost spontaneous. She could think of nothing to say.

*   *   *

But Lucy's warning stayed with her. In spite of her fervent desire to emulate Gabe's skepticism, she could feel herself blowing with every wind. What she believed seemed to depend, to a shameful extent, on whom she had talked to last. She spent half the night tossing and turning, arguing herself this way and that, and finally fell asleep to dream fitfully of vague, sinister shapes that formed and dissipated and formed again. It seemed she had barely closed her eyes when there was an insistent tapping on her bedroom door.

"What?" She was grumpy and her head hurt.

Glancing at the clock, she could see it was just past seven. "Christ," she said. "What *is* it?"

Gabe's voice on the other side of the door was muffled. "There seem to be some horses wandering around your backyard. Aren't they supposed to be fenced up?"

"Shit." Nan jumped out of bed and ran to the back window, looking down to see Merlin, Little Bit and Jolie below, nosing around the wooden bin that contained the trash cans. "Oh, shit."

By the time she had pulled on clothes and run down to the kitchen, Stephen was up, too, bouncing up and down beside the window. Gabe seemed to be restraining him from rushing outside.

"What's the drill?" he said when she came down the stairs.

"Beats me. They've never done this before."

Stephen and Gabe were right at her heels as she opened the back door. The squeal of the screen startled the horses; they scattered in a flurry of flattened ears and flaring nostrils. Nan put her hands on her hips. "Now how did you get out?"

The sound of her voice seemed to reassure them. The ears came forward and Jolie started to move toward her. She could almost see a cartoon thought-bubble floating over the white mare's head: *Carrots?*

Bribery seemed as good a way as any to effect a capture. "Stephen. Look in the vegetable crisper and get some carrots, will you? Let's put these beasts back where they belong."

He turned back into the house and Gabe eased out through the screen to join her on the back step. "Aren't there supposed to be four of them?"

Nan looked around uneasily. "I don't see Scheherazade. Damn it, I wonder how they got out."

She held out her hand to Jolie as the mare came close and felt the velvety muzzle search her empty palm. "Don't tell me that damn gate came open again. I thought I fixed it."

She said even when she didn't see him, she used to find that gate open ever' so often, like he'd been there.

Impossible. She pushed the thought away. Jolie was nickering softly and she said, "Carrots are coming, sweetheart."

Behind them the screen shrieked, startling the horses again and revealing Stephen with a bunch of carrots like a bridal bouquet in his fist.

"Mom, I saw Scheherazade. She's in the front yard."

"Terrific," Nan said. "Let's deal with this group first."

The horses wore no halters. Sky had showed her how to throw a short length of rope around their necks and lead them, but she didn't think even that would be necessary—the carrots should do the trick. She broke one into pieces and fed it to Jolie, seeing the ponies prick their ears as the mare crunched the treat between her teeth.

"Shouldn't I get a rope or something?" Gabe said.

"I don't think we'll need one. Can you just go ahead and make sure the pasture gate's open? I don't see how else they could have gotten out. Unless they've learned to fly."

"Mom, can I give them some carrots?"

"Honey, I want you to stay in the house until we get them back into the pasture." If there was some kind of unexpected stampede, she didn't want him underfoot.

"But—"

"No buts, Stephen," she said, and Gabe chimed in. "Mind your mom, champ."

Stephen faded back inside, scowling, while Gabe started for the gate. Nan saw his head swiveling back as if he would have preferred to be in charge of the situation. She passed out carrot pieces and then moved after him, praying the animals would follow. They did. She rounded the corner of the house to see Gabe hovering by the gate.

"Was it open?" she said.

"Sure was."

Concentrating on willing the horses to follow her into the pasture, she ignored the qualm his blithe assurance gave her. Never mind, for now, how the gate had come to be open. She had more immediate worries. But Jolie and the ponies passed docilely through the gate, and she shooed them in the direction of the barn as Gabe closed the gate and hooked it shut.

"Well, that was easy enough."

Nan felt her smile fade as she looked past him into the front yard. Scheherazade stood motionless under the oak tree, a black marble statue watching them. "Oh, I think the fun's just starting."

He turned to follow her gaze. "Oh yeah, the wild mustang. Stephen told me about him."

"Her."

"Sorry. Her. Do we try the carrot trick again?"

Nan took a deep breath and released it audibly. Left to herself, she would have phoned Sky and asked him to come over and deal with Scheherazade. But in Gabe's presence she needed somehow to prove herself. And she was self-conscious as well; he would only have to lay eyes on Sky to guess the nature of their relationship, and she didn't want him knowing her private business.

A cautious voice at the back of her mind, sizing up the black horse's watchful shape under the tree, told her she might be risking more than the loss of her privacy if she tried to accomplish this task on her own. She recalled Sky telling her that Scheherazade was barely halter-broken. Yet unlike the other horses the mare was at least wearing a halter, its leather straps loosely framing her delicate head.

Nan eyed her, then turned to Gabe. "Might as well try the carrots. Maybe they'll work."

"Want me to do it?"

He had picked up on her reluctance and she supposed he was trying to be helpful, but she couldn't help resenting the inference that she couldn't handle her own animals. After all, this was her place; she had spent the last six weeks living here. Who was he to come waltzing down from the big city and try to show her how it was done?

She shook her head without answering and started toward Scheherazade with a carrot temptingly displayed on her outstretched palm, saying a silent, fervent prayer that this one would be as easy as the others. Without moving a muscle the mare let her approach, pricking her ears as Nan began murmuring a litany of insincere endearments.

"Good girl. Thatsababy. Pretty baby."

It seemed to be going well, and then she must have crossed some invisible, forbidden line. Suddenly Scheherazade rolled her eyes, their whites gleaming wickedly in her dark head as she snorted and moved away abruptly, sidestepping out from under the tree to trot across the front lawn in the direction of the orchard, her long tail streaming and smooth black hide glittering in the sun.

Nan stood under the tree, the carrot clutched tightly in her fist. Her knees felt hollow. She had been completely unnerved by the brief, hot touch of the horse's breath on her skin. All at once its size and power, its restless energy, were overwhelming.

Dangerous. You've got to call Sky.

But her stubborn streak refused to let her give up yet. Gabe was here; surely, between the two of them, they could manage to catch Scheherazade, or at least trick her into returning to the pasture. The mare had come to a stop and was eyeing her again. Nan made herself move forward, offer the carrot.

"Mom!"

She froze and glanced back over her shoulder. Stephen was on the top step of the front porch.

"Honey, I told you to stay inside."

"Let me give her the carrot. She likes me."

"Stephen, I said no."

"Stephen, you heard your mother."

Her backup man again, over by the gate. He had given her more support this morning, she thought with passing bitterness, than in the whole of their time together as parents.

"Listen, Gabe," she called. "She's not interested in the carrot. I'm going to try to get behind her and herd her your way. Maybe you can head her off if she tries to bypass the gate. But be careful. She's kind of a nut job."

He threw a casual salute and moved into position. Nan made a wide circuit of the yard, moving around behind Scheherazade to cut her off from the orchard. The mare's hooves beat a restless pattern in the grass as she turned to watch, tossing her head with a jingle of the halter's metal rings.

She knows what I'm up to. And she's not going to let me get away with it.

Nan quelled the thought. This was just an animal, one belonging to a species that, she recalled Sky saying, wasn't particularly smart. She found herself still holding the carrot and dropped it on the ground, then took a step toward Scheherazade and clapped her hands.

"Go on, you. Move it!"

Another jingling head toss. Scheherazade held her ground. Her dark eyes were fixed on Nan, who cursed softly.

"I said move it!"

The horse made a squealing noise in its throat and stamped a forefoot on the grass. Nan's heart was pounding, her palms slippery with sweat. A horrifying scenario, in which Scheherazade escaped past her down the driveway and out onto the road, flickered through her mind and she suddenly flapped her arms and yelled, "Get!"

The mare reared onto her hind legs. Nan had a dizzying view of a towering black silhouette, chiseled head like a chess piece sculpted against the cloudless blue sky, front hooves wildly pawing the air before they came back to earth a scant yard away, with an impact that jarred every bone in her body. Vaguely she heard Gabe shout, saw him come running toward her from his post by the gate.

Before she knew what was happening he had grabbed the horse's halter and the two of them were tussling, Scheherazade starting to rear up again—Nan saw Gabe's feet actually leave the ground before the mare gave up and tried to run instead. She heard herself yelling "Let go of her, for Christ's sake! Gabe! Let go!"

The milling fracas terrified her; it seemed impossible

that he wouldn't be killed. The horse's hooves scattered gravel in every direction as it skittered across the driveway, dragging Gabe along while he clung grimly to the halter.

And then all at once it was over.

Without warning Scheherazade simply gave up and stood still, sides heaving and head bent submissively to Gabe's hand on the halter. Nan could scarcely believe her eyes. She swallowed, vaguely aware that her throat was raw from screaming. "Can you lead her over to the gate?" she said hoarsely.

His breath was coming in grunts and his glasses were wildly awry, but otherwise he seemed unharmed. "Sure. Why not?"

Nan went ahead on unsteady legs, glancing back once or twice to see Scheherazade keeping step with Gabe, docile as a carousel pony.

It was only after she had closed the gate, after Gabe had released the black mare into the pasture and climbed back over the fence, that they noticed Stephen sitting white-faced and silent on the porch.

Gabe waved a hand. "It's okay now, son. Everything's fine."

"You didn't hurt her, did you, Dad?"

Gabe went over and hugged him, giving Nan a crooked smile over the small dark head. "No, Stephen. Of course not."

"She's really a nice horse."

Gabe winked at Nan. "She's a sweetheart all right."

That smile and wink seemed to unseal a hot pocket of anger somewhere inside Nan. "You were damn lucky," she said tightly. "That was a really stupid thing to do."

He gave her a level look, then a little shrug. "Well, it worked out all right."

"Lucky for you. Otherwise you could be dead right now."

His eyebrow went into action. "From the look you're giving me, I'd say you might have preferred it that way."

He clearly thought he was some combination of John Wayne and Tarzan. Her chest felt like a pressure cooker. "I'm glad it happened to turn out okay," she said. "Just don't act like you did something smart."

Gabe sighed. "Look. I was just trying to help. That's all. It looked like things were getting out of hand."

The last phrase made Nan see total, unqualified red. "And that's what you came here for, right? To help me get everything under control, because I certainly wouldn't be able to do that on my own. Well, thank you so much."

Gabe said nothing. He just looked at her with his mouth open, and Stephen's face, right below his, mirrored its expression in miniature.

She went riding. She needed to get away from Gabe, to be by herself for a while. She knew he had acted on impulse, without thinking about the danger. She knew it was impossible to expect him not to feel satisfied with himself for having saved the day when she had made such an obvious hash of it. But she couldn't escape the feeling that it was partly his presence that had undermined her confidence and kept her from being able to handle the situation herself. He expected her to fail, and so she did.

Part of her anger came from the fright he had given her. In the brief space of that horrifying scuffle with the horse there had been plenty of time for her to imagine him trampled and killed. But behind the anger and the fear, fueling them both, was the question, rubbing like sandpaper along her nerves, of how the gate had come to be open in the first place.

There's nothing wrong with the catch. I fixed it.

Then who opened the gate? The horses?

Impossible. They're not that smart.

There was nothing to explain how it could have come unfastened. Nothing—except the explanation Lucy had given her.

She shook it off. Right now she needed action, not thought. Jolie was still grazing near the fence; it was easy to catch and saddle her, and Nan did it in record time, fingers flying over the straps and buckles that had once seemed complicated. She mounted and rode down the driveway at a gallop, hearing the gravel fly from under the white mare's hooves. A rabbit, flushed from the trees, darted in front of them. At the road she crossed and rode the quarter mile south to Sky's property, where she turned up the drive, past the weathered apple-packing shed, and entered the orchard beyond.

Once among the trees, the horse carrying her effortlessly down the long leafy aisles, she began to feel better. Dew still glittered on the grass, and above the trees with their clusters of ripening apples the sky was blindingly blue. Distant birdsong was the only sound, barely ruffling the surface of a vast early morning peace that leached her tension away as she rode down one gentle incline and up another. She was starving, but it didn't seem to matter. The neat rows of gnarled trees on either side of her were as soothing as a formal garden; she closed her eyes and relaxed to the motion of the horse beneath her, invisible sun warm on her face.

The sound of approaching hoofbeats broke the spell. She opened her eyes and glanced behind her to see a mounted figure approaching between the green rows. Sky, on Joker. She reined in and waited, feeling her tension level start to rise again. The last thing she wanted right now was company. Especially the company of a man she couldn't trust. That business about Watkins—

Sky pulled Joker down from a canter and trotted up to her. "Hey there."

"Hi." She couldn't sound glad to see him and didn't really try. She had the feeling his grin was supposed to melt her bones or something. He must take her for a fool, so gone on him that he could tell her anything he wanted and she would believe it.

"Saw you goin' past the shed," he said. "I hollered, but I guess you didn't hear me."

"No, I didn't."

The horses walked side by side.

"You're up mighty early. How's things over at the house?"

"Just fine." She felt him looking at her and stubbornly kept her gaze between Jolie's ears.

"Hey." He grabbed her wrist, reining Joker in close to Jolie. "What's got you so riled up?"

In her current mood it was too much. Furious, she tried to twist away. The abrupt motion startled Jolie; Nan saw the mare's ears go back, saw her turn her head, bare her teeth and sink them into Joker's neck. The big gelding squealed and shied away, nearly unseating Sky and breaking his hold on Nan's wrist. She gathered Jolie's reins and kicked her hard. The mare bolted.

Nan bent low, feeling the flying mane sting her

face, seeing the trees flash past in a green blur. At some point she turned Jolie down another row; at some point she started laughing and couldn't stop. She heard a shout: Sky was following her. She urged Jolie on. The rhythmic hoofbeats, the rocking motion of the saddle between her legs excited her, and she leaned into it and closed her eyes, trusting the horse to look out for them both.

Jolie was tiring. Gradually she slowed to a trot and then to a walk, her sides heaving. Sky came pounding up behind them and reined Joker in, jumping out of the saddle like a wrangler in a TV Western. He grabbed Nan and dragged her off Jolie; together they half fell to the ground. Nan was still laughing. The horses moved away from them, dropped their heads and began to graze.

Sky wasn't laughing. He was lying on top of her and she could feel his erection, but he didn't move, just lay staring down at her until she ran out of breath. They studied each other. Her throat was suddenly dry, and when she tried to swallow she couldn't. She didn't trust him and at this moment she wasn't even sure she liked him, but her body didn't seem to care about anything but its own specific desires. He saw her difficulty and a grim little smile touched his lips.

"Now let's see how loud you can holler," he said softly.

There on the grass among the apple trees, he tested the limits of her capacity. There was nothing tender about the transaction; it was like a contest between them, a clash of wills, and Nan was astonished at the strength of her resistance. Nonetheless she found herself steadily losing ground. As she approached climax he pulled back, leaving her stranded while he stared down into her face, his own devoid of expression. It humiliated her and she hated him, and still she found herself aroused beyond anything she had ever experienced, even with him. When he thrust into her again, she locked her legs around him and begged him not to stop. His teeth bared in a snarling grin.

"You want it bad, huh? Real bad?"

"Yes. Yes."

He took her at her word. His savage rhythm pounded her, taking her breath away. At the moment of orgasm a dizzying black tide rose behind her eyes; her head spun and she thought she was going to faint. As she hovered at the edge of consciousness there was a sensation of plummeting downward, into bottomless depths—down toward some obscure, fearsome thing awaiting her there. A faint wailing cry sounded inside her head, sending a burst of terror through her, and desperately she began to struggle upward, sobbing for breath, mindlessly fleeing that sound . . .

Running and not getting anywhere, seeing my breath clouding the air in front of my face . . .

She clawed her way back to consciousness, becoming groggily aware of Sky on top of her—of clinging to him and feeling the shudder of release that shook his body from head to foot.

He rolled off her. She lay without moving, all thought suspended, seeing the sun wink among the silvery leaves overhead and hearing a sound she only gradually recognized as the interlocking pattern of his breathing and her own. Behind it she could hear a leisurely tearing and munching as the horses grazed nearby.

Turning her head she found him watching her, the blue eyes unreadable. At last he said, "Your husband get here?"

Her thoughts stirred sluggishly. She nodded.

"And?"

"And what?" The terror was gone, along with every other sensation: she felt drained, as if she had run a marathon. In an effort to pull herself together, she made herself sit up and start putting her clothes in order. Sky did the same, turning his back to her.

"And, what's the story? Y'all still separated?"

"Yes," she said. Behind her torpor, irritation began to stir.

"So how come you're bein' so damn snooty to me?"

Nan hesitated, watching the back of his coppery head. "Maybe," she said softly, "because I don't like liars."

She remembered Stephen calling him a liar over the story of the deer with the cherry-tree antlers, and herself reprimanding him. It seemed like a century ago.

Sky had grown very still. There was a silvery jingle as one of the horses shook off flies. He turned slowly to face her.

"What the hell you talkin' about?" His eyes were cold and she felt a flicker of apprehension, but anger pushed it aside.

"I'm talking about Mister Jerry Ray Watkins, who is apparently a friend of yours, since I saw him riding in your truck. And who was doing *something* over at Annabel's when he almost ran Stephen and me down in our own driveway—*something* besides picking up his tools, because he never worked for Annabel. Even though you told me he did."

Halfway through her outburst she saw his gaze slide off hers and knew there was no simple, harmless explanation for the deception. But apparently he was going to try.

"Look, Nan, okay. Fact is, Jerry Ray was pickin' up

some stuff of mine I left over at Annabel's. Sorta runnin' an errand for me."

"So why not just say so?"

He shrugged. "Hell, I thought you might not like me sendin' him over there, now it's your property and all. While I was lookin' after the place I sorta got used to treatin' it like it was mine. I sent him over without thinkin', but then when you asked me about it, I got worried you might feel like I was makin' too free with your property."

This reasoning struck her as feeble, but she decided to let it go. "So just how close are you two? I mean, you *pretended* you barely knew him."

He ignored her gibe. "We do a little business now and then. Like I said, he might run me an errand once in a while."

"And what do you do for him in return?"

"Hell, I've lent him a little money when he's short. What's it to you?"

He was starting to show annoyance, but it seemed calculated, as if he had started to run out of easy answers and wanted her questions to stop.

"I think you're lying," she said. "I think you've lied about him all along, and you're still at it."

She felt reckless saying it, wondering if there was a chance he would get violent. Who could possibly hear them out here, amid acres of trees? She got to her feet and stood looking down at him, her knees a little shaky.

But when he stood up at last, it was to move away from her. He yanked Joker's head up from the grass in midmouthful and swung himself into the saddle.

"Fine. You think what you want."

*   *   *

When she got back to the house, Gabe and Stephen were watching television. Stephen didn't look up; Gabe did. She could intellectually recall her outburst at him but could not recapture the anger itself. It seemed to have been experienced by someone else. Whatever his faults, at least he had never lied to her.

"Where'd you disappear to?" he said. "Lucy Talbot called."

"I went riding," Nan said briefly. She was aware of his eyes on her as she went toward the stairs.

"Looks like somebody else did most of the riding," he said.

She cursed herself for the second's hesitation in her step, for letting him get to her. But how could he know? Reaching the top of the stairs she put her hands to her face; it was burning. Damn him. How could he tell?

It wasn't much of a mystery: solved when she went to change her clothes and saw the back of her white shirt covered with grass stains.

Looks like somebody else did most of the riding.

Damn Gabe. She didn't have to answer to him, not in her own house. She threw the shirt on the floor.

"You don't have to act so guilty," he said from the bedroom door. "I knew you were fucking somebody. I knew it as soon as I saw you. You've got the glow."

The way he was looking at her made her forget what she had been planning to say. She noticed that she was half naked. After nine years of cohabitation it seemed a little absurd to start worrying about modesty in front of Gabe, but she felt at a tactical disadvantage. She retrieved a towel from the back of a chair and draped it around her neck.

"I'm going to take a shower."

He followed her to the bathroom. "You know, it could explain a thing or two about Stephen's problems if you're sneaking out to get laid by some good old boy—"

"Gabe, shut up. I didn't go looking for this thing with Sky, okay? It just happened. So please shut up." The previous half hour in the orchard came back to her and she winced at the memory. "I think it's over anyway. Now would you get out of here and let me take a shower?"

It was strange how a raised voice could echo in the small room, as if each single tile caught the sound and threw it back at a slightly different moment, making it jangle inside her head. Her heart started pounding and her vision went black. Suddenly she could feel the pull of that inner darkness once again, the suffocating senseless fear, and she reached out and gripped the edge of the basin. The touch of the cool porcelain oriented her. She could hear Gabe's voice fragmented among the echoes.

"What"

"matter with"

"y—?"

Her sight cleared slowly. She was leaning against the bathroom wall. Gabe was holding her shoulders and the towel had slipped and it didn't matter because he couldn't be less interested; he was looking into her face with concern and she remembered that once upon a time he had been her best friend.

"You okay now? What happened?"

"I got a little dizzy, that's all."

He peered at her over the tops of his glasses. "You're probably just hungry. Too much exercise on an empty stomach."

Nan wasn't sure if that was supposed to mean the horseback riding or the sex, and didn't want to know. To hide the quick color in her face she bent and picked the towel up off the floor, wrapping it around her shoulders and holding the door for him with exaggerated politeness. "I'd like to take my shower now. Do you mind?"

Chapter 17

They drove into Breezy for lunch at Bev's and spent an hour giving Gabe a tour of the town, including a visit to Books, Etc., where he met Cooper and admired his inventory of windup toys. Stephen clung to Gabe's hand as they left the bookstore and crossed the street for a closer look at the monument in front of the courthouse. He hadn't mentioned Woody since his father's arrival, and Nan could tell Gabe thought she had been making a mountain out of a molehill. And she had to admit it seemed almost as if Woody had faded out of existence the moment Stephen had better things to do.

"So here we are at the Tornado County Courthouse." Gabe had been keeping Stephen entertained by pretending to be unable to remember the name of the town, calling it variously Windy, Gusty, and so on.

The boy was giggling. "Dad, it's Breeeezy."

Nan rolled her eyes. Ordinarily the exchange would have amused her, but just now she found herself unable to shake off her rotten mood. Much as she would have liked to put the topic of Schuyler Barnett out of her mind, it wouldn't go. Aside from his lying, and whatever shady activity it was designed to hide, there was the disturbing memory of what had happened during their sexual encounter—what seemed disturbingly like a psychotic break on her part. She supposed it wasn't fair to blame Sky for her own psychological kinks. But she could certainly blame him for the lies.

The next day it rained early, then cleared around nine-thirty. Gabe slept late and Nan found him at the kitchen table drinking coffee when she came up from working in the darkroom. She thought he looked incongruous against the green backdrop of pasture and mountains outside the window—the way Sky would look on a sooty, busy New York City street. Or maybe it was just her vision that was limited. The thought of Sky made her wince.

"Where's Stephen?" Gabe asked her.

"Across the creek. With Woody."

He grunted and rubbed a hand over his face. Nan cocked her head at him. "Did you really think you were going to get rid of Woody that easily?"

He grunted again. "Maybe I'll go over and give old Woody a little competition. See if maybe I can edge him out."

"Should I expect the three of you for lunch?"

Gave favored her with a sour look as he went out the back door, wincing at the screen's rusty squeal. She watched him let himself through the pasture gate, fasten it carefully behind him, and start off toward the creek. She bit her lip. Maybe if she had done something along these lines, paid a little more attention to Stephen, fulfilled her responsibilities as a good parent, the whole issue of Woody would never have arisen.

Within the hour Gabe was back.

Swirling a print in the developer, she heard someone banging around in the kitchen overhead and went up to see what was going on. She had a crazy idea it might be Sky, and found herself nervous at the thought of seeing him.

But it was Gabe causing the ruckus—Gabe clearly in a foul mood, getting a glass from the kitchen and stomping into the library to grab the brandy out of the cabinet and pour himself a drink. Nan trailed after him, glancing at her watch. It was half-past eleven. She looked more closely at him. He was soaking wet.

"What happened?"

He drained his brandy and poured another. He was shivering. "What does it look like? I fell in the fucking creek. That water is goddamn cold."

"Did you see Stephen?"

"No, goddammit. But I swear the little bastard made me fall in."

Nan sat down on the sofa, trying not to smile. "Why don't you change into some dry clothes? Then you can tell me all about it."

He couldn't seem to get warm. His lips were blue and he couldn't stop shivering. In the end he climbed into the shower and stood under a scalding spray.

"I went across down there where it's shallow," he shouted over the drumming water. "Didn't see him so I climbed up the hill. No sign of him. I went down and poked around in the woods on the other side of the hill. The creek's deeper there. I saw this fallen tree, a natural bridge—figured I'd use it to cross."

He prided himself on his balance. In the loft he had used a tall stool, set precariously on the seat of a chair, to change lightbulbs in the fifteen-foot ceiling. "I could have been an astronaut," he would say. When he moved out she'd bought a ladder.

Now he turned off the water in the shower and Nan passed him a towel. He pushed the curtain back on rattling rings and faced her, rubbing himself down. The casual intimacy of their years of marriage had reestablished itself without their noticing.

"He must have been following me. I was halfway across—thought I heard rustling in the trees on the bank behind me. Then the log rolled. I swear it rolled under my feet. I hit the water ass-first. By the time I got out there was nobody in sight."

"You're sure you didn't just slip?"

He stopped drying himself long enough to give her a dirty look. "I heard him. Little bastard was laughing his ass off."

*   *   *

Stephen had laughed so hard he almost choked. He and Woody had fled from the telltale sound, running headlong through the woods until it caught up with them at last and they collapsed, gasping and giggling, on a thick bed of pine needles. Every time Stephen started to get his breath, he would look at Woody and remember how funny his dad

(trespasser)

had looked, arms and legs flailing in the air as he struggled to get his balance, then the big splash

(teach him a lesson)

he had made hitting the water. They had spotted him almost as soon as he crossed the creek, and Woody had whispered that he was a dangerous convict, escaped from Brushy Mountain State Prison. The excitement of the game had made a tight knot in Stephen's stomach. They had followed the trespasser for a long time, creeping up as close as they could without showing themselves, holding their breaths every time he stopped or turned. When he had started across the log, Stephen had known exactly what to do.

The splash and the long stream of curses came back to him now. He hadn't heard his dad say so many bad words all in a row since the time their neighbor's visiting kitten had taken a dump in one of his running shoes.

His dad.

Stephen stopped laughing. Slowly he drew his knees up to his chest and hugged them. "Woody? He was okay, wasn't he? He didn't hurt himself?"

Woody's grin faded. A breeze blew and the scattered light around them danced, sliding over his pale hair. "Naw. Anyhow, who cares?"

Stephen was taken aback. "He's my dad," he said.

Woody shrugged and his eyes shifted away. "Yeah. But he don't want you playin' with me." The muttered words themselves were scarcely audible, but Stephen felt the other boy's loneliness sweep over him.

"That's not true," he said. Was it? He remembered the way his mom had acted, the night Woody wanted her to say hi to him. His mom had never liked Woody; he knew that. His dad . . . he wasn't sure. But—

"Don't worry, Woody," he said stoutly. "It doesn't matter what anybody else wants. You're my friend."

Unconsciously he touched the faceted head of the horseshoe-nail ring on his finger. Somewhere at the back of his mind there was a kind of whisper, just two words, and without thinking he found himself repeating them aloud.

"For always."

Chapter 18

Over the next few days Nan had ample opportunity to remember—if she had ever been in danger of forgetting it—Gabe's tendency to take charge of any situation that confronted him. From ten minutes spent scanning the Methodist Church bulletin board in Breezy, he had come up with the idea of augmenting Stephen's social life by enrolling him in a program of summer activities run by volunteers from the church membership. It was the type of thing she would never have thought of in a million years—and, even if she had, would never have been able to persuade Stephen to attend.

But Gabe made a phone call, found out the details (activities varied from day to day, including art, singa-longs, and puppet shows) and decided the morning sessions sounded perfect. Stephen did kick up a fuss about going, but it was minimal and Gabe dealt with it. Nan was left feeling woefully inadequate, remembering how she had racked her brain for ways to get him connected with other children, when all along this quick and easy solution had existed under her nose. So far he didn't seem to like it, but he had been only twice and things were bound to improve. Maybe eventually he would make a friend less problematic than the boy he called Woody—whoever or whatever he might be.

Today, instead of heading across the creek as usual, he had stuck around the house, seduced by Gabe's promise of a ride on Annabel's minitractor. As Nan changed the sheets on the beds upstairs she could hear the growl of the engine ruffling the peaceful afternoon air. The lush front lawn, untended since Sky had cut it nearly five weeks ago, was knee high by now, a daisy-studded green sea lapping at the old white house. Gabe, on the tractor seat, was letting Stephen stand in front of him and steer, and the kid was in heaven.

Her own mood continued to be shadowed by what had happened between her and Sky. She still hadn't come to terms with it, but it was never far from her thoughts. Whatever his reasons—whether it was because of Gabe's presence, or because he didn't want to answer any more questions about Jerry Ray, or because he too had been offbalanced by their sexual encounter, he hadn't shown his face since. And she wasn't sure if she was sorry or glad.

As she took a clean sheet from the laundry basket and spread it on Annabel's bed she heard the engine sputter and die, then Stephen shouting from the yard.

"Mom! Mom! Look out the window!"

She went to the alcove window and looked out. They sat on the tractor waving up at her.

"What?"

Gabe gestured expansively. "We made you a present."

A number of random swaths had been mowed in the grass. Nan leaned her elbows on the sill. "You're not finished."

Stephen bounced up and down between Gabe's knees. "No! We wrote something! Read what it says!"

Nan squinted. The trimmed spots, darker than

the rest, still looked random to her. She hazarded a guess. "Hi?"

"No! It says 'Mom'!"

"It does not."

"It does so," Gabe said. "Woman, can't you read?"

She supposed one of the jagged patches might pass muster as an *M*. The other, in relation to it, seemed to be lying on its side.

"It says 'Mo-3.' "

This hit Stephen's eight-year-old funnybone and he started to giggle wildly. "Hey, Mo-3! What's happening, Mo-3!"

It was, she thought, the kind of idyllic moment they had never really achieved as a family back home in New York, probably because she had always been too busy or too distracted. Now Gabe had moved on emotionally and, appearances to the contrary, they were no longer a family. Were they? The pair of them sat on the tractor in the middle of the green lawn, matching bespectacled faces laughing up at her.

From the window's vantage point she saw the car before they did: the Talbot station wagon coming down the drive. She waved. Gabe and Stephen turned to look.

"I'll be out in a minute," she called. She saw Gabe lift Stephen down from the tractor and climb off himself, then turned away from the window and headed downstairs to the kitchen. Guests meant lemonade. She couldn't stomach the stuff herself, but she had learned to keep a supply on hand in the refrigerator for unexpected drop-ins, since "viztin' " seemed to be a way of life in this part of the country. She took out tall glasses, filled them and set them on a tray, her spirits lifting. Nan Lucas, country hostess. Who would have thought she could pull it off?

She carried the tray out to the front porch. Gabe stood by the car chatting with the Talbots; Lucy caught sight of her and waved. The men turned and Whit lifted his hat. As usual the old-fashioned gesture charmed her. She set the tray down on the broad porch railing and beckoned. "Come and get it, folks."

They came across the mutilated lawn, passing Stephen, who had climbed onto the vacated tractor seat and was fiddling with the controls, pretending to drive it. She could hear Gabe complaining to their guests about how hard she was working him on this visit.

As they reached the porch steps Whit smiled up at her. "Nan, that lemonade looks mighty good on this hot afternoon."

"There's beer, if you'd rather have one."

"Bless you, honey. No, if I was t' drink a beer right now I'd fall dead asleep here on your porch."

"Well, I can think of worse ways to spend the rest of the day," Gabe said. "I wouldn't mind a beer. Got to replace my electrolytes. All that manual labor."

He settled comfortably into the porch swing and smiled up at Nan, apparently expecting her to wait on him. The smile annoyed her; she connected it somehow with Jennifer. She was on the verge of telling him to get his own beer, but his last remark made her hesitate. He *had* been working, after all—if sitting on the tractor could be called work. The presence of Whit and Lucy was another factor restraining her from putting him in his place. She shrugged and went back into the house, Lucy trailing after her. Nan got a cold Guinness out of the refrigerator and turned to the older woman with a wry look.

"Think he deserves a glass?"

Lucy smiled vaguely but didn't answer. Nan

decided against the glass and opened a drawer, rooting through a tangle of utensils for the bottle opener. She had just found it when she heard Lucy say, "Honey, I'm so glad to see you're keepin' your little boy in sight."

Nan slid the drawer shut and looked up. "Oh—uh, yeah."

"And now your husband's here, and you all seem so happy together. Maybe things will come right somehow. Maybe Tucker'll move on to where he belongs."

Nan felt a fake smile plaster itself to her lips. She despised herself as a hypocrite. But what could she possibly say?

"Hey, where's my beer?"

Gabe's shout from the porch saved her. She looked down and busied herself with taking the cap off the beer bottle. When she had replaced the opener in the drawer, she glanced up and saw Lucy beaming at her.

"You're a doll, Lucy," she blurted. At least it was an honest statement. The older woman broke into her cackling laugh.

When they returned to the porch Stephen was nowhere in sight. Gabe, lolling in the swing, took the bottle from her and gave her a mock salute of thanks without pausing in his conversation with Whit.

"So I'm walking down Bleecker Street and I see this woman with a dog coming toward me—one of those really emaciated dogs, a greyhound or something. And the dog is wearing this polyester leopard-skin coat. So I say to the dog—"

Nan found herself trying to follow the story's thread with one part of her brain, while another kept wondering where Stephen had gotten to. Sitting with the others on the shady front porch, surrounded by voices and laughter, air sweet with honeysuckle and new-mown grass, she couldn't account for the mounting tension she felt. Was it only the somber warning implicit in Lucy's well-meaning words?

I'm so glad to see you're keeping your little boy in sight.

"Gabe, where's Stephen?"

Gabe, interrupted in midsentence, gave her a blank look. "Huh?"

Nan gestured at the empty yard. "Your son? Where'd he go?"

He stood up to survey the half-mowed expanse of green. "Damn if I know. Whit? Did you see him go?"

Whit shook his head, broad forehead creasing in concern. " 'Fraid I wasn't lookin'."

Nan and Lucy exchanged a look in which she could read the older woman's thought as clearly as if the words had been spoken aloud. Ain't that just like a man? But the humor that should have been intrinsic to the exchange was undercut now by worry. Where was Stephen?

Gabe took a swig of beer, set the bottle down and went to the top of the porch steps. He raised his voice a notch. "Stephen?"

In reply there was only silence, a silence in which Nan found herself holding her breath, aware for the first time that the sound of the crickets, so constant that she had long since ceased to hear it, had stopped. She felt sweat pop out on her skin.

"Stephen!" Gabe bellowed. The sound jolted along her nerves and she opened her mouth to protest, to say that screaming wasn't going to help. But just at that instant, there was an answer.

"Dad?"

The small, scared voice came, apparently, from nowhere—they all looked wildly around them and saw nothing. Nan began to panic.

"Stephen? Wh—"

Whit pointed suddenly at the oak tree. They all looked. Stephen was not visible. But high in the tree there were branches stirring, and as they stood staring at the slight movement, the small wavering voice came again.

"I'm up here. In the tree."

*   *   *

It had been okay as long as he hadn't looked down.

Stephen had gotten bored pretending to drive the tractor. His dad was blabbing with Cousin Whit, his mom and Cousin Lucy had gone into the house, and there was no one for him to talk to, nothing to do. He wished he had gone down to the creek this afternoon to play with Woody, instead of hanging around with the grown-ups, who would always rather blab than do anything fun. He slid off the tractor seat and wandered toward the oak tree, sitting down to rest his back against its thick trunk, feeling boredom settle over him like a stifling blanket.

"Hey!"

Woody's whisper sounded very close. Stephen scrambled to his feet and rounded the tree to find his friend sitting there, knees drawn up to his chest—a mirror of Stephen's posture a moment before. His boredom vanished instantly. "Hey, Woody! Want to go down to the creek?"

Woody shook his head. "Let's climb up to the tree house."

"The tree house?" Stephen felt his eyes flick up and

as quickly dropped them. The tree house tempted and terrified him at the same time. Every so often, out of nowhere, he would feel it tugging at his imagination—the little house cradled high up in the oak's green branches, surrounded by rustling leaves. And then the idea of the long, scary climb would intervene, making his stomach writhe and his knees feel woozy.

"Come on," Woody was saying.

"I can't," Stephen said. "I can't reach the bottom branch."

"I'll give you a boost," Woody said.

At first it had been okay. Stephen had kept his gaze fixed on the rough bark a few inches from his nose, concentrating on scrambling from one thick branch to the next, following Woody's lead. But as they got higher, it became harder to block out the impression of vast space all around him.

And above.

And below.

A breeze parted the leaves and a dizzying vista shimmered momentarily at the edge of his vision. He was almost as high as the roof of the house. His father's voice, audible at first from the porch, had been drowned out by the stirring of leaves all around. He shut his eyes and felt his stomach heave.

"Come on!"

Woody's voice sounded high above him. From the ground the tree hadn't seemed nearly so tall. By now he should have reached the tree house, should have been sitting safely beside Woody, pretending the climb hadn't scared him at all. But instead he was still climbing, the bark scraping his hands and knees, heart banging against his ribs as he imagined himself falling, plummeting down through the air to hit the ground with a horrible crunch. His mouth felt as though he had eaten glue; when he tried to swallow he couldn't. His crotch ached from straddling the branch beneath him.

"Woody? Is it a lot farther?"

There was no answer. Stephen drew one trembling leg up to the limb where he sat, got his foot on it, and forced his hands to creep up the trunk to the next branch. The breeze returned, fluttering the leaves around him. He thought he could feel the whole tree swaying. Hot tears came into his eyes and he blinked them back fiercely.

He got his hands around the next branch and pulled himself up.

*   *   *

I'm up here. In the tree.

Nan's skin turned to ice beneath its film of sweat. She heard Gabe say "Holy shit" under his breath; then he was down the porch steps and across the lawn, and without having consciously willed herself to move she was running after him, stumbling forward involuntarily as if someone behind her had suddenly jerked the ground backward beneath her feet. At Gabe's side beneath the tree, she craned her neck to peer up into the maze of leaves and branches above.

"Son, I think you'd better come on down," Gabe was saying. There was no answer and he said, "Stephen?"

"I—I can't."

"What do you mean, you can't?"

"Woody wants to show me the tree house."

Nan felt a cold hand grasp hers. She lowered her eyes from the branches overhead to find Lucy standing beside her. The old woman's chin was visibly trembling. "Lord have mercy," she whispered. "Lord have mercy."

Gabe's hands had gone to his hips. "Look, Stephen. I don't care what Woody wants. I want you to come down from that tree. And I want you to do it right now."

The pause this time was excruciatingly long. Nan saw Gabe's mouth open again, then close as Stephen spoke.

"Woody?"

The branches rustled. From high over their heads a child's voice, not Stephen's, drifted out of the tree.

"Come on. You're slower'n cold molasses."

The local drawl was unmistakable. But it was the quality of that voice, the scuffed treble with its impatient inflection, that connected some circuit in Nan's memory with a blinding flash that made her brain reel. *Tucker's voice.*

Over the past weeks it had sounded again and again in her memory, and she recognized it instantly now. The realization brought a cataclysmic wave of dizziness, followed by nausea, and for a second she thought she was going to pass out. But there wasn't room now for such self-indulgence. She met Lucy's eyes and saw her own terror mirrored in the old woman's gaze. This was not her imagination: Lucy had heard and recognized the voice as well. She took a deep breath and glanced at Gabe. He was standing with his head tilted back, staring up into the tree. Whether it was surprise or just the sharp angle of his neck, his mouth hung open. When he spoke at last, his voice was gentle.

"Now, listen to me, son. I want you to come down now. Maybe you can visit the tree house another day. We'll talk about it, okay? But right now, you need to come down."

There was no answer.

"Stephen. Did you hear me? Right now."

"I'm stuck, Dad."

"No, you're not. Listen. I want you to do exactly as I say. Don't look down. Just reach below you with one foot until you can feel a branch there."

Silence from above: then a tentative rustling.

"Stephen?"

"O-okay."

"Feel the branch?"

"Yeah . . ."

"Fine. Now put your other foot down on it."

Branch by branch, step by agonizing step, he talked Stephen down from the tree. Vaguely Nan heard Whit say something about fetching a ladder. She had a dazed impression of hours crawling by. She stood with her hand in Lucy's, listening to the intermittent cautious rustling in the tree above, once in a while catching a glimpse of shadowy movement. She was aware of her body only as a stiff carapace of fear enclosing her hot, pounding heart. Occasionally loose leaves floated down to land soundlessly on the grass.

"Dad, there's no more branches—"

"Sure there are, son. You got up there, didn't you? You can get down exactly the same way."

"But what if I fall?"

"You're not going to fall. Because if I have to catch you, and put my back out doing it, you won't be eating chocolate cheesecake for a month."

The quavering sound from above might have been an attempt at a laugh.

A broken twig tumbled down and landed at Nan's feet. She glanced down, getting a vicious twinge in her neck muscles, and then looked back up into the tree.

There was unmistakable movement among the lower branches now. As she watched, Stephen's sneaker-clad foot came in sight, feeling blindly, tentatively for purchase below. He was maybe twenty feet up, and she held her breath.

Please . . .

He eased his way down onto the branch. For an instant she caught sight of his scared little face peering down.

"Da—ad—"

"Don't look down, son. What did I tell you? Just keep looking at the trunk. You'll be on the ground in one minute. Okay?"

It seemed more like twenty—but at last he reached the lowest branch and Gabe, who had seemed as cool as a cucumber all this time, lunged forward to snatch him down so roughly that Stephen shrieked and burst into tears.

Gabe hugged him close to his chest, laughing and swearing. Nan felt Lucy hug her. She wanted to go to Stephen, but all at once her knees were shaking too much to hold her and she sank on her heels into the grass. She was dimly aware of Whit coming across the lawn with a ladder over his shoulder, slowing from a run to a walk when he saw it was no longer needed. Lucy had gone to hover near Gabe and Stephen. And then there was a sound in the tree above them.

Soft at first, a tentative rustle, escalating in an eyeblink to a series of thuds and snaps and tearing sounds as something came plummeting headlong down through the branches.

"Jesus!" Gabe said. He ducked and stumbled back, still clutching Stephen in his arms. Whit, just reaching Nan, grabbed her arm and dragged her to her feet. But

Lucy didn't move. Lucy stood as if transfixed, looking up with arms half extended as if to catch whatever it was. And the thick board falling out of the tree, plunging into sight with startling suddenness, struck her upturned face with brutal force.

"Nan. Take Stephen inside."

Gabe was speaking urgently in her ear, and she blinked. He was pushing Stephen into her arms. For a moment her thankfulness that her little boy was safe blotted out everything else, and she could not remember the cause of the cold horror that lay just beneath it. Then she became aware of Whit making soft choked noises, kneeling next to something on the ground not far away.

She turned her head.

Saw.

Remembered.

Lucy lay very still. Her eyes were wide open and there was a deep indentation in her forehead just below the hairline where the falling board had struck her, knocking her head straight back with a force that must have broken her neck. The board, a weathered two-by-six that had obviously formed part of the tree house, lay on the ground beside her surrounded by a litter of leaves and bark, debris knocked loose by its fall.

A small amount of blood had pooled in the depression on Lucy's forehead. Either the blow or the fall had caused her long white hair to come loose from its pins, and Nan couldn't help noticing, even in the midst of her shock and horror, that in spite of its disfigurement Lucy Talbot's face had somehow regained the elusive look of youth it had possessed the night of the square dance in her barn.

* * *

Stephen was crying, tears streaking his face. "I didn't mean to do anything bad," he said.

There was a lead weight in Nan's chest that made speaking, thinking, even breathing seem like an enormous effort. From moment to moment she lost track of what had just happened, and each time she remembered, it was as bad as watching it for the first time. Stephen crouched on his bed and she sat next to him. Gabe and Whit were dealing with the situation in the yard, details she preferred to keep unclear in her mind. She had shut the window against the sounds that carried too clearly on the quiet country air.

The sense of what Stephen was saying reached her slowly. She put her arm around him. "It wasn't your fault, honey."

"Woody said it was an easy climb."

Nan shut her eyes, found the replay too vivid against her lids and opened them again, drinking in the room around her like an antidote. Wrinkled old quilt on the bed beneath them, dragonfly lampshade on the table nearby. An involuntary shudder went through her; she hoped no trace of it was discernible in the hand that stroked her child's shoulder.

Woody?

Come on. You're slower'n cold molasses.

That scornful young voice, impossibly familiar, floating down from the high reaches of the tree. Her head reeled again and against a swirling dizziness she saw Lucy's body sprawled on the ground, long white hair loose around her face. Then Lucy in the kitchen of her home, a few nights ago when they had gone there for dinner. Her urgent hand on Nan's wrist.

It's not natural for the dead and the living to keep company.

The shudder passed through Nan again. This time it didn't die away but diminished to a weak trembling that seemed to begin somewhere below her heart and move out to her fingertips in waves.

What was up in that tree with Stephen?

Not *what*.

Who.

She flinched back from the thought and tried to concentrate instead on something practical, like persuading Stephen to lie down. Finally she succeeded. He fell into exhausted sleep almost at once and she covered him with the quilt, then sat down again at the foot of the bed, listening to him breathe noisily through his mouth and staring at anything that would keep her from connecting the thoughts that chased through her head. The faint sounds outside the window had ceased, and the house was so still she could hear the clock ticking across the hall in her bedroom.

Woody said it was an easy climb.

Come on! You're slower'n cold molasses!

She found herself starting to shake again and rose carefully from the bed, afraid she would jar Stephen awake. She didn't want to think anymore. As if from an enormous distance, she saw Gabe and herself sitting with Whit and Lucy on the porch less than an hour ago, drinking lemonade and laughing, a group of hazy figures suspended in a bright bubble of safety and innocence. She closed her eyes tightly until the image was the only thing in her mind, pretending that if she tried hard enough, desperately enough, she could wish herself back inside.

Chapter 19

The Hope of Heaven Baptist Church in Breezy was packed. It was a hot day, and people were using everything from hats to hymnals to fan themselves. Brother Fesmire, the minister, had a white handkerchief the size of a dishtowel, which he used to mop his pale sweating face at intervals during the service. During the hymns he blew his nose in it.

Nan, sitting with Stephen and Gabe in a pew behind Whit and his family, welcomed the physical discomfort—welcomed even the small bead of sweat making its ticklish way down the back of her neck. Anything that distracted her from thinking about the past couple of days. Gabe had located some man who had come and dismantled the remainder of the tree house to prevent further accidents, driving off with the rotten boards piled in the back of his truck—but the horrifying recollection of the tragedy could not be removed so neatly. Her brain kept visualizing the accident over and over again, making it happen differently. Making Lucy stumble out of the way and the board land in the grass, so that the whole incident ended harmlessly and Stephen got a spanking.

The temptation was to see the dozens of innocent directions in which the sequence of events could have gone instead of ending in disaster. But she had discovered that concentrating on trivia was best. It seemed to shift her brain into neutral, to ease the heaviness in her chest to a not-unpleasant numbness.

Once the drop of sweat had been absorbed into the collar of her dress, she looked at the pew in front of her and resumed counting the plastic cherries on Irene Talbot's hat. She had counted them twice already and come out with two different totals: twenty and eighteen. There were six tiny plastic bananas as well, wildly out of proportion to the cherries.

Brother Fesmire was talking now about Lucy Talbot's warmth and kindness, her many years of Christian service to the community. Nan heard his nasal, high-pitched voice, a lot like Frank Perdue's, from a distance. From time to time she stole a glance at Stephen beside her, hands clasped in his lap. She couldn't tell if he was listening or not.

For the final hymn they sang "Shall We Gather at the River?" During it Whit broke down and cried, bending his tall frame to hide his face on Irene's shoulder. She patted him and kept on singing, a hooting soprano that went flat on the top notes. Before the service Whit had made a point of speaking to Stephen, shaking his hand—even making some little joke about the two of them wearing neckties. He didn't blame Stephen. No one did. It had been an accident. But if they had never come here, Lucy would still be alive.

Woody said it was an easy climb.

Come on! You're slower'n cold molasses!

Stephen stood beside her, holding a corner of the hymnbook, small thumb with its bitten nail pinching down the page. Hard to tell if he was singing or not.

His head was bowed, silky dark hair fringing his shirt collar. Bending closer Nan could hear him making a sound, a wordless crooning that more or less followed the melody. She straightened and tried to join in the singing.

> Shall we gather at the river—
> The beautiful, the beautiful river?
> Gather with the saints at the river
> That flows from the throne of God?

Yew trees shaded the little graveyard on the hill behind the church. Sky was one of the pallbearers, somber-faced and handsome in a dark suit, bearing the coffin's weight along with Lucy's three sons. The crowd from the church followed quietly until Nan heard someone near the back break into sobs, a desolate sound on the sun-baked hillside.

She held Stephen's hand. At the graveside, under the trees, it was cooler. There was shade and a whispering breeze that brought the smell of humid grass and funeral lilies.

At the end of the service in the church, the preacher had invited the family to approach the open casket for what he called "last good-byes." Nan could tell Gabe had some idea of dragging Stephen up there; when he shifted around in the pew she had fixed him with a look that said *No way*. The three of them had stayed in their seats, watching a long line of people shuffle up to the coffin and bend over it, murmuring a few words to the dead woman within, many of them turning away in tears. She saw Sky's brother and his family, Cassie and Tom and their brood of children, Cooper sweating in a jacket and tie, Mr. Ikenberry from the general store, ancient Uncle Jim still in his faded overalls, the fiddling couple from the square dance, and more than a dozen others she could recognize but not name.

Now, as she looked at the closed lid of the coffin waiting beside the freshly dug grave, the finality of the whole business struck her with a force that threatened, for a moment, to override the numbness she had summoned to shield her.

Lucy is dead. Dead.

She let the words repeat inside her head until they became a formula, meaningless syllables without power to hurt. Beside her Stephen's head was lowered in concentration on the toes of his shoes, his hand in hers limp and damp. She squeezed it but got no response.

Sky stepped forward from a group at the head of the grave and cleared his throat.

"Whit's asked me to say a prayer."

His voice was hoarse. He was obviously distraught and Nan was suddenly ashamed of her own emotional cowardice. His eyes, passing over the crowd, met hers in a brief flash of blue and moved on without lingering. In that moment she regretted the ugly scene between them, and its aftermath of estrangement, with a bitterness that stunned her like a blow.

Sky bowed his head and the rest of the mourners followed suit. "Lord, you know Lucy was pretty special to us. We're asking for your help in gettin' along without her. She was a part of our lives and we're goin' to miss her.

"Help us to understand that in a lot of ways, she's still here with us. We're all a little better off than we woulda been if we hadn't known her. Lord, thank you for lettin' us be the ones to share Lucy Talbot's time here on earth. It was a privilege. Amen."

He stepped back. Nan found a knot in her throat. When she tried to swallow it, her eyes filled with tears. In its brevity and simplicity the prayer seemed to have slipped past all her defenses. The comforting numbness was fast eroding, leaving her with a grief so overpowering she could scarcely draw breath.

Fighting back tears, she turned away from the sight of the coffin being lowered into the ground, pushing her blurred gaze over the faces of the crowd in an effort to recover her detachment. The majority of those present were still unfamiliar to her; she knew she had met many of them, was probably related to them, but had no real sense of who they were. It struck her that Sky and Lucy had been her closest contacts here and that she had effectively lost them both.

Tears welled up again and she blinked them back fiercely, finding herself gazing across the open grave at a boy standing opposite her, head bowed so that his longish blond hair concealed his face. His hands were clasped in front of him. On the right one was a crude ring made from a bent horseshoe nail. Just as that fact penetrated her distraction, he lifted his head and looked at her.

Their eyes met for a long moment. His lips parted. There was a chip off the inside corner of his left front tooth.

Tucker.

Recognition slammed into her, knocking her breath away as she stood staring at him, feeling each deliberate beat of her heart against her ribs. She could see him clearly: the faded overalls, one hand clasping the other wrist in front of him, the dull glint of the ring on his hand. A few strands of his sun-bleached hair lifted in the breeze. He stood just in front of two men she did not know, and in some corner of her mind she was numbly aware that she could see their bulky dark-suited bodies right through him. Beneath her crawling skin, her body heat was rapidly draining away, replaced by a seeping cold. Across the open grave the pale-haired boy lifted his hand as if to reach out to her. His lips moved soundlessly, in syllables she recognized.

Annabel—

"Ashes to ashes," the preacher's high voice said, sounding very far away. "Dust to dust."

There was a whisper of dirt falling on the coffin, a shifting of the crowd; Gabe's shoulder bumped hers and she blinked and started. Men were moving forward, throwing a few loads of dirt into the grave and then passing the shovel on to someone else. The two men she had seen standing behind Tucker had stepped forward, but the boy himself was gone.

She searched the faces around her. He seemed to have vanished into thin air. But she had seen him.

And he had seen her.

The grave had been filled, a low mound of fresh earth dark against the grass. Two men wrestled the headstone into place and she read the newly chiseled inscription beneath the name and dates.

Lucinda Vail Talbot
1915–1988
"She lived with us a little while,
An angel from above.
She's gone to heaven whence she came
But left behind her love."

Brother Fesmire, a thin, black-clad figure standing behind the stone, raised both hands in the air and people bowed their heads. For a moment the only sound on the hill was a rustle of leaves from a breeze too faint to register on hot faces.

"The Lord bless you and keep you. The Lord make His face to shine upon you. The Lord lift up His countenance upon you and give you peace. Amen."

The preacher dropped his hands. The crowd stood still a moment longer and then began to turn away, some people moving toward Whit and his family, others starting down the hill. Nan looked frantically among the straggling figures for some glimpse of Tucker. Gabe was at her side, saying something, but she didn't hear the words. At some point she had let go of Stephen's hand and now she moved down the hill alone, hurrying through the crowd, looking for a blond head. She passed one little blond boy—plump and sweating, already moving ponderously like the fat man he would become—and another, much too young, carried by his father.

Then she saw him.

He was up ahead, walking by himself, hands in his pockets.

She ran to catch him.

She put her hand on his shoulder.

He turned to face her and she almost cried out from the shock of seeing not Tucker but a stranger—a boy with dull eyes, half his face disfigured by a bright pink birthmark. They stood staring at each other. From somewhere a woman in a frumpy black hat and veil appeared and gave Nan a worried half smile, half frown, took her son by the hand and led him away. As they went off down the hill Nan could see he was dressed, unlike the boy she had seen, in a Sunday suit and shoes. She stood on the hillside in the sunshine, the hot grass tickling her sandaled feet.

"Nan!"

Sky was coming toward her. She turned to look at him with the foggy sense that they existed in separate universes. He reached her and took her hand, his face registering shock. "Lord, but your hand's cold! You feel faint?"

"I'm fine," she said numbly.

"Look, we got to talk."

By an immense effort of concentration she was able to remember that there had been some unpleasantness between them, but the details were beyond her at this moment. She stared at him, seeing the lines of pain and concern in his face. And another face super-imposed upon it. The face of a young boy with sun-bleached hair and a chip off one front tooth. The face of Tucker Wills.

"Nan?" Gabe was at her elbow, Stephen in tow. She saw a glance pass between him and Sky, the two men sizing each other up but neither speaking. After a moment she found Sky had released her hand.

"You ready to go?" Gabe was saying. She wasn't aware of answering, but the next thing she knew he was leading her off down the hill.

Chapter 20

On the way home from the funeral she was in a daze, scarcely aware of where she was. Gabe drove; Stephen kept to himself in the back seat. Nan stared out the car window, a single image repeating itself ceaselessly in some no-man's-land between her eyes and her brain: the boy facing her across Lucy's grave, the ring on his finger and the pale strands of his hair lifting in the breeze, his chipped front tooth visible as he soundlessly spoke a familiar name.

Annabel—

Again and again she saw it happening. A trick of memory, a product of her imagination? Or some kind of perceptual blip—hallucination? He had been so close. So unmistakably *there*. With dazzling clarity the details were branded onto her optic nerve.

When they got home she sleepwalked into the library and poured herself a brandy. Gabe came in as she was downing it and pouring another.

He eyed her critically. "Is that smart?"

Nan stopped pouring long enough to give him the finger. "I saw him, dammit. I *saw* him."

Eyebrow up. "Saw who?"

Vertigo rose suddenly inside her and she sat down abruptly in the nearest chair, miraculously without spilling her drink. "Tucker."

In extreme slow motion, Gabe's hands went to his hips. He didn't say anything, just stood there looking at her.

"At the grave," she said. "Standing right across from me. One minute he was there. Then he was just—gone."

" 'Gone'?" He managed to make the word sound ridiculous.

Nan shook her head. She wasn't making herself clear. She didn't even know why she was bothering; he wasn't going to believe her anyway.

"Listen," she said. "Lucy was right. There really *is* a ghost. Tucker's ghost. And he's made some kind of connection with Stephen. I think it's through Woody."

Vertigo came swirling back and she closed her eyes, but that made it worse. She opened them again. Gabe was staring at her.

"Christ," he said. "How did you get drunk so fast?"

"I'm not drunk."

"Then you're hysterical." He regarded her steadily for a long moment. "Not surprising, considering the past couple of days. Now"—taking the chair opposite—"let's start over. You say you saw a boy at the funeral."

She nodded.

"And you thought he was Tucker."

"It *was* Tucker," she said, speaking clearly to counteract any more accusations about being drunk.

"What makes you so sure?"

"For Christ's sake. I recognized him. That white-blond hair, the chipped tooth—he even had a ring like Stephen's!"

"Nan! Half the rug rats in the county have blond hair and chipped teeth!" He paused and made an obvious effort to soften his tone. "Look. Your memory of what

Tucker looked like is *two decades old*. You saw a kid, okay. Somebody who resembled Tucker enough to make you *think* it was him. But it wasn't. It was some real flesh-and-blood kid."

"Fine," she said. "If there's no ghost, then who was up in that tree with Stephen? You heard him talking, didn't you? Because I did. And Lucy did."

He was shaking his head. "What I heard was Stephen, acting out the part of his imaginary friend."

"Gabe, it was Tucker's voice!"

"In your head, maybe. The way some kid at the funeral had Tucker's face. Nan—how can you possibly remember the quality of someone's voice, someone you knew for a few months, twenty years ago? You're just filling in the blanks with whatever's at hand!"

"Who threw that board out of the tree?"

"Threw, schmoo! The damn thing fell. Stephen must have grabbed onto it and loosened it a little. While he was climbing down, it worked itself loose the rest of the way, and—"

"Fine, okay." She waved a hand. "I assume you're willing to admit Stephen *was* up in the tree. Or did I imagine that too?"

He scowled. "What are you getting at?"

"I am getting," she said, "at the fact that Stephen is *too small* to get up in that tree by himself. His best jump is about a foot short of the lowest branch. I saw him try it, the day we got here. Gabe, he couldn't do it by himself."

"Maybe not the day you got here. But that was over a month ago. He's grown since then, Nan. I noticed it as soon as I saw him. You're taking a bunch of perfectly normal occurrences and building them into some wacky scenario—"

He went on, but she didn't bother to listen with more than half an ear while he told her that she was overwrought with grief and guilt about Lucy. That she couldn't trust her memory right now, or her perceptions either. The boy she had seen could not possibly have disappeared into thin air. And whoever he was, he had certainly not been the ghost of Tucker Wills. While he talked she remembered the boy's intent gaze, saw his lips form those familiar syllables.

Annabel—

The memory made her head start to swim—or maybe it was the brandy starting to get to her—and she mumbled something and bailed out to go upstairs for a nap. Lying on the bed, she could hear Gabe and Stephen talking downstairs in the kitchen while Gabe fixed the kid a snack. The casual murmur of their voices made a strange counterpoint to her wildly skittering thoughts. After a while there was silence.

It seemed she had just drifted off to sleep when something jounced the bed roughly and she opened heavy eyelids—her throat closing in sudden horror when she saw what it was. Lucy Talbot was sprawled across the foot of the mattress, her hair in disarray, a thin trickle of blood running from the terrible dent in her forehead to stain the white bedspread. As Nan lay staring, frozen with shock, Lucy sat up and twisted her long hair into a semblance of its customary knot.

It's Tucker, honey, she said. *He wants Stephen. He knew I was on to him, and that's why he pried that board loose and dropped it down on me. You have to stop him. He's lonely. He wants somebody to play with. Nan, he wants your little boy.*

Lucy, Nan tried to say, but the word caught in her throat. Lucy smiled at her and shook her head gently from side to side, blood dripping down her face to stain the front of her dress as she gradually faded from sight.

At that point Nan woke up, for real this time, and found Mister Mustard sitting at the foot of the bed, washing the back of a furry thigh. Her heart was pounding and her head felt as fragile as blown glass. The dream had seemed so horrifyingly real that she found herself examining the bedspread for bloodstains. The cat stopped its bathing process to give her a yellow-eyed blink. She glanced at the clock: she had been asleep for over an hour. From downstairs came the murmur of the television. She got out of bed and slowly descended the kitchen stairs.

"Oh. You're up." Gabe was closing the refrigerator door, a beer in his hand. In the living room there was a baseball game on TV. "Feeling better?"

"Where's Stephen?" she said.

He took a swig of beer, keeping his eyes on her. "Off playing."

The words hit her like a dull blow. "With Woody?"

Shrug. "Who else?"

The dream welled up again, overlaid by the image of Lucy's open grave and the boy facing her across it.

He wants your little boy.

Nan's knees went fluttery and she sat down hastily at the table. "Gabe—"

"Now don't get started." He brought his beer over and sat down across from her. "I've got an idea, okay?"

She looked at him speechlessly, unable to imagine what he was going to say. Events had gone wildly, impossibly out of control in a very short space of time, and he seemed completely unaware of the fact.

"We're going to find this kid you saw," he was saying gently. "We're going to find out where he lives, and go see him, and you can touch him, and then you'll know he's real, and that he's not Tucker."

She kept on looking at him. He patted her hand.

"While you were sleeping, I called the people at the church—the ones who run Stephen's summer program. I thought they might have some idea who this kid is. They didn't know anybody answering that description, but they said he probably lives back in the mountains, in a place called Stepp Hollow. They gave me the name of the local preacher there, a Brother Woolbright. Said he might know the kid. I got directions to his house. Tomorrow we'll go check it out."

Nan looked down at his hand on hers. He patted it again. Then a roar from the stadium crowd got his attention, and he pushed back his chair and headed for the living room.

She went on sitting at the table in the wash of afternoon sun. Shimmering heat lay over the pasture; birds called in the hazy distances. Gabe's scheme struck her as a bad idea. Even if she had cherished any hopes of finding the boy she had seen at the funeral, she still would have doubted the wisdom of venturing into the mountains. The residents of Stepp Hollow were bound to be aloof and clannish. Without an introduction from someone they knew, they were likely to resent any intrusion by outsiders. It occurred to her that Sky could have acted as a liaison, but his help was no longer something she could count on.

There's times when things go a certain way and you can't do a blessed thing but just lay back and let 'em.

She remembered him saying that, early in their relationship, commenting on the sense of superiority she had made little effort to conceal. In the context of the last couple of days the words had taken on a sinister coloration, seeming to mock the fact of her powerlessness, her sense of things going out of control.

Was it possible Gabe was right—was she letting her imagination run wild? Had her vision of Tucker at the grave been just another of those vivid memory flashes?

No. I saw him. He was there.

Again she saw his lips move, saw his hand reach out. What did he want? The memory of her grotesque dream, Lucy sprawled on the bed upstairs, came to her as if in answer.

He's lonely. He wants somebody to play with . . . he wants your little boy.

*   *   *

"Woody? Woody!"

Even to his own ears, Stephen's voice sounded as high and reedy as the rust-colored bird that was always circling high in the air over the hill. Woody said it was called a kestrel hawk. It always sounded as if it was frantic, and Stephen felt frantic right now, because he couldn't find Woody.

He had thought if he sat still on the top of the hill, Woody might come. But he had been sitting here half an hour or more, and there was still no sign of him. Stephen shaded his eyes and looked down toward the creek, watching a breeze scatter sunlight across the feathery yellow grass. But there was no sign of Woody. Maybe he was afraid he was in trouble, because he had been up in the tree when the board from the tree house had fallen and hit Cousin Lucy and—

(killed her)

Stephen flinched away from the memory. Dad had said it was an accident. No one's fault. Not his, or Woody's either. He wanted to find Woody and tell him so.

"Wood—ee!"

This time, far away, he thought there was an answering call. Like an echo of his own voice, but not quite. It seemed to come from the pine woods, and he ran down the hill toward them, seeing the green branches stirring even though now there wasn't any wind. As he approached the trees their cool fragrance came to meet him, suggesting shade and silence even on the hottest day. His mom and Cousin Sky had said never to go into the pine woods, but he had gone in anyway with Woody, a couple of times. With Woody he was in no danger of getting lost. Woody knew his way around.

"Woody?"

There was no answer. Only the pine branches whispering together.

"Woody, my dad says it was an accident. The thing that happened. He says it wasn't anybody's fault. Not mine. Not yours." He swallowed. "Nobody's."

He peered into the woods and for an instant he thought he glimpsed Woody—a shadowy figure standing far back among the trees. Woody held out his hand as if beckoning him. But then Stephen must have blinked or something, because all at once the dim figure was gone.

The branches were motionless now, and around him the whole world was still with the immeasurable stillness of a tree-covered hillside on a sunny July afternoon.

Chapter 21

The sign for 617 was half hidden by the shaggy branches of an enormous pine, and Nan might have missed the turn if Gabe hadn't said, "There it is."

State Road 617 was a gravel track that wound between fenced fields in the direction of the ridge. She slowed and turned onto it, wishing it was a nice day. Under cloud-heavy skies the mountains had a forbidding look. They no longer sheltered; they loomed. And the unbroken ranks of trees that radiated serenity in the sunlight seemed to conceal menace instead. Or maybe it was just her state of mind.

She looked over at Gabe. He was fiddling with the radio, trying without success to get rid of the static on the dial. He had high hopes for this expedition and she was keeping her mouth shut, going along with him because she wanted to give his theory a chance. Because she actually *wanted* this whole business to be all in her head. Wanted the boy she had seen to be some real live little hillbilly, some local Jethro or Jim-Bob, and her reading of the situation to be completely off base. Because in this particular situation, the discovery that she was losing her mind would come as an enormous relief.

As they began to ascend the ridge the road curved sharply to the right and the trees closed in on either side, their leaves a peculiar lurid green in the flat light. They were heading almost due north now, the valley opening below on their right as they went higher. Nan drove carefully. The road surface was rough, not much better than the one up Sleepy Gal leading to the Larkin cabin, but unlike Sky she was taking it at a reasonable speed.

They followed the rolling top of the ridge for nearly a mile before the hollow came in sight. Beyond thinning trees to their left, a deep well of land nestled among the forested slopes, a few rooftops visible in its green depths. It amazed Nan to see it there, so completely hidden from the outside world, only minutes away from the bottomland, yet wrapped in an air of remoteness that might have suited a hamlet in Tibet. She kept her foot on the brake as the road began a winding, precipitous descent, the mountains seeming to rise from their haunches and tower over them as they entered the hollow.

She was starting to feel claustrophobic when the appearance of a dwelling on the right-hand side of the road distracted her—a trailer, robin's-egg blue in color, set on cinder blocks at the center of a small area of cleared ground. One tree had been allowed to remain in the clearing, tethered by a clothesline to one corner of the trailer. Nan saw overalls, shirts, ragged dishtowels, before her attention was caught by what seemed to be a menagerie inhabiting the yard.

Gabe was crinkling his jotted directions with an air of dissatisfaction. "Pull over, okay?"

She stopped the car. On the side of the tree opposite the clothesline, a crude two-dimensional dog made of painted plywood stood with its forepaws planted on the trunk, nose lifted as if it had treed a cat. And sure enough, now that she looked, there was a matching plywood cat attached to a branch above. Nearby a couple of pink plastic flamingos on sticks protruded from the scanty grass. From the top of a nearby mailbox labeled HARMON, a ceramic raccoon grinned a Disney grin, and near the trailer's front door a glossy Bambi, easily two feet high, cocked its head sideways with unnerving cuteness.

"My God," Gabe said. "We're in Queens."

The door of the trailer opened and a dirty-faced little girl looked out at them, then disappeared back inside. A moment later a woman with a baby in her arms came to the doorway, making no move to approach the car, just watching them. She was young, under thirty, sallow and tired-looking, wearing a cheap print dress. Her lusterless brown hair was long, past her shoulders, and looked as if she hadn't got around to brushing it yet. The little girl peeked out from behind her.

Gabe leaned out the car window. "Hi. Can you tell me how to get to Mr. Woolbright's house?"

The woman didn't answer. He pulled his head back into the car and glanced at Nan. "Okay, time for the famous Phillips charm. Cover my back."

He opened the passenger-side door and climbed out, leaving it ajar. Nan wondered if she should accompany him—if maybe the woman was intimidated by a stranger, a man. She tried to see Gabe through unfamiliar eyes: a bearded, average-size guy starting to spread through the middle, hairline in retreat and wire-rimmed glasses riding the end of his nose. It was hard to see how anyone could be intimidated, but she turned off the engine and got out of the car, remembering to smile. It was all wasted effort; the woman wasn't looking at her. Gabe had come to a stop beside Bambi and was delivering his prepared speech.

"My name is Phillips, Gabriel Phillips, and my wife and I recently moved into the valley. We're looking for a Reverend Woolbright. Does he live around here?"

The woman shifted something in her mouth from one cheek to the other and at the same time, in a perfectly symmetrical movement, transferred her baby to her other hip. Her eyes flicked toward Gabe's crotch and away.

"Two mile up th' road," she said. The little girl started out from behind her, toward Gabe, and she reached down and pulled her back. The baby started to cry. From inside the trailer there was a muffled thump and the woman's eyes cut briefly to one side and then the other, but she didn't turn. "Two mile," she repeated.

"Okay, thanks." Gabe, backing up, barely missed tripping over Bambi. The woman smirked, shifting her gaze to meet Nan's across the distance between them. The look was unfathomable. Nan gave a little wave, feeling foolish—doubly so when the woman didn't respond. She ducked back into the car and started the engine.

Gabe joined her a moment later, muttering. "So much for Southern hospitality. Maybe we should have brought one of your relatives along as an interpreter."

"Maybe," Nan said. But she was no longer in a position to ask favors of Sky, and she couldn't imagine who else there was. Cassie was always much too busy, and there was no one else she knew well enough to ask. Lucy would have been perfect. But Lucy would have been the first to warn them that their expedition was in vain.

The rutted road ducked beneath a dark canopy of trees, awakening her claustrophobia again. The whole excursion already seemed doomed, the hostility of the woman in the trailer merely a harbinger of worse to come. Nan was following her thoughts, only a modicum of attention on her driving, and she would have driven right past the next house but for Gabe's yelp of "Stop!"

She stepped on the brake too hard and saw him, out of the corner of her eye, brace himself against the dashboard. The car rocked. He shook his head at her, opened his door without further comment and got out.

This one was a real log cabin, like Pen and Flutie Larkin's, spaces between the logs filled with yellowish plaster and the roof made of rusty tin, but set among close-growing trees it had a hooded, secret look. Underbrush grew right up to its door. Nan thought that even if she had been paying proper attention she might have missed the place. It was deserted, probably abandoned. Gabe poked around it, knocking on the crude plank door and trying to see in the windows.

"Nobody home." He came back to the car and climbed in, picking burrs off his pants. "Let's keep going."

As they pulled away Nan glanced in the rearview mirror and saw a car come around a bend in the road behind them. Primer-splotched hood, damaged front grille—she felt a qualm in her guts. Jerry Ray Watkins. He was driving slowly, as if he had no intention of passing them or even catching up. Just following them. She watched the car in the rearview mirror, checking it every few seconds until another twist of the road hid it from sight.

"We're being followed," she said. Gabe turned around to look. "Back there around that bend," she told him. "I know the guy. He's a local yokel. A real lowlife."

He grunted. "Probably lives somewhere around here. You're getting xenophobic, my dear."

Maybe. After all, Watkins hadn't actually done anything to her. Their near collision had been an accident.
Sky's series of lies, she realized, were mainly what she
had against the man. As they drove on she kept checking
the mirror, but Watkins's car did not reappear. They hit
a patch of fog, white wisps hovering eerily on the surface of the road, then drove out of it as the road began to
climb. Emerging from the woods onto higher ground,
they found themselves overlooking the hollow from the
south. Another house came in sight up ahead, perched
on the steep wooded mountainside, a long rickety flight
of steps mounting to its front porch. Nan glanced at the
mailbox and abruptly hit the brake, evoking another
spluttered curse from Gabe.

"What the—"

"Wills." She indicated the crude letters painted on a
mailbox that leaned drunkenly to one side of the porch
steps. "That was Tucker's last name. Wills."

"Yeah?"

"Well, these people are probably relatives of his."

"Maybe they are." His tone was one of heavy
patience. "What's that got to do—"

A voice hailed them from above. "Howdy, folks.
Y'all lost your way?"

By craning her neck out the window Nan was able to
catch sight of the speaker, an elderly man leaning over
the porch railing high above them. She got out of the
car. Gabe climbed out on his side and shaded his eyes to
look up.

"Well, no, not exactly. Actually, we're looking for
someone who lives around here. My name is Gabriel
Phillips. This is my wife, Nan."

The old man wore a straw hat, ancient colorless pants
with suspenders, a sleeveless T-shirt. A hefty potbelly

seemed to have drawn its sustenance from his stick-thin
arms and legs. He nodded. "Virgil Wills. Why don't you
folks join me up here on my perch?"

As they ascended the stairs—there were at least
twenty of them, ladder-steep—he kept up a running
monologue.

"Call this my perch, see. I'm so high up here, I feel
just like a bird sittin' in a tree. Soon as supper's done
most nights, I say to my wife, 'Goin' out on the front
perch now, and set a spell.' She don't like it out here.
Bugs eat her up. They don't bother me none. 'Too
tough,' I tell her. 'I ain't sweet like you.' "

He seized the back of a rickety-looking chair and
pushed it in Nan's direction as she reached the top of the
steps. "Have a seat, honey. Who y'all lookin' for?"

Nan sat down, relieved by his cordiality. It had made
her more nervous than she cared to acknowledge, all this
driving around in the backwoods, accosting strangers
and questioning them. But she was somehow reassured
by this unexpected encounter with what was almost certainly a branch of Tucker's family. However flimsy, it
was still a connection.

She looked down the road. If Watkins was still following them, he should be along any minute. But his car
failed to appear and she found her gaze irresistibly rising
to the vista beyond. She was surprised by how high up
they were: she could see over the entire hollow. The fog
they had driven through was visible as a swirling
witches' cauldron of mist among the trees below.

Behind her Gabe was saying "We're looking for a
guy named Woolbright. Someone at the Methodist
Church in Breezy suggested we get in touch with him. I
understand he lives around here."

"Well, son, that's right. But I'm sorry to say Brother

Woolbright's not at home today. He's up at Gaylesville till the weekend." He winked. "Between you and me, he's gone courtin'. It's took his mind clean off God."

Nan smiled, but Gabe was too focused on his mission to notice the pleasantry. "Then maybe you can help us. We're looking for a little boy who might live around here. Blond, around ten or eleven, with a chipped front tooth. Sound like anybody you know?"

Virgil Wills tipped his hat back and scratched his forehead. "Not offhand, but don't you take my word for it—folks round here got more chi'ren than a hound dog's got fleas. I mighta missed one or two. Towhead, you say? Let's ask my wife. She knows 'em all."

He crossed the creaky porch to the screen door of the cabin and opened it to lean in. "Janey? We got us some company, honey."

They heard light footsteps come from the back of the cabin.

"Why, Virgil," a voice said, "I thought you were out here talking to yourself. He does, you know," said Virgil's wife, closing the screen door quickly behind her (the action eloquent of years of arguments about letting insects into the house) and turning to hold out her hand to Nan. "I'm Janey Wills."

"Nan Lucas," Nan said. She found she had gotten to her feet. Janey Wills was extraordinarily beautiful in what must be her late sixties; as a young woman she must have been nothing short of spectacular. Familiar with the world of high fashion, Nan would have said she had encountered every known variety of female beauty, yet this old woman's face astounded her with its timeless purity of line, as simple as a seashell's. White hair and aging skin had only added a poignant quality to its perfection. Janey had turned to Gabe now and was greeting him graciously. Nan saw his stunned face and knew he was thinking, along with her, What is *this* doing *here*?

"May I offer you something to drink? There's lemonade, or you might want to try some sweet birch tea—Virgil and I prefer it on days like today, when the air's so heavy."

Her accent, Nan realized, had only a trace of the local twang, as if she had been born here but educated outside the valley. She found herself mystified by this exquisite, apparently educated woman, living here in a cabin in the mountains with a man who, pleasant as he seemed, was still your basic hillbilly. Her curiosity came as a welcome relief from the past few days of grief and shock. When Janey invited her to the kitchen to help brew the tea, she jumped at the chance to talk with her, leaving Gabe to whatever rapport he cared to establish with Virgil.

"We don't get many visitors here," Janey said, leading the way through the cabin's front room toward the kitchen at the back. Nan had an impression of gleaming plank floors decorated with bright hooked rugs, handmade curtains at the windows and a sturdy pine bookcase bulging with hardback volumes. The kitchen was, if not modern, at least twentieth century, with a gas range and a refrigerator several generations younger than the one in Pen and Flutie Larkin's cabin.

Janey filled an old tin kettle at the sink and set it on the stove to boil, choosing a glass canister of tea from among half a dozen on a shelf over the counter. She took cups and a chipped blue china teapot from a pine hutch and set them on a tray, hands moving deftly among her possessions with a rhythm born of many years. Nan watched her, wanting to broach the topic of Tucker but not knowing how.

"Well, we're not exactly visitors," she said. "My son and I moved into the valley a little over a month ago. My grandmother died last winter and left me her house and land."

Janey turned and looked at her. "That's it—now I know who you put me in mind of! You're Annabel Stephens's granddaughter. Why, I remember when you visited her that summer—how long ago was it?"

"Twenty years," Nan said.

Janey was spooning tea into the pot. The water in the kettle began to whisper, on its way to a boil. Outside the window a jay's harsh squawk cut the air.

"Twenty years," Janey said at last. "It doesn't seem that long." She shook her head a little. "I hadn't seen much of Annabel for a good while. But now she's gone, I feel her absence. She was a good person. Some of the bottomland folks act like we don't exist up here on the ridge, but Annabel wasn't like that. Way back in 1947, when I graduated from Teachers' College in Knoxville and came back here to start a school, she gave me money to buy books."

"You started a school here?"

"And kept it going thirty-six years," Janey said. "Men came from all up and down the ridge and raised me a cabin just above Silverleaf Falls. A lot more folks lived up here then. Ed Luther donated a wood stove so we wouldn't freeze to death when the cold weather came on. I had fifteen children in my first class, and Rufus Bessey. Rufus was thirty-eight and set on learning to read. His mother had always read the Bible out loud on Sunday mornings, but she was going blind so Rufus figured he'd better learn to do it for her." She smiled and Nan smiled back.

"Did he learn?"

Steam was billowing from the kettle's spout. Janey wrapped a dish towel around the handle and lifted it off the stove, poured boiling water into the pot. "Oh, he learned." She set the kettle back on the stove. "But except for the primer, I don't believe he ever read anything but the Bible, and only on Sundays. That's how it was in these parts back then. Folks thought if you got your dose of the Good Book, that was reading enough."

She looked down, smiling faintly as she stirred the tea. The spoon clinked against the ceramic pot. Nan watched her profile, wishing she had her camera, then realized she was staring and forced her gaze away. She heard Janey say, "So you're Annabel's granddaughter. What brings you to Stepp Hollow?"

"Well . . ." Unable to think of any smooth transition to the subject on her mind, Nan gave up and blurted, "Could I ask you something? Was Tucker Wills related to you?"

The other woman nodded slowly. "Tucker was Virgil's nephew. His brother Caleb's son."

Nan swallowed. The vague idea that had begun to form as soon as she saw the name on the mailbox was now taking definite shape. She took a breath. "Do you . . . have any photographs of him?"

She knew how odd the question must seem, coming on top of this out-of-nowhere visit. But if Janey was surprised, her manners were too good to let it show.

"I believe there must be some in our family album," she said. "Let me just fetch it."

While she was gone Nan sat watching steam curl

from the teapot's spout, her thoughts a busy, incoherent whirl. If Janey had a picture of Tucker—if the picture resembled the boy she had seen at the funeral yesterday—if she could be certain it wasn't just, as Gabe claimed, a matter of her imagination filling in the blanks in her memory—

There were quick footsteps and Janey was back, a thick black photograph album open in her arms. She pushed the tea tray aside and laid the album on the table in front of Nan.

"There aren't many of Tucker, and that's a fact. Now that I recall, most times he wouldn't hold still long enough to have his picture made! But here's one of him with Caleb."

A bony young man in a baseball cap stood against a white clapboard wall, holding the hand of a boy about four or five. The two of them squinted into the sun, their eyes reduced to dark slits by the glare. The child's light hair came close to blending into the white wall behind him. He looked completely generic. Disappointment washed through Nan.

"Are there any of him from the time when—when I knew him? When he was around ten?"

Janey turned a page or two and pointed, and this time Nan felt her heart begin a hard, measured pounding. The boy in this picture was the right age, the right size. . . . Again he stood with his father, this time holding up a fish he had caught, the two of them with broad grins on their faces under a shady tree with a glint of water in the background.

Nan bent closer. Captured more than two decades before, by the interaction of light with sensitized silver nitrate particles, Tucker's face in the photograph was no bigger than the nail on her little finger. Yet beneath the booming of her heartbeat in her ears, she had not a shred of doubt that it was the same face she had seen yesterday, looking at her from the other side of Lucy Talbot's open grave. All at once the uncanniness of the whole business, its sheer impossibility, was borne in upon her with sudden dizzying force. She covered the photograph with a shaking hand.

After a moment she heard Janey say quietly, "What brings you here? After all this time?"

Nan swallowed and sat back in her chair, hugging her elbows with cold hands. The task of framing an answer to that question was so daunting she couldn't even begin to try. But the same cloudy impulse that had made her stop at the sight of the mailbox, the same thing that had prodded her to ask about the photographs, was still driving her. There was information here. And maybe a chance of fathoming the impossible events that seemed to be closing in around her.

"You know—" The words stuck in her throat and she had to stop and swallow once more before she could go on. "I don't really remember much about—about the accident. It's pretty much a total blank to me."

Janey closed the photograph album and set it aside. "That's only natural. Whyever would you want to remember something so painful?"

"But I do," Nan said. "I mean, I feel like I ought to." She hesitated, unnerved by her own sudden need for the details, afraid of seeming like a ghoul. Janey took the top off the teapot and gave it another stir. She shook her head slightly and Nan said, "Please."

The urgency in her voice stopped the clinking spoon. Their eyes met, and slowly the other woman put the spoon down and lowered herself into the opposite chair.

For a long moment, except for the chattering birds outside, the kitchen was completely silent.

"It happened late in the day," Janey said at last. Her soft voice seemed hardly to break the stillness. "You and Tucker had been out playing all afternoon, and it was already starting to get dark when Caleb said they heard you screaming from clear across the creek. When they ran down there, Caleb and Annabel, they found you just soaking wet from head to toe." She paused and gave Nan a close look. "You're sure you want to hear this?"

Nan nodded shakily. She had no conscious memory of the events Janey was recounting—no recollection at all, and so far these details seemed completely alien, rousing no echoes in her memory. It was still difficult for her to believe she had ever made that winter visit. But nonetheless her heart was pounding and her palms were slippery.

"Well, Annabel took you back to the house and Caleb went running toward the quarry, following your footsteps in the snow. He said when he got there, his heart just died inside him. Because there was broken ice in the middle of the quarry, and no sign of Tucker anywhere.

"He said it was all written there in the ice and snow, what had happened, plain as words. That big jagged hole in the ice, with the black water just oozing over the edges, and the snow all trampled where you'd gone running through the woods, looking for a branch to reach Tucker, to pull him out. The branch was still there, lying on the ice. But he'd gone down too quick for you to save him. Just too quick."

Blurred images had begun to stir at the back of Nan's mind, grainy and jerky as an old newsreel. She saw a small figure running headlong through the frozen white woods. Saw it find a broken branch on the

ground and retrace its steps, dragging the branch awkwardly along.

*Trying to run and getting nowhere ... seeing my
breath form icy clouds in the air in front of me ...*

"Caleb said when the two of you fell into the water,
Tucker must have been able to push you out. But he was
bigger than you, and the ice was too thin to take his
weight—must have just kept on breaking under him
every time he tried to climb out. The branch was a good
idea. But that water was too cold, and he just went down
too quick."

Inside Nan's head the silent film continued, showing
the figure of a little girl stumbling back to the edge
of the quarry. Close-up of her terrified face—the eyes
widening, then the mouth, in a soundless scream. Cut to
the black, ragged, empty hole in the ice. The camera
zooming in on that horrifying splintered shape.

A touch on her arm made her jump. She found herself
looking into Janey's worried face.

"Drink this," the older woman said, and put a
steaming cup of tea in her hand. Nan sipped and felt the
hot liquid scald her throat. "Lord, honey," Janey said. "I
declare I don't know what I was thinking of, telling you
that story. Here you haven't been in my house ten minutes and I've practically made you faint."

Nan took another, more cautious sip of tea. It had a
bracing, decidedly herbal taste.

"No, I'm glad you told me. I can remember it now, I
think, some of it. It still doesn't seem real. But it's
better than having just a—a blank where the memory
ought to be."

And yet had the blank been as total as she had
thought? The recollection of frantically searching the
woods for a fallen branch, hurrying to find one and

return in time to save Tucker, had been encoded in the nightmare whose origins had until now been a mystery. She hesitated. Then: "I'm sorry. Sorry I couldn't save him."

"Oh, mercy! No one blames you—it was an accident! If anyone at all was to blame, it was Tucker. He was older. He should have known better than to go out on that ice. I just thank the good Lord you didn't both drown."

Nan shrugged. Janey took her hand and squeezed it. "A young woman like you—you ought to be looking forward, not back. The past is finished. Over and done with."

Oh, don't I wish.

But she didn't say it. The moment hung awkwardly until the sight of the tray seemed to remind Janey that the menfolk were still out on the porch, waiting for their promised refreshments. She pushed back her chair, rose briskly and picked up the tray. "Why, I almost forgot about their tea! Will you get the door?"

Nan scrambled to her feet and went ahead to hold the screen, remembering to shut it promptly behind her. On the porch Janey set the tray down on a low pine table and poured the cups, handing them around. Nan saw Gabe set his cup down on the porch beside his chair. He hated herbal tea.

Virgil had turned to Janey. "Do you know that young'un they're lookin' for?"

Janey looked puzzled. "What?"

"A boy around ten or eleven," Gabe said. "Blond hair, a chipped front tooth. He was in Breezy yesterday, and the people at the Methodist Church seem to think he might be from around here."

Janey had turned to look at him while he spoke. Now

her gaze returned to Nan. Their eyes met and held as Janey said quietly, "No. He's not from around here."

"Ain't she somethin'?" Virgil said. "Why, she remembers every name of every child that's growed up here on this ridge since Lord knows when, and can tell you stories on 'em, too. Why, there was one young fella put a dead skunk in the schoolhouse stove one time—"

Janey rose abruptly to her feet and moved toward the far end of the porch, motioning Nan to follow her. Nan did so, hearing Virgil's chatty voice rambling on. She felt numb all over, except for her hardworking heart. Janey was standing at the porch railing, looking out over the treetops. When Nan reached her side she said, "Why did you come here? Tell me the truth."

At least the railing provided a solid support to lean on. Nan said flatly, "I saw Tucker yesterday."

At this point she was past caring if anyone believed her or not. Janey said nothing for a long interval. When she finally spoke her voice was light and almost dreamy.

"My grandmother told me a story once. She said that during the winter of 1900 there was a terrible influenza epidemic up here in the mountains, and everybody in the family came down sick except her. My grandfather, my father and his brother, and their little sister who wasn't but seven years old. My grandmother nursed them. The boys weren't so sick, but my grandfather was real bad, and so was Rebecca, the little girl. Finally she died. For a while my grandfather looked like he was going to die, too, but then he began to get better."

Her fingers kneaded the railing as she talked. "He'd been so sick, he didn't even know Rebecca had died. When my grandmother thought he was strong enough, she told him. He didn't say much, but she said she could see he took it hard. It was like a light went out in his eyes.

"She said things went on, the way they do regardless of any trouble or sorrow. Then one day my grandfather mentioned he'd seen Rebecca, standing out by the pump in the yard. She asked him what did he mean— Rebecca was dead and gone. He just sort of smiled. A few weeks later, he told her he'd seen Rebecca sitting cross-legged by the hearth, the way she liked to do when she was alive.

"That was when my grandmother started to get mad. She said he was talking crazy, and she wouldn't have any more of it. She said it was bad enough Rebecca was gone, without having him pretending she was still around. After that he didn't say anything about Rebecca for a long time. Then, one fall afternoon a year or so later, my grandmother was in the kitchen making an apple pie and she heard him calling her to come out to the porch. When she got out there, he pointed into the yard and said, 'Look there. You see her now?'

"My grandmother said she looked, and all she saw was a whirl of dead leaves—you know the way the wind will pick them up and spin them in a circle? That was all she saw. But then she said the afternoon sunlight struck through them, and just for a second she saw her little girl, standing there in the middle of those whirling gold leaves."

Janey fell silent. Above her own heartbeat Nan could hear, without being aware of the words, the drone of Virgil's voice continuing behind them. At last Janey said, "That was the only time my grandmother ever saw her, but my grandfather kept on seeing her for years. My grandmother said she thought in a way he was keeping her there. She'd died, you know, without him knowing, and it was like he just couldn't let her go."

She was silent again. Nan understood what she was trying to say, but the message seemed wide of its mark. It was not her refusal to part with Tucker that was holding his spirit here on earth. According to Lucy, he had been haunting Annabel's property since his death—while all the time she herself had virtually forgotten him.

Glancing out over the tree-covered mountain slopes, the hollow shrouded in mist, again she had a fleeting but heartfelt wish that the sun would come out. The rumble of an engine reached her ears, distracting her; a moment later, Jerry Ray Watkins's car sped past on the road below the Willses' cabin, going much faster than was sane on such a poor surface. Leaning forward over the porch railing, Nan got no more than a glimpse of Watkins's fat, ginger-bearded face bent close to the wheel. Then the car was past, hidden by the trees, the sound of its engine gradually diminishing up the mountain. She glanced at Virgil, who had gotten up to join them at the rail. He was shaking his head.

"Wonder what's got ol' Jerry Ray so riled up?"

Janey made a *tsk* sound. "He's worse than ever since he went to prison. You know, I believe he's gone and built himself another still somewhere. You'd think he'd learn his lesson. Most folks would. But not Jerry Ray."

"He's a moonshiner?" Gabe said in disbelief.

Virgil nodded. "You see how jumpy he looked? Must think y'all are the law, come snoopin' after that still of his."

Gabe snorted. "Do we look like law enforcement officers?"

Virgil gave a dry cackle. "Maybe not, son. But any

stranger's face'll do to make that boy jumpy. When you got a business venture that runs afoul of the gov'ment, you just naturally feel a little bit nervous all the time."

Gabe drove on the way home. They didn't talk. Nan sat lost in some process more akin to mental nail-biting than actual thought. The neat theory of mistaken identity had been more or less blown away by Janey Wills's flat denial of knowing anyone who answered Tucker's description. Now Gabe was in a bad mood—but it was nothing compared to what it would be if she should tell him about seeing the photograph that had confirmed her side of the story. Or about the ease with which Janey had accepted the idea that Tucker's ghost might be hanging around. He might dismiss Lucy Talbot as a gullible old woman, but Janey was educated, obviously intelligent . . .

"We've got company," Gabe said suddenly.

His eyes were on the rearview mirror, and Nan twisted around in her seat to see what was bothering him. Another car had appeared at a distance behind them on the narrow road, and her heart sank as she recognized it. Jerry Ray Watkins again.

"What does *he* want?" she said.

"Maybe he doesn't like us trespassing in his neck of the woods. Wants to escort us out."

The reflection of sky and leaves on the windshield behind them rendered Watkins invisible, but Nan had a clear picture of his face in her mind. It was easy to imagine that face emblazoned across the cover of one of the true-crime books her friend Genevieve back in New York was always reading: the patchily whiskered jowls, the piggish eyes with their flat, mean look.

"Well, we're going," she said shakily. "That ought to make him happy."

The blue trailer appeared up ahead and she noticed that the laundry had been taken off the line. A quick glance back showed her Watkins's car beginning to close the distance between them.

"Gabe. He's catching up."

"Well, there's not much I can do about it on this road. If we want to leave him behind, we can't do it till we get on a paved surface."

Nan tried to convince herself she was overreacting. What could Watkins do to them, after all? Rear-end them, okay, but any collision would cause far worse damage to his rusty rattletrap than to the solidly built Volvo. No, he was just trying to intimidate them. And she had to say he was doing a damn good job. All at once Janey's disapproving remark about his moonshine business came back to her, accompanied by a mental picture of Watkins dumping something into the back of Sky's truck, then climbing into the cab beside Sky. Was *that* the secret of the association between the two men— was her cousin a silent partner in the illegal brewing business?

Right now it was hard to feel much satisfaction from guessing the probable cause for Sky's inept series of lies about Watkins. She was finding that she was powerless to prevent her head from swiveling around to look back every few seconds as they climbed the steep road out of the hollow. Watkins was maintaining an even distance behind them now, maybe twenty feet, and she could make out a silhouette of head and burly shoulders behind the windshield. An ugly thought occurred to her.

"Gabe. Do you think he has a gun?"

The Volvo's transmission gave a distinct groan of relief as they reached the top of the ridge and the road leveled off.

Gabe threw her a glance. "He's a redneck, isn't he? I'm sure he has a gun. But it's probably a shotgun and, since this is not the movies, he can't possibly operate it while he's driving. Besides, maybe he'll lose interest in us now that we're out of his territory."

But he didn't. As they drove back along the ridge the junkmobile continued to cruise behind them—too close for comfort but never catching up, never dropping back. Even when she forced herself to look away from it and face the road in front of them, Nan could still feel its presence looming behind them. Gabe said nothing, but she could see from the twist of his lips, the way his eyes kept flicking to the rearview mirror, that he was annoyed. And yes, scared.

They made their descent into the valley, bumping at last onto the gravel road. Gabe maintained the same speed for a few moments, watching the other car in his mirror. "Go home, you idiot."

Watkins kept coming. Gabe's eyes shifted to Nan. "Okay. Time to lose this turkey."

The Volvo surged forward and she felt her pulse rate do the same. Her shoulder harness clutched her. She clutched back, holding the strap with both hands as the green countryside flew past in a sudden blur. Gabe hunched grimly over the wheel, slowing but not stopping as they made the right turn onto 622, then speeding up again to send the car flying over the narrow road, hugging the curves and zooming up and down the hills like a roller coaster.

Nan peeked over at the speedometer and saw they were really going only a little over sixty, but it seemed like ninety on the virtually shoulderless road lined with tall woods on one side, barbed-wire fencing and a rocky drainage ditch on the other. Behind them Jerry Ray Watkins, taken by surprise, was nowhere in sight.

Fortunately for them, State Road 622, winding and narrow as it was, had no sharp turns and the Volvo seemed to negotiate it easily even at high speed. They were nearing Annabel's, passing the culvert where the creek ran under the road, and then her woods came into view as they hurtled toward the entrance to the driveway.

"Hang on," Gabe snapped. "Bailout time."

He braked and turned sharply right, but the driveway's surface offered poor purchase for the wheels and Nan was thrown hard against her shoulder harness as the car skidded wildly on the gravel. There was an ominous *thump* from underneath, a brief rattle of branches against the windshield as they sideswiped the woods on the side of the drive. They came to a rocking stop.

The engine died. In the momentary silence they could hear another engine, growing louder and then deafening as Jerry Ray Watkins roared past on the road behind them. Looking out the window, Nan saw his head turn in a startled movement as he caught sight of them.

For a split second she saw the fat jowly face with its scraggly reddish beard and dirty cap pulled low, and felt his eyes take in her features as well. It gave her a jolt, a sense of violation, as if he had touched her. She flinched, but his car didn't stop. They sat in stunned silence.

At the house, Gabe stopped swearing just long enough to announce that he needed a drink.

Nan looked at her watch. "I'd better go pick up Stephen."

Church camp didn't end till noon and it was barely ten-thirty, but in spite of the fact that she could have used a drink herself after this morning's adventures, she had her reasons for wanting to go to town early. She desperately needed to talk to Cooper. And so she headed down the porch steps toward the car, faltering to a stop as she noticed an ominous dark stain on the gravel underneath it.

"Gabe? Can you come here a minute?"

He came out of the house grumbling. She pointed and he bent stiffly to peer under the car.

"Goddammit. I need a flashlight."

Nan fetched it and hovered, awaiting a diagnosis, while he knelt and examined the Volvo's underside. At last he grunted and sat back on his haunches. "Damn oil pan looks like it's punctured. Must have happened when we pulled into the driveway. Double-damn that asshole hillbilly. We're going to need a tow truck."

"Great. How am I going to pick up Stephen?"

He jerked his head at Annabel's car, still parked beside the house where Sky had left it. "Does that thing work? Or is it just a lawn ornament?"

Nan remembered Sky bragging about tuning up Estelle's engine. Theoretically the grand old dame was in tiptop condition for someone her age. Peering into the car, she could see keys dangling from the ignition. When she got in and turned the engine over, it caught smoothly and settled into a well-bred mutter like an elderly lady talking to herself. Nan looked up to see Gabe watching her, hands on his hips.

"Don't get kidnapped by any antique auto buffs."

Nan repressed the image of Jerry Ray Watkins's

junkmobile speeding past, his startled face turning to look at her. She gunned Estelle's engine and offered Gabe her best Southern drawl with a levity she was far from feeling. "Now honey, don't you fret."

Chapter 22

Someone in the back of Bev's Valley Luncheonette was washing dishes. Sitting across from Cooper in their usual booth, Nan took a certain comfort in the ordinary clatter of crockery and utensils, set against the craziness of what she was telling him. She had started with Stephen climbing the oak tree, and the voice she had seemed to recognize, and finished with Janey showing her the photograph of Tucker. Cooper listened without interrupting, his green eyes never leaving her face.

"Of course," she finished, "I haven't told Gabe about the photograph. I know he's going to say it doesn't constitute any kind of proof—that any similarities are all in my head." She sighed. "So far as I can tell, all we accomplished by chasing around in the mountains this morning was to piss off that creep Watkins."

Cooper smiled faintly. "We had this old black lady working for us when I was a kid. Her name was Dovey. When you'd tell her something she thought was farfetched, she'd say 'One see is worth twenty hears.' Gabe's not going to believe in ghosts until he sees one with his own eyes, and probably not even then. But Nan—you've had your one see. I've had mine. And I think your grandmother was right. I think what you saw yesterday at the funeral was the ghost of your friend Tucker."

She released the breath she hadn't known she was holding, feeling a mixture of terror and odd relief flood her without being able to tell which was uppermost. Mind-boggling as the whole business was, it was helpful to be able to discuss it without being told every two words that she was stressed out, hysterical, or just plain nuts. She was profoundly grateful for Cooper's existence. She supposed, given a completely free choice of advisers, she would have preferred that bearded old party in all the vampire movies who knew just when to start waving the garlic and the crucifix. But she would take whatever she could get.

"He saw me too, you know. He spoke to me," she said softly. She had held that part back until now because it sounded so crazy, but at this point she couldn't imagine why she was bothering to split hairs. It all sounded crazy, every blessed bit of it. She saw Cooper's eyes glint.

"What did he say?"

"My name. Or at least the name he used to call me. Annabel. That's what my grandmother called me, so everybody else did, too." She shifted suddenly on the booth's spongy seat, feeling a shudder run through her, mixed fear and incredulity. "You know, I can't believe this. If I've actually seen a ghost . . . a *ghost*—then what about modern science? Modern science says there's no such thing. No ifs, ands or buts. Just no . . . such . . . thing. But I've seen one. And now I feel like the bottom's dropped out of everything I ever believed."

He smiled crookedly. "Tell me about it."

"What *are* they, really? I mean, if they're just spirits, how can we see them?"

Cooper poked at the remains of the questionable omelet he had ordered. "Well, the theory is that they're sending some kind of signal and you're receiving it, but with some subliminal part of your mind instead of with your eyes. So the person—the ghost—*seems* to be there. But it's not. Not physically."

"Coop, that's just not possible. I mean, what kind of signal could—"

"Hey," he said. "We're talking about something that's been denied by science, and so the whole subject has remained almost completely untouched by any kind of serious investigation. But just because we don't understand it, that doesn't mean it's not happening. Think about radio for a minute. Somebody on the other side of the world says something, and you hear it. How? Because of these invisible wa-a-aves floating in the air." He waggled his fingers suggestively. "Sounds pretty weird, doesn't it? *Not possible.* But it happens."

"Okay." She was willing to concede that, put in those terms, the theory was slightly more palatable. "All right. So it happens. But *why*? What makes it happen? Why aren't they just *dead*?"

He shrugged. "Nan, all I can give you is more theory. And what it says is that a death like Tucker's—sudden, traumatic—can cause the spirit to go into something similar to shock. He's disoriented, confused—he doesn't know where to go, what he's supposed to do. So he just stays put. He clings to what was familiar to him in life. That's what a haunting is. The place is crucial. He's lost his body, his physical cohesion. The place is literally what's holding him together."

The place.

Hill. Creek. Stephen's room. The oak tree in Annabel's front yard.

"Then what was he doing at Lucy's grave?" she said.

"I don't know." He gnawed his lower lip. "That's a good question. And here's another one. You say he called you by name. Now, isn't it interesting that he seems to know you in spite of the fact that your physical appearance has changed considerably since the last time he saw you? I mean, you were nine years old when you knew him, right? Yet he recognized you yesterday, after a lapse of twenty years in which you went from a little girl to a grown woman. Apparently he was able to recognize your *psychic* self even though your *physical* self has altered radically. And you have to admit that's interesting."

A musical crash sounded from the kitchen as a pile of dishes toppled in the sink, startling her back into awareness of her surroundings. She discovered a grease spot on the Formica beside her coffee cup and polished it with her paper napkin. "I wouldn't really choose that word, Coop. Weird, yes. Scary. But I'm not advanced enough for interesting."

He smiled sympathetically. "Yeah. The subject does take a little getting used to."

"Can I get y'all something else today?" Bright-faced Bonnie, the teenage waitress, had appeared beside their booth, pad at the ready. Cooper glanced up at her, then down at his watch.

"Guess not, Bonnie. We've got to be going." He accepted the check and tucked a dollar under his coffee saucer, then slid out of the booth and headed for the register by the door.

Nan trailed after him. "Hey, let me get that. You're the one giving the free consultation."

He shook his head, got his change and pocketed it.

"Can you come on back to the store for a minute? There's something I'd like to give you to read."

At Books, Etc. Nan collected the book (a tattered paperback; she barely glanced at it before shoving it in her bag) and accepted condolences on Lucy's death from two customers who entered the store as she was leaving. A glance at her watch told her it was time to pick up Stephen. Out on the sidewalk, she paused and looked stupidly up and down the street for the Volvo before the sight of Estelle's ample pink tail fins reminded her that it was Annabel's car she had driven to town.

And why. The conference with Cooper had pushed the memory of Jerry Ray's threatening behavior to the back of her mind, but now it returned. Getting out of her parking spot she gave Estelle too much gas and nearly backed into the car behind.

She jammed on the brakes just in time, swearing inwardly. Jerry Ray was Gabe's fault. It was his quixotic jaunt into the back hills that had aggravated the moonshiner's paranoia and set him on their trail. But it wasn't only Jerry Ray who had her on edge—he was just the icing on the cake, tangible trouble in contrast to the far-out stuff she and Cooper had discussed. Her hands were shaky on the steering wheel.

He seems to know you in spite of the fact that your physical appearance has changed considerably. I mean, you were nine years old when you knew him, right? Yet apparently he recognized you yesterday, after a lapse of twenty years in which you went from a little girl to a grown woman. He was able to recognize your psychic *self, even though your* physical *self has altered radically.*

He recognized her, yes. He knew her. But what did he want?

She drove the four blocks to the Methodist church in a daze, pulling up in front of the church to the sight of children gathered on the sunny lawn. Their treble voices, wavering in the vicinity of a melody line, drifted across the grass as a long-haired young couple, man and woman, led the singing, accompanying it with guitars. Nan turned off the engine to listen.

Tell me the stories of Jeeeeesus
I love to heeeeeeear

The young man, who actually looked quite a lot like Jesus as depicted in Protestant Bibles, smiled and bobbed his smooth head to the beat as he sang. His companion put her whole body into the act, swaying back and forth with an energy that had her long yellow braids moving like twin pendulums.

Nan picked out Stephen sitting near the back of the group, wearing a red T-shirt, shoulders hunched up to his ears. She couldn't tell if he was singing or not. She wondered if it was just personal paranoia that made her imagine a kind of force field of isolation surrounding him: in the group, but not part of it. The song ended and Jesus led the children in a round of self-congratulatory applause. The group broke up: children began to dart and scream on the lawn, a blur of colorful motion. Stephen caught sight of the car and came running over.

She found herself greeting him with false gaiety, trying to override her worries. "Hi honey! Have fun today?"

He shrugged and mumbled something inaudible. On

the way home, all she could elicit to her questions were monosyllabic replies. At last she gave up. He obviously disliked the camp, and it was pretty clear by now that he was not going to replace the friend he had with some new acquaintance. Woody—Tucker—was all he wanted.

(Late afternoon sunlight stretching two shadows long on the crest of a golden hill . . . child's voice calling from the depths of the dusky orchard, pale apple blossoms trembling against a lilac sky—here I come, ready or not!)

Against the upwelling images came the clear, cold memory of Lucy Talbot lying open-eyed, her head at a wrong angle, white hair spilled around her in the grass. Her grave marker with its sentimental verse chiseled deep in silvery Tennessee limestone. Nan glanced over at Stephen's small profile and bit her lip. It was time to heed Lucy's warnings—now, before anything else happened. Again, as she had been doing half consciously all the way home, she glanced in the rearview mirror to reassure herself that the road behind them was empty. All she needed right now was for that idiot Watkins to reappear and start trying to force her off the road.

But there was no sign of him, and when they reached Annabel's at last and pulled up at the house, Gabe and Mister Mustard were waiting on the porch. Gabe announced with a flourish that he had made a ratatouille for lunch. It would be ready in twenty minutes.

Stephen slumped down on the top step and the cat jumped into his lap. "Can I just have a sandwich? I want to go find Woody."

Gabe struck a pose, twirling the tip of an imaginary mustache. "You insult ze famoose Chef Gabriel! Ze five-star chef zat make onlee one ratatouille each year!"

Chef Gabriel was new to Nan, but apparently not to Stephen; he reached up and patted Gabe's arm, a curiously adult gesture. "Come on, Dad. Gimme a break."

"Okay, okay. How about a sandwich?"

Nan shifted the groceries in her arms. "Mind giving me a hand with these, Mister, uh, Chef?"

He relieved her of one bag and followed her inside, where a bubbling, fragrant mixture on top of the stove testified to Chef Gabriel's talents. She turned to him. "I don't want him playing with Woody anymore."

"For Christ's sake, Nan." The grocery bag he had set on the counter started to fall over and he caught it.

"Gabe, listen to me—"

"And you listen to me." His face had reddened and he was starting to breathe audibly through his nose. She was suddenly acutely aware of the difference in their respective heights and weights. "If that kid went to all the trouble of inventing himself a friend, it's because he's desperately in need of one. You don't just pull the plug on that kind of fantasy. Not until you're willing to give him some alternative. Until you're willing to put his needs ahead of yours and stop balling that good-looking cousin of yours long enough to spend a little time with your child."

Furious tears sprang to Nan's eyes; she felt as if he had punched her. She couldn't speak.

He pushed past her and opened the refrigerator. "I'm going to make him a sandwich."

Nan fled upstairs to her room and sat on the edge of the bed, shaking from head to foot and willing herself not to cry. When she was finally able to form words, she whispered over and over again, "Bastard. Fucking bastard."

The rage helped drive back the pain. She was under

no illusions about Gabe's opinion of her as a mother. But the irony was that it was *his* attitude that had become a danger to Stephen. He was convinced Woody was a harmless, even beneficent fantasy. And he had science on his side, and reason, and common sense. While all she had was the gut feeling of something terribly wrong. And the dazzlingly clear image of a sunny-haired boy reaching out to her across Lucy's open grave.

It hovered before her now. In the silence of her sunlit bedroom she almost could hear that soundless whisper.

Annabel—

It was blotted out by a bone-chilling scream.

And another.

And another.

They kept on coming, the screams—long enough for Nan to shake off the paralysis caused by the first and to register the fact that they were coming from the front yard. As she bolted off the bed and started for the window, she heard Gabe's footsteps thud across the living room beneath her. The front door banged. Reaching the window she saw him below her, running toward the center of the yard. Toward a blur of violent, screaming motion. Against the green of the grass she could see flashes of red, of tawny gold.

Stephen—and Mustard—

Just as Gabe reached them, the cat tore itself free from the boy's grip and streaked across the lawn toward the house. Gabe caught Stephen's flailing arms and pinned them. Even from where she stood, Nan could see the blood.

She tore downstairs and met Gabe coming through the door with the boy in his arms. Stephen had stopped screaming, but one look at his blood-streaked face nearly started Nan on a bout of her own.

"His *eyes*—"

"They're okay—I checked. But I think he's going into shock. Where's the nearest hospital around here?"

"About sixty miles away," she said. "Listen, the local guy's okay, and he's seen Stephen before. Let's get him to Breezy."

Gabe drove. Nan sat in the back seat with Stephen cradled against her, making automatic soothing sounds. About halfway to Breezy he started to cry. The worst of the scratches were on his forearms, one particularly long and deep that refused, in spite of the towel they had wrapped tightly around it, to stop bleeding. The ones on his forehead, although they bled copiously, didn't seem that deep.

Doc Hales took stitches in the deep gash on Stephen's left arm and another near his thumb.

"I can do the one on his forehead, too, if you want. Otherwise there could be a pretty bad scar." He addressed Stephen, lying on his back on the examining table. "Want a big, ugly scar, young fella?"

"Maybe." There was a tremor of interest in the small voice.

Hales cackled. "Boys—they never change."

"I'd prefer you to go on and stitch it," Gabe said heavily.

"Aw, Dad—"

"Humor me, son."

The rest of the wounds needed only cleaning and bandaging. Hales worked quickly, talking over his shoulder to Nan the whole time. "You'll need to change these dressings twice a day at first. Keep a lookout for infection. No baths for a couple of days—I know that'll break the boy's heart."

He installed the newly repaired Stephen on a sofa in the waiting room with a pile of Spiderman comic books, then motioned Nan and Gabe into his consulting room. They sat down. His reddened eyes peered over his glasses at them. "Cats are dirty things, even if they do spend half their lives washing themselves. And some of those wounds are bites. You'll need to get that animal checked for rabies."

The word rendered Nan speechless. Gabe said, "Rabies?"

The doctor glared at him; the business about the scar seemed to have engendered an instant dislike. "Cat goes outdoors, don't it? Could've been bit by a raccoon, possum—plenty of rabid wild critters around this time of year."

Nan made an effort to swallow the dryness in her throat. "Wouldn't Annabel have had him vaccinated?"

Doc shrugged. "Probably. But with something like this, you don't want to take a chance."

"So how do we have him tested?"

The doctor made a sour face. "Ain't exactly a test. They cut the cat's head off, send it to Nashville. Lab there can check the salivary glands."

Nan was appalled. "Can't we just find out if he's been vaccinated? I mean—"

The old man shrugged. "Maybe. I'm no vet. Call Tompkins. He'll know."

On the way home in the car, Stephen was calmer and Nan took the opportunity to try to extract the details of what had happened.

"I was patting Mustard, and Woody came. Mustard tried to run away, but I thought Woody might want to pat him. So I held on to him. But he just kind of went crazy."

Nan recalled the afternoon she had seen the cat crouching flat-eared and hissing on the floor of Stephen's room. Recalled the prickling sensation she had felt running like an electric current over her own skin. "He didn't mean to hurt you, honey. He was scared. Why didn't you just drop him?"

"I don't know. It all happened so fast—"

Surprise must have tightened his grip, and after that, in terror and pain, he had been unable to let go. Nan smoothed his hair back from the white bandage covering the sutures in his forehead. "Don't worry, sweetheart. It's over now."

But it wasn't, not quite. Stephen wanted to watch TV when they got home, and Gabe settled him in the living room before coming into the kitchen where Nan was trying to get Dr. Tompkins, the local vet, on the phone.

"I sure as hell hope we can *find* the damn cat."

"What?" The vet's phone was ringing in her other ear. Why didn't he answer? She glanced at her watch: barely four o'clock. This day seemed to have lasted forever.

"He took off like a bat out of hell," Gabe was saying.

"He was scared," she said.

"Scared of what?"

She glanced sideways at him. He was scraping the charred, forgotten remains of Chef Gabriel's ratatouille out of its pot into the garbage. He had heard, as clearly as she had, Stephen's remark about Woody. But to him Woody was completely imaginary, existing only inside Stephen's head—certainly nothing a cat could perceive or fear. *Animals don't like ghosts.* She had read that somewhere, had considered it an entertaining bit of folklore. Yet now—

"Office." The brusque voice at the other end of the phone was unexpectedly loud, pitched over a frenzy of barking in the background.

"Dr. Tompkins?"

"Put him on the table, Willie. Damn. Might have known he was going to piss. Use that towel." The barking subsided to whimpering.

"Dr. Tompkins?"

"Yeah."

"My name is Nan Lucas. I'm Annabel Stephens's granddaughter. I need some information about her cat."

"Annabel . . . Stephens's . . . cat." He repeated the syllables as if they were complete gibberish, a sentence in another language.

"I need to know when it was last vaccinated for rabies."

"Ma'am, my receptionist is off getting married this afternoon, and I've got a waiting room full of sick animals. Call me tomorrow."

"Please," Nan said desperately. "The cat attacked my son this afternoon. Doc Hales said we should check with you. In case—"

"Hold on."

She held, hearing voices in the background. A door slammed; there was more barking. A child's voice said, "Down, King. Down, boy." There was a crash. A cat yowled mournfully.

"Red male tabby, six years old, called Mustard?" said a sudden loud voice in her ear.

"Yes—"

"Vaccinated rabies last November."

"And it's good for how long?"

"One year."

"So I don't need to worry?"

"No, hon. You don't need to worry."

The sudden, unexpected kindness in the drawling voice brought a lump to her throat. She had to try twice before she could get out a reply. "Thank you. Thank you so much."

"Okay." He hung up, cutting her off. She sank into a chair at the kitchen table beside the phone and rested her head in her hands.

"Well?" Gabe said.

"It's okay. He's had his shots."

"Thank God. But Nan, even if he's not rabid . . . do you really want to own an animal whose behavior is that erratic?"

"His behavior is not erratic. He was scared."

He gave her a long look without answering and she managed to hold it. Finally he turned away.

During supper they spoke only from necessity. Nan was realizing there was no possible hope of convincing Gabe of her version of what was happening. Her thoughts returned briefly to the photograph Janey Wills had showed her. Should she have asked to borrow it? Maybe she could have showed it to Stephen, asked him if the boy in the picture looked like Woody. . . . But she knew Gabe would be ready with some pat explanation, something about suggestibility and imagination.

She shrugged. She was a little surprised to discover that she didn't care anymore about what he thought, and with this realization came a certain sense of freedom. After supper she took an exhausted Stephen up to bed, returning downstairs to find Gabe on the phone in the kitchen. He looked up guiltily when she came in.

"Do you mind? I'm on with Jennifer."

Nan made a sarcastically expansive gesture and left the room, retreating to the library to pour herself a brandy and sit nursing it, and her thoughts.

What had happened to her glorious plan of finding a haven in the green countryside, a place to heal and renew? It hadn't taken long for the pastoral idyll to collapse. A friendship between two children . . . one living and one dead? It went against all reason; it was impossible—yet here, in the fastness of the mountains, the line between possible and impossible seemed to blur as it never had in the city. Walking down Park Avenue, between rows of magnificent skyscrapers, it was easy to credit humanity with total knowledge, total power. But here the balance was reversed: the wilderness overshadowed all else, and the deep places of the psyche seemed to mirror the landscape, resonating with echoes beyond the reach of reason. Somehow, the various faces of reality—memory, dream, imagination, and something that looked disturbingly like the paranormal—had intersected in a way that was proving dangerous.

And I thought I had problems in New York.

Nostalgia swamped her. All at once it was tempting to click her heels together three times, to whisper: *There's no place like home . . . there's no place like home . . .*

Should she cut her losses and head back north? The thought of leaving the valley caused her a wrench. She had experienced a renewal here—a reconnection with a part of herself she couldn't afford to lose touch with again. Her book of photographs was starting to take shape. She was, in spite of what Gabe said, in the process of forming a genuine relationship with her child.

And she had realized, seeing Sky at Lucy's funeral, that she wanted another chance with him.

But in the scales against this agenda was the undeniable fact that the situation here was going rapidly out of control. Running away was clearly the safer choice.

Hearing someone drive up outside, she got up and went to the window, cupping her hands around her eyes to peer out into the dusk. Speak of the devil—Sky's truck, and his tall figure mounting the front porch steps. She went to open the door. He stood there, just the way he had that first morning, if possible looking even better than he had then.

"Nan, I got to talk to you."

"About what?" She spoke curtly, struggling to resist the traitorous wave of desire passing through her.

He grimaced and ducked his coppery head. "Can I come in?"

She backed up to let him enter. He closed the door behind him and turned to face her. "Bad doin's about Lucy. Real bad."

"It was an accident," she said tightly.

"Hell, I know that. I ain't blamin' y'all." He put his hands in his pockets and looked at the floor, then up at her. "Seems like everything's been goin' bad lately. Nan, what happened with you and me?"

She shrugged, too emotionally unsteady to speak, afraid she might start bawling. There was a sound in the doorway leading to the kitchen. She looked up to see Gabe standing there.

"Gabe. This is Sky Barnett."

Somehow she pushed the words out past the tightness in her throat. She wasn't up to a more fulsome introduction and doubted she ever would have been. Gabe offered a guarded nod and took two steps into the room.

"And what can we do for you this evening, Mr. Barnett?"

Sky shifted his weight. "I came t' talk t' Nan."

Was he exaggerating the country drawl for Gabe's benefit? The two of them were already bristling; she was reminded of two male dogs vying for disputed territory.

Without taking his eyes off their visitor, Gabe said, "Nan? Do you want to talk to him?"

The preemptory question took her so much by surprise that she didn't answer right away.

Sky crossed his arms deliberately over his chest and rocked back on his heels. "If she don't, I guess she can damn well tell me herself."

Gabe looked him up and down, then turned to her. "What's he supposed to be, your knight in shining armor? I thought you said you were finished fucking him."

Things were moving too quickly for Nan. She glanced at Sky. His face was impassive but she had seen his eyes flicker.

"Shut up, Gabe," she said. "Leave him alone."

"Well, let him state his business, then. And make it quick."

Sky slowly uncrossed his arms. "What th' hell're you gettin' so feisty for, ol'-timer? From what I hear, you ain't even in th' picture no more. So why don't you just butt out?"

Gabe's face turned bright red. He lunged across the space between them, thrusting an awkward fist at Sky's jaw. Nan heard herself gasp, but Sky slapped the attack casually aside, then planted his other hand on Gabe's chest and shoved him hard. Gabe lost his balance and stumbled back. One windmilling arm hit a lamp and rocked it on its base, knocking the shade askew as he flailed, regaining his balance at last to stand with his feet planted wide apart, both hands making and unmaking spasmodic fists. He glared murderously at Sky but made no further move, obviously realizing he was no match for the younger man. The room was silent except for his labored breathing.

"Wonderful," Nan said. "Now can I say something? This is my house, and my son needs rest. He's had a rough day, and he doesn't need a couple of overgrown roosters crowing and carrying on down here while he's upstairs trying to sleep. And I don't need it either. So if you two can't control yourselves, I suggest you go outside and beat the shit out of each other, or whatever it is you're so desperate to do. But don't do it in here."

The burst of hot anger that had carried her on its crest sank away suddenly and left her exhausted. But it seemed to have done the trick. Sky had his hands jammed in his pockets; Gabe was looking off into a corner of the room. He muttered something. She couldn't understand the words, but it sounded apologetic.

"I'm going up to check on Stephen," she said. As she left the living room she saw Sky heading for the door.

Chapter 23

The next morning at breakfast, Gabe offered Stephen a deal that Nan assumed was Jennifer's brainstorm. He would attend church camp two more times, making every effort to enjoy himself. After that, if he wanted to stop going, he could.

"Really, Dad?" His face brightened in obvious relief.

Told you so: she beamed the thought at Gabe and it must have reached its destination, because he gave her a dirty look. Stephen was saying, "Dad?"

"Yes, son."

"Do you think maybe I could stay home today? I don't feel so good."

"All right," Gabe said heavily.

Nan seized her chance. "If you don't feel good, then you need to take it easy, Stephen. Stay in the house. Okay?"

He was so happy to be staying home that the restriction didn't seem to make a dent. "Sure."

She avoided Gabe all morning, but after lunch he came looking for her upstairs. Down in the living room she could hear some video game blasting away, Stephen at the controls. For once the sound came as a relief. Gabe entered her bedroom cautiously, as if he thought it might be booby-trapped.

"Listen, Nan. We need to talk."

"I'm listening."

She put down the catalog she had been leafing through, shifting her position on the window seat. He started to fiddle with the things on top of her dresser and she resisted the urge to tell him to stop.

"Jennifer thinks Stephen ought to be in therapy," he said at last.

She leaned back and folded her arms. "And?"

"Well, there's nobody around here even remotely qualified to treat him. In New York he can get the best."

"And who's the best? Jennifer?"

"Don't be an idiot," Gabe said. "Jennifer wouldn't see him professionally even if we begged her to. She's much too ethical to treat someone she has a personal relationship with. But she could certainly recommend someone."

The idea of *begging* Jennifer to do anything made Nan's blood pressure start to rise. She stood up abruptly from the window seat and had the dubious pleasure of seeing him recoil slightly.

"Nan, the kid needs help. There's nothing wrong with having an imaginary friend. But for some reason Woody has gone from positive to negative. He's become a danger to Stephen. And since Stephen created him, we have to start wondering why Stephen feels a need to punish himself."

"Punish himself? For what?"

"That's what we need to find out. That's why he needs therapy." He put his hands in his pockets and then took them out again. "Nan, please. Let me take him back to New York."

She bit back a hot refusal. How could she blame Gabe? He was trying, as best he knew how, to take care of Stephen. To protect him. And the way things were going, she couldn't say she was having much success in that department. Maybe, for Stephen's own safety, she *should* let Gabe take him.

She walked to the window overlooking the pasture and stared out toward the ridge. He seemed to sense her weakening, because he moved closer and touched her shoulder gently. "We have to do what's best for him."

She looked at his earnest face and then out the window again. Caught in the late sunlight, the golden hill blazed in the distance above the dark trees along the creek.

"You'll have to ask Stephen," she said finally.

*   *   *

Summoned to sit beside his father on the sofa in the library that night as soon as supper was over, Stephen looked impressed and a little apprehensive. Gabe had a real flair for the dramatic; Nan remembered from high school how, during slide shows in his class, he used to edge over to the light switch and turn on the lights unexpectedly, accompanying the sudden blinding illumination by some succinct comment on life as art. She had fallen for it at seventeen. Stephen was eight.

"Son, we have to talk."

Stephen's eyes were as round as the lenses of his glasses. "About what, Dad?"

Nan had insisted on being present for this talk. Every cowardly instinct she possessed, and they seemed to be legion, yammered at her to slink out of sight until it was all over. But here she was, tucked into a corner chair with a book, Lady Low Profile. She had caught the quick, tentative smile Stephen had sent her as he took his seat beside Gabe.

"About the future, champ. The fact is, I have to get back to New York."

Stephen flinched. Clearly he had expected something like this. He sat without speaking, his misery almost palpable. Nan ducked her head to the unread page in front of her; she hadn't even looked at the title of the book she had picked up. She didn't want to leave Tennessee, even after everything that had happened. Her half-formed picture of a life here, away from the craziness of the city, still exerted a powerful pull. She wanted that life for Stephen, too. But suppose Tucker was part of the package?

"Listen to me, son," Gabe said. "I want you to come with me."

"Back to New York?"

"Yes. Back home. We can be on a plane first thing in the morning, Stephen. Maybe even get there in time for hot chocolate and croissants at Bruno's. How about that?"

Stephen picked at one of the bandages on his arm. "Are you coming too, Mom?"

Startled, Nan temporized. "I—I'm not sure, honey. But even if I do, it doesn't mean your dad and I will be living together again. It'll be the same as before. You'll be with me during the week and spend weekends with Jennifer and him."

She wanted no more confusion on that front. Stephen was swinging his feet, watching the movement with desperate concentration.

To her surprise, when he finally spoke, it was to her. "I want to stay here, Mom," he said. "I want to stay here with you and Woody."

Gabe had been sitting forward with his elbows on his knees; now he leaned back, letting out an explosive breath. Stephen flinched a little at the sound, then looked up at his father.

Gabe made an effort to soften his frown. "Look, son. Woody can come with us."

Stephen shook his head. "He wants to stay here."

Nan took a slow breath. Wants to—or *has* to? Cooper had babbled something about a ghost being a collection of fragments held together by a specific location . . . a familiar place. If Stephen left, Tucker couldn't follow. There was comfort in *that* thought, anyway.

Gabe and Stephen had locked gazes. One young and one aging, the two profiles in matching granny glasses might have made her laugh if the situation had been less fraught with tension.

At last Gabe sighed. "Well, then maybe you'll have to leave him behind."

"But, Dad—"

"Look, Stephen." His frown had deepened again. "Maybe Woody's not such a good friend to you anymore. Remember when he asked you to climb that tree? Remember how scared you were? And what about the business with the cat? Woody made you squeeze the cat, didn't he? And you got scratched."

"It wasn't his fault."

But he sounded a little shaky, and Gabe homed in. "Son, please trust me. I'm your dad and I have an obligation to do what's best for you. Okay?"

Stephen was quiet; the concept might have been beyond him, but there was no way he could miss the weighty tone.

"Okay?" Gabe said again, and under pressure Stephen's lips moved in silent echo: *Okay*.

"Good. Then you and I are going back to New York. Tomorrow."

Stephen just sat there, and for a long moment Nan thought it was over. Then his head started to move from side to side with a determination that bordered on violence. "No. No! I'm not leaving! I won't leave Woody! You can't make me!"

Gritting his teeth on the words as he jerked his head from one side to the other like a dog shaking a shoe in its jaws. As Gabe reached out, he flinched away and stumbled off the sofa to stand swaying on his feet.

Nan found herself out of her own chair, putting out a tentative hand, almost afraid to touch him. He had stopped the violent headshaking, but his shoulders were hunched up to his ears and both hands were clenched in fists. "NO!"

He shouted this last refusal into his father's face. Nan saw Gabe flinch and his eyes fill with tears—but Stephen, blundering noisily up the enclosed staircase to his room above, wasn't there to see them.

She went up a little later to put her child to bed and found him uncommunicative except for a fierce good-night hug that nearly strangled her. Leaving his door ajar she crossed the hall to her own room, aware all at once that she was physically exhausted. The day's stresses had just about finished her, and the shouting match between Gabe and Stephen had drained her last reserves. There were dirty dishes downstairs in the sink but they could wait until tomorrow. Even though it was not quite eight, she was ready for bed.

But once there, she couldn't sleep—her body tired but her mind racing, running a ceaseless loop of Lucy lying in the grass, then Stephen's bleeding face, then Tucker reaching out to her across Lucy's grave. As far as she could see, matters were deadlocked. Unless Gabe was willing to take Stephen against his will . . .

Abruptly she remembered the paperback Cooper had given her to read. It must still be in the car.

Going back downstairs she glanced through the darkened living room and saw the light still on in the library, where Gabe sat sulking by the cold fireplace. Outside, the night sky was a vast canopy of velvety black, pricked by stars above the dark bulk of the ridge. The creek muttered in the distance. She avoided looking into the darkness around her, keeping her eyes down as she made her way quickly across the shadowy lawn to Annabel's car, noticing how furtive her own footsteps sounded on the grass.

Was it out there now, somewhere in the vast darkness, unable to rest—the spirit of the boy she had known twenty years ago? What did he want? Why was he haunting the place where they had played together as children? Janey Wills had dispelled the mystery surrounding his death, offering her facts in place of the blank space in her memory; and even though the facts still seemed dry and distant, at least now she knew what they were.

Is he out here now, in the darkness, aware of me?

What does he want?

It was an accident.

Ducking into the car, she fumblingly retrieved Cooper's book, then turned back toward the house. Behind her, a sound came out of the night, sliding along her nerves to leave a raw seam of panic in its wake.

A slow and rusty creaking, as if the pasture gate were slowly swinging open.

"No," she whispered. Her legs felt numb. She forced herself to turn and look over her shoulder.

The gate was closed.

Imagination?

*   *   *

Back inside the house, propped up in bed on pillows with the book in front of her, she bored her way into the text with a vengeance, trying to blot out that rusty creak of hinges. But it was heavy going. She slowed down and began to leaf cautiously through the pages, reading a paragraph here, one there, seeing names she recognized—Einstein, Oppenheimer, Williams James; others, like Planck and Heisenberg, that rang a faint bell; and still others— Meister Eckhardt, Vivekananda, that were totally unknown to her.

Gradually her eyelids began to droop. She shifted and reached behind her to plump the pillows. This was obviously Cooper's bible; dozens of its tattered pages had turn-down marks at the corners and there were underlined passages everywhere. Out of a sense of obligation she focused her now-bleary eyes on one of them:

We see this world with the five senses, but if we had another sense, we would see in it something more.

It was the kind of thinking Gabe held in contempt, equating it with incense, seven-grain bread, and people who wore glitter in their eyebrows and asked, "What's your sign?" Until recently she would have said she agreed with him. But her skepticism had been second-hand; under pressure of recent events it had tottered, and by now she was ready to admit it was in a state of complete collapse. She would have liked to believe there was nothing out there other than what she could see, taste, touch, smell and hear. But she could no longer afford the luxury of believing what she liked.

On that note she put the book on the table beside the bed, turned out the lamp and felt the vast darkness outside the windows come flooding in.

Chapter 24

"So Jennifer says Stephen is using Woody to punish himself for some unknown reason. She says he really needs therapy. Professional help."

Across from her in their regular booth at Bev's, Cooper sat watching the steam curl above his coffee cup. He sighed and reached behind his head to touch his ponytail. "Nan, listen. At some point you have to start trusting your own sense of what's going on."

Trust in her own perceptions was a variable she couldn't predict from one minute to the next, but for some reason his vote of confidence brought her dangerously close to tears. She delved into her handbag for something resembling a handkerchief and instead found the book he had lent her.

"Oh, I brought your book back. It was—well, I didn't get far in it. I guess I'm too distracted to be able to concentrate on anything."

She passed the ratty paperback across the table and he received it reverently.

"I just thought it might help you accept what's happening," he said. "One of the things that was a comfort to me, when I first blundered into this stuff, was that there are some very smart people out there who take it seriously. Know what Einstein said? *The stuff of the world is mind-stuff.* And really, once you take something as wild as the theory of relativity—"

Her eyes must have glazed, because he stopped. "How far along did you get?" he said.

Nan groped for her coffee and took a sip. "Not very far."

"Let me just tell you how I think it might apply to your situation. Okay? I'll try not to rant or rave."

"Okay," she said.

He put his elbows on the table and leaned forward. "It's basically about expanding your definition of reality. Getting rid of the notion that if we can't taste, smell, see, hear and touch something, that means it doesn't exist. You have to think of the senses as a filter. They pare down our perception of the world to manageable proportions, to optimize our chances for survival in the biological sense. But in doing so, they make us miss a lot of what's going on—a much broader spectrum of reality that's just not accessible through the physical senses."

He paused and Nan said, "Like ghosts."

He smiled. His hand was behind his head again, playing with his ponytail. "Not just ghosts. Whole areas of reality that exist, as surely as this table"—he tapped the greasy Formica—"only most of us are missing them, because we haven't developed our ability to perceive them. We have the ability. We're all born with it. But because we don't need it to survive, we neglect it and it atrophies, the same as a muscle that's never used. We just lose it."

Impressed by his earnestness, she tried to frame an intelligent question. "But what would we do with it? If we kept it?"

He took a breath and met her gaze squarely. "See the future. Read each other's minds. Talk to the dead."

Up to now Nan hadn't noticed if anyone was sitting near them, but at this point she looked around to see if they could be overheard. An elderly man sat two booths away, apparently absorbed in his newspaper. Up at the corner Bev was joshing two truckdrivers about something to do with a tattoo one of them had.

Nan looked back at Cooper and took a deep breath.

Talk to the dead.

"So now we're back to ghosts," she said. He nodded.

"Remember how we talked about Tucker's ghost as a kind of signal received by your brain? For you, it was a flash, a fluke in which the two frequencies, yours and his, somehow intersected for a few seconds. Same with Laura and me. And that's about what you could expect for people like us, adults who've had years of practice at ignoring anything that's not literally in front of our noses. But for a young kid like Stephen, extrasensory reality is no less genuine than the sensory kind. It takes kids a while to pick up our prejudice against anything we can't see or hear or touch. So they're able to tune into things that the rest of us have completely blocked out."

"What about Woody?" she said abruptly. "How does he fit into all this? I mean, if it's really Tucker Stephen's perceiving, why call him by the name of an imaginary friend he invented three years ago? How can he think it's the same kid?"

Cooper shrugged. "Nan, I can't pretend to know exactly what's going on. It's pretty clear that the being Stephen calls Woody is really the ghost of Tucker Wills, but only Stephen can tell you how he got the two of them connected in his head. Woody may have been shadowy enough for Tucker to slip into his shoes, so to speak. A private friend, a friend no one else can see. . . .

Who knows where the imagination stops and nonsensory reality begins? There may be no clear boundary between the two, only some kind of transitional area. And that may be where Tucker and Woody overlap."

This conversation, she thought, was getting more and more like something out of *The Twilight Zone*. She glanced around Bev's again, half expecting to see Rod Serling leaning against the jukebox, but saw only Bonnie the waitress perched behind the cash register filing her nails.

She turned back to Cooper. He was just sitting there, looking normal: a born-too-late hippie with a nice smile. By rights he ought to be talking about carrot juice or dance therapy. But instead—

"It's like he's getting stronger," she said. "More active. Annabel told Lucy she saw him only about a dozen times over a period of twenty years. But since we've been here—"

Cooper was nodding his head. "Yeah, I've been thinking about that. About how he was able to manifest at Lucy's grave, and how he was able to recognize you after twenty years. And here's what I think.

"The classic ghost is supposed to be a kind of echo or shadow, not really conscious. Somebody, I forget who, called them 'dream-fancies of the dead.' And I think that's what your grandmother was seeing. But as you say, Tucker seems to have changed recently. And I think it may be because of you."

"Me?" Her heart seemed to slip a notch.

"Yes. You've mentioned your memories of him— how vivid they've become since you've been back here. Nan, those memories of yours may be providing a kind of substance he was missing before. In a sense they function the same way the place does, to orient and define him. But unlike the landscape, your memories are active, not passive. We talked about Tucker's 'signal.' Your memories may actually be amplifying that signal."

"That's insane," she whispered. But it sounded somehow familiar. Hadn't Janey Wills, of all people, suggested something similar?

"Maybe," Cooper was saying. "But obviously there's an active psychic link between the two of you. That's how he recognized you in the graveyard. What else could be providing the connection, if not your memories?"

"But a memory is just ... it isn't real! It's just something inside my head. How—"

He was shaking his head, smiling a little. "There you go again, same old trap. If you can't see or touch it, it doesn't exist. But remember: the physical spectrum isn't all of reality. Just a tiny slice of it."

Nan felt panic rising in a sudden wave that nearly swamped her before she forced herself, with an effort, to concentrate on the noisy coffeeshop and Cooper's intent face. Her napkin was a crumpled ball beside her plate; she picked it up and began to smooth it out with shaking fingers. Her own memories, adding substance to a phantom ...

"Annabel thought he was harmless," she said. "And maybe he was—before. But not anymore. Look what happened to Lucy. And Stephen could have been killed, too, if he'd fallen out of that tree." Images swam behind her eyes: her child's terrified face peering down from the leaves. His forehead gashed and bloody from the cat's claws. White face beneath the moving water of the creek.

"What does he *want*?" she whispered.

Cooper toyed with his fork, then put it down. "I don't know. In some primitive societies, the dead are feared because they're lonely. They're looking for company."

There was an unpleasant sensation in Nan's chest, like the flutter of tiny wings beneath her breastbone. She remembered hearing a child's whisper on the stairs. Finding the horseshoe-nail ring on the floor, like an offering. Hearing a voice call out when she fell, that time in the barn.

Looking for company. Unable to reach her, had Tucker settled for her child instead?

"Jesus Christ," she breathed.

"Look, Nan, let's not panic." Having scared her wit-less, Cooper seemed anxious to undo the damage. "It's perfectly possible Tucker doesn't intend anyone any harm. Maybe he threw the board down from the tree on impulse, because he was angry at the rest of you for not letting Stephen join him in the tree house. He probably didn't intend it to hit anyone. Or maybe it fell on its own."

"He made the cat attack Stephen," she said.

"Maybe. Or he may not have understood his pres-ence would have that effect. Don't forget—he may be a ghost, but he's the ghost of a child. Maybe he just wanted to pet the cat."

She grimaced. "Make up your mind, Coop. One minute you say he's trying to make Stephen into some kind of permanent playmate. Then you say he's com-pletely innocent."

"Well, he may *be* innocent. It's hard to imagine him plotting ways to put Stephen in danger. The theory says a ghost's existence is probably pretty much a moment-to-moment thing, with no real continuity of thought or action. We can't assume—"

All at once Nan had had enough. "Look," she said.

She could feel her heartbeat thumping in her temples. "The *why* doesn't really matter, does it? The bottom line is, we have to stop what's happening. Can't we get rid of Tucker somehow? I know it sounds heartless. But can't we do an exorcism or something?"

He pursed his lips. "There might be a way, at that . . . Miz Flutie's a natural medium, you know. If she's willing, we could hold a séance."

The suggestion jolted Nan. "Wait a minute. Flutie Larkin is mentally retarded."

"Well—" He spread his fingers out on the table-top and looked at them, then up at her. "It's true her mind isn't like ours. She's given priority to a mode of perception that's nonstandard, so we say she's mentally retarded. But in India she might be considered a wise woman. Even around here that's true to some extent. People go to her when they want to know something they can't learn through normal channels." He paused. Then: "She might be able to make contact with Tucker."

"And then what? We can—send him away?"

He nodded. "It wouldn't be a bad thing, Nan. He doesn't belong where he is—stuck between our reality and wherever he ought to be. And it might have to do with the way he died. You know? Waiting for you to come back with that branch and save him. In a way, it's like he's still waiting. . . . But if we can help him understand what happened, maybe he'll be able to go on." She saw him swallow. "God knows, if Laura'd been trapped like that, I'd have wanted somebody to help her find her way. To reach—wherever it is they go."

"And then he'll stay put?"

He nodded slowly. "It seems like once they get there, they just forget about all this. About us." She saw tears in his eyes as he said, "Laura called it *home*."

Chapter 25

It was past six o'clock when Nan got back to Annabel's. Coming in sight of the house she kept an eye out for Gabe and Stephen. Earlier this afternoon they had made plans for constructing and flying a kite—both of them shaken by last night's argument about returning to New York, anxious to make up— and she fully expected to glimpse some idyllic father-son tableau in the shadowed bowl of pasture. But there was no sign of them. Had the project been a failure, or had they finished with it and gone on to something else from Gabe's seemingly limitless list of activities? He always had time for Stephen, always had something to teach or show him; no wonder the kid preferred his father. Yet remembering with vague amazement how he had turned to her yesterday in his moment of crisis, she thought the balance might be shifting. And Gabe seemed to sense it, too: his attitude toward her, following Stephen's refusal to leave, had been wary—as if she were purposefully exerting some secret, undermining influence. He had made it pretty plain he didn't trust her to take proper care of their child. If he couldn't remove Stephen to New York, he would stay here where he could keep an eye on things.

She pulled up beside the house and got out; the slam of the car door sounded loud in the stillness. The lowering sun dazzled just along the top of the ridge, stretching the oak tree's shadow extravagantly across the lawn. Nan winced at the sight, reminded of Lucy. The old lady's death was still a physical ache in her chest, sometimes dull, sometimes acute. But standing there in the wash of tender light that caressed the old white house in its lush green setting, she felt somehow soothed. It was so beautiful here. If only they could stay. If only things would somehow work out . . .

The first thing she saw as she came through the front door was Gabe, fast asleep with his mouth open, sprawled in the easy chair in front of the television. The evening news was playing at barely audible volume. Nan looked twice around the room before her brain would accept the fact that Stephen wasn't there. She crossed the room in three steps and jogged Gabe's shoulder. He blinked.

"Wha-uh—"

"Gabe. Where's Stephen?"

"Huh?" His glasses had slid down to the end of his nose; his eyes were bleary and unfocused as he gaped at her. He looked old and disoriented, and the sight shocked and angered her. She watched him rub a hand over his face, knocking his glasses loose so they dangled from one ear. He fumbled them back into place. "Shit. What time is it?"

Nan showed him her watch, heart starting to thump against her ribs. "Where's Stephen?"

"He went—he said he was going—" He heaved himself to his feet and stood glaring at her as if it were all her fault. "That was three frigging hours ago!"

"He said he was going *where*?"

"Down to the creek. He said he knew where to find some long, thin sticks we could use to make the kite.

He was supposed to come right back. I just sat down for a minute—Christ, I must have nodded off."

He went on talking but Nan had stopped listening. She dropped her handbag on the floor and ran for the stairs. "Stephen? Honey, where are you?"

But his room was empty and there was no answer. She knew he wasn't in the house. Heading back down the kitchen stairs, she went out the back door at a run.

Gabe caught up with her at the pasture fence. "Look, don't panic, okay? Let's not panic. He's probably just over on the hill."

She looked toward the hill, its crest blazing with the last of the day's light above the green treetops along the creek, and heard Cooper's voice inside her head.

In some primitive societies the dead are feared because they're looking for company.

Company.

"With Tucker," she said.

They reached the creek in record time, stopping briefly at the crossing to glance up and down the stretch of water winding out of sight among the trees. No sign of Stephen.

Once on the hill, Gabe took the lead, charging up the steep slope at a pace Nan couldn't match. As she watched his broad back dwindle ahead of her, leaving a wake in the tall yellow grass, the thought occurred that maybe he wasn't so old after all. Her legs ached from trying to catch up with him but she pushed them without mercy, concentrating on the physical discomfort to keep herself from thinking.

Stephen was not at the top of the hill. Reaching the crest at last, she found Gabe shading his eyes to look down the far side toward the pine woods. The sun, sinking behind the ridge, sent out a starburst of rays and she shut her eyes against their dazzle.

An intricate pattern of colored spots on the inside of her lids made her head swim. Her temporary blindness seemed to intensify the heady, familiar fragrance of pines and ripe blackberries on the hill. A breeze rustled the tall grass around her, and for an instant she was nine years old, her best friend a skinny pale-haired boy who could perfectly imitate a bobwhite's call or catch a drowsing blacksnake in the fork of a stick. In that instant, summer surrounded the two of them like an enormous golden cloud with no beginning and no end, and she could feel Tucker's presence as surely as she could feel the sunlight's fading warmth on her skin.

Those memories of yours may be providing a kind of substance he was missing before. In a sense they function the same way the place does, to orient and define him.

The echo of Cooper's words seemed to reach her from far away. She opened her eyes with a jolt. Gabe was starting down the far side of the hill, toward the dark trees that began halfway down its slope. She hurried after him. Abruptly he stopped and turned to face her.

"If he's in there, we'll never find him—not until he wants to be found. You know what I think? I think he's getting me back for confronting him about Woody. I think he'll show up when he decides I've had enough."

Nan lifted her eyes to the ridge looming against the sky, its forested folds now deep in shadow. Somewhere, back there among the close-growing trees, was the quarry where Tucker had drowned.

The quarry.

"What if he's gone to the quarry?" she said. "Gabe, we have to find him. It'll be dark soon."

His hair was standing on end where he had raked his hands through it. "Why the quarry? What makes you think—"

"Just trust me for once," she said fiercely, and he blinked.

"Okay, all right. But how do we get there? It's not going to help Stephen for us to get lost in the woods ourselves."

She remembered Sky saying the quarry was reachable from the hill, but the specifics eluded her at the moment. Gabe was right; it wouldn't help matters for them to go stumbling around the woods with dusk rapidly coming on. They needed someone to guide them. Someone who knew his way.

"Let's go back to the house," she said. "I'll have to call Sky."

He said he would be there in five minutes. They went out to the front porch to wait for him, too keyed up by now to talk, straining their ears for the sound of the truck. Nan stood on the top step, unable to keep from picking the peeling paint on the railing beside her. Gabe chewed his thumbnail.

In some primitive societies, the dead are feared because they're looking for company.

She thought of the steep cliff hidden among the green ranks of trees, the silent bottomless water at its foot, and her throat closed with fear.

Looking for company.

Sky's truck came barreling down the driveway at that moment, pulling up beside the house with a jerk. Nan ran down the steps, Gabe at her heels, and caught the passenger-side door of the cab as he swung it open. As she climbed into the truck, Gabe close behind her, she saw the two men exchange a look she recognized as the counterpart of their earlier friction—some kind of male fellowship thing based on rallying to the crisis of Stephen's disappearance, rising above any issues they might have with each other around her. Fuck you, she wanted to say. Fuck you both. She bit her lips instead.

The ridge loomed dark against the sunset sky as they tore along the road toward it. Sitting between the two men, Nan tried to hold herself rigid but ended up getting thrown against one and then the other. No one spoke. She stared straight ahead through the windshield, watching the road. At one point she felt Sky glance at her but didn't meet his eyes. At this moment it was unimaginable to her that she had ever had sex with him; he seemed like a complete stranger. And Gabe on her right was another stranger, both of them alien in the face of the tight-coiled dread inside her, the sense of events moving too fast for her to catch up.

As they rattled over the rickety bridge across the creek she caught sight of a car parked off the road among the trees. Her heart jumped as she recognized it: rundown, primer-spotted, sitting there like a bad dream come true.

"What the hell? What's Jerry Ray Watkins doing on my property?"

She wasn't sure if she was exactly asking Sky, but he shrugged in response. In any case the car was behind them now, out of sight, and her worries returned to Stephen. She could find out about Watkins later.

The road had begun to climb and Sky shifted gears, the truck rattling and bumping as he manhandled it around the tight turns. Nan dug her fingers into the front edge of the seat, trying to steady herself. Even though there was still plenty of light in the sky, the mountainside was already in deep shadow and he was forced to switch on the headlights for better visibility. Nan felt her eyes straining as if trying to see around each curve. Just when it seemed the ride would last forever, Sky swung over abruptly and brought the truck to a stop.

"Is this where we walk?"

He nodded curtly. His next actions did nothing to make her feel better. Once he had killed the truck's engine and motioned Gabe and her out, he reached behind the seat and released a double-barreled shotgun from its rack.

"Sky?" She could hear the quaver in her own voice.

He shrugged. "Better safe 'n sorry."

They entered the trees in single file, Sky leading, then Nan and Gabe. In his right hand Sky carried the shotgun at an angle, gleaming barrels pointing at the ground. Nan's nerves were singing like wires, her anxiety tuned by now to an excruciating pitch. Green dusk laced the woods around them, although looking up she could still see light overhead whenever a patch of sky became visible through the close-growing branches.

She found herself crowding Sky on the overgrown path, vaguely aware of Gabe's thrashings and muttered curses farther behind as he untangled himself from the thick undergrowth. He was making more noise than an army; she twisted around to shush him. He gave her the finger and she turned away from him, almost colliding with Sky, who had stopped.

"What?" she said. "What is it?"

He shook his head. "Just takin' a listen."

At some point during the last hour, her heart seemed to have gotten stuck in a spot just at the base of her throat, where it was now beating extravagantly, preventing her from being able to draw a deep breath. As they moved forward again she tried to will it back to its proper location, but it was like trying to swallow a glob of peanut butter.

Soon afterward they reached the quarry. As the deep pit opened ahead, Sky extended a warning arm in front of her and she moved forward carefully, watching her footing, taking hold of a sapling to anchor herself. The open sky above the excavation was beginning to fade, although the far side of the valley was still tinged with sunset light. She stood scanning the quarry's forested rim, too wound up to make a systematic survey, her eyes jumping back and forth to take in haphazard chunks of territory. Beside her Sky, gun in hand, was doing his own reconnaisance.

She heard Gabe come up behind them, his breathing labored. "See him?"

Nan shook her head wordlessly. He had brought the fieldglasses; he lifted them to his eyes and moved them in a slow sweep. At last: "I don't see him. You want to take a look?"

Through the powerful glasses the sudden proximity of the quarry's far side dizzied her. She swayed a little and felt a steadying hand—Sky's—on her shoulder. "I'm okay," she said, and he took it away.

She found the focus knob on the glasses and adjusted it. The low edge opposite sprang into sharp clarity; she could see the dark trunks of the trees, their shadowy leaves. There was no movement among them and she found the utter stillness ominous, the mountainside twilight unbroken by so much as a distant bird-call or falling twig, even the ubiquitous crickets for once mute. Only the violence of her heartbeat lent a kind of false movement to the scene before her, making it seem to pulse under her gaze.

No sign of Stephen anywhere. She moved the glasses, scanning the edge again, seeing the place Sky had pointed out to her on their first visit, where the wall had crumbled in a rocky cleft that led down into the water.

The water.

She swept the glasses over its surface, searching but refusing to think about what she was searching for. Dark and murky, its patches of pale algae apparently undisturbed. She had nearly finished her scan when suddenly a hoarse shriek split the stillness, coming from somewhere below the cliff where the three of them were standing.

In that instant Nan's thoughts jumped to the faint, wailing cry she had heard before. But this was different: loud and scared, unmistakably human. Meanwhile her heart executed what felt like a double backflip against her ribs; she dropped the fieldglasses and heard them hit the ground at her feet with a muffled thump. She wanted to call Stephen's name but found herself unable to make a sound. Near her, Sky and Gabe stood frozen. There was no doubt they had heard it too.

For a long moment they all stood waiting, but the only sound now was a long-drawn whisper of rustling leaves. The forest seemed to have swallowed the cry completely. In the silence the last gleam of sunset faded from the valley below. Nan felt the skin crawl between her shoulder blades. At last Gabe said hoarsely, "What the hell was that?"

Sky lifted his hand to point; even in the poor light Nan could see it shaking. "Came from down there."

She took a breath. "Stephen?" It came out a whisper, but he heard her and shook his head.

"That wasn't Stephen. No way. But the sooner we find him, the better. Best go down and take a look."

The path through the woods had brought them to the highest point of the crannied limestone cliff. Sky motioned them back into the trees and led the way, skirting the pit at a distance of several yards from the edge. Brush and fallen leaves made for treacherous footing; twice Nan slipped and had to grab at nearby branches for support.

The ground sloped sharply as they rounded the northern lip of the quarry and began to descend the mountainside. Sky set a fast pace. It seemed to Nan they were plunging headlong down through the dusky woods, caroming off tree trunks and skidding on dead leaves—that any moment she would slip and fall and go rolling down the mountain and bash her brains out on a rock or a tree. The steep descent was murder on her leg muscles but she was scarcely aware of the pain, only of feeling trapped in an endless gray nightmare, afraid to imagine what might come next.

The ground began to level off at last. Sky, in the lead, silently called a halt with an upraised hand. They moved close to him. Here in the depths of the woods, dusk had already gathered. His face was shadowy except for a gleam of eyes as he looked from Nan to Gabe. When he spoke his voice was pitched low. "Creek's yonder. Let's take a look along it."

As they went forward Nan found herself straining to hear the murmur of the water, but beneath the crackle of branches underfoot the woods were silent, except for the soft hoot of an owl audible somewhere in the distance. Then she realized with a start that the creek was beside them on the right, a wide glimmer flowing silently between deep-cut banks. Its stealthy movement seemed threatening, another part of the nightmare. She quickened her pace to catch up with Sky. "Where are we?"

He motioned across the creek. "Just northwest o' Annabel's house, comin' up on the far side o' the hill. That yell sounded like it mighta come from the pine woods over 'cross the creek. We'll be there in a minute."

A little farther on, he led them down the bank and across a shallow place where the water barely covered their ankles. Nan's nerves were in shreds. She dogged Sky's heels; Gabe trailed some distance behind them, heavy breathing broadcasting his whereabouts. They moved up the opposite bank among the shadowy shapes of the pines, breathing the trees' sharp fragrance, their feet sinking into the thick carpet of needles underfoot. The light was so poor that when Sky came to an abrupt stop, Nan bumped right into him.

His hands steadied her; she felt his whisper tickle her ear. "Listen."

She strained—heard nothing, then a child's distant high-pitched voice. Stephen's.

Dizzy relief flooded her; she clutched Sky's hands. Her little boy was singing to himself—a wordless tune in radical yet reassuring contrast to the wild shriek they had heard earlier. She started toward the sound. Sky caught her arm and held her back.

She tried to jerk free. "Let *go*."

His fingers dug into her arm, his whisper vehement. "Remember that yell we heard? You want t' run into whoever made it?"

That sobered her. The woods around them suddenly seemed twice as dark. Measureless, swarming with unseen menace. Gabe caught up with them, puffing and panting. Sky whispered to him and Nan could see Gabe shaking his head violently. She moved closer to hear their conversation.

"No, dammit," Gabe was saying. "We need to stay together. What if—"

"Look." Sky's dry whisper cut him off. "No offense, but I can move a lot quicker and quieter on my own. I'll find Stephen and be back here with him in two shakes."

"I'm coming with you." Gabe was adamant. He had held himself in check so far, but now it seemed he couldn't stand the thought of Sky saving the day all by himself.

"Gabe," she said. "Maybe he's right."

His glare was invisible in the darkness, but she felt it anyway. "I'm telling you it's crazy to split up! It doesn't make sense. Now let's go find Stephen. We're wasting time."

He turned and plunged into the trees and Nan hesitated, then followed. It was true that splitting up didn't make much sense; in the dark they might not be able to find each other again. In any case, Sky seemed to have capitulated. He was bringing up the rear now, right behind her, his progress barely perceptible in contrast to the racket Gabe was making up ahead. If the shrieker was still in the vicinity, maybe all the noise would alert him to stay clear of them.

Stephen's voice was no longer audible, and she was seized with a sudden certainty that they were moving away from him. Without Sky's guidance they could be walking in a circle; in the twilight, among the trees, it was impossible to get any sense of direction. All at once this whole business was disturbingly reminiscent of her first morning in Tennessee, when she had lost Stephen in the woods by the creek. Ahead of her, Gabe had started to lose momentum. And then they heard Stephen singing again.

This time he sounded quite nearby. Without

thinking Nan blurted, "Stephen?" Her own voice startled her: young, scared, a little girl's.

"Mom?"

She pushed past Gabe and stumbled forward. A shadowy structure appeared ahead, uprights and a low roofline looming in the dimness. She stopped.

A rustling sound. She thought she made out movement under the overhang of the roof. Hurried toward it—relief flooding her as she made out Stephen's indistinct shape.

"Mom, how'd you find me?"

"Honey, are you okay?"

"Sure." He wriggled in her embrace as she knelt and hugged him, trying to be careful of his bandages.

"Mom, lookit this neat place I found. It's some kind of factory or something."

Gabe and Sky emerged from the trees and she felt Stephen's startled movement as he recognized his father.

"Dad!"

"Son, what on earth are you doing here? You were supposed to get the sticks for the kite and come straight back!"

Stephen ducked his head. Nan released him and he stood shifting his feet. "Me and Woody started playing hide-and-seek and I just forgot. Are you mad at me?"

"A little. Haven't you been told not to play in these woods?"

"Aw, Dad. I was looking for Woody."

"Did you find him?" Nan said.

"Not yet. But I found this neat place."

Hide-and-seek. Nan turned and looked around her at the woods, shadowy shapes of trees melting together in the dark. The wind rose. There was a sudden rustling in the trees, a stirring like a sigh growing steadily louder, raising goosebumps on her skin. Finally the leaves subsided into stillness. She saw Stephen gaping at the unmistakable shape of the shotgun in Sky's hand. "Hey, is that a rifle?"

"Nope. Just an ol' shotgun." Sky hefted it. "Didn't see no cherry-tree bucks runnin' around out here in the woods, did you, Stephen?"

The boy shook his head, still staring at the gun. "No. But there was somebody yelling."

"Yeah, we heard him." Sky's tone was casual in contrast with his suddenly alert posture. "You know which way he went?"

"No. I only heard him yell. Then a lot of noise, like he was running away. Maybe he saw something scary. Like a bear."

There was a beat of silence in which no one spoke.

"Maybe," Sky said at last. He unhooked the flashlight from his belt and switched it on. The small circle of light was friendly as a firefly in the encompassing shadows. He played it briefly over the interior of the open shed, illuminating a crude brick furnace surrounded by a hodgepodge of barrels from which copper piping protruded at various angles.

"What *is* it?" Nan said.

"I believe we done found us Jerry Ray's place o' business. Sly bastard musta put it here after Annabel died. Thought he'd have plenty of privacy. Didn't figure on you folks movin' in."

Jerry Ray Watkins. On their way to the quarry, Nan recalled, they had passed his car parked by the bridge farther down the creek.

"You mean this is a still?"

"Mighty right." Sky's tone was noncommittal and she wished she could see his face.

"What's a still?" Stephen said.

Sky cleared his throat. "Well, son, a still's where you make moonshine. You know what that is?"

Stephen's scowl was clearly visible at the edge of the flashlight's beam. "You're lying. People don't make moonlight. It's reflected from the sun."

Relief made them all laugh. After a moment Stephen, confused, joined in. Sky shook his head. "Once a liar, always a liar, I guess. Y'all want to get on home to supper now?"

His flashlight guided them out of the woods and up over the hill through a summer dusk suddenly alive with crickets and twinkling fireflies. Knees shaky, Nan kept Stephen's hand in hers as they walked, listening to him chatter without really hearing the words.

They reached the creek and Stephen pulled free to splash confidently ahead. Nan swallowed her protests, watching him scramble safely up the opposite bank before she followed. The water's coldness made her shiver as it sluiced past her calves.

There was a curse and then a splash behind her—someone was floundering in the shallow creek bed—Gabe, she saw, as Sky's skittering flashlight beam picked him out. Gabe, clambering to his feet with his pants sopping wet and a grim look on his face.

"What—?"

"I slipped, okay? I just—ouch!" He pitched forward; Sky reached him and caught his arm just in time to steady him. "Twisted my goddamn ankle."

Back at the house he refused to let Nan look at it, insisting he was all right. She gave up: one child was all she could deal with at the moment. Stephen was filthy and she sent him to the bathroom to wash up. Gabe shook Sky's hand, muttered what must have been thanks, then limped off to the library to pour himself a drink. Nan and Sky were alone in the kitchen.

"Well, what can I say? Thanks. I appreciate it." A sense of obligation spurred her into adding, "Would you like to stay and eat with us?"

"Thanks, but I got to be goin'. Can I trouble you to drive me back to where I left my truck?"

"Sure."

She told Gabe she would be back shortly. Sky was waiting for her outside under the stars, a shadowy outline like the ghost of a Minuteman, gun in hand. She indicated Estelle and they got in without speaking. The last time they had been in this car together, Nan remembered, he had made love to her. She felt a perverse stirring of desire for him and quelled it angrily, starting the engine with a roar and seeing, out of the corner of her eye, Sky give her a startled look.

They didn't talk during the drive. The road seemed very different by night and Nan found it rough driving. When they crossed the bridge she glanced quickly into the trees and saw that Watkins's car was gone.

Sky's head had turned, too, and now he cleared his throat. "Listen, Nan—"

"I know," she said. "You're in the moonshine business with Watkins." The mountain road loomed ahead and she switched on her brights. "Is that why you told me all those lies? Why didn't you just tell me the truth? Did you really think I'd care if you're a part-time moonshiner?"

He sighed. "I didn't know what you'd think."

"God," Nan said. "I thought it was only New Yorkers who didn't trust anybody."

"Hell, if I'da known Annabel was goin' to leave you the property, I never woulda let Jerry Ray put his damn still in them woods. Ever since y'all got here, I been tryin' t' get him to move it. But he's done turned stubborn on me."

"So whose idea was it to put it there in the first place? Yours?"

He gave a grunt that sounded like assent. "It's a sweet setup. We float the stuff down the creek on a raft, right up to the bridge yonder, then just load it in the truck."

"And who are your customers? Local people?"

"Mostly. It's good stuff. Jerry Ray's a mite crazy, but he can purely brew."

Nan's arms were beginning to ache from guiding the car around the sharp bends in the road. "So why didn't you just offer me a complimentary jug? After all, it's my property. The two of you must owe me some back rent."

He let out a surprised snort of laughter. "You don't care?"

"Look, Sky." There was the truck at last, at the far limit of the headlight beam. She slowed the car, pulling over to the side of the road. "I'm not happy about having Watkins on my property. Like you said, he's a mite crazy, and what he's doing is a mite illegal. But what I'm *really* unhappy about is having him trying to scare me away or whatever he's trying to do. I don't need this shit. I have enough problems already. So tell him to get off my back."

She stopped the car behind his truck, but he made no move to get out. "Hey, Nan. I'm real sorry 'bout all this."

She shrugged. Set against her worries over Stephen, it hardly seemed to matter. They sat in silence while crickets chirped in the night woods around them. She wished he would get out of the car so she could get home to her child. At last he opened the door.

"Thanks for the ride."

She suddenly recalled that he had just done her a big favor. Without his help, she and Gabe would still be searching for Stephen.

"Thank *you*," she said. "I mean it."

In the feeble interior light of the car they exchanged a guarded smile.

She arrived home to find a variety of sandwich makings spread out on the kitchen table. Gabe and Stephen had already eaten and were parked in front of the TV watching *Jeopardy*. Gabe had his ankle propped up on a chair and a drink in one hand, gesturing with his glass at the screen, where one of the contestants had just hit the Daily Double.

"Bet the ranch, asshole!"

"I'll risk a hundred, Alex."

"Chicken," Gabe muttered, and then glanced over at her. "Hero get back to his chariot okay?"

She suspected he had been drinking steadily since her departure. "Fine," she said blandly, and then, to Stephen: "Bath time for you, buddy. Then bed."

Stephen's grumble was perfunctory; he was half asleep already. Upstairs Nan started the bathwater running. The doctor had said to keep the bandages dry, and she took a plastic bag and rubber band from the supply she had stocked in the bathroom cabinet. Paradoxically, now that she was home with Stephen, her mind kept returning to her conversation with Sky just now in the car. So her cousin was in the moonshine business. It explained why he had wanted Gabe and her to wait in the woods while he went to find Stephen. He would have liked to keep his secret. Yet he hadn't let that wish interfere with his concern for Stephen's welfare.

"What's that place in the woods for, Mom?"

As if Stephen had picked up the topic from her thoughts. Well, hadn't Cooper told her that psychic ability was common in children?

"Sky told you." She motioned for him to hold out his injured arm. "It's for making moonshine—illegal whiskey."

"You mean *booze*?" His face fell: he had clearly imagined something infinitely more interesting.

" 'Fraid so." She slid the plastic bag over his left arm. The bandage was filthy; she would have to change it. As Stephen helped anchor the rubber band over the bag with his free hand, her eye was caught by the dull glint of metal on his ring finger.

Now we've both got one. That means we're friends for always.

She spoke abruptly to silence the echo in her head. "Honey, do me a favor. Take that ring off. Okay?"

"Why, Mom?" He frowned up at her.

Nan forced a smile. "Just . . . because."

He looked away without answering. She tried again. "Please, sweetheart. As a favor to me."

She reached for his hand and he let her have it with obvious reluctance. But when she tried to slide the ring off his finger, his small grubby hand clenched in a sudden fist.

"Stephen—"

"Annabel."

The syllables came unmistakably from her child's lips. But the whispered name, the look in his eyes—

She dropped his hand and took an involuntary step back. For what seemed like an endless interval they stared at each other. Then Stephen wrinkled his nose in puzzlement. "Mom?"

The roaring in her ears might have been nothing more than the bathtub filling—looking past him, she saw it on the verge of overflowing. She moved to shut the water off and remained there, trying to force down the panic squirming inside her, clinging to the faucet handles as if they were the only solid point in a shifting universe.

Chapter 26

Once she got Stephen into bed, she went downstairs and called Cooper. Her hands were shaking and she felt very close to jumping out of her skin. Cooper made no comment while she told him about this evening's escapade in the woods, and about what had happened when she tried to get Stephen to take off the ring. Listening to herself talk, she wondered vaguely if any of it had really happened—or if maybe, instead, she had simply lost her mind.

"It was as if, for a split second, Tucker was talking *through* him. But Stephen wasn't even aware of it. Or at least he didn't seem to be. How could that happen? What the hell is going on?"

"I don't know, Nan. It sounds as though Tucker temporarily took control of Stephen, the way a spirit controls a medium during trance."

A medium . . .

A memory surfaced in the midst of her jitters, and she seized it. "Coop—what you said about Flutie Larkin, about her being a medium. About holding a séance. I want to do it. Do you really think we can contact Tucker?"

There was a pause and then he said, "If she's willing, we can sure try. When?"

"Now," Nan said.

*　　*　　*

So now, less than two hours later, here they were, bumping through the dark woods in Annabel's car, straining to catch sight of the lit windows of the Larkin cabin through the last stretch of trees. Estelle's elderly suspension didn't take kindly to the rutted road; Nan felt as if she and Cooper were bouncing around inside like Ping-Pong balls in a lottery drawing. She gritted her teeth in silence, afraid she would end up biting her tongue off if she opened her mouth to speak. She let out a sigh of relief when they reached the clearing at last and the ground leveled off.

She parked beside the cabin and they got out, Cooper peering curiously into the darkness. Their approach must have been more than audible in the peaceful mountain night, yet except for the glow of light behind the threadbare curtains there was no sign of life from the cabin. Nan felt her anxiety level rise a few more notches.

She mounted the cinder-block step to the porch and knocked tentatively on the door. "Hello? Anybody home?"

No answer. Where on earth could Pen and Flutie have gone? Were they out on some arcane hillbilly expedition, hunting possums or gathering herbs by moonlight; or had Sky's fears finally been realized—had the two isolated old women met with some emergency that had left them helpless? She heard Cooper step onto the porch behind her.

"Aren't they here?"

"I don't know where else they could be." She knocked again, harder this time. "Pen? Flutie? It's Nan Lucas."

Inside the cabin there was a scraping sound, as if someone had bumped against a piece of furniture. Nan tensed. She caught a flicker of movement in the window to the left of the door—the edge of the curtain being moved—and took a step back, squarely onto one of Cooper's feet. He grunted softly.

"Nan?" said a quavering voice. "That you?"

The door opened a crack and a face peered out: Pen Larkin's.

"Pen! Are you okay? What's going on?"

"I declare to never," Pen said, sounding more like her crotchety self as her voice steadied. "You like to scared us half to death."

Once inside, seated on the ancient couch in the welcome light of a pair of glass-chimneyed oil lamps, they got an explanation. It seemed Estelle was to blame: peering out the window, the two Larkin women had recognized the car's familiar silhouette and been seized by the notion that they were receiving a visit from its original owner.

"Well, not exackly—we didn't rightly know just *what* to make of it." Pen seemed anxious to repudiate the notion that she herself, at least, had been more than passing prey to such foolishness. "Lord knows, I ain't seen that crazy ol' car since your grandmaw passed on. It just give me a turn, that's all."

Flutie, seated in the rocking chair opposite, hadn't once taken her eyes off Nan. When Pen stopped talking she said softly, "It's come time, Annabel."

"Her name's Nan, Flu! You know that. She ain't been called Annabel in years!"

Flutie seemed oblivious to her sister's scolding. Her pale eyes caught and returned the steady golden light of the lamps. Below her shining gaze a half smile came and went on her lips. Nan, unnerved in spite of herself by the mountain woman's unblinking stare, was about to look away when Flutie spoke again.

"Come time to make things right."

"Don't you pay her no mind." Pen waved a dismissive hand. "She has days, I guess this is one of 'em, when she don't make enough sense to fill a jam jar."

And speaking of not making sense . . . Nan nudged Cooper. "Maybe you'd better explain why we're here."

*   *   *

On the drive up the mountain, he had done his best to answer her frantic questions about exactly what had happened in the bathroom, when Tuck had seemed to speak to her through Stephen. The car's headlights and glowing dashboard panel were the sole illumination on the dark mountainside, Cooper himself only a disembodied voice to Nan's right as he talked.

"It's like a spirit can borrow someone's body temporarily, the same way I could borrow your car. Some professional mediums actually have specific spirits who speak through them on a regular basis. It's like a partnership."

She slowed for a sharp curve, wishing there was some analogous pedal she could press to regulate her heartbeat. "Coop. We're not talking about a professional medium. We're talking about Stephen. My eight-year-old son."

"I know," said his voice from the darkness beside her. "But it's possible a similar partnership may exist between Stephen and Tucker. Partly through Woody . . . but maybe through the ring as well."

"The *ring*?" Nan wanted to laugh, but she was too tense. "What are you telling me? That it's some kind of magic device?"

"Not magic. But Tucker made the ring. And didn't

you tell me there was some emotional significance attached to it?"

Friends . . . for always.

Her abstract desire to laugh faded away. "Yes," she whispered.

"Nan, there's a theory that physical objects are capable of receiving a kind of emotional imprint. The stronger the emotion, the stronger the imprint. A person with the right sensitivity can actually read incidents from an object's past by handling it. It's like the object forms a link between past and present. So I'm thinking, maybe . . ." He broke off, and the darkness seemed to deepen inside the car.

Finally Nan said, "Thinking what?"

"Well, what if an object—the right object—can enhance a connection between different levels of reality as well?"

"Now," Pen directed. "Each o' you take one o' her hands. If she should pull away when the spirit takes her, don't you try to keep ahold, just let her go. But for right now we need t' make a closed circle. That's what brings 'em. A closed circle."

Flutie sat in the rocking chair, the seeing quilt unfolded on her lap, Nan and Cooper on either side of her in rickety chairs brought in from the bedroom. Pen put one of the lamps out and turned the other's wick down until it gave out only a faint glow. Taking her seat on the couch opposite her sister, she reached out both hands to close the circle. Flutie herself had lapsed into silence, staring vacantly into space. Now that the proceedings had actually begun, she seemed scarcely aware of where she was.

Left hand in Pen's, her right clasping Flutie's, Nan

was besieged by sudden doubt. Her earlier panic had begun to fade—routed by, of all things, embarrassment. There was something painfully low budget about all this, something so rinky-dink it made her want to laugh or cry. Here she was, parked on her butt in a cabin in the uttermost boondocks, summoning spirits with the help of two old hillbilly women who probably couldn't even read or write. If she had told Gabe where she was going tonight he would have accused her once again of losing her mind, and she supposed there was a better than even chance that she had.

But it was too late to back out now. She glanced across at Cooper's absorbed, serious face. He was clearly immune to the sudden squeamishness she felt, having been through this, or something similar, before—in trying to contact the spirit of his dead wife.

The lamp's low flame had transformed the cabin's interior into a place of shadows. In the dimness Flutie looked astonishingly young, a girl in her teens or early twenties. She sat quietly, eyes closed now, the folds of the seeing quilt spilled across her lap, her cool, bony fingers exerting only the slightest pressure against Nan's. In spite of her growing discomfort Nan couldn't help being fascinated by the quilt. Patches of fabric had been cut and stitched to mimic the exact line of the ridge against a sky of faded purple. Below the mountains were the fields and orchards of the valley, patches of green and blue, pink and tan and gold, a few houses set among them.

She was craning her neck, trying to identify one of the houses as Annabel's, when she heard Cooper clear his throat.

"We want to contact the spirit of Tucker Wills," he said softly. "Is there anyone here who can help us?"

Uncannily like a response to his question, the thin curtains in the open window behind the sofa filled with a breeze. Nan gave an involuntary start. It might have been the tensing of her muscles that made Flutie's fingers slip out of hers; the mountain woman gave a deep sigh and began to pass her freed hand over the quilt in her lap, smoothing and stroking the fabric. Remembering Pen's instructions, Nan did not try to touch Flutie again. Her own hand felt cold and she tucked it between her knees to warm it.

The curtains hung limp now. After a moment Cooper spoke again. "We want to tell Tucker his time in this world is finished. There's nothing to hold him here anymore."

There was no noticeable response. Nan watched Flutie's hand smooth the quilt over and over again as if searching its folds. The repetitive movement began to grate on her already frayed nerves and she gritted her teeth, wishing she could release Pen's hand as well. She felt desperately foolish holding it. Cooper, across from her with his hands linked to the two old women's, looked ridiculous talking to thin air. The whole business had begun to seem like a parlor game, pitiable and embarrassing. What had possessed her to think anything meaningful could be accomplished by such a farce?

Flutie's chin had sunk to her chest. Her hand lay motionless now on the quilt, fingers twitching slightly.

Cooper cleared his throat again, but it didn't seem to help; he still sounded hoarse when he spoke. "Tucker might not remember what happened," he croaked. "He might not remember the ice breaking in the quarry. He might not remember falling into the water, or waiting for his friend Annabel to find a branch and pull him out."

His voice petered out on the last word and Nan looked at him with sharp misgiving, suddenly convinced she had made a bad mistake in bringing them here, in asking him to go through with this. His experience with Laura had imparted a crushing emotional weight to the idea of a loved one surviving bodily death, and to him there was no question that Tucker existed in some limbo between life and death, a lost youngster desperately in need of rescue. His eyes were closed and the expression on his face was that of someone in the grip of some kind of religious fervor. Embarrassed, Nan looked away.

Flutie mumbled something incomprehensible, then lapsed into a silence that stretched, as they sat there, into an interval long enough for Nan to become aware of the chirp of crickets in the summer darkness outside the cabin. She stared at Flutie's bent head, at the crooked part in her gray-streaked hair, wanting this to be over. She was bone-tired, annoyed in spite of her fondness for these people, and mortified by their naïveté. And she was freezing. She should have remembered to bring a sweater; it got cold in the mountains at night.

A lone tear seeped from under the closed lid of Cooper's right eye and made its way slowly down his cheek. He made no move to wipe it away; Nan thought he was probably unaware of it. "She couldn't save you, Tuck," he whispered. "She did her best. There just wasn't time."

Shifting on the hard seat of her chair, Nan hunched her shoulders against the chill. The noise of the crickets had stopped and a ringing silence seemed to surround the cabin. All at once, completely without warning, she was invaded by a dizzying certainty that the world outside had simply fallen away, leaving this small dwelling adrift in some dimension unconnected with conventional time and space. She had the wild notion that if she were to jump up and look out the window, she would see nothing but swirling emptiness. Her skin prickled into gooseflesh; she squeezed her knees together painfully on the bones of her hand in an effort to drive the sensation away.

But it didn't go. Instead she could feel her tension mounting to an unbearable pitch, sweeping away all traces of skepticism and leaving her quaking in her chair, overwhelmed by a feeling of invisible presence close at hand. She moistened her lips and tried to speak. At first nothing came out. Then she managed a dry whisper.

"Tuck?"

The threadbare white curtain suddenly streamed inward, letting in a gust of icy air, and at that moment the glass chimney of the lamp shattered with a musical *pop* and its flame went out, plunging the cabin into darkness.

"Annabel, help me!" A child's voice, ragged and scared, sounding so close to her in the dark that she could have reached out and touched—*what?*

"Please, Annabel!"

Nan felt the blood congeal in her veins. Pen had released her hand, and Nan floated anchorless in the darkness shrouding the cabin's interior. She could feel herself shaking all over, with no more control over her own jigging limbs than a marionette. She clutched the chair beneath her, blinking frantically against the blackness. Her heartbeat hammered in her ears like frantic running footsteps, and in the encompassing darkness it suddenly seemed she could see the smoky shape of her own breath—

A sudden muffled *thump* in the dark made her yelp aloud. To her left she heard an answering, half-stifled shriek. There were various bumps and creaks in quick succession, then the scrape of a match—and all at once the lamp's wick flared into blessed light. Behind the leaping flame Pen's scared, wrinkled face was visible as she looked across at Nan, then at her sister, who sat blinking in the rocking chair—and finally down at Cooper, who lay sprawled unconscious on the floor.

Nan was still shaking half an hour later when she started the car and turned on the headlights, illuminating the dark wall of forest that edged the clearing. From the porch of the cabin Pen's squat figure offered a farewell wave, and she returned it. Cooper was a subdued presence beside her in the passenger's seat. And a wet one: the elder Larkin sister had restored him to consciousness by upending a pitcher of cold water over him.

Now he let out a heartfelt sigh. "I can't believe I passed out."

Nan put Estelle into cautious motion. The darkness disoriented her; at last she spotted the break in the trees that marked the road and headed for it. Cooper twisted to look back at the cabin once more. For the tenth time he said, "You heard it too, right?"

A tree branch smacked the car roof and they both flinched. Nan tightened her grip on the steering wheel and nodded, as well as she could in the jolting car. She didn't know if he could see her and didn't care. If he came out with some theory or other at this moment she would slap him, she really would. She didn't want to think about the frightened young voice in the darkness, or the moment in which she had seemed to feel the cabin drifting in space. She didn't want to think about any of it. She concentrated instead on her driving; the twisting track through the trees deserved her full attention. Beside her, Cooper's teeth were chattering. It was chilly in the car, and she turned on the heat without comment.

They bumped along in silence, reaching the relative smoothness of the dirt road at last. Nan turned onto it, dreading the hairpin turns down the dark mountainside. She was exhausted, mind and body. A shiver passed through her. The heat didn't seem to be functioning right; the air from the blowers was frigid and she wondered if she had somehow turned on the air-conditioning instead. She slowed the car and squinted at the dashboard display, keeping half an eye on the road.

Several things happened simultaneously.

She remembered that Annabel's car was not equipped with air-conditioning.

She saw a flash of white in the headlights.

Cooper said, "Nan—look out!"

She jammed on the brakes and the back end of the car slewed around, sending the front wheels into the underbrush on the road's nonexistent shoulder. The engine stalled into sudden silence. In the stabbing beam of the headlights a swath of the night forest showed startlingly green.

"What was *that*?"

Cooper was halfway out of the car. "It was a kid."

"No," she said half to herself.

He was already too far from the car to hear her. "He just—disappeared," she heard him say. She got out of the car and saw him on the other side of the road, looking down the dark mountainside into the trees.

"Coop?" she said, shivering, seeing her breath make a white plume in the night air, reminder of that indescribable moment when the lamp had gone out. "Are you sure?"

She reached him and he turned toward her, hugging himself with both arms, showing his teeth in a tight little grin that said he was scared. "He was real pale, and not very big. That's all I saw. Nan, he was just standing there in the road. Didn't you see him?"

"Not really. I saw something, but not clearly." Her mind showed her a replay: flash of white in the head-lights. Showed it again in slow motion so that the flash became a small pale figure, one she recognized. But that was just imagination. "I didn't see," she said.

"Jesus," Cooper said. He came closer and touched her arm; she could feel him shaking.

"Let's get out of here," she said. Whatever the flash had been, she had no wish to investigate it further. She had had more than enough for one night. She hoped the car would start again; she didn't relish the idea of hiking down the mountain in this wintry cold. She didn't remember it having been so cold the other night when they had been out looking for Stephen. But it was later now, past ten; the moon was high in the sky overhead, a chilly white disc surrounded by a vaporous ring.

She turned back to the car. Cooper was scanning the trees. "Maybe we ought to take a look around."

"You really think he's out there?"

"I don't know. But if we saw him, maybe it's because he wants something from us."

Her hands were freezing. She tucked them into her armpits. The idea of crashing around in the pitch-black woods made her cringe; already she was having unpleasant feelings of déjà vu from the other night's hunt for Stephen. It wasn't that she was *afraid* exactly

(that frightened yell they had heard echoing through

the woods below the quarry, and Stephen's casual words: *Maybe he saw something scary*)

but she and Cooper didn't know what they were doing. They didn't even have a flashlight. Getting lost would be the least of their worries; they could fall, break something—you name it. She had a moment's violent nostalgia for the crowded, noisy, dirty streets of New York City, where, in spite of all the bad press about apathy, there were always at least a dozen people willing to stop and comment on your troubles.

She peered into the leafy blackness of the forest again. The reedy sound of crickets was like a scratching on the surface of a bottomless stillness. If the figure had ever been there at all, it was gone now.

"I don't think we're going to find him, Coop," she said.

He didn't answer, just stood there staring into the woods until she touched his arm. Then he turned abruptly and slouched back toward the car, footsteps crunching on the gravel. Nan followed.

"Annabel—!"

This time the thin cry came from some directionless distance, sending a series of echoes into the mountains around them.

"—el—el—el—"

They froze, their faint shadows sprawled across the moonlit road, staring at each other. In the silence that followed, during which even the crickets ceased their piping, Cooper said hoarsely, "Did you hear that?"

Nan nodded. Her heart was hammering, pumping blood like icewater through her veins. *Annabel.* She could feel the desperate cry reverberating inside her, an echo endlessly circling in the fog that shrouded Tucker's death in her memory.

Panic descended on her all at once: a moment's total awareness of the dark, looming wilderness surrounding her, trackless in more senses than she could comprehend. She broke and ran for the car, fumbled with the door and got in, praying it would start. Cooper slid into the passenger's seat beside her just as the engine caught with a roar, barely getting his door closed as she backed out of the bushes and accelerated down the mountain. Her grip on the steering wheel felt weak as a baby's. Some instinct of self-preservation overrode her impulse to put pedal to the metal; she drove as fast as she could without losing control of the car. Beside her Cooper was silent, hands braced against the dashboard.

They had reached the base of the mountain when she noticed she wasn't cold anymore. Heat was pouring full blast out of the vents: heat like an unrelenting desert wind on her face and bare arms. She reached over and switched it off, taking her foot off the gas and letting the car slow down. With a rattle of boards they coasted over the bridge across the creek. She brought the car to a gradual stop and they sat without speaking while the song of the crickets gradually penetrated their daze. At last Nan rolled down her window and felt the balmy air outside flowing past her face.

*   *   *

Stephen was dreaming. The dream had started off being about New York, about going to school one morning and finding all his classmates transformed into enormous rabbits.

But then it changed. The rabbits disappeared and he was in an unfamiliar place. He had the impression that he was supposed to be playing hide-and-seek with Woody, but it was dark and he couldn't see. Then he heard Woody calling, his voice loud and blurry as if he were standing too close to a microphone. The voice got louder and louder inside Stephen's head until he thought his skull would burst.

He tossed his head on the pillow and let out a muffled groan. The moonlight streaming in through his window fell across his face, washing his features in white light, but he was not aware of the light. In his dreaming brain, he was trapped in a bewildering, shadowy world of indistinct shapes and murmurs in which he was terrifyingly aware of only one thing.

He was alone.

Chapter 27

Nan woke knowing, before she even looked at the clock, that it was late. It had been past one when she had finally gotten to bed. And then, exhausted as she was, she had lain awake for another hour, her mind like a tangled ball of string, her thoughts so many inefficient fingers picking and picking and getting nowhere but unable to stop. When she finally drifted off, she had slept like the dead.

Except that around here, the dead were pretty damn wakeful.

The clock on Annabel's dresser showed a quarter to ten. Outside it was raining, a light sprinkle barely dampening the grass. She listened uneasily to the quiet house and thought that, unless Gabe had waylaid him somehow, Stephen must have already gone across the creek.

Gone to meet Tucker.

The memory of the white flash by the roadside, the cry in the dark woods, got her moving. She slid out of bed, feeling a tight, sick knot forming inside her, and hurried out onto the landing. The sight of Stephen's closed door startled her. Was he still asleep? He was usually awake much earlier than this. What—

She opened the door. There he was in bed, curled in a ball beneath the quilt. Relief flooded her and then subsided, leaving a trickle of misgiving. Why was he still asleep? Crossing to the bed, she reached down to smooth back his hair.

"Stephen? Wake up, honey."

He didn't stir.

"Stephen?"

Still no response. Nan grasped his shoulder and shook it—gently at first, then harder. "Stephen, wake up! Stephen!"

An icy suspicion brushed her. Was he breathing? She dropped to her knees beside the bed, putting her face close to his, holding her own breath to listen. There was a paralyzing instant in which she heard nothing, and then came the soft intake of air through his nose. Nan drew a shaky breath of her own.

He was alive. But why wouldn't he wake up?

"Stephen," she whispered. "Honey, please—"

But the dark lashes fringing his cheeks never even quivered. She pushed herself to her feet and went to the door. "Gabe!" No need to worry about raising her voice to shout—if it woke Stephen up, all the better.

"Gabe!"

It seemed like a long time before there was any response; then she heard a muffled answering yell. A moment later she heard his slow, limping approach through her bedroom from the spare room on the far side. He must have been still asleep. He appeared across the landing, rubbing a hand over his face and scowling.

"What the hell—?"

"It's Stephen."

"Stephen?" He lurched forward abruptly. "Goddamn ankle— what about him?"

"He's asleep. And I can't wake him up."

*   *   *

Doc's opinion was that they should just let him sleep.

She and Gabe had tried for another twenty minutes to rouse Stephen. To no avail. Although he appeared to be breathing normally and there was color in his cheeks, he remained as limp as a rag doll. At last they called Doc Hales at his office.

Doc had driven out at once. Arriving, he bustled up to Stephen's room—checked his temperature, pulse, blood pressure and reflexes, lifted his eyelids and peered into his eyes with a little flashlight. At last he covered the boy again with the quilt and squinted over the tops of his Ben Franklins at Nan and Gabe, who were hovering nearby.

"All I can say is, his vital signs are normal. He ain't in shock, nor nothin' like that. Now, suppose you folks tell me how come he's so blessed set on stayin' asleep?"

They exchanged a look. Doc saw it and barked, "Well?"

"He's been under a lot of emotional stress recently," Gabe said at last. "Spends most of his time playing with an imaginary friend. In the last couple of days I've been trying to get him to come to terms with the fact that the friend isn't real."

"Any partic'lar reason you felt the need to do that?"

Gabe scowled defensively. "Yes. The friend encourages him to do things that are dangerous for him."

Doc scratched his stubbly chin. "Okay. I ain't saying you was wrong. But you want my opinion, here it is. He's havin' a tough time with what you told him. He don't want to face it, pure and simple. So he's takin' a little time-out, like they do in the big football games when the goin' gets too rough. More'n likely he'll wake up in a few hours. If he don't, you give me a call."

This didn't seem to satisfy Gabe. "Shouldn't we take him to a hospital—just to be on the safe side?"

Doc Hales grunted. "Better for him to wake up in a place he knows. You just watch him. Like I said, if he ain't up and around by nightfall, call me."

He was more affable with Nan, who walked him to his car and tried to say how much she appreciated the house call.

"Never saw the sense in asking sick folks to climb in a car and make a long trip." He leaned into his dilapidated Chevy and dropped his bag on the seat, then faced her again. "One of your neighbors from out here come all the way into town to see me, though. Just this mornin'."

Dazed with worry, she was having trouble following him.

"One of my neighbors?"

"Mountain boy name of Watkins. Fell and busted his wrist runnin' through the woods. Had a wild story about seein' a spook or some such foolishness."

The surrounding vista did a slow lazy circle with Nan as its axis. She stared at the intricate pattern of broken blood vessels on the end of Doc's nose. Inside her head Stephen's high voice said clearly, *Maybe he saw something scary. Like a bear.* Her mouth felt cottony. "A spook?"

Doc Hales nodded. "Musta been drinkin'. You got to be drunk or crazy, one, try and run in the woods. Roots'll trip you up for sure. Fella like that, raised up in the mountains and all, ought to've had more sense. Nasty fracture, too."

Nan murmured something in reply.

Gabe was sitting at the kitchen table, staring at nothing, when she came back into the house. She went past him and up the stairs to Stephen's room, where he lay curled in the same fetal ball. The sight of the ring on his hand made her wince. If she could just get that off . . .

Around one-thirty Cooper phoned and she brought him up to date on what had happened.

"Jesus," he said when she had finished. "Do you think . . . ?"

His thoughts obviously paralleled hers, connecting Stephen's condition with last night's séance.

"I don't know," she said. "Doc seems to think it's just part of some emotional process. A reaction to what Gabe told Stephen about Woody—Tuck—being imaginary."

"Did you tell Doc about the séance?"

"Oh, sure. Sure I did. What, do you think I'm crazy?"

There didn't seem to be much else to discuss. They listened to each other's breathing for a moment or two. Finally he said, "Listen, let me know how he's doing, okay? You know I'm real fond of Stephen."

"I know," Nan said.

She waited by her son's bed as the afternoon slowly moved toward dusk. The sprinkling rain stopped, leaving a flat gray sky that made the ridge into a cardboard backdrop. Little by little shadows gathered in the corners of the room, while she sat wrapped by a numb exhaustion in which even the effort of leaning forward to turn on the lamp seemed beyond her means. Only her thoughts moved, cycling endlessly. Suppose Gabe was right after all—suppose this was some kind of psychological thing, a desperate appeal for help. But the timing seemed to argue a connection with the séance, as if Tucker's crisis had somehow precipitated Stephen's . . .

At some point she heard the phone ring and the murmur of Gabe's voice; some time later there were cautious footsteps on the enclosed staircase, and she looked up to see Cooper shifting his feet in the doorway.

"Hi." His voice was just above a whisper. "How is he?"

"I don't know." She kept hers low as well, even though it didn't make sense, when all she wanted in the world was for Stephen to wake up.

"I called a little while ago. Gabe said it would be okay if I came out to see him." He exhaled audibly. "I feel like it's my fault somehow."

"Don't be silly," Nan said.

He shrugged. "Well, I went monkeying around, not knowing what I was doing. I was trying to help, but it looks like I just made things worse."

"We've probably got delusions of grandeur to think the séance had anything to do with this," she said.

Cooper's eyes were on Stephen's face. "I wish I could believe that."

Later, when dusk had fallen, Gabe limped up and joined them. In the dim light she could see him looking at his watch. "It's past seven, Nan. Have you tried to wake him?"

"Not yet." She had been too afraid of the result. Gabe moved to the edge of the bed and bent over Stephen.

"Hey, champ. Time to wake up." A pause. "Stephen?"

Still no response. Gabe's shoulders sagged. He remained there without moving, both hands planted on the edge of the mattress, as if he lacked the strength to stand upright.

"Maybe we should call Doc now," Nan said.

Gabe straightened and turned to glare at her. "The hell with Doc. He's nothing but a country quack. I say we get Stephen to a hospital where they can figure out what the hell is wrong with him. What if this entire business with the imaginary friend, his weird behavior this whole summer, is some kind of physical problem, some brain disorder that's come to a crisis—and we're just letting him lie there, hoping he'll sleep it off? He needs to be looked at by someone who got his M.D. in this century."

The sound of a car coming up the drive saved her having to answer. When Gabe had hobbled off downstairs to see who it was, she turned to Cooper. "Do you think he's right?"

He twisted his ponytail. "I just don't know, Nan. Maybe so. Maybe a hospital would be the best thing."

"Maybe."

She tried to weigh the factors involved, but her thoughts refused to add up to any conclusion: it was like trying to complete a structure with blocks that kept falling down. Everything that went through her mind collapsed into a mute, helpless plea for Stephen to just *wake up*.

She became aware of voices downstairs, Gabe greeting what sounded like a crowd of people at the door. A few minutes later he came limping up the stairs and stopped in the doorway.

"More company."

"Who?"

"Two old hillbilly women and your Cousin Sky."

Nan was confused. "What on earth do they want?"

"One of them says she wants to see Stephen."

The words jabbed Nan like something sharp, pushing her up out of her chair. The light in the hallway was behind Gabe and it was impossible to see his face. "Wants to see Stephen—why?"

"How the hell should I know?" He folded his arms. "She didn't elucidate."

Nan was shaken by the unexpected arrival of the Larkins, Flutie's apparent knowledge of their crisis. How could the old woman possibly have known?

"Let me go down and talk to her," she said.

Cooper followed her downstairs, where the two old women stood with an uncomfortable-looking Sky in front of the library fireplace. As Nan reached the bottom of the stairs, Flutie came straight over to her.

"I need to see your boy, honey. After y'all left last night, I got a bad feelin'—"

"And wouldn't shut up about it neither, not for one blessed minute," Pen said loudly from across the room. "It was either get her down here or knock her over th' head with a stick o' firewood. Thank the good Lord, Sky Barnett showed up in his truck this evenin'. I told him, I said, for pity's sake drive us down t' Annabel's before I commit murder on my own sister."

Sky met Nan's eyes briefly with a little grimace that said none of this was his fault. She tried to reassure him with a nod but Flutie was between them, commandeering her attention. The mountain woman's pale eyes were clear as glass.

"Honey," she said. "I got to see him."

There seemed no reason to refuse her request. Nan took her up while the others stayed downstairs. In Stephen's room nothing had changed; Nan switched on the lamp by the bed while Flutie stood looking down at the little boy, her chin sunk in the folds of her scarf. Her scrutiny lasted a long time. Nan felt her tension level rising. What was this about? No matter how lucid Flutie had appeared downstairs just now, it was hard to have any real confidence in her sanity.

All at once Stephen's head moved on the pillow. He muttered something. Nan's heart jumped; she held her breath. The mumbled syllables came again.

"Annabel . . . help me . . ."

Nan's skin broke into gooseflesh. The relief that he had moved, had spoken, was canceled by the words themselves. *Annabel, help me.* Just like last night, when she had tried to remove the ring, and—

Her cold hands clasped each other as if for comfort. Flutie took her arm, drawing her out into the hallway. Through the open door Nan could see her child's shape, motionless once more under the old quilt, lamplight falling in a band across the nubbly texture of the material but leaving his face in shadow. She glanced at Flutie. With her shabby clothing and flower-child hair, it should have been easy to dismiss her as comical, a weirdo—but at this point Nan found herself incapable. There was an urgency about Flutie now in contrast to her usual vagueness. She had a natural dignity, a surprising air of calm authority. She spoke softly.

"You got to be strong now, honey. Tucker's spirit has done took hold o' your boy."

Nan felt her heart jump like a shot deer. "But Flutie—why?"

"Tucker's scared, Annabel. You got to help him."

"But how?" Her insides started to tie themselves in complicated knots. *You got to help him.* "I don't know how," she repeated.

The mountain woman only stared at her in silence.

* * *

Downstairs in the library there were varying reactions when Flutie repeated, at Nan's request, what she had to say.

Cooper's face turned ashen. "She's talking about possession," he said.

In contrast, Gabe had turned bright red. He flung up both arms. "I can't believe I'm hearing this. I thought you were an educated man."

Cooper swallowed. "I've seen it happen—a spirit taking control of a medium in a trance. It's like they borrow the body for a little while, while its owner just sort of takes a back seat. They—"

Gabe's face darkened to purple. "Look, pal. My son is not a medium, and he has not lent his body out to some fucking disembodied spirit! He's a sick little boy who belongs in a modern hospital. And that's where I'm going to take him. If I can find such a place in these godforsaken boondocks."

Cooper shrugged. No one said anything. Pen's withered-apple features were without expression. Sky, at the foot of the stairs, folded his arms across his chest; Nan saw him wet his lips. Gabe favored them all with a scorching look and limped out of the room.

Nan turned to Flutie beside her. "You said I can help Tucker. How?"

The old woman opened her hands, as if to display their emptiness. But her gaze was disconcertingly steady, and finally Nan was forced to turn away.

When she went up to check on Stephen a few minutes later, he hadn't moved—still lying flat on his back and breathing quietly. She stood in the darkened room looking down at him, fighting formless dread. He didn't look any different. But those muttered words—

Annabel . . . help me . . .

Faintly she could hear Gabe haranguing someone on the phone downstairs in the kitchen. Outside the window by Stephen's bed the moon was beginning to rise, and around it the night sky was filled with summer stars that seemed to cluster above Sleepy Gal's shadowy bulk.

Folks down in the valley'd see his lantern shinin' on the mountain, searchin' all over for that gal. One day he just never come back . . .

Tucker's spirit has done took hold o' your boy.

Possession.

Like a nightmare from which she couldn't wake, impossible but inescapable, confronting her no matter which way she turned. *Possession.* Before this summer she would have laughed at such a word, but after what she had experienced . . .

Looking down at Stephen she caught sight of the horseshoe nail ring on his hand. On impulse she reached out. Maybe if she could remove it—

But the first gentle tug made his hand close into a fist, as it had last night in the bathroom. She swallowed and gave up. Taking a final look at her sleeping child she went out, leaving the door ajar. She didn't want to go back downstairs, didn't want to face Gabe and his frantic need for action, any action. Instead she stopped in the bathroom for a glass of water to moisten her dry throat. After a couple of swallows she set the glass on the edge of the basin and stood staring at her own face in the tarnished mirror.

He's scared, Annabel.

You got to help him.

But how? Her heart began to hammer again. It was as if Flutie knew, but would not or could not communicate her knowledge. As if she, Nan, must come to it on her own.

The face in the mirror stared back at her, the eyes unreadable.

You got to help him.

Cooper's words—was it just yesterday? *It might have to do with the way he died . . . Waiting for you to come back with that branch and save him. In a way, it's like he's still waiting . . .*

You got to help him.

Far inside her, something stirred. A shudder in the depths of her memory. The nightmare. Trying to run, seeing her freezing breath—

But I tried to help him.

I tried.

The eyes in the mirror flickered. *It's like he's still waiting . . .*

A faint sound of children's voices seemed to reach her, far away but shrill and clear in a landscape of pure black and white, where spidery leafless trees stood in sharp silhouette against the snow-blanketed ground.

See, I promised you I'd show you something neat.

What is this place?

It's the old quarry where they used to cut limestone. They dug so deep they hit an underground river, and the whole thing filled up with water.

Look, it's frozen over. If only we had some skates!

You crazy, Annabel? That water's about a million feet deep.

So what? The ice will hold us. Come on! Even if we don't have skates we can still slide on it. It'll be fun.

Yeah, lots of fun—if we don't get killed.

You're just chicken.

Am not.

Then come on!

I dunno, Annabel—

Chicken!

I ain't neither!

I dare you . . . chicken!

Nan's heart was pounding. Suddenly the shape of the memory was very close, looming behind the barrier that had obscured it for so long. Her instinct was to defend herself from it, bury it once again—but for Stephen's sake, and for Tucker's, she had to let it come clear. She stared at her own reflection, seeing only the eyes. Seeing the knowledge return to them.

We start out being careful, staying near the edge, placing our feet gingerly and listening for any faint cracking sounds before we commit our weight. But the ice seems solid enough and gradually we start to relax. Tuck's foot slips and he falls flat on his belly, arms and legs splayed out comically—we both start laughing and he rolls over and against the cold white ice I notice how red his cheeks are, the fringe of pale yellow hair sticking out from under his blue knit cap. He gets up and takes a running start and sliiiiides across the ice, arms windmilling for balance, and it looks like so much fun that I imitate him, feeling the icy wind lift my hair.

See? I told you we don't need skates!

It's even more fun than I thought it would be. He pushes me unexpectedly and I almost fall, catching myself just in time to push him back. We're laughing so hard we can't even talk, never noticing we're getting farther away from the edge, closer to the middle. My winter boots grip the slick surface better than his, and

*even though he's bigger, I end up being able to push
him down more than he does me. The last time, he
lands bang on his butt, the painful impact showing in
his face, and I'm about to ask if he's okay when we
both hear the series of pops and snaps, like far-distant
firecrackers.*

*And it happens too fast for us to move. One instant
I'm standing there, staring down at Tuck—and then the
bottom drops out of the world, plunging me into blackness. Without warning, in that split second, everything—light, air, breath, life—is jerked away, out of my
flailing reach. For an eternity I hang in the void. And
then a hand grabs the shoulder of my coat and drags
me, coughing, to the surface.*

*Tuck's clinging to the jagged edge of the hole in the
ice with one red-mittened hand, clutching me with the
other. Black water swirls around us, so cold my whole
body shrieks in outrage. I can see his lips moving, but
my ears seem frozen and I can't hear him. Then all at
once I can.*

*"Go on, Annabel! You gotta climb out. I'm gonna
give you a push. You ready?"*

*I force my frozen arms to move, extending them on
the unbroken ice in front of me, and Tuck lets go of the
soaked shoulder of my coat long enough to shove me
hard from behind. I hear another crack, and suddenly
the pressure of his hand is gone. But I'm almost out,
and I claw my way onto the ice and turn to see him
floundering in a jagged pool of black water, grabbing
onto the newly broken edge.*

"Tuck!"

*I reach out my hand and he grabs it. I pull—but
when he tries to climb onto the ice, we both hear the
ominous crack.*

"*Look out!*" *He lets go of my hand and slips back a little, clutching at the new edge and gasping as the black water makes oily ripples around him. "This won't work. Listen, Annabel. You gotta find a b-branch, a long one. You can s-stay back where the ice is th-thicker . . . hold it out to m-me. O-k-kay? You g-g-gotta go f-f-find a long b-b-branch.*"

"*Okay. Hang on, Tuck. I'll be right back.*"

"*H-h-hurry.*"

Running as fast as I can among the skeleton shapes of trees, floundering through knee-deep snow that drags at my legs, making it feel like I'm moving in slow motion. My gasping breath makes crackling clouds in front of me in the freezing air and I can feel my heart beating with trip-hammer terror.

I find one at last, a fallen branch sticking out of the snow that blankets the ground. When I get back to the quarry Tuck is waiting, clinging to the edge of the ice. His cheeks are blue now, no longer red, and his lips match. Clutching the branch I start across the ice, but after only a few steps something seems to happen to my legs and they move more and more slowly until at last they stop altogether.

"*Annabel! Come on!*"

With shaking arms I extend the branch out in front of me. It's too short. I can't reach him from where I am. But my legs won't take me any closer.

"*Annabel, please!*"

I know I have to go closer. But if I do, the ice might break. And I know it's waiting, that cold black water. It has Tuck, but that's not enough. It wants me, too.

"*Annabel, help me!*"

But I can't move.

Can't move.

*   *   *

The sensation of something cool and hard under her hands reached Nan slowly. She blinked and looked down at the basin below her and gradually released it, fingers bloodless from their grip on the unyielding porcelain.

Her knees were wobbly and the back of her throat stung. Her hands were beginning to prickle with pins and needles but her mind was still numb, still unable to accept the terrible knowledge it had buried for twenty years.

She moved to the open window and stood leaning on the sill, taking gulps of the cool night air, feeling her eyes fill with hot tears.

I dared him. And he saved my life. But I didn't have the guts to save his.

There was a faint sound behind her. Still reeling from the shock of the memory, she turned groggily to look.

Stephen was standing in the doorway.

His eyes were open and he was looking at her. But there was something about the way he was looking—something wasn't right. It took a beat before the answer clicked in.

He wasn't wearing his glasses, yet he was looking at her . . .

. . . looking at her *as if he could see her.*

The wide blue eyes were focused and clear. She opened her mouth but no sound came out, and then he was gone, ducking out of the doorway with an unfamiliar fluid grace. She heard his bare feet thud across the floor of her bedroom and down the stairs to the kitchen. The screen door gave its raucous squeak and banged shut, and at the sound her voice came back and she screamed.

When she came pounding down the stairs to the kitchen Gabe was standing there gaping, the phone in his hand.

"What the hell is going on?" he yelled. Everyone else came racing in from the library, babbling and exclaiming.

"Did you see him?" she shouted back. "Did he go outside?"

He dropped the receiver and it dangled there, swinging back and forth at the end of its wire. "Who?"

"Stephen, for God's sake! He woke up. I was in the bathroom, and he came to the door and looked at me. Then he ran off."

"Ran off? Why the hell—?"

"We have to stop him," Nan said. She ran for the door.

Chapter 28

Outside in the moonlit pasture there was chaos. The moon, close to full, gave off what struck Nan as an astonishing amount of light—but it was a light in which shadows took on a deceptive substantiality and solid objects seemed to soften and melt into their surroundings. The others had followed her out of the house and now they were all looking for Stephen, stumbling and shouting and chasing things that turned out not to be there at all. The horses, spooked by all the noise and activity, went galloping off into the darkness. Sky was the only one with a flashlight, and its beam skittered futilely across the pasture's expanse, temporarily blinding anyone who got in its path. Against the darkness of the trees hundreds of fireflies twinkled, tiny points of light mirroring the stars overhead. But there was no trace of Stephen.

. . . Or whoever was in Stephen's body, Nan thought bleakly, finding herself down near the creek at a distance from the general pandemonium. In between the shouts she could hear the babble of the water, its likeness to a human voice intensified by the dark under the trees. Slowly she moved forward until she stood on the bank. Quiet as it was, the sound of the moving water blocked out all others as she stood there. Odors seemed stronger too: damp earth and rotting leaves mixed with

the rank green smell of summer growth. On the opposite bank the hill seemed to float in the moonlight.

Race you to the top, Annabel!

Last one there's an ol' maid . . .

Only the creek, mimicking the syllables to her suggestible mind. Yet she found herself moving irresistibly forward, stepping into the water and feeling its
cold tug around her ankles, then her knees. She
stumbled on the rocky bottom and almost fell, then got
her balance and kept going, scrambling up on the other
side and stopping to catch her breath.

. . . race you to the top . . .

. . . Annabel

Her legs seemed to move of their own accord, carrying her up the steep hill toward the rounded crest
shining against the night sky. Once she reached the top,
she stopped to catch her breath and stood shivering,
noting vaguely that her sandals were sopping wet from
the trek through the creek. In some corner of her mind
she was aware that what she was doing didn't make
sense—but she seemed driven by something outside
herself, blindly following its agenda. As she stood
looking down the far side of the hill into the pine
woods that hid the creek's northern fork, all at once
Sky's voice sounded in her head as clearly as if he had
been standing beside her.

*If you go through the pine woods on the far side of
the hill, then cross the creek and follow it a ways,
you'll come out over there on the low side.*

Low side of what?

The quarry.

Nan moved toward the trees, hearing more voices
now, a mingled babbling in her head.

The dead . . . looking for company.

Tucker's spirit has done took hold o' your boy.

Reaching the woods, she hesitated only a moment before entering them. Among the pines it was dark, but she made her way by the scattering of moonlight visible through the feathery branches—a tentative advance from one patch of illumination to the next, arms extended to ward off unseen branches. The downhill slant of the ground seemed to indicate that she was heading in the right direction. And then, somewhere ahead, she caught a faint crackling sound.

She froze, listening. Silence now. Had it been Stephen, or just some animal on its nightly hunt? In any case it wasn't repeated and she started forward again, hurrying as best she could in the dark. The downward slope underfoot obligingly propelled her forward; she stumbled over a root and barely missed falling, hearing Doc Hales's voice join the others in her head.

You got to be drunk or crazy, one, try and run in the woods. Roots'll trip you up for sure.

Cross the creek and follow it a ways . . .

She was glad of this chorus. It provided a kind of company on this dazed, dreamlike journey through the dark. As long as the voices kept on talking, nothing outside her own head was quite real—not this nightmare search for her lost child, which seemed to have been foreshadowed as long ago as that first morning by the creek, not the enormous country night or the dark rustling woods around her, gradually becoming easier to navigate as her eyes grew accustomed to the filtering moonlight.

There it was again. The sound of someone moving through the trees ahead.

"Stephen?" she called, and it ceased. She stumbled forward. Oh God, please let me find him . . . but remembering those focused eyes, that unfamiliar physical grace, she couldn't help wondering exactly *whom* she would find. She made herself move faster. And then, without warning, a hand reached out and grabbed her arm.

She let out a stifled shriek. The fingers digging into her flesh seemed to cut through the fog in her head, jarring her out of her daze, and as they tightened and yanked her around to the right, she recognized the shadowy figure of Jerry Ray Watkins.

"Hey there, little lady. Out all by y'self tonight?"

His breath stank. Nan's heart started a sudden hard pounding, throwing itself against her ribs like a maniac in a cell. Her gaze, skittering away from his face, fixed on the shotgun in the crook of his arm.

He gave her a shake, as if to get her attention, and she nearly gagged on another wave of cheap-whiskey breath. "You sure seem fond o' me, little lady. Ever'where I go, there you are."

To her disgust, Nan found she couldn't speak. The bill of his cap was pulled low and she couldn't see his eyes, only the fat jowls covered with scraggly beard, and the white cast on the wrist of the arm cradling the gun.

"You want t' watch how you go chasin' around at night. Lot o' wild critters in these here woods. You could get hurt." He released her suddenly, but as she stumbled back she saw the gun barrel shift toward her. "What the hell you doin' out here, anyway?"

Nan put one hand on a tree trunk to steady herself. If she tried to run, would he shoot her? Inside her head, Sky's voice said helpfully, *Jerry Ray's a mite crazy . . .* She took a breath and managed to say shakily, "Look, Mr. Watkins—"

("Anna-bel—!")

It came just as her voice trailed off into nothingness. Like an echo, so faint she couldn't be entirely certain she had heard anything at all. But Jerry Ray's frozen posture told her he had heard something. She held her breath. The cry came again.

("Anna-bel—!")

It seemed to come from no direction and all directions. Watkins twisted around and looked over one shoulder, then the other. Nan caught the scared gleam of his eyes.

"What th' hell was *that*?" His voice had jumped registers to falsetto.

"Look, maybe you can help me." For someone who had been unable to speak scant moments before, Nan was astonished at how businesslike she sounded. "My little boy's out here somewhere, and he's lost. Can you help me look for him? I'll pay you. Whatever you want."

"That's your boy hollerin'? Don't sound like no human child t' me." The words were a whine, and she saw him take a quick glance down at his broken wrist. "Sounds like a damn *haint*."

"Please," Nan said. "Please help me find him."

Whatever else Watkins might be, he knew these woods. He might be her only chance. But when she moved toward him, he actually cringed away.

"Let me alone—I seen me enough haints t' last a lifetime! Damn woods're crawlin' with 'em. Shit!"

He backed up a few steps, took another wild glance around, then ducked between two shaggy pines and was gone. Nan heard him crashing off through the trees.

You got to be drunk or crazy, one, try and run in the woods.

She moved forward again, still headed downhill, and in fewer than a dozen steps found herself at the silent creek. Its surface glimmered faintly between deep-cut banks in the moonlight. She stopped and peered across the water at the impenetrable forest on the other side.

Cross the creek and follow it a ways, you'll come out over there on the low side.

What about the cry she and Watkins had heard? The night was completely quiet now, not even the piping of a single cricket. The moon hung like a spotlight in the night sky overhead, leaching color from the landscape, rendering it in stark black and white. The smell of pine needles was sharp in the cool air. In the stillness she could hear her own heartbeat as she stood on the bank, waiting . . .

("Anna-bel—!")

The sound jerked her forward. Rang in her ears as she slid down the muddy bank and splashed through the creek into the woods beyond, fighting her way through a jungle of close forest growth, stumbling and grabbing wildly at branches to keep herself from falling. Vines tore at her feet; leafy tendrils swiped across her face. The darkness was darker here, where moonlight could barely penetrate the dense canopy of leaves, but she forced her way forward—seeing at last a kind of radiance up ahead. All at once the way was clear. There was the high quarry cliff, rising skyward across the expanse of water at its foot. Summer trees ringed its edge, their foliage silvered by the moonlight that made a mirror of the dark water within.

A mirror not of this moment, but another. As she stumbled closer she glimpsed the reflection of a white winter landscape, tree branches showing black and bare against the snow.

"Annabel!"

Vertigo swamped her and she sank to her knees at the edge of the quarry to stare down the image in the water. Vertigo gripped and spun her as the reflection rushed upward to meet her, obliterating all reality but its own.

All the trees were bare. Snow covered the ground and powdered the spidery black branches etched against a sky pink with the last traces of winter sunset. Some part of her brain resisted what she saw and yet she accepted it in a kind of waking trance, her mind wiped clean of judgments about what was possible or impossible, real or unreal. Her sense of the rational had been outraged so many times that it had gone limp, like an exhausted muscle.

The air was crisp and cold. Her breath made little crackling clouds in the air in front of her and an uncontrollable shivering ran through her limbs as she knelt at the quarry's edge.

"Annabel!"

He clung to the edge of a hole in the ice near the center of the quarry, black water oozing over the jagged fracture around him. His lips were purple with cold, eyes wide and staring in his white face. He wore a dark blue knit cap on his pale hair, a scarf and a bulky jacket. The hands scrabbling at the broken ice were red-mittened.

"Tuck," she whispered. "Oh God—*Tuck.*"

"Annabel, help me!"

To her left was the place where the quarry wall had

eroded in a rocky seam down to the water. She ran toward it and scrambled down the narrow channel, slipping on the frozen surfaces, feeling one knee strike hard stone with no sensation of pain. She didn't want to take her eyes off him. She was afraid he would lose his grip, sink into the water . . .

When she set foot on the ice it was slippery and she flailed wildly for balance.

"Please, Annabel—"

"I'm coming, Tuck. Hold on."

She stumbled, half sliding toward him. The treacherous footing kept her progress painfully slow and awkward. She could hear his teeth chattering. As she made her way closer, his figure became less clear, seeming to pulse—bright one moment and almost invisible the next. On the bright pulses his frightened face was so clear that she could have counted the freckles standing out against his bloodless skin.

Only a few yards remained between them when she heard the ice crack under her feet. His lips parted but no sound emerged.

"Tuck!"

She stumbled and went belly down, a slide into home plate that any major leaguer would have envied. The boy in the water lunged forward and she felt his hand touch hers, the frantic clasp of his fingers inside the icy wool—

"Jesus Christ! Nan! *Nan!*"

The shout echoing from above exploded in her consciousness, shattering the fragile reality cradled there.

The winter landscape surrounding her shuddered and vanished.

The last thing she saw was Tucker's thin freckled face, flaring up like a beacon once before it was gone.

Then she found herself chin deep in cold water and sinking, going all the way under before her arms and legs instinctively began to flail. She sucked in water and came up choking, gasping for breath, seeing night sky above, the ring of moonlit trees towering above her at the quarry's edge. Vaguely she heard splashing nearby; then rough hands grasped her under the arms and maneuvered her into a life-saving tow. She became aware that her right hand was gripping something harder than she had ever gripped anything in her life. Another hand, smaller than her own.

A child's.

*   *   *

"Jesus," Cooper said. "For a minute there I thought I was too late."

The three of them sat huddled, dripping wet, under a tree well back from the quarry's edge. Nan held Stephen against her. He was disoriented without his glasses and his sopping pajamas were in tatters. But the recovering wounds on his face and arms seemed no worse—although his legs, like her own, were criss-crossed with angry new scratches from his trek through the woods. Otherwise he was apparently unharmed. He didn't ask where they were, and she wondered to what extent he had been aware of what was happening. Now, incredibly, he seemed to be falling asleep.

Shivering more from the adrenaline rush than from cold, she noted remotely that when Cooper's hair was plastered wet to his skull like this, it was obvious he was starting to go bald. It seemed like an uncharitable observation to make about someone who had just saved their lives.

"I saw you go down toward the creek," he was saying. "I followed you."

The words reached her slowly. She licked her lips and the rank taste of the quarry water supplied an instant antidote to the fog inside her head.

"Did you hear him?" she said. "He was calling—the way he did on the mountain the other night. You didn't hear him?"

He shook his head slowly. "I didn't hear anything. You left me behind on the way up the hill—you were going like a bat out of hell. When I finally got to the top, I thought I heard voices down there in the pines, so I went that way. But you were long gone. I barely caught up with you in time to pull you out of the water."

He leaned closer, trying to get a better look at her face. "Nan, what happened? Did Stephen . . . fall in?"

She told it the way she remembered it, aware of how crazy it sounded—especially in view of the fact that Cooper had arrived to find Stephen and herself on the verge of drowning in the flooded quarry. Yet he didn't seem to doubt a single word, interrupting only to ask for details. When she was finished he let out a slow breath.

"That seems to fit the theory. You know? That a ghost exists just moment to moment, with no real continuity. The Tucker who played with Stephen on the hill and along the creek probably had little or no conscious memory of his own death. But when we held the séance, when we reminded him—well, that unresolved moment at the quarry became all that existed for him."

Nan swallowed. "But how did he end up in Stephen's body, Coop? What made him . . ."

For once he had no tidy theory to offer her. "I don't know. Maybe it was some kind of attempt to escape. Maybe Tucker panicked—and Stephen was there.

After all . . . thanks to Woody, he was almost a part of Stephen already."

Nan drew her sleeping son more closely against her and they sat for a time without speaking, hearing the soft rustlings of the night woods around them. The moon's reflection floated on the dark water of the quarry, an immense white circle.

Annabel, help me.

"I remembered something earlier tonight," Nan said at last. "Something that fits in with what you said about Tuck's death being unresolved. I finally remembered what happened the day he died." She glanced at Cooper, meeting his intent gaze briefly before looking back at the moon shining on the water's glossy surface.

"The story his father reconstructed, from the hole in the ice and the footprints in the snow, was pretty accurate. When the ice cracked and we fell in, Tuck managed to push me out. Then I went hunting for a branch to pull him out. Later, when it was all over, they found the branch out on the ice. But they just assumed he had already drowned by the time I got back." She took a shaky breath. "What they never noticed was that the branch really wasn't long enough to reach him.

"I *did* get back in time, Coop. But the branch wasn't long enough, and I would have had to go out where the ice was too thin. And I couldn't make myself do it. I was afraid it would break under me. I was too scared. I ran away."

She heard his intake of breath but didn't look at him. The image of Tucker's pleading face hovered before her.

Cooper's voice broke into the memory. "You can't blame yourself, Nan. You were nine years old. But tonight . . . you tried to help him. Maybe that's all he needed. Maybe now he'll be able to go on."

She had no answer. They went on sitting there—for how long Nan had no idea. She seemed to drift between past and present, one reality and another, with no anchor anywhere. Cradled against her Stephen snored softly, his mouth open.

A commotion in the woods roused her. A flashlight beam pierced the trees at their back; there were voices and the sound of bodies crashing through the underbrush. Cooper stood up. "Over here!"

"I'll be damned," Gabe's voice said. "They *are* here."

The blinding beam picked them out; behind it, several shadowy figures emerged from the trees, Gabe's immediately identifiable by its limp.

"Y'all find him?" Sky's voice, issuing from the tallest of the shapes. The beam dropped lower and Nan saw, as they all came forward, that the other two were the Larkin sisters, their eyes as pale as the moonlight. Then Gabe limped forward and hunkered down beside her, looking at Stephen as if he was afraid to touch him.

"Is he . . . ?"

"He's okay," Nan said. "He woke up for a while. Recognized Coop and me. I think he's just exhausted."

Gabe's hand gently traced Stephen's cheek, and in his sleep the boy smiled. Gabe gulped and grasped Nan's arm, then did a double take. "Christ, you're soaking wet." He reached out for Cooper. "You too? And Stephen? What the hell's going on?"

She had her own question. "How'd you find us?"

Gabe jerked his chin in Flutie's direction. "She said you'd be here. What in God's name happened?"

Nan opened her mouth and closed it again, then

looked at Cooper and shrugged. In Gabe's presence the past hour seemed more than ever like delirium. It was summer; it was the present. If the moment of Tucker's death had existed at all tonight, even for an instant, maybe it had been only in her mind.

Gabe was still looking at her and she shook her head. "I'll tell you some other time." She felt a light touch on her shoulder and found Flutie beside her. The mountain woman was smiling.

"What y' got in your hand, honey?" she said softly.

Nan looked down. The fingers of her right hand were clenched around something. She was aware all at once that they were numb—that she hadn't opened them for a long time, maybe since she had felt that small hand in hers in the dark water. She could feel something hard pressing into the center of her palm. Slowly, almost fearfully, she uncurled her fingers and looked down. For a moment there was silence as they all looked.

"What's that?" Gabe said.

Nan brought her hand closer to her face and looked. "Just Stephen's ring. It must have come off when I grabbed his hand." She shivered suddenly. "Let's go home. I'm cold."

She nudged Cooper and he rendered up a convincing shudder of his own. "Me too. Brrr."

Gabe peered suspiciously at them both, but Sky had heard enough. "Fine. Let's get goin'."

He swung his flashlight to send a bright path through the trees, plunging everyone behind him into darkness, and started back toward the creek. Pen and Flutie followed, and then Cooper, carrying Stephen. Nan motioned Gabe ahead of her. Alone at the quarry's edge she examined the ring.

In the bright moonlight she could see it clearly: fashioned from a bent horseshoe nail, a crude circle small enough to fit a child's hand. She looked from it to the flooded quarry, where the moon floated on the bottomless water within, its white disc wreathed by the reflections of trees no longer bare. A shadow swept the water and she glanced up to see the dark feathered shape of a hunting owl. In the woods at her back, a single cricket began to sing, and then another.

Nan took a deep breath. With a quick motion she flung the ring into the water's depths, watching as a few ripples wrinkled the surface of the floating moon. Then she started after the glow of Sky's flashlight, still visible ahead in the dark.